Praise for Ian McDonald

DESOLATION ROAD

"Wild, original, exuberant, profound, moving . . . You're going to want to read more of Ian McDonald."
—*The Denver Post*

KING OF MORNING, QUEEN OF DAY

"*King of Morning, Queen of Day* carries such a rich wealth of language and story, of character and concept, that I don't doubt it will rank among the best works the genre will produce over the next ten years. This is a brilliant book; do yourself a favor and read it."
—Charles de Lint, author ... *art*

"

"McD ... *ooklist*

SCISSORS CUT PAPER WRAP STONE

"[McDonald] does more in a page than most writers do in a chapter."—Neal Stephenson, author of *Snow Crash* and *The Diamond Age*

TERMINAL CAFÉ

"An astonishing, dazzling book."—*Locus*

"Punk, funky, and frightening: a fantastic acid trip to the end of the world."—*Kirkus Reviews*

"A whirlwind of imagery and emotion that immediately pulls the reader in and won't let go until the last page . . . in the best science fiction tradition."—*Publishers Weekly*

Books by Ian McDonald

The Broken Land
Desolation Road
Evolution's Shore
King of Morning, Queen of Day
Out on Blue Six
Scissors Cut Paper Wrap Stone
Terminal Café

Short fiction

Empire Dreams
Speaking in Tongues

Evolution's Shore

Ian McDonald

BANTAM BOOKS

New York Toronto London Sydney Auckland

EVOLUTION'S SHORE

A Bantam Spectra Book

PUBLISHING HISTORY

Bantam trade paperback edition / December 1995

Bantam mass market edition / January 1997

Library of Congress Catalog Card Number: 95-21474.

ISBN 0-553-57309-8

Published simultaneously in the United States and Canada

Bantam Books are published by Bantam Books, a division of Bantam Doubleday Dell Publishing Group, Inc. Its trademark, consisting of the words "Bantam Books" and the portrayal of a rooster, is Registered in U.S. Patent and Trademark Office and in other countries. Marca Registrada. Bantam Books, 1540 Broadway, New York, New York 10036.

PRINTED IN THE UNITED STATES OF AMERICA

OPM 10 9 8 7 6 5 4 3 2 1

To

Rachel Ellen Bankhead

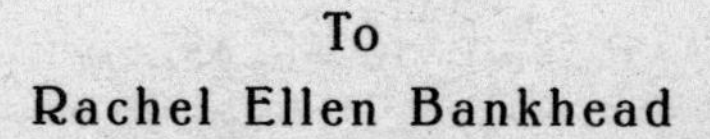

contents

preface

Though this book shares the same setting, background and many of the same characters and situations as my 1990 novelette *Towards Kilimanjaro,* it is not a direct sequel to that story but rather an expansion and refinement of its ideas. Readers of both may notice a number of seeming inconsistencies; these are deliberate; *Towards Kilimanjaro* should be read as a working prototype for this book.

Thanks to CEM Computers, who saved a sizable portion of the book from cybernetic nirvana. (Always back up. *Always* back up.) Thanks also to Trisha for her inestimable help in the early stages of this work, and in all things.

a tapestry of stars

The light was almost gone now. Late-summer purples lay across the Point's heathlands and salt marshes. An edge of cumulus outlined the hills across the lough. The aircraft warning beacons on the television mast were blinking.

The dogs went bounding out into the setting dark. Freed spirits. Primeval forces. Rabbits scattered for their sandy bolt-holes among the gorse roots. Horace was too old and arthritic to kill. He ran for the joy of running; while he still could run. The vet had diagnosed CMDR. The process was irreversible. The myelin sheaths of the lower spinal nerves would deteriorate until his hindquarters were paralyzed. He would not be able to walk. He would piss himself. He would shit himself. Then, the one-way ticket to the rubber-topped table. The girl hoped she would not have to be there for that.

Until then, let them run. Let them hunt. Let them catch what they can, if they can.

"Go, Horace! Go, Paddy!" Gaby McAslan shouted. The dogs flew from her like twin thunderbolts, the big white-and-tan, the smaller black. Crossing a scent, they plunged into the dense gorse thickets, crashed about in the dry brown rustling spines of last summer's growth.

The hills of Antrim rose black against the indigo sky: Knockagh with its cenotaph; Carnmoney; Cave Hill that was said to have a profile like Napoleon's, though Gaby had never been able to see it; Divis; Black Mountain. Belfast was a hemisphere of amber airglow at the head of the lough; grubby, phototoxic. Beneath the black hills a chain of yellow-and-white lights clung to the shoreline. Fort William. Greenisland. Carrickfergus with its great Norman keep. Kilroot, Whitehead, ending with the pulse and flash of the lighthouse that marked the open sea. Its counterparts on Lighthouse Island and at Donaghadee responded. There is a moment, one moment, her father had said, when all the beams flash as one. She had been watching the lights all her life and she had never yet seen that moment of synchronicity.

The sky seemed vast and high tonight, pierced by the first

few stars. The summer triangle: Altair, Deneb, Vega. Arcturus descending, the guide star of the ancient Arab navigators. Sinbad's star. Corona Borealis; the crown of summer. One of those soft jewels was a cluster of four hundred galaxies. Their light had traveled for a billion years to fall on Gaby McAslan. They receded from her skin at fifty thousand miles per second.

Knowing their names and natures could take nothing from them. They were stars, remote, subject to laws and processes larger than human lifetimes. By their high and ancient light you saw the nature of your self. You were not the pinnacle of creation beneath a protecting veil of sky. You were a fierce, bright atom of selfhood, encircled by fire.

The dogs came plunging from the gorse, panting, smiling, empty-jawed. She whistled them to her. The path turned along a ruinous drystone wall past the marshy ground. Yellow flag and tattered bullrushes. Diamondback tracks of mountain bikes in the dirt, but also the heavier tread of scramblers. Her father would not be pleased. Let people enjoy the Point by their own power, foot or pedal; that was the spirit he had tried to build for this place. The gobble of motorbike engines, the shriek of gear trains shouted it down.

Marky had never caught the thing about this place. He could not understand what a day smells like, or what it is to know you are tiny but brilliant beneath the appallingly distant stars. He left scrambler tracks on the world, or car tires; not bicycle treads or bare footprints.

She climbed the low, lichen-covered rocks and stood at the edge of the land. The dogs splashed and frolicked in a gravelly inlet, pretending to swim. Paddy, the small black one, ran in circles with a kelp stalk in his mouth, inviting Gaby to play. Later. She breathed in the air. Sea salt, dead things desiccating on the shore, the sweet land smells of gorse and bog iris, the scent of earth that has soaked in the heat and light of the day and in the twilight gently exhales.

Down at the edge of the sea she built a ring of stones and set a small fire in it. It was a cardinal sin on the Point, but the warden's daughter should be permitted some license. She sat on a rock and fed driftwood to the flames. Bleached branches, slabs of old fish boxes tarry and studded with nails, pieces of forklift pallet and old cork fishing floats. The wood popped and crackled. Sparks showered up into the scented night.

"No, I'd rather not, not tonight, Marky," she had told him on the phone. The video-compression chip amplified his facial movements. Gaby always thought of silent-movie actors. Heavy heavy makeup; big big expressions. Love. Hate. Fear. Rejection. Marky's emotions matched his videophone face; that was the problem. "I have to think. I need some time for me; just for me. No one else. I have to get distant from everything and maybe then I can look back and see what I want to do. Do you understand?"

She knew that all he understood was that saying no to him on a Sunday night was saying no to him forever. He already had her going up the steps to the airplane.

The dogs came to stand by her. Water dripped from stalactites of belly hair. They were panting. They wanted her to give them a task to do.

"Sorry, lads. In a minute, right? Go off and kill something yourselves."

Out to sea, black guillemots skimmed the water, calling to each other in fluting, querulous voices.

They had refused to let her sleep late the day the results came out. First her father, back from his dawn survey of his little kingdom, with tea that she let go cold. Then the dogs, cold noses under warm duvet, heavy paws on ribs. Then the cats, fighting for a place between her breasts. Last of all, Reb pulling the corner of the quilt, shouting, "Come on, come on, you have to go and see."

The old school is strange when you are no longer a part of it. Its rooms and corridors are suddenly smaller than you remember. The staff you meet are subtly changed; no longer authority figures, but fellow survivors. She had not wanted to open the slim brown envelope in front of her friends. In the privacy of her father's wreck of a Saab she had unfolded the single sheet of paper. The grades were good. More than good enough for the Network Journalism course. And that was perhaps worse than them not being good enough because now she would have to decide between going to London and staying.

Rebecca and Hannah had respectively hugged and shrugged. Her father had popped a bottle of real champagne he had bought on faith. His long-term girlfriend, Sonya, who was too wise to move into a house so full of women, came to the celebration meal. Marky too. Everyone had been certain she would go to England, except Marky, and herself.

Her fire was burned down to red coals crusted with powdery white ash.

Marky. He had a job in a bank. He had a Ford. He had money when everyone else was broke. He had good expensive clothes, he had just-past-fashionable music and machinery far too impressive to play it on. In winter he played hockey, in summer he windsurfed. In either season he expected his girlfriends to stand back and admire him. Someday he would have a beautiful house and a beautiful wife and beautiful children and a life as dead dead dead as that empty crab husk lying claws-up on the gravel beach.

Gaby flicked the dead crab into the fire. Its chitinous shell squeaked and hissed, its legs curled up and withered in flame.

Marky imagined that thrice-weekly fumbles with her bra strap and a condom dropped out of the car window could hold her back from London and Network Journalism. He was a fool. It had never been a man that would keep her here. She had made him an excuse. It was this place, this Point she had known all her life, in all its seasons and climates. It was the thick walls of the Watchhouse on its promontory, watching over land and sea and the lives those walls contained. It was the golden light of rare autumn days; it was the silver frost on the dead brown bracken on January mornings; it was the shudder of the little headland beneath the storm waves when the wind seemed to push at the house like a pair of huge hands and got inside through crannies and vents to blow the carpet up like a heavy green sea. It was the little beaches on the seaward sides of the low islets known only to those who have paddled through the shallow tidal lagoons. It was being rooted in the land. It was the fear that her strength came from the physical presence of place and house and people, and separated from them she would become pale and transparent. An unperson.

''There are two, and only two ultimate fears,'' her father had told her one September storm night with the wind bowing in the window glass. ''The annihilation of solitude or the annihilation of the crowd. We lose our identities if we are alone with no one to reflect us back on ourselves and tell us we exist, we are worth something, or we lose our identities if we are in a mass of others; anonymous, corporate, overwhelmed by the babble.''

Gaby was old enough to understand that hers was the fear of the annihilation of the crowd. In solitude, in this place among the elements, she existed. To go would be to join the mass. That was the nature of her dilemma.

''Give me a sign,'' she said. Insects whirred. She flicked them away from her face and long, straight mahogany hair. So many stars. The dark-adapted eye can see four thousand stars on a clear night. A constellation crossed heaven; an aircraft, following the line of the coast into the City Airport.

It was not a sign.

A cluster of lights moved against the far side of the lough. A night ferry, decks aglow.

It was not a sign either.

Saturn and its moons were still under the horizon, beyond the hills of Scotland. That was the thing that most exemplified Marky. Mysteries that would inspire anyone with a functioning sense of wonder were happening out there. To Marky, they were too far away, too small to be seen with the naked eye; irrelevant. How many times had she told him he had no soul? The biggest question occupying him was whether Gaby would let him get his hand down the front of her jeans. She felt pity for people who were never touched by things greater than themselves.

''Come on, dogs.'' They appeared out of the darkness, eager for something to be happening at last. ''We're going back.''

She poured yellow sand over the embers of her fire and walked back to the house beneath the brilliant stars. The dogs went streaking out before her, catching the scent of home.

In the living room that looked out over the harbor, Reb was curled comfortably on the sofa, half watching the Sunday-night sports results on the television while she stitched at her tapestry. It was a monumental work: a map of the zodiac eight feet long. Cats purred, nested in the blue-and-gold folds of Capricorn and Aries. She had been at it six months; it would take another six to complete at her rate of a sign per month. Gaby admired her youngest sister's dedication to long, exacting tasks. In many ways, Rebecca was the best of them.

''Two nil,'' Reb said, without looking up from the needlepoint. ''They lost.''

''Shit,'' said Gaby McAslan.

''Marky left a message on the machine.''

''Double shit. I'm making coffee. You want?''

''Hannah's in the kitchen tacklin' with one of her wee Christian boyfriends.''

"Thrice shit. Dad?"

"Upstairs, trying to get a look at what's going on out at Saturn."

"Anything about it?"

"Some boffins on the news just now with some new theory or something. I'd be more bothered about two nil."

"Season's young yet."

"Gab."

She stopped, hand on the door frame where all their heights had been scratched indelibly with a steel ruler and pair of dividers.

"You should have better than Marky. Dump him before he dumps you."

Strange, wise child. Four years separated them, but Gaby was more kin to Reb than Hannah, the middle sister who had spent most of her life on a long and solitary search for belonging. Playgroup, GymClub, Brownies, Guides, school choirs, sports teams and now a multitude of little Christian groups that kept her running from meeting to meeting. Sound theology, Gaby thought. If they stay too long in one place, they might start having ideas about sex.

What would the small-group leaders have to say about the mystery out at Iapetus? Something to do with the end of the world, probably.

The Watchhouse was the best kind of house in which to grow up. It had enough windings and twinings and crannyings for privacy and enough openings to the seascapes outside to draw you out when you felt you were curling in on yourself. These qualities met in the Weather Room. Tradition in the village was that each generation of occupants add something permanent to the Watchhouse. The previous resident had built the new dining room that smelled of beeswaxed wood paneling and had views on its three sides of harbor, headland and open sea. The current resident had put his contribution directly on top of it. It was a kind of conservatory-cum-observatory-cum-study-cum-wizard's-den. Glass walls gave unparalleled panoramas of the coastline on both sides of the lough. You felt like you were standing on the bridge of a stone ship with waves breaking on your rocky bows. In autumn the storm spray would drench the windows and the wind would howl under the eaves and wrench at the chimney pots and satellite dish and then you were Vanderdecken flying forever with his crew of the damned into the eye of the eternal hurricane.

"Two nil, Gab."

"I know. Reb told me."

Her father sucked his teeth in mock regret, shook his head. At least tonight he was not playing those terrible punk records of his from the 1970s. "Golden years," he would insist. Every generation reckons the music of the time when it gains social mobility to be the golden years.

"Give me a hand with this."

They dragged the telescope on its stand to the open window. It was a good telescope; the best you could buy for the money. That had always been her father's way, to buy good, to buy expensive, but never to buy indiscriminately. It was one piece of parental wisdom his daughters had learned. A still-unsolved domestic mystery was how he always had vastly more money than his many little occupations—a spot of wardenship, a bit of writing, a little boat chartering—could account for.

"Marky left a message."

Gaby hoped he could see her grimace in the dark room. The only light was from the monitors.

"How did he look?"

"Rudolph Valentino plays Jilted Nobility. Here, click on this, would you?"

The lower screen displayed coordinates for the seventeenth moon of Saturn. The upper showed a videostill of what remained of Iapetus's brightside.

"Is that from Hubble?"

Her father nodded.

"Those must be costing you a penny or two."

"They're handing them out free. Loss leader to get new subscribers to the Astronomy Net. It's not every day a moon goes black."

Gaby moved the mouse. The screen flashed at her. The telescope moved on its computer-controlled mounting. Gaby's father bent to the eyepiece.

"Perfect."

"You'd be much better off with the pictures from Hubble. All you'll get on that is a white dot that suddenly vanishes when it drops below resolving power."

"Sometimes I'm ashamed to think I may have raised such an

unromantic creature as you, Gabriel McAslan. If full occultation is tonight, I want to witness it with my own naked and bloodshot eyeballs.''

''So have they decided if it's Interior Vulcanism or Black Snow?''

''The money's on Black Snow, but I don't buy it. Where does this space snow come from all of a sudden? How does it get round the trailing side of the satellite? And why is it building up symmetrically on all sides? If you read the bulletin boards, you'll get theories from alien redevelopment to God with a pot of cosmic black paint. Everything's a racing certainty until the NASA probe gets there in 2008.''

Gaby looked through the telescope. She hoped her father would not smell the wood smoke in her hair. As a precaution she had changed her T-shirt. It was the one with the masturbating nun on it. She loved it, though her father disapproved of her wearing it around younger and impressionable sisters. She adjusted the eyepiece. At the age of eighteen she could find her way around the solar system better than the capital of her own province. In the solar system you could not end up with the wrong name in the wrong district. No one sprayed *Iochaid Ar La* on the slopes of Olympus Mons or painted the edges of the craters on the moon red white and blue.

The enigma of Iapetus with its dark and light hemispheres had fascinated generations of astronomers, science-fiction writers and lovers of mysteries. The *Voyager* missions had only deepened the mystery. Hubble had squinted Saturn-ward and added a few more lightside features to the atlases of the solar system but nothing to the Casini Regio debate. The new generation of big orbital telescopes had turned away from planetary astronomy to the grandeur of star birth and star death among the glowing gas sheets of the inner galaxy. With them went the professional star-watchers. The celestial backyard was left for the amateurs to play in. It was an Italian postman and part-time planet-spotter who noticed that there seemed to be less of the brightside of Iapetus than the last time he had looked at it. He had logged his observations into the Astronomy Nets. They had lain gathering data-dust for almost a month; then, when they began to provoke gossip, had drawn professional ridicule until someone had the courage to sneak a peek with the Mauna Kea reflector at the Saturnian System.

While the professionals bickered and prevaricated, sixty percent of Iapetus's surface had turned black. This could not now be ignored. Projects were canceled, time slots reassigned, funding found. Hubble and her sisters were swung back to Saturn. What they saw out there made lead lines in every prime-time news slot. It was not so much that Iapetus was turning black, it was how it was turning black. The dark was closing in equally on all sides: the circle of bright white ice was dwindling like a focused-down spotlight.

Ten days later all that remained was a white dot fifty miles across, threatened on all sides by the dark. Someone had calculated that the black was advancing across Iapetus at ten miles per hour.

The upper monitor displayed the nature of the catastrophe. NASA had overlain the dark disc with a topographic map. Iapetus's surface features were named after figures from the *Song of Roland.* Roland himself had been among the first to fall; his soul-friend Oliver and mighty King Charlemagne not long after. The battle plain of Roncevaux was taken; only Hamon stood against the encircling dark. Soon he too would fall and there would be no more heroes anymore.

"What is that stuff?" Gaby whispered. The light from the Copeland Islands beamed across the room. She thought of Marky, out there in the night in his car with his friends and his fast food and his expensive stereo playing his cheap music. It is a poor kind of human who is not a little afraid of the powers in the sky. You can hide from them and pretend that they do not exist and limit your life by your ignorance, or you can go out from your strong, safe house into the night and call them out and maybe make sense of them to yourself and to the world.

Her father replaced Gaby at the telescope. "Thirty miles to full occultation," he said, fiddling with the eyepiece.

The pictures from Hubble were being updated every thirty seconds. The upper screen abruptly blanked. A new message appeared. Gaby read it.

"Dad. There's something here I think you should see."

"I think we're going to miss full occultation. It'll just be below the horizon. Damn."

"Hyperion's disappeared."

He was there in an instant.

It was on the screen. A Net-wide bulletin: at 20:35 GMT September 8 2002 researchers using the Miyama Small Object orbital observatory reported the disappearance of Saturn's sixteenth moon, Hyperion, from their monitors. Instantly. Totally. Inexplicably.

"Jesus," said Gaby's father reverently.

"How can that happen?" Gaby asked.

"I don't know. I don't think anyone knows."

E-mail icons winked into existence along the top of the screen; the informational equivalent of the Irish Astronomical LocalNet shouting all at once.

"The whole of the moon," Gaby said. Fresh information flooded downline from NASA. *Voyager* flyby photographs and simulations of Hyperion: a blighted potato of a moonlet three hundred and fifty by two hundred and fifty by two hundred miles. Gone. The satellite's final seconds came through image processing from Miyama Control, frame by frame. For twenty frames nothing happened. On frame twenty-one, Hyperion seemed to throw off its surface like the peel from an orange. Light glowed from the cracks, fanned from the torn open ridges and dorsae. Frames twenty-two to thirty-two were white. Pure white. Frame twenty-three was nothing. Just space and stars without any sign of the several trillion tons of rocky ice called Hyperion.

Total elapsed time of the moon's destruction was 4.38 seconds.

The oak door to the Weather Room opened. The dogs came rushing in, running around and wagging their tails. Something had excited them. After them came Rebecca. She looked fearful.

"It was on the news," she said. "They interrupted *Spitting Image* for it."

"Nothing left bigger than a hundred feet across," Dad read from the sceen. "Or the Small Object Array would have picked it up. They're trying to tell us it was a cometary impact."

"And the next moon out goes black all over?" Gaby said.

"I think sensible people should be afraid of this," Reb said.

"Sensible people are," her father said. On the monitor, Hyperion's final seconds were repeated, over and over.

They are trusting that they will find answers there, Gaby thought. They are trusting that those answers will make sense, that there are people who can explain why the world constantly surprises them. It does not have to be logical, forgivable or even sane, but eventually explicable in some way or other. That is why you must go away, because you want to be the person who has the answers to the question *why?*

It was easy now. It was surprising how little decision there was to be made when it came to it. A fire on the Point and the death of a moon had helped her, but she had always known since she had posted off the application for the Network Journalism course that in the end she would go. She wanted to tell them she was right and she was ready, but her father was showing Reb what all the information coming through the Net meant.

Horace came and stood beside her, beseeching attention. She ruffled the fine, soft hair behind his ear. She pointed out to him the way she would be going; out there, past the lights of the ferry she had seen from the Point, far beyond the glow of the land, beyond even the reach of the lighthouses, to the open sea and the country on the other side of it. But he was only a big tan-and-white dog with a degenerative nervous disease, who understood nothing.

african night flight

1

Videodiary Entry: March 23 2008.
Ten thousand feet over the Equator.

Now we'll see if it's true. The Coriolis effect thing. Dr. Dan probably thinks I'm either insane or have amoebic dysentery, but if you've got a Personal Data Unit that can give you exact time and location anywhere on the planet, how could you resist testing the old Plughole and Hemisphere Experiment?

God, I hope no one really has amoebic dysentery and needs to get in. Muttering from the portside toilet. Probably think I'm scoring lines, or applying for the Mile-High Club.

What we are now seeing is the wash-hand basin of a Kenya Airways Airbus A-330. The PDU says we are traveling at eight hundred and eighty miles per hour; our location is twelve kays north of the equator. Which—just a moment while I press a few buttons—is fifty seconds or so.

T-ten. I pull the plug. Lo! The water spirals clockwise. Three, two, one: equator. And the water is running straight down the sides of the plughole. Now I'm in the southern hemisphere and, *tadah!* The water spirals anticlockwise. Gaby McAslan proves that the earth moves in space.

You know, I wasn't totally convinced it would do that.

Gaby McAslan switched off the visioncam. The cabin staff were getting restless out there. They had obviously all read *Airport.* She sniffed the soap, rejected it, emptied out the clever little lockers and plundered them. The disposable razors would be useful. The men's cologne did not smell too bad. Condoms. *FlightMates.* She took a handful more as a hope than a precaution. Her malaria/yellow fever/HIV 1 and 2 inoculation scab itched sympathetically.

Back in executive, Dr. Dan had ordered her another whiskey on his government account.

"Well, did it?" he asked. His voice was gentle and very deep.

"It did."

He stirred his drink with a plastic swizzle stick shaped like an elongated giraffe.

"I suppose it is a kind of cancer," he said. Executive class was being woken up with passion-fruit juice and microwaved croissants. The plane was well into its descent path. "The Chaga, I mean. As there are sicknesses that eat a person's life away from inside, so there are diseases of nations. It invades the land, draws strength from it, kills what it finds and duplicates only itself. While we sit here contemplating our croissants, it is growing, it is spreading. It never sleeps. Even the name you have given it is not its own, but has been taken from the people who once lived there: what else can it be, Ms. McAslan, but a cancer?"

He glanced out the window. Nothing to see in the predawn dark but engine glow and the flicker of warning beacons.

"So early in the task of nation building too. Why, we have scarcely fifty years of history behind us and suddenly *boom!*" He softly smacked heel of hand into palm. "Surely, God is not kind to Kenya; just as the information revolution was allowing us to take our true place in the world, we find we must go hand open to the United Nations. We shall certainly not have fifty more years. What is it they are estimating? Twenty more until the country is overrun? Seventy years is not time to be a nation. Why could it not have come down in France or England, where they have too much history; or China or India, where they have so much past they do not know what to do with it? Or America, where at least they could turn being made into another planet into a theme park."

In the course of her professional travel, Gaby McAslan had come to dread airline booking computers and their malicious humor. They put you next to terrible people. The noisiest eater in the world. The man with the one long hair coming down his nose that you couldn't take your eyes off until you wanted to reach over and tear it out by its follicle. The teenager whose Discman would hiss and whisper away in the high treble notes. The person who had memorized every word of Monty Python's *Life of Brian.*

Sometimes the computers relented. Then their favor shone upon you.

"You will pardon me if I blaspheme," the big, heavy black man in the next seat had said as the Airbus turned onto Heathrow's main runway and throttled up. "I am not a very good flier, I am afraid." He had sunk his fingers into the armrest and stared at his feet. As the plane lifted off he very reverently whispered, "Jesus."

He was Dr. Daniel Oloitip. You would not think it to look at him, but he was Masai.

"I have become a city creature, sleek and soft," he had apologized. "But mostly old."

"I like your ear," Gaby had said, looking at his right lobe, which had been pierced and stretched into a loop of flesh that hung to his jawline. Dr. Daniel Oloitip had taken a Fuji film can from the bag under his seat and slipped it through the loop.

"This is the current fashion. They throw them out of safari buses by the thousand. It does not create quite the right image for the Overseas Development Agency."

Dr. Dan was a politician, the member of Parliament for Amboseli and Kajiado South constituency. He was returning for a daughter's wedding from an aid-begging mission around the capitals of the European Union. A waste of time, he reckoned. The Europeans had been civil, but there would be no more money. They would not lend to a nation that might not be there by the time the first interest payment became due.

"It is ironic that they send me with the alms bowl, whose constituency will be the first to go. Already half of it is lost, though I draw some small satisfaction from knowing that I will be the first Parliamentary representative for another planet. Next election I shall be canvassing aliens."

Dr. Dan set his yellow plastic swizzle giraffe at the end of a line along the edge of his folding table. Gaby sipped the whiskey he had bought her and imagined Kenya slipping away beneath the belly of the Airbus. Dark Africa, down in the underdawn. Wonderful names: Eldoret and Kisumu, Longonot and Nandi Hills, Nyeri and Ngong. Lake Nakuru, Lake Naivasha, Lake Baringo. Mt. Elgon and Mt. Kenya; the Aberdares that were now the Nyandarua. The Rift Valley. These were among the first places to be named by human voices. Powerful, ancient names.

She could feel the descent in her inner ears. The captain bing-bonged. Should be down in about so long. Temperature about so warm, wind speed so fast. Please set your watches to East African time; non-Kenyan nationals, please have your landing cards ready for collection, and we advise you that under exchange regulations all foreign currency brought into the country must be declared on arrival and that it is illegal to import any Kenyan currency. Thank you.

They were going down and all the anticipation that had pretended it was only anxiety about the long journey became a fist of excitement in the base of her belly. The big Airbus was dipping down over all those strong, ancient names toward a new city, new friends, a new job, new life. Toward SkyNet, and Nairobi, and to the south, not so far on the map but on the very frontier of the imagination, the Chaga. Like the Chaga, none of it could be stopped. Not now. Her hands were shaking so badly she could hardly fill in the landing card. Dr. Dan smiled as he saw her write *On-line Multimedia Journalist* in the space that asked her occupation.

"Westerners have always come to my country because of something," he said. "It used to be because of the animals, because of the coast. Now it is because of the Chaga. No one comes because it is Kenya. That does not seem to be enough, unfortunately. Be good to my country, Gaby McAslan; it is a good country. The world should know that, if it knows nothing else."

The plane rocked a little.

"Oh, dear me." Dr. Dan closed his eyes and gripped the armrests. Sweat had broken out on his forehead. The captain came on again. If you look out the left, those lights are Nairobi. That's where we'll land. The plane rocked again. Up went the flaps. The Airbus banked steeply. Gaby looked down at the yellow lights, scattered like grain on the high, dark plain.

The plane slammed sharply to the right. Engines screamed. Gaby shrieked and seized the seat back in front of her. Dr. Dan grabbed for the window frame, trying to brace himself, but there is nothing you can hold on to when you are sliding toward the ground at three hundred miles per hour. All the plastic giraffes fell off the table. Hostesses went reeling. Landing cards scattered like frightened birds. Gaby saw a shape loom in the window, a ghostly pale winged thing far closer than any shape should have been. For an instant the other aircraft's lights lit up the Airbus's cabin, then it was gone.

Gaby and Dr. Dan stared at each other. It was the stare of people who have felt the wind from beneath the wings of the angel of death, who is white, and fast, and always closer than you think.

"I saw another plane," Gaby whispered. "A big white plane. Coming right at us."

Dr. Dan nodded.

"A near miss," he croaked. "It was a UNECTA aircraft."

The captain apologized on the PA and said that there had been a close approach situation but everything was under control and they would be on the ground in three minutes. He sounded like he would be personally very glad to be down there. FASTEN SEAT BELTS/NO SMOKING pinged on. Gaby felt the reassuring rumble of wheels going down and locking. Three minutes later they were on the ground. They taxied a long way to find a stand. They all seemed to be occupied by enormous transport aircraft hastily painted white with the blue-mountain-and-paired-crescents symbol of UNECT*Afrique* on their tails.

Gaby and Dr. Dan waited for the plane to empty before gathering their things. On the concrete it was colder than Gaby expected equatorial Africa should be. Streaks of gray and dull red lightened the sky behind the main tower. Dr. Dan shook Gaby's hand at the foot of the steps.

"Have a good wedding," Gaby said.

"I doubt it, somehow. Her betrothed is not a good man. Then again, my daughter is not a good woman. So maybe it will work well. If it does not, I shall want the fifty cattle I gave that good-for-nothing as dowry back." A black Mercedes was approaching from under the passenger pier. "It was a pleasure to have met you, Gaby McAslan. Doubtless, given the nature of our vocations, we will meet again. I look forward to it. I shall certainly never use an aircraft washroom again without thinking of you." He smiled wickedly and was driven away in the black Mercedes.

Don't go, Gaby wanted to shout, alone on the apron among the huge white aircraft. Don't leave me.

They had lost her luggage. She waited for it to appear in Reclaim until the man came to shut the carousel off. He told her where she could make a report, and not to worry. The immigration officer was just settling down for a doze when she came through. He stamped her passport, checked her inoculation certificates and assured her with a wonderful, generous smile that her bag would turn up very soon. She would see. The smart woman with the very good English at the airline desk gave the same assurances and smile. It would be brought to her hotel. Where was she staying? The PanAfric. But only for three days until she found somewhere more permanent.

There was one figure in the whole big arrivals hall. He was a short, stoutish, middle-aged man in the rumpled linen suit that was uniform for male East Africa staff. His black hair was receding at the front but had been let grow long at the back. It looked as if his scalp had slipped. He wore round spectacles that with everything else gave the impression of an owl on a long-haul holiday. Rather needlessly, he was holding a cardboard sign with *Gabriel McAslan* felt-markered on it.

"T. P. Costello?"

"Gabriel McAslan?"

"Gaby."

They shook hands.

"Is this all you've got?" the short man asked. He was the Nairobi station chief of SkyNet News but had never lost his native North Dublin accent. Easier to take the boy out of Barrytown than Barrytown out of the boy.

"They lost my luggage."

"It'll turn up. That's the amazing thing about this country. It looks like bloody chaos, but things get done all the same."

It was even colder in the car park than on the apron. Gaby's breath steamed. The gray dawn light was just strong enough to make the white floods dazzling and surreal. The SkyNet logos on the sides and hood of the big Toyota Landcruiser gleamed.

I am here, Gaby McAslan told herself as she fastened her seat belt. *This is me, this is real.* No. She could not believe it. There was still a pane of glass like a television screen between her and the reality that she was in Africa.

"Good flight?"

"Apart from losing all my worldly goods and a near miss with a UNECTA plane on the way down, about as good as any long-haul flight can be."

"Those bloody Antonovs," T. P. Costello said, sliding his credit card into the car-park reader. "Things should have been scrapped twenty years ago, but as usual the UN's running the whole damn show on a shoestring. It'll take hundreds of dead bodies before they wise up."

"There almost were." Soldiers in blue helmets waved them through the sandbagged permanent checkpoint. "I met an interesting guy, though. Could be useful. Dr. Daniel Oloitip."

T. P. Costello laughed.

"Dr. Dan. He's all right. One of the white-hats, I suppose. At least he doesn't have his head so far up UNECTA's ass that every time it yawns you can see him singing 'God Bless America.' An African problem with an African solution, he says. I agree with him."

"Except it's an Asian and South American and Indian Ocean problem as well."

They were on the main road now, a good two-lane highway. Most of the streetlights were still working. It was early, but traffic was heavy. A stream of taxis flowed out from the city, some with biogas compression tanks fitted into their trunks. Big gasoline tanker trains hurtled inbound through the morning dusk. Oil products were precious with the connections to the coast under threat. Everywhere were small Japanese microbuses with baggage-laden racks welded to their roofs. Each was filled to bursting with passengers. Some brave souls clung to the sides or hung from the sliding doors. The road surface was inches from them and the vehicles seemed only to have one speed, which was flat-out, but the hangers-on were blasé enough to wave and grin and waggle their tongues at the white woman in the big Landcruiser.

"Matatus," T. P. Costello said. "Something between a bus and a taxi. Cheaper than either and a hell of a lot less safe. They go all over the damn country: up mountains, across deserts, through swamps. There're probably ones trying to make it through the Chaga. Everybloodywhere. Only use in dire emergencies." He braked and blared simultaneously as a green Hiace bus cut in front of him. The matatu flashed its hazard warning lights impudently and accelerated. Faces grinned in the rear window. *The Lord Is Thy Salvation* said a sticker on the glass.

Shanties crowded the airport road on each side. The rows of tin shacks and cardboard lean-tos stretched farther than Gaby could see in the gray light. The township had been awake and busy since before dawn, as the poor must. Women lined up with plastic demijohns at the community standpipes or stood battered margarine cans to boil on wood fires. Some carried sacks of grain on their heads. The sacks read A GIFT FROM THE PEOPLE OF THE UNITED STATES. Some women scrubbed children in the porches of their shacks, others pounded washing and hung it out to dry. Ten thousand trickles of pale blue wood smoke rose up and mingled in a veil that hung low in the cold morning air.

Children were everywhere. Standing by the side of the road with fingers in their mouths, rolling heavy tractor tires up the twining alleys, driving away leprotic dogs or mangy goats with well-aimed stones. They were thin and poorly clothed, but Gaby did not see one who was not smiling.

She wound down the window and unfolded her visioncam.

“I’d put that away if I were you,” T.P. said. “Or you’ll end up with a rock up it. Not that that matters to me, but they might miss and I don’t want to have to pay for another new windscreen for this buggy. You think this is bad? I tell you, this is one of the good ones. You should see Pumwani. Jesus. Ten million people; Nairobi’s population doubles every five years. If it was me, I’d take my chances with the Chaga, but the UN says evacuate and so we evacuate. One day they’ll run out of places to evacuate to. It’s not an if, it’s a when, but they can’t see that. This is what happens when you try to apply military thinking to something totally outside its conceptual framework, like an alien colonization.”

Traders had spread plastic sheets on the oily red earth verges and laid out their wares for inspection. Piles of misshaped oranges, unsteady pyramids of Sprite cans, knobs of maize blackened over hubcaps filled with charcoal. Flies were shooed from grilling skewers of meat with whisks of shredded newspaper. Seeing white faccs, children sprang up, shimmering bangles looped over their fingers.

“Karma bracelets, they call them.” T.P. hooted savagely and swerved around a homemade water cart that was little more than an oil drum on car tires hauled by an emaciated pony. “Hokum for the New Agers. They’re actually optical fiber. Grab the stuff up faster than Kenya Telecom can lay it down. Funny thing is, there are people not even five minutes into the country who’ll stop and buy one. That’s the thing about this place, there’s always someone trying to sell you some damn thing or another.”

A white aircraft appeared over the slum. It came very low, very fast. Its wheels hung down like the talons of a bird of prey. It seemed far too huge and heavy to be kept aloft by those ridiculous wings. Gaby cringed as it passed over the highway in a howl of engines and dropped toward the threshold lights.

“Was a time when all this was open bush,” T.P. said. “Dead Tommy’s gazelles all over the place. No road sense. Giraffes used to saunter right across this. You stopped for them. Okay. Catechism time.” He glanced as long at Gaby as the traffic would allow. ''Rule one. With your complexion, never ever go out without a hat for six months at least. Melanoma you can do without. What'll you do?''

''Wear a hat.''

''That's correct. Two: you've got green eyes, right? Wear shades. All the time.''

''Don't need to. I got an eye job done. Pupils photochromed; it lasts a year.''

''Not out here it doesn't. You'll get six months max with the UV levels at this altitude. Don't forget to get them redone; crow's-feet you don't want. Underwear.''

''Cotton. No artificial fabrics. Don't breathe.''

''And what'll you get?''

''Thrush if I'm lucky. And no bodysuits either.''

''That's correct. And if you do get fungus?''

''A tampon dipped in live yogurt.''

''Not likely ever to try it myself, but that's what I'm told. Money.''

''Keep it in your shoe, but always have a hundred shillings handy for mugging money. Avoid conspicuous wealth.''

''Current scam is threatening you with hypodermics filled with HIV-infected blood. Whether you believe them or not is your call, but don't trust your jabs. HIV 4 farts in the face of the Pasteur Institute and you're home in a body bag in six months tops. Therefore, no unprotected cocks, white, black or any other color. What'll you do?''

''Be a nun.''

''That's correct. And be careful about things like going to the dentist, or getting your hair cut, which you should. Half an inch all over.''

''I'd sooner stick needles in my eyes.''

''Be permanently hot and sticky, then. Your choice. Water.''

''Don't trust it, even in hotels. Wash your teeth with bottled. No ice in drinks, peel all fruit and treat salads with extreme caution. And don't drink beer out of the bottle.''

''Those two guys.'' He pointed at two men walking hand in hand along the side of the road. ''Gay or just good friends?''

''Just good friends. African men have no problem showing same-sex physical affection.''

''Good girl. I think you might actually do here. Of course, culture shock never hits right away. It waits until you think you're comfortable and feeling you know all there is to know. Then it goes for you. It can kill you. You're booked in for three days at the PanAfric. Sorry it can't be longer, but unlike UNECTA, we have to operate to strict commercial principles. Bad news is UNECTA's pushed the private rental market right up into the ionosphere. Best advice is book into a cheap guesthouse and be prepared for a lot of footwork. What should you do?''

Gaby McAslan did not answer. The sun had burned away the dawn mists. Golden light spread across the tin roofs of the shanties: in the middle distance, the towers of Nairobi rose sheer from the encircling townships. Light caught their many windows and kindled them into pillars of fire rising from the dark earth. Gaby lifted her visioncam and videoed through the Landcruiser's filthy windshield. It would not catch it; video never could catch it. The act of putting a frame around it killed the magic, but perhaps an echo might be held on the disc, enough for a moment of a moment.

They were into the urban traffic now: private cars—4X4s mostly—and buses, yellow-and-green behemoths that had never been washed, belching black diesel smoke. Their windows had been replaced by steel bars. T.P. swore expressively as one cut in front of him on a roundabout—*keepie-leftie* in Swahili, he informed Gaby. They passed a big church and a covered market, the national football stadium and the country bus station. They crossed the railway and turned onto a tree-lined highway with parkland on one side and downtown Nairobi on the other. Gaby watched a beautiful tall black woman in a red one-piece run along the side of the road. She moved with a liquid, unconscious grace that made Gaby feel angular and badly put together. The sun was high now. Shafts of light fell between the buildings into the avenues. T.P. turned the Landcruiser onto Kenyatta Avenue and drove against the flow of the morning traffic up a shallow valley wooded with tired eucalyptus and acacia. Pedestrians thronged the red earth footpaths where the edge of the highway had crumbled away. Posters for toothpaste adorned the bus shelters. T.P. threw the Landcruiser up a curving concrete drive that opened abruptly on the left. It led to an anonymous international-style hotel perched on the hillside.

''This is you. My advice is go straight to bed and sleep it off. These overnight flights bugger your clock gene. We aren't expecting you in until tomorrow anyway. We'll fix you up with an

EastAf Teleport account, but it takes a little time, so your PDU won't be doing much for a day or so." He leaned across and opened Gaby's door. "Sorry to have to boot you out like this, but I've got the end of the world to attend to." As she got out she heard him mutter, "What is it with this place for Irish girls anyway?"

The door slammed. The wheels spun. He was gone. She was alone with an overnight bag and the clothes on her back. Her feet had swollen inside her boots on the flight. A porter in a red fez arrived to carry her bag the twenty feet to Reception.

"Is this all you have?" he asked.

The room was comforting and depressing for the same reasons. You can fly faster, higher, farther, but the rooms at each end are still the same. This one seemed to have been built by a set designer for *Star Trek*. A batik of feeding giraffes and the Nairobi LocalNet directory were the only concessions to this being Africa. Gaby arranged her airline booty in the bathroom. There was a big insect in the upper corner of the shower cubicle. Someone had folded the toilet paper into a point. There would be a little foil-wrapped chocolate on the pillow. She would have to be careful not to fall asleep on it. She did not want to have to wash it out of her hair with the big insect watching balefully for a chance to pounce.

She switched on the radio. Bright guitar music poured forth. The deejay rattled out swaggering pop-Swahili. Encouraged, Gaby opened the window to look at her new city. The bustle on Kenyatta Avenue had not abated. The grubby buses swung amiably along; matatus and little moped tricycles darted impudently between. Everything was way too overloaded. Five men struggled a trolley laden with wood down the road, piling up a long line of traffic as they tried to make a right turn. A convoy of armored vehicles in UN white came up the road from the city center. A continuous grumble of engine noise, sirens and the ghosts of diesel and biogas drifted into the room.

In Uhuru Park the trees were dismembered stumps, pillaged for firewood. Beyond the worn, parched green the inner-city skyline began abruptly. In the high, strong light the towers that had seemed to glow with a golden inner fire now looked shabby and hard-worked. High above the sky was that clear and infinite kind of blue you only see on the hottest days. It was down at street level that it began to take on the orange haze of photochemical smog.

Gaby fetched the camcorder and framed a tracking panoramic from the elegant white bungalows of the well-to-do across the valley from her to the concrete-and-glass sunflower of the Kenyatta Center headquarters of UNECT*Afrique.*

"Hi, Dad," she said. "I'm here."

2

Three thousand years of history gives a perspective on human truths. The Chinese are right. It is a curse to live in interesting times. World events have dangerous slipstreams in which many lives can be swept away. Gaby McAslan was one fated to follow the lights in the sky. Saturn's moons had drawn her to London; the Kilimanjaro Event would drag her across whole years and continents.

Like the death of Kennedy, or Elvis, or the *Challenger,* the Kilimanjaro Event was one of those points where world and self touch and you can remember exactly where you were and what you were doing.

Gaby McAslan was bouncing around in her singlet and panties on her bed, very full of Australian Sémillon-Chardonnay and pretending to avoid the undressing fingers of Sean Haslam, her boyfriend of eight days. He was a part-time network media tutor. The other part of his time he freelanced multimedia overlay for Reuters. Therefore Gaby McAslan had uncorked the uncheap Sémillon-Chardonnay and invited him to bounce on her bed.

"Do you have to have the television on?" he had asked.

"It's going to distract you?" she had asked, smothering him in winy kisses and the mahogany hair that hung to the small of her back.

She had been the distracted one. The late-news presenter had had the look of a man asked to read something he could not believe. So had the correspondents in Washington and Dar es Salaam and at the foot of the mountain. American spysat shots were incontrovertible. On the second pass the resolution was enough to show things the size of a domestic oil tank. Not that there were any oil tanks on Uhuru Peak on the Kibo snowcap. Not that there was anything remotely recognizable there at all after the impact. Gaby had knelt on the bottom of the bed, resting her chin and hands on the carved wooden footboard, watching the news coming out of Africa. She had felt the stretch fabric of her panties slip down across her rump, followed by the inquisitive press and prickle of dick and pubic hair.

"Go away. This is important."

"More important than this?"

"A hell of a lot more important. What kind of multimedia pro are you anyway?"

The camera had taken a few vertiginous, swooping shots of something that looked a little like a multicolored rain forest and a little like a drained coral reef but mostly like nothing anyone had ever seen before. Then the Tanzanian soldier had put his hand over the lens and there was a scuffle of sky and camouflage and the presenter in London was saying that the *infection zone* (he had seemed uneasy with the hastily devised terminology) was expanding outward from the site where the meteor hit Kibo at an estimated fifty feet per day.

He had then shuffled his papers, looked embarrassed and gone on to the rest of the news.

Suddenly sobered and unsexed, Gaby went to the Net. Screen after screen of information unfolded from the on-line news services. Schematics, stills, simulations, animations. Page after page of text. Skywatch satellites hunting for Near Earth Orbiters and Planetbusters had spotted the bolide ten days ago: an atmosphere grazer, a little out of the ordinary in that it had made three complete orbits before entry, but otherwise unremarkable. Its ion trail across the Indian Ocean had been observed by U.S. defense systems, but they no longer mistook meteors for MIRV warheads. It had impacted on the peak of Kilimanjaro, near the camp of a German hang-gliding expedition. Storms had closed off the mountain for three days. Then the stories began, from the local Wa-chagga people and the remnants of the hang-gliding team.

Something was growing up there.

The Tanzanian government might have succeeded in hushing the thing up had an Earth Resources platform not been ordered to turn its cameras on equatorial East Africa. What NASA saw sent them straight to the White House to ask Mr. President if he could ask the Pentagon to loan them a few minutes on the military spy satellites.

The Tanzanians could not have kept it secret for long. Not even the Pentagon could. Not growing at fifty feet per day.

Gaby had not noticed Sean dressing and leaving. After an hour or so she no longer noticed even the images unreeling across her screen. Here was the way to make the world know her name. Her star with her name on it, fallen from heaven. If she was true to it, it would honor her, but she must come to it. That was why it had fallen so far away, so that she would have to prove her worthiness of it. It was patient and enduring—who knew how many billions of miles it had crossed to come to her—but it would not wait forever.

Her tutors were astounded by the enthusiasm with which she addressed her work. They did not see the shining star with her name on it; they saw only her fierce, dark determination. She was racing not against the demands of Network Journalism, but the inexorable growth of the alien flora. When the second biological package came down in the Bismarck Archipelago, to be followed a month later by the Ruwenzori Event, her pace became frenetic. Her tutors told her to slow down. She could not. The United Nations was out there now, in the form of UNECTA, poking and prying and sampling and sniffing her alien rain forest. She had to get there before it was all named and numbered and known and there was no mystery left for her to explain.

Time and inexperience frustrated her. Trapped in gray London, she wished she were the Hundred-Foot Woman who could push the dirty buildings apart until new, strange life sprang through the cracks in the street and the light of a brighter, kinder sun shone through the tear in the sky.

Her semester project on UNECTA as agent of Western industrial neocolonialism earned her a summer placement with SkyNet Multimedia News. It was the first step southward to the plains of East Africa. That summer she determined that she would give SkyNet no possible grounds for declining her a job when she graduated in a year's time. She grew pale and vampirish while the rest of her class flourished in sunny climates. She cultivated relationships, not all of which ended in bed. She shook hands. She did lunches. In the end, she succeeded.

Her father and Reb came to the graduation. First of all her year, she went up to collect her degree. When her father jokingly referred to her ruthlessness, she was startled. She had never thought of herself so. She was a frustrated visionary. The next day she moved into the glass-walled menagerie of SkyNet's London office among the architectural wet dreams of Docklands. It was a junior compiler's post in the economics division, but it was another step south.

The Chaga continued advancing outward at fifty feet every day. Gaby charted its progress on a big map of Africa on the wall of her flat. She stuck photographs around the map: elephants with the snows of Kilimanjaro behind them; aerial views of the great disc of colored mosaic dropped onto the dun landscapes of northern Tanzania. Neither friends nor her brief lovers were allowed to see her little shrine to the Chaga. It was not that she feared them thinking she was pathetic, it was that it was hers and hers alone. Others would profane it.

Beneath the towers of London she maneuvered, she manipulated, she percolated up through the dense hierarchy of SkyNet like ground water rising in an artesian basin. Opportunities opened; promotions appeared: she let them go. They were too easy, she was not ready. There was still the possibility of failure. That would have killed her. She would move only when victory was assured, though every day's wait was a tap of the needle another millimeter deeper under her thumbnail.

Six hundred and forty taps. Six hundred and forty silent chokes of frustration. And because she had honored her star, it honored her. The position was a junior one; had it not been in the Nairobi Station, it would have been a demotion and she would have been fatally overqualified. It was the third step, the sideways step that took you over seas and mountains and deserts to the land of heart's desire.

She put in her application, called in all her overdue markers and went home to Ireland. The answer was there on the Watchhouse's computers as she came in through the door to be greeted by leaping, wagging black Paddy and weeping, hugging Reb and Hannah.

She had a week to get visas, injections, do research, pack bags, buy a new wardrobe and book tickets. Her father uprated her Kenya Airways booking to executive class.

"If you're not coming back, then you must go in style," he said. "It is better to travel first class than to arrive." Then he turned away quickly so that Gaby would not be embarrassed to see how he felt about that.

He gave her a present at the departure gate. It was wrapped

in dark blue paper patterned with stars and moons and ringed planets.

"Open it when you're airborne," he ordered, then hugged her and kissed her in a burly, beardy way and pushed her through the security check. When the little feeder jet had leveled off and Northern Ireland was an edge of white foam on black rocks, she unwrapped the present. It was a minidisc viewcamera; a beautiful little thing, solar-charged, top of the range. Stuffed underneath it was a Manchester United scarf. *It can get cold at two thousand feet, even on the equator,* said the note. *Love Reb.*

3

The rhythmic knocking woke her. *Tap-ta-ta-tap tap tap. Tap-ta-ta-tap tap tap. Tap-ta-ta-tap tap tap.*

Gaby came out of sleep with a start. Purple twilight filled the room. She did not know if it was evening or morning twilight. She did not know what room this was in which she found herself, or how she was in a very big bed covered with a sticky sheet. She did not know why it was so hot.

She fumbled out of bed and gingerly opened the door. On the old-fashioned carpet stood her suitcase. She looked left, she looked right. There was no sign of who had put it here and knocked her into wakefulness and it was a very long corridor. She quickly stepped outside and retrieved the case. The baggage labels were exceedingly interesting. While she had slept her suitcase had been to Mauritius and back.

4

Gaby McAslan came out of jet lag wanting a drink. Food would have been good, but you met more valuable people in hotel bars than restaurants. Hemingway kitsch. Zebra skins on the walls, sad antelope heads begging sympathy. Spears and shields and photographs of great white hunters and their memsahibs squatting on the running boards of ancient Bentleys, dead things at their feet. Wicker tables and chairs, of course. Black staff, white clients. Feeling conspicuous in fashionable silk blouse, jodhpurs and riding boots, Gaby McAslan approached the bar. A short, solid woman with shoulder-length dull blond hair sat on a stool talking with the barman. She wore a sleeveless plaid shirt, combat cutoffs and biker boots. She looked the only other professional in a room of Chaga hangers-on.

"Excuse me, what do people drink around here?" she asked the barman.

"They drink this," the blond woman said. She pushed a bottle along the bar. It had an elephant on the label. "Only beer with picture of factory on bottle. Old joke." She spoke with a pronounced Slavic accent. "I get you one. Moses."

The barman flipped up a dewdropped bottle and uncapped it with his teeth.

"Slainte agus saol," Gaby said to her new drinking companion.

They clinked bottles.

"Big cocks and vodka," the blond woman said.

The beer tasted nothing at all like elephant piss. Drinking from the bottle. Less than twenty-four hours in the place, and you are already sinning against T.P.'s catechism.

"You have funny accent," said the woman. "Know most English accents, but yours . . ."

"Northern Ireland. *Norren iron,* in the local dialect."

"Norren iron," the small woman said, making it sound almost Japanese.

"Russian?" Gaby ventured.

"Fuck no!" the small woman exploded. She ripped open her plaid shirt. Underneath was a much-washed muscle top with a picture of an ugly jet aircraft taking off and something in Cyrillic. "Siberian. Proud of it. Never forget."

Sibirsk, that was what was written on the T-shirt. Part of your research, Gaby McAslan. First generation Aeroflot offspring. They have the air transport franchise for UNECTA. They almost turned you into a five-hundred-mile-per-hour fireball this morning.

"I had a close encounter with one of your comrades coming into Kenyatta Airport," Gaby said.

The Siberian woman sneered.

"Bloody 142s. Need five kays to get down and another ten to get up. Boring boring boring. Only thing you can do on 142 is drink whole damn flight." She patted the aircraft on her T-shirt: a stubby, high-wing, T-tail jet with a big engine mounted over each wing root. "An72F. Now that is airplane. Take them anyplace. Anyplace at all. This town full of old white hunter wankers; talk all about old days when they go all over place in Cessnas. Cessnas. Toy airplanes. Model kits with engines. I tell you anywhere you take pissy Cessna, I take An72; proper airplane."

"You fly."

The Siberian woman smiled with a mixture of pride and modesty that Gaby recognized and admired. She had time for people who did their work, however lofty or low, proudly and well. It was a small sacrament, like those monks who served God by washing dishes. Dishonesty she despised; those who bought and sold, or were parasitic on others, and did not create. Only people who *did* something were truly human. Gaby felt herself warming to this Siberian flier.

"Gaby McAslan."

The blond woman stuck on the surname glottal several times.

"Well, I am pleased to meet you, however you say your name. I am Oksana Mikhailovna Telyanina, of Irkutsk."

The barman lined up two more elephants. They clinked bottles and drank to Siberian-Ulster friendship. She drinks and dresses like a gay man, Gaby thought.

"You are here for Chaga, yes? Of course, everyone is here for Chaga, one way or other. Tourist or worker?"

"Worker. I'm with SkyNet. Start tomorrow."

"Good people. Jake Aarons, he is good man. Good man. Big waste. Ah, they are all good. Better than fucking UNECTA—well; Administration who tell us where we can and cannot fly."

"Death to administrators."

"And accountants. Up against wall, *boom boom boom*."

They drank to the mass liquidation of the administrative and accounting classes. The empty bottles lined up along the bar. Glass elephants on parade.

"What do you think it is?" Gaby asked. "The Chaga."

The little Siberian woman shrugged expressively.

"You mean, another planet? I don't know. Easy to talk about other planets, other worlds out in cosmos, make stories about them, make movies when they are far away. When you can see it, touch it, walk through it—fly over it—is harder to believe. Too close, understand? Maybe is one big big movie set. Industrial Light and Magic, all that. I tell you, right here in this place, is very hard to believe in aliens and other worlds, yes? Oh, meant to say, I love your hair.'' She gently stroked Gaby's hair.

''Blood of the Celts flows in me,'' Gaby said, touched.

''Blood of Finno-Ugarics flows in me. Well, my father's side, generation or so back. Mighty people, long before damn Russians. Proud people. Look.'' She pulled down the ragged neck of her Sibirsk T-shirt to reveal a tattoo of two intertwined circles on her right breast. ''Apprentice shaman. Or should it be sha-woman?''

''Sha-person? No shit?''

''No shit, Gahbee UmmicAzlan. Father had no sons, so passed on mysteries to eldest daughter. Me. Oksana Mikhailovna. Already I can fly. No problem! In time, I will heal the sick, see into human hearts, speak with voice of forest, take on spirits and shapes of animals. See.'' She moved the stretched neckline. The left breast bore a wolf-mask tattoo. ''Maybe is why I cannot believe in aliens, other planets, colonization, all that. I know earth is still strong, can still surprise us. Most of all here in Africa, where everything is born. Ah! Moses! You are great man. What are you doing afterward?'' The great Moses set them up and kept setting them up and the two women kept drinking them and they talked men and money and football and tried to teach each other mouthfuls of Finno-Ugaric and Irish, which of course ended in beer spitting and laughing because they only taught each other to say dirty things.

''Go to bed, Gaby McAslan,'' Oksana Telyanina said as the line of bottles reached the end of the bar. ''You have big day tomorrow: new city, new job, new workmates. Need sleep. Me too. Have to fly tomorrow, early.''

''After all this?''

Oksana turned her right forearm up. She tapped a swelling under her wrist.

''Diffusion pump. Cleans it out of blood as fast as I drink it. Piss pure alcohol. Tomorrow I fly to Ruwenzori sober as judge. Soberer.''

Ruwenzori. The Mountains of the Moon. The white on the map of darkest Africa. *Terra Incognita.* Since the Kilimanjaro Event the cartographers had been forced to redraw those unknown regions marked *Here Be Dragons.*

''We do this again, yes?'' Oksana said. ''When I get back, God knows when. Me, I am only here because I am babooning.

Moving out of place so friend can *fiki-fiki,* yes?'' She made thrusting gestures with thumb. ''You on EastAf Teleport?''

''SkyNet's fixing it. You'll have to leave a message so I can find you; I'm only booked in here for a couple of days. After that, I don't know where I'll be.''

''I will find you. You'll see. Ah, damn. Moses, are you closing that thing up already? Is too soon. Maybe we have one more, yes? Moses!''

His gleaming teeth showed no obvious signs of distress at having uncapped fourteen bottles of Tusker.

''Big cocks and vodka!''

''Big cocks and vodka!'' Gaby McAslan agreed.

5

She woke bright, sober and decided to walk to work. Any town she visited, she needed to walk over, claim it like an animal marking its territory with a rub of musk. She crossed Uhuru Park, and the highway, steering by the open flower of the Kenyatta Center rising out of darkness into the morning light. *Something growing,* Gaby thought.

She videoed the big bronze UNECT*Afrique* horns-and-mountain colophon in the center of the plaza. People of all colors and races and nations hurried past her, all on the business of the Chaga. As she was. All part of this magnificent machine, unfolding the heart of a great mystery.

She walked on.

In three intersections she was lost. Every turning she took brought her back to the same Indian bookstore. Time was ticking away. Taxis would have been flagged down, but they did not seem to prowl these streets. Nor were there any policemen to bribe for directions. It would have to be a choice between the homeboys in street-fashionable flares and patch leather jackets hanging around their good friend's shoeshine stand, or the smart-casual, studenty types waiting for the pedestrian lights. She remembered T. P. Costello's pointed warnings about HIV-infected hypodermics.

''Excuse me, could you tell me the way to Tom M'boya Street?''

The tallest of the student types smiled broadly.

''Certainly. In fact, we are going that way ourselves. We

could walk with you; it is not really safe for a white woman to be on the streets on her own."

As they walked they asked her questions: was she on holiday or was she working here, where did she come from, how long had she been here, had she ever been to Africa before, what did she think of Kenya so far? Gaby's answers were interrupted by the arrival of a friend every hundred feet or so, necessitating lengthy greetings and handshakings. Within half a mile what had been three were now six. They did not seem to be making very fast progress in the direction of the SkyNet offices.

"This is a quicker way to go," said the tall, bearded one with the expensive clothes who asked all the questions. Friend number eight joined the party. "I am wondering," the bearded one went on, "if maybe, like we are helping you, you can help us. You are a journalist, an educated woman, you will understand our problem."

The problem unfolded over the next quarter of a mile. A good friend of theirs, a political science student, had got himself into trouble by speaking out against corruption in UNECTA. "As you know, the Americans clap their hands and our beloved government dances. They will not allow any criticism of the UN presence in our country—and so our friend is in grave danger. His life has been threatened, his wife and family have been visited, if you understand what I mean. Even we are taking a grave risk in talking to you. You will be all right, you work for a Western news agency, they will not touch you."

"What do you want me to do? Run a story?"

"That would put him in more danger, I am afraid," said the bearded student. "His only chance is to get away with his family, go south to Mozambique, where he will be safe to carry on the struggle. There is a boat he can catch from Mombasa; unfortunately, these days, no one goes anywhere without *magendo.*" He rubbed fingers against thumb, the universal gesture of black money. "He needs five thousand shillings to get his family out. Only five thousand shillings for a new life."

"We would not ask you for that much," said a flat-nosed, very black man who had not spoken before. "Five hundred shillings would be a good start. It would get him and his family to Mombasa."

Gaby stopped on the street. The eight men stopped with her

and stood in a circle around her. They felt very big, very close. She knew, they knew, it was a scam. But nobody said so.

"I don't have that much," she lied, twitching her toes in her left boot.

"That does not matter," said flat nose. "You have traveler's checks?"

"No," she lied again. "Not on me. Back at the hotel."

"A credit card, then. You are a journalist, you will have a credit card. You can get money out of a cash machine. There is one not far. We will take you to it."

There is a fatal passivity in being conned, Gaby realized. You know it is happening, yet you go along with it, you play it to the end, because it is the only way to make it stop. They know you will pay them their five hundred shillings to be free of them and they will go back to their street corner and tell the same tale to the next mark who comes along asking the way to Tom M'boya Street. It would not have been so bad if they had simply cut the straps of her bag and roared off on a moped. That would have been an opportunity seen and taken in an instant; there would have been nothing personal about it, not like this slow drawing-out of your trust and then gang-raping it.

There was a dispenser she could use. As they had said, it was not far. She fumbled her card out of her bag. A white man in chinos and a faded denim shirt was coming down the street. She did not want him to see the final sting. He was looking at her. He adjusted his course toward her. He was smiling at her. Beaming.

"Honey! There you are!"

The stranger swept her off her feet and kissed her hard on the mouth.

"When you didn't turn up, I came looking. I know how easy it is to get lost in this town." He had an American accent. He seized Gaby's hand and drew her away from the hustlers. "Excuse me, guys, hope you don't mind, it's just we're running a little late."

He did not let go of Gaby's hand until they were around two corners.

"Jesus. Whoever you are, thank you."

"Was it the Rwandan refugee story?" the American asked. He was averagely tall, averagely built, averagely handsome. His accent was averagely midwestern. But his eyes had the same blue twinkle that had made Paul Newman Gaby's first true love, and that redeemed all the averages into superlatives.

Gaby could still taste his kiss.

"It was the student-on-the-run-from-the-government story. How did you know?"

"They got me too. Fresh off the plane and they scammed me for a hundred dollars. I was so ashamed I couldn't admit it to anyone for a month."

Gaby shuddered as if they had laid hands on her body. She could understand such shame.

"All I did was ask the way to Tom M'boya Street. I reckoned they looked safer than the boys in funny outfits."

"Like something from an old blaxploitation movie?" Gaby nodded. "Should have asked them. They're *watekni;* they might have flirted a bit but they wouldn't have tried to fleece you. The Sheriffs insist on good manners in their posse members."

"Watekni?"

"Semilegal hacker gangs. Information brokers. Cyberpunk caste. They take *Shaft* as role model, but they're sound enough. Tom M'boya Street." They had walked a hundred feet and two right turns. Gaby could see the intersection where she had been picked up by the hustlers. It was less than a block away.

"Whereabouts?" asked the American.

"Right here." They were at the door of SkyNet News. She put her card back in her bag and found her identity pass. When she looked up, the American in the chinos and denim shirt had vanished as utterly as if he had never existed. Paul Newman as angel?

She did not even know his name.

Gaby McAslan fastened her identity to her shirt and trotted up the steps. She was only ten minutes late.

6

Videodiary entry: March 20 2008.

Pan around a very large room filled with desks, workstations and people. The camera is stopped down for interior fluorescents: the windows blaze with light. If there was such a thing as smell-o-vision, there would be a strong aroma of coffee. Over the high level of ambient noise, Gaby McAslan's voice can be heard.

Well, this is it, Ma. Top of the world. Well, seventh floor, SkyNet News Nairobi, English Language Section. Germans are next to the window, Scandinavians are back against the wall, which is kind of glum but satisfies their national characteristic. That glassed-in office-ette is where Great White Chief T. P. Costello presides over us all. He's supposed to be lovable and huggable and everyone's big daddy: can't say I've found that yet. Maybe he's still pissed at me for being late on my first day, but professional instincts tell me it's something more, though I don't know what I've done to offend him.

The camera moves to a tall, dark-haired white man in his middle years. He is thin, his face is all planes and angles, his hair is suspiciously less gray than it should be, but it may be due to the personal energy that shines out of him even when he is sitting at a desk drinking coffee. He is smartly dressed. On the window ledge behind him is a row of unattractive trophies and awards. He notices Gaby surreptitiously videoing him, visibly straightens, smartens and waggles his fingers: hello, camera.

This man, of course, needs no introduction, being the one and only Jake Aarons, SkyNet's chief East Africa correspondent and darling of a million late-evening-news special reports. Please note that video evidence to the contrary, he does in fact exist from the waist down. Apparently there is a cute little Somali boy who can personally testify to this same fact, but one shouldn't repeat office bitchery. Sexual peccadilloes aside, he gets the angles on the news that no one else gets: no one, however, seems to get angles on him, which I suspect is how he likes it. Something of a man of mystery, our Jake, despite—or is it because of?—his very public persona. OK, Jake, you can stop posing for the camera now.

An olive-skinned woman in her late thirtysomethings is leaning over a researcher's desk. Her hair is Latin black, as are her eyes. There is something predatory in the way she dominates the researcher's space. She is expensively and smartly dressed, too expensively and smartly for Nairobi. She wears perhaps too much silver.

Abigail Santini. On-line features editrix, and my boss. She does not like me. That's all right, because I don't like her, and it's always refreshing to be mutual about these things. At least I have good reasons not to like her. One: she insists on being called "Abby" and there is not room in this office for two names ending in *aby*. Two: she enjoys the power of executive authority with none of the creative responsibilities of those she lords it over. Three: she looks good, and damn well knows it, and has Mediterranean features that tan beautifully and never freckle, burn and then peel, and has a classic aquiline nose of the type that built the glory that was Rome and not the snub thing of a race whose idea of civilization was stealing each other's cattle. Now you can see why I don't like her. What I can't understand is why she shouldn't like me.

The eye of the lens comes to rest on two black men at a video editing suite drinking coffee. One is small, wiry, bearded; he is sitting on a chair. The other is so extraordinarily tall you can tell it even though he is sitting on the edge of the desk. It is quite obvious that they are of different tribes, different races and are the closest of friends. The tall one sees Gaby's lens on him and waggles his tongue and makes a phallic gesture with his fist.

My heroes. My buddies. My adopted family. Tembo and Faraway. Cameraman and communications engineer. SkyNet's number-one team. They grew up within five miles of each other up in the north near Lake Victoria, but Tembo is Luhya and Faraway is Luo. This apparently is important. Something to do with Bantus as opposed to Nilo-Hamitics.

Faraway's name is self-explanatory. Even among a race of basketball players, he is exceptional. *Tembo* means "elephant" in Swahili. Memory like an elephant? I ask. No, hung like an elephant, Faraway tells me with great delight. No wonder he's never been able to steal Tembo's wife away from him, he says. Faraway is a career flirt. He has turned sexual harassment into high art. His life is ruled by the politics of cool and, he says, his dick. He cannot meet a woman without trying to talk her into his bed.

Neither they, nor he, take him seriously. That he occasionally succeeds surprises him most of all. He tells me I am a demon-woman sent from hell to tempt him into unspeakable sin because of my red hair and green eyes. There is only one way he knows to exorcise the demon in me, he says, which involves pelvis pumping and a lascivious grin. Dream on, Faraway.

On the other hand, Tembo is good livin', as we say back home. He's a born-again Christian. He directs the choir in St. Stephen's Church. It's good enough to make an atheist believe in God, Faraway says, with genuine pride in his friend. He has two wee girls so gorgeous you'd want to eat them; he shows his photographs at the drop of a hat. In his lunch hour he's always editing videos he's shot of them.

For some reason they have decided to teach me to be African. Unlike most of the people here, they think I have the capacity. Maybe it's because one of the first things I did here was put my name down for the SkyNet football team—only four whites and no women. Tembo is a useful left-winger, and Faraway, by virtue of his height, is goalkeeper, which he might actually be good at if he stopped showing off and chatting up women spectators long enough to actually stop a ball. Problem is they can't decide whether I should be a Luhya African or a Luo African.

I get my real lessons in how to be African at my new lodgings. The barman at the PanAfric recommended it: Mrs. Kivebulaya, the proprietrix, is a cousin of a cousin of something of his, and likes Irish girls. And what's more, it's just up the hill on First N'Gong Avenue. I didn't think I could settle in something that calls itself the Episcopalian Guesthouse, but Mrs. Kivebulaya runs a trim ship. OK, so I rode up in the taxi with that night's dinner—a goat—tied up in the backseat, but there's a pool, the gardens are quiet and good to work in, though missionaries back on R&R from the country speak a completely different kind of English to mine, one full of bishops and rural deaneries and Theological Education by Extension.

It's the little, trivial things that I miss most about home. Things like buying sanitary towels, or proper chocolate that hasn't gone musty in old-fashioned purple foil wrappers. Diet Coke, in cans, not bottles where you pay more for the deposit on the bottle than its contents. Rock and roll. For the first ten minutes Kenyan radio sounds like the Greatest Thing You've Ever Heard, and then after that you'd kill to be able to sing along to the

''Mama Mia, Let Me Go'' bit of Bohemian Rhapsody. Late-night shopping. In a mall. I miss a horizon. I don't like feeling I'm in the middle of a vast tract of high, flat land. I want *terrain.* Like the sea around the Watchhouse; even if you couldn't see it, you always knew it was there. I want *landmarks.* Is this homesickness?

Mrs. Kivebulaya does her best to make me feel at home—hospitality is her mission from God; I can agree with that—with cozy chats and the best coffee you have ever tasted at the table in the garden where I like to work. She worships with coffee and banana cake. Her most important contribution to my happy and successful integration into a new land, new culture and new job are the tales of the bizarre and wonderful that seem to be everyday life here in Kenya. Yesterday she told me about a friend of a relative of an acquaintance of hers who is a complete rude boy and a glue-sniffer. Seems he broke into the Yellow Imp Glue Factory on Jogoo Road for the biggest high of his career, leaned too far over a vat and fell in. Overcome by fumes, he climbed out, lay down on the floor to recover and passed out. Next morning the staff found him stuck fast to the floor and had to cut him free with a power saw. This morning over breakfast, she told me about a group of Christians returning from a rally by canoe across Lake Victoria. They encountered a boatload of rude boys out for a pleasure cruise with their girlfriends, who jeered at them and told them they were no good Christians, they had no faith, going in canoes, why they should walk on the lake like their God. Valiantly responding to the challenge, fifteen leaped up and stepped over the side. ''They sank like stones,'' Mrs. K said, rocking with laughter, which reminds you of a sailing ship in heavy weather. ''They were pulling bodies out of the water for days. Six were never accounted for, but there are a lot of crocodiles in Lake Victoria.'' There seems to be no end to her supply of stories of the bizarre and wonderful. Which is a good thing, as I've just sold them to T.P. as an idea for a series of humorous (or just plain surreal) end-of-news fillers: ''And Finally'' tales from the Nairobi Station. It may not be much, but it's another step closer to the Chaga. Oops. Captain on the bridge. Better make as if I'm writing up these text overlays of Jake's interview with UNECTA's chief of operations.

7

''It's the hardest thing in the world to get a good picture of,'' said Tembo, passing the bowl of irio. As part of his Africanization lessons, he had invited Gaby to dinner with his family at their house out by Limuru. As extended uncle to Sarah and Etambele, Tembo's daughters, Faraway had, of course, been invited too.

It was a good house in a good neighborhood. SkyNet paid its senior cameramen well. It had a veranda; this was where they ate. Moths fluttered around the tin candle lanterns. The dark garden twittered with night insects. Screening trees muted the traffic; the air was warm and smelled of Africa, which is not one smell but many smells: wood smoke and red earth and fruit and shit and night-blooming flowers, but is more than the sum of all the things that make it up, as the perfume of a woman is more than the perfume of the scent she puts on.

Faraway uncapped a beer and passed the bottle to Gaby.

''I do not just mean the actual physical difficulties,'' Tembo continued.

''Like bribing your way past the soldiers,'' Faraway said heathenly.

''Like the way it attacks plastics, which means your camera breaking out in flowers if you do not wrap it up carefully. But that is only part of it. It is just a hard thing to get a good image of. For a start, under the canopy there is very little light; and then, what do you video? It looks the same wherever you point the camera. And there are things in there so different from what we understand as *living* that we find it hard to comprehend them. We cannot *see* them like we see a tree and know what it is and what it does, what the bits we cannot see will look like. Everything is different: what is it the people at Ol Tukai have worked out? They have cataloged over fifteen thousand different species in the Chaga. And of course, every time you go back, they have changed into something else.''

Mrs. Kivebulaya's ''And Finally'' stories had won Gaby critical appreciation, grudging acknowledgment by T. P. Costello and a place at a table in the Thorn Tree bar of the New Stanley Hotel, where the real journalists went to drink, but those were not the things for which she had come to Africa. That thing was still denied her. She worked in the Chaga every day, in the gigabytes of images, documents, reports, simulations stored in archives. She knew all that was humanly knowable about the air reefs, the pseudo-corals, the hand trees, the things that looked like marine radiolaria for which no one had yet invented a name; except how they felt, how they smelled, how they tasted. She felt trapped beneath Nairobi's smog layer while her star burned bright in the south. Tembo and Faraway could not understand her impatience. "It will wait," they said. "It is not going anywhere. Well, actually it is, and in the best direction, toward you."

Tembo's children arrived on either side of Gaby with dishes of chicken.

"You are to have the gizzard," said Sarah, the older one. Both were beautiful and serious and funny. "It is always kept for the guest of honor."

Gaby looked at Faraway to see if he had put his extended nieces up to a joke on the poor ignorant *m'zungu.* If so, he was playing it mightily deadpan.

"Actually, I don't know what a chicken gizzard looks like," she said. "In my country we don't eat them." Etambele, the younger girl, whose name meant "Early Evening, Just After Teatime," which was the exact time she was born, looked amazed and whispered something to Sarah.

"My sister wants to know if your hair is real," Sarah said.

"Etambele, don't ask rude questions about our guest," her mother said. She was a small, silent woman, very beautiful in traditional dress, but peripheral to this men's world of news and affairs and events.

"I know how I could find out," Faraway said, which was as much as he could get away with in the company of a Christian family.

"It's real," Gaby said to the staring sisters. "It goes all the way down my back. I haven't had it cut in seven years, which is older than you are, Etambele." The girls went round-eyed in astonishment. Gaby let them touch her hair. They giggled and fled to fetch the sweet potatoes.

Chicken gizzard was very much better than she had feared.

"UNECTA is reevaluating its security position," Tembo said. "They are getting scared about the refugee problem. Sooner or later someone will decide to disbelieve what UNECTA is telling them about the Chaga, and reckon it is a better chance than the squatter camps. That is why they are thinking about military patrols inside the Chaga.''

''That is not because of the refugees,'' Faraway said. ''That is because they are afraid of what the safari squads might find.''

''Safari squads?'' Gaby asked.

''They operate out of the Tacticals, the gangs that run the townships,'' Faraway said. ''They go in, they find things, they bring them out. They laugh in the face of United Nations quarantines. That is why they want to put soldiers into the Chaga, to stop them. If the United Nations can show that those who go in deep never return, then people in the squatter camps will say better Pumwani than the Chaga. It will work for a time. But the day will come when the people start to say, better the Chaga than Pumwani. It has to come, my friend. It has to come. The United Nations cannot stop the Chaga, neither can it evacuate ten million people.''

''More, by then,'' Tembo said.

''What will you do, Tembo?'' Gaby asked, seeing his wife in her beautiful dress, seeing his children on their too-high seats with their too-big cutlery.

''I will trust SkyNet to look after us.''

''You trust SkyNet, I will trust myself,'' Faraway said. The beers were making him outspoken.

''You'd take your chances with the Chaga?''

''*M'zungu,* in the end everyone will have to take their chances with the Chaga. Maybe even you. Just because the packages have all come down within three hundred miles of the equator does not mean they always will. The very next one could come down in Paris, or New York, or even Ireland. And why does everyone assume that the Chaga is confined to the tropics? Maybe it will just keep growing, out of Africa, across the desert, across Europe, over the pole until there is nothing left, only Chaga, and we are all swinging from the trees and playing knucklebones with the aliens.''

''Faraway, please, you are scaring the children,'' Tembo's wife said softly but firmly.

''If there are aliens,'' Tembo said.

''My friend here has a theological problem with intelligences from other worlds,'' Faraway said. Mrs. Tembo and the children had cleared away the main-course dishes. A hiss of seething oil and the smell of deep-frying finger bananas from the kitchen louvers meant dessert. "Given that God created the aliens behind the Chaga, the question is, were they created in a state of grace, or are they fallen creatures, like us? If they are angels, then they run the risk of falling should they come into contact with sinners like us. Me, I like the idea of being responsible for the fall of an angel. If they are already fallen, then do they have a means of salvation, or must we evangelize them?"

"A Chaga Messiah?" Gaby asked. The bananas arrived, piled high on serving plates, sprinkled with sugar and cinnamon.

"There are no aliens," Tembo said a little impatiently. He was accustomed to his friend's boasting, he did not like to see him massage his big male ego at the dinner table, in front of guests and family.

"If they could put an entire ecology into something the size of a small matatu, I am sure there is room for a couple of aliens in the ashtray," Faraway said, undeterred. Mrs. Tembo's cooking succeeded in silencing him.

The children were made ready for bed while coffee brewed. They came to say good night. Faraway tousled their hair and hugged them beerily. Tembo kissed them. Gaby showed them photographs she had brought of her sisters and dogs and father.

"This is the house where I grew up, and here we all are in front of it. This was taken the day I left to go to London to learn to be a reporter."

"Did your mother take the photograph?" Sarah asked.

"No, it was my father's lady friend. My mother died a long time ago, when I was quite young," Gaby said, and then folded the photographs quickly away before they let loose things that had no proper place here among hosts and friends. "Good night, sleep tight and don't let the bugs bite," she said to the children. They giggled appreciatively.

Gaby's offer to help with the dishes was politely but firmly turned down.

"It is woman's work, and tonight you are an honorary man," Tembo said.

You guys have a lot to learn about feminism, Gaby thought as coffee came around. *And you girls too.* Faraway produced Russian cigarettes. Gaby took one.

"I did not know you smoked."

"Only after dinner."

"I smoke after sex," he said.

Gaby was listening to the sound of the mother in the bedroom singing her children to sleep with a song a thousand years old. It made her feel very close to and very far from home at the same time. The candles burned low in the tin lanterns. The traffic noise lessened. The honorary men talked work, about Jake Aarons, whom they all liked, and Abigail Santini, whom no one liked, and T. P. Costello, whom everyone liked but Gaby, because she said he did not like her. Tembo stared at his coffee grounds as if trying to divine the future from them, then said, "There is shadow on his memory. I do not know it all, it was back before I joined SkyNet, when he was East African station chief for Irish News Services. There was a woman, an Irish woman, like you. She disappeared into the Chaga. That is all I know, but I think you remind him of things he would sooner forget, Gaby."

She smoked another Russian cigarette and listened to the rattle of insect wings against the lantern glass.

"Did he love her, Tembo?"

"He has not said so."

"He loved her. So that's why he won't put me in front of a camera."

"Is that what you really want?"

Gaby's frustration blew up in her like the candle flames when the night wind blew across the eaves and through the lanterns' ventilation slits.

"What I want is to do something. Make something of my own, that I have experienced with my own senses. Not someone else's report, someone else's technical brief, someone else's image or experience. Not someone else's stories about cabinet ministers disappearing and reappearing under the name of 'Mr. Shit,' or weddings in country churches that turn into tribal warfare because someone can't stop farting during the marriage vows."

"Those are good stories, Gaby," Faraway said.

"Yes, they are good stories, but they aren't my stories. They come to me; I want to go and get them. It doesn't have to be video reportage; just as long as it means me acting for once and not reacting." She took another of Faraway's cigarettes and lit it from a candle lantern. "It's like an old story my dad made up for me when I was wee. There was one of our cats—we had five—who used to stare up the chimney all the time. My dad told me that he was waiting for the night when a voice would come down the chimney saying, 'The King of the Cats is dead! The King of the Cats is dead!' On that night, when that voice came, he would leap up, say, 'Then I am King of the Cats!' and run up the chimney and over the rooftops to claim his crown. That was why he was looking up the chimney all the time, waiting for the call.

"I feel like that stupid cat."

Faraway exhaled a plume of smoke and looked long at Tembo before speaking.

"What if I were to say that the King of the Cats is a personal friend of mine?"

"Be careful, my friend," Tembo said.

"To get stories, you need to know what is going on before anyone else, friend Gaby. To know what is going on before anyone else, you need good information. I know a man—we are the same tribe, almost the same village—who deals in that kind of information: hard to get; useful. Valuable."

"Are we talking about the Sheriffs?" Gaby asked.

Every day on her way in to the office she saw people in the hundreds crowd the dirt streets of the slums around the soft, silent Mercedes of the software brokers as they did their day's hiring. The first time she had seen it she had stopped and opened her visioncam as the cars disappeared beneath the surge of bodies, hands snatching for the slips of paper with the password for the day of whatever Western life-insurance or savings-and-loan company needed data processors. The informational superhighway had promised so much to Africa, and delivered only the daily scramble to do the world's paperwork because an African data processor cost less than a European or East Asian. The combination of the primeval and the technological had disturbed Gaby. She had watched the hired minibuses arrive to take the few away to the warehouses and enough money for a week's food, if they worked hard. The others had returned to their homes and children. This was the public face of the East African Teleport. It was no wonder that so many turned away from it, seeing a better, or at least more glamorous future with its private face: the posses. You saw the kids everywhere, the boys in flares and long-collared shirts and platform soles, the girls in leatherette and nylon. They looked cool, they looked street, but they were merely the runners, the dealers, the minders and enforcers. The Sheriffs, known to most only by their titles, held the power, but they were no more the posses than their boys and girls. The true posse, like the True Church, was invisible, spiritual, virtual. It was the boy in

Pumwani whose teenage sister sells herself on the street to pay for the deck and connection charges that will buy them both a way up and out. It was the girl living on the houseboat on Lake Victoria with a mother who tells her she is useless and a father who fucks her and grandparents who sit around all day staring at her and nine siblings who eat her food and push her out of her space, the one who dreams of someday pulling on the leather jacket and sliding on the Ray Bans and becoming a Name in a nameless city. It was the Likoni ferryman who comes home every night to hang out on the cybernetic street corner until the dawn comes up out of India, high-fiving with dudes you only meet in dreams; it was the woman whose children have all been lost to religion, crack or HIV 4 who finds a bigger marketplace in which to sell her goods and swap gossip. It was all of these, bound together in a virtual community—the posse—under the patronage and protection of their Sheriff.

"We are talking the Sheriff of Sheriffs," Faraway said.

"Mombi would disagree with you," Tembo said. His wife appeared with fresh coffee. She looked suspicious: seditious talk on her veranda.

"Mombi's girls look better on the street, no one would disagree with that, but she has no breeding, no pedigree in this thing. Look how she made her money: cybersex salons. Haran is class, Haran is Sheriff of Sheriffs."

"Haran is a bad man and a damn rude boy," Tembo's wife said with unexpected vehemence. "He is no good to anyone, none of them are, worthless posses."

"Anything you want," Faraway whispered confidentially to Gaby. "Haran can get it for you. And he does not deal in cash. He is a gentleman, my friend Haran. He does you a favor, you do him a favor, someday, when he needs it. Maybe never."

"The devil is a gentleman too," said Mrs. Tembo. "Very polite. He does you a favor, and then one day the favor he asks back is your immortal soul."

"Woman, you are prejudiced and computer illiterate," Faraway said. "You insult him, you insult all Luo. Who do you think brought Net technology and the information revolution to this poor country? Luo, that is who. Woman, you should be thanking Haran, not cursing him."

She scowled and returned to the kitchen.

"Faraway."

"Well, it is not illegal," Faraway said to Tembo.

"Neither is it totally legal."

"All right. I will apologize to her. It is the beer, it is the warmth of the night, it is the excellent company of my good friends, it is the superlative food!" This he shouted in the direction of the kitchen. "Gaby McAslan, believe me, you need this man. He can help you get what you want. I know where he is to be found, I can take you to him, introduce you. We are the same tribe, we are blood."

8

Gaby carried the Ethiopic gospel box carefully on her knees as the taxi driver swerved to avoid a crater in the road. In Kenya you could tell the drunk drivers. They were the ones driving straight down the roads. The box was a beautiful thing, the best in the shop. It had been made with the eyes and hands of faith. The side panels were illuminated with the four evangelists. On the top was a wide-eyed St. George slaying a dragon that did not look as if it had put up much resistance. Gaby had balked at the price—half a month's wages—but Faraway had insisted that nothing less than the best would be acceptable to Haran.

"That is where a lot of big businessmen go wrong," he told her as the taxi negotiated the late-night downtown traffic. "They think they can buy a cheap Somali fake knocked up yesterday in a sweatshop in Mogadishu, stuff it full of hundred-shilling notes, or diamonds, or cocaine, and Haran will eat out of their hands. Such men receive the reward their small souls deserve. Haran, he is an aesthete. A connoisseur. A most spiritual man."

He practiced a strange form of *magendo.* Haran did collect Ethiopic scripture cases, with suitable inducements inside. He would receive the donation and beg to be excused a moment while he compared the case with his large, probably unparalleled collection. If he returned with the reliquary saying that he regretted that he was already in possession of one similar, you knew that for unspecified reasons your petition had failed. If he returned empty-handed and told you your donation was a grace to his collection, you knew that you had become a client of his posse. Either way, the cash inducement inside would be gone.

"It is really a question of whether he likes you or not,"

Faraway said. The taxi swept past the huddled mounds of Nairobi's street-sleepers, piled in doorways, wrapped in cardboard and tattered blankets and laid out like victims of a small holocaust along the sidewalks. "And he will like you. He likes beautiful, intelligent women. Women like him. I do not know why, given what happened to him."

"And you just have to tell me, don't you?"

"It was the *khat,*" Faraway said, ignoring Gaby. "Everyone knows that bad things can happen if you chew too much, but we never thought it would be anything like that. It began back in Kisumu when he was just starting out. He used the *khat* leaves to help him concentrate; he was working with up to five simultaneous screens of information. No one had ever seen anyone chew that much *khat.* People used to warn him that no good would come of it, and staying up, staring at screens day and night. They were right.

"He was smitten with a plague of orgasms."

The taxi abruptly veered where there was no pothole. The driver had a sudden coughing fit. Gaby caught sight of his astonished eyes in the rearview mirror.

"He could not help it. At home, at work, on the bus, out with friends, anywhere, anytime: *bam!* An orgasm. Thirty, forty a day. The doctors had never seen anything like it. They had all kinds of explanations, but everyone knew it was too much *khat.* But in case you think that this is the greatest thing that could happen to man, something terrible happened. After three months at forty orgasms a day, they suddenly stopped. Just like that. Gone! Since that day he has never had another. Not in five years. He cannot even get it hard anymore. Complete impotence. The doctors are as baffled as they were by the plague of orgasms. But I think that it is because every man has a certain number of orgasms in him, like bullets in a gun, and he can either fire them like a hunting rifle, at one target at a time, or spray them around like a machine gun. Haran used up his lifetime of orgasms in one big go.

"And you, you no good damn rude boy!" Faraway leaned forward and poked the driver in the shoulder. "Stop listening to the conversations of your betters and drive this heap of rust. That is what we are paying you for, not to see your ugly face grinning away in the mirror."

Gaby McAslan wished Faraway had not told her that story. It

would make everything so much harder, having to deal with a man who had been cursed with a plague of orgasms.

"What is this Cascade Club anyway?" she asked.

"You will find out soon," Faraway said. "We are here."

It betrayed no secrets from the outside: a big off-street retail block fronted by an Asian supermarket, a CD store and a haberdasher's. Blue neon waterfalls framed a door from which a bouncer in an ankle-length leather coat and the biggest Afro haircut Gaby had ever seen scrutinized the street. There was no name, no flashing sign, just the tumbling neon waterfalls. The doorman stopped two middle-aged white men in fashionable hacking jackets, riding breeches and boots.

"Boys' night Thursday and Sunday," Gaby heard him say. He and Faraway traded fives and bantered in Swahili. Gaby wrapped the black lace shawl she had brought for the cool of the morning more tightly around the scripture box. Faraway slipped the doorman a fistful of shillings and ushered Gaby up the steep stairs behind the door.

"Faraway, am I imagining it, or can I actually hear a waterfall?"

Faraway grinned his irresistible grin and opened the zebra-skin door at the top of the stairs.

The Cascade Club was built on two levels. The upper level, where the bar, dance floor and tables were situated, was a wide balcony that extended all around the hollow interior of the retail block. Patrons were crowded three deep at the bar. All the tables were occupied. The clientele was almost exclusively female. Barboys in gold lamé pouches, boots and bow ties moved dexterously between bar and kitchens. There was a lot of champagne being drunk. Some of the boys had cash poked down the fronts of their posing pouches. They smiled a little too hard.

The biggest crowd had gathered around the balcony rails, looking down into the lower section. It was down there, in the pit of the Cascade Club, that the action was to be found.

Floodlights gleamed from the pristine white tiles on floor and walls. The cages were black iron with dramatic chrome spikes. Some of the men inside were white. One was Native American. All had big muscles, no body hair and were naked. They clung to the spiked bars and arched their backs and shook out their long hair and pretended to be in that hybrid state of ecstasy and despair pornographers think is the pinnacle of sex as the high-pressure hoses played over them. Some ran from one wall of their cages to the other, like wild animals. Some crouched on all fours, trying to hide away from the water. Some rattled the bars and roared back at the roaring jets. Some were bound hand and foot in a variety of dramatic bondage devices.

Behind the splash guards the women shrieked and laughed as they swung the hoses across the caged models. One of the men had had an erection; three different women targeted it with their jets. Every so often a stream of water would slacken and collapse. Then the woman behind the trigger would hunt in her purse for more tokens and, if she had none, reluctantly hand over her weapon to the woman waiting behind the spray barrier while she hurried to the change booth with her credit card. Some of the women were soaked through, expensive cocktail dresses clinging to their bodies, hairstyles plastered flat, earrings dripping. They laughed hysterically.

Faraway joined a fascinated Gaby at the rail. He had brought piña coladas. "Compliments of the management," he said. "There are automatic cutouts on the hoses to stop them trying to shoot up onto the balcony. They can do what they like to the boys, or each other."

"I can see why Haran bought into this place," Gaby said, sipping her thick, semeny cocktail and thinking Freudian thoughts about water jets and a man who had used up a lifetime of orgasms in three months.

Wails of disappointment rose from the tiled pit. The hoses were all failing at once. No quantity of tokens would restart them. Muscular scene-shifters in wet suits with the tops pulled down and tied around the waist unshackled the cages from the floor bolts and carried them away on wheeled pallets. The big white floodlights went out. A single pinspot lit the pit. In it stood a smiling black man in a naval uniform. Loud music started. The man in the naval uniform began to dance to it. Yelling, the women leaped to their hoses. In one instant he was drenched, but he was still smiling. Piece by piece, he stripped. Water dripped from his oiled pectorals. Gaby hoped the water was not too cold, amazed at the profligacy. Even the resourceful Mrs. Kivebulaya had to ration showers in thirsty Nairobi and pray that the rains would be early.

A tall man in flares, a blue denim safari jacket and a floppy cap came across the crowded bar to the rail.

"If you will please follow me, the Sheriff will see you now."

He led Gaby and Faraway through a door marked PRIVATE in English and Swahili. Gaby clung to her Ethiopic scripture case like it was her own soul. The *m'tekni's* platform soles clumped on the steep stairs. Do not laugh at these people, Gaby reminded herself. They dress like a classic episode of *Kojak*, but they run the corridors of the Pentagon and no one sees them; they play Find the Lady with the European Central Bank. They do not hesitate to kill to protect what is theirs. There is a top-range smartgun slung crosswise for a fast pull under that denim safari jacket.

At the door to the penthouse suite a second posseboy sniffed them with a snooperwand.

"Please excuse me," he said. "Everywhere there are government stool pigeons wearing wires. You are clear."

What struck Gaby first about Haran's penthouse was the floor. It was the glass-tile ceiling of the Cascade Club. She could just make out the bright square of the pit surrounded by the dark fringe of the balcony. The big fans that kept the moist air circulating turned slowly beneath her feet. There was no other light source in the big room than what escaped from the club below. It was like walking on a pane of luminous ice beneath which were trapped, drowned souls.

Haran sat in a massive black Makonde chair behind an ebony desk. One hand rested lightly on the carved chair arm. The other held an antelope-tail fly whisk, the traditional symbol of authority and wisdom.

"My cousin Faraway, isn't it?" The voice was soft, cultivated. "It is a long time since I last saw you. I hope you are well."

"Better for seeing you, friend Haran."

"Who is this *m'zungu* with you?"

"My name is Gaby McAslan," the *m'zungu* answered for herself. "I work with Faraway for SkyNet."

Haran rose from behind his desk. He made Faraway look small. Gaby would have felt dwarfed had he not been so thin. With the paleness of his skin—cosmetic lightening, she reckoned—and the Cuban grandee's frock coat, cravat and wide-brimmed hat, he looked like an avatar of some long-suppressed

Afro-Caribbean animist sect. He had a pencil-line mustache and a permanent collagen pout.

He bent and kissed Gaby's hand. His nails were French-manicured. There was lace at his cuffs.

"And what do you wish from me, Ms. McAslan?" He indicated chairs for them to sit. Coffee appeared, poured by yet another *m'tekni.*

"A favor. In my line of business, information is life. I'm new in your country, I don't have the contacts, the names, the numbers, and I want to move up quickly. I'm not ashamed to admit I am ambitious; it is not a sin. What you can provide me with can make the difference between me getting what I want, and being average."

Haran pursed his lips, steepled his fingers.

"I presume we are talking about a long-term relationship of patronage."

"In the news business, you never know what you will need to know next, or when you will need to know it."

"It is not just in the news business," said Haran.

Faraway nudged Gaby's foot.

"I believe you are something of a connoisseur, Mister . . ."

"My parents named me Haran."

"Haran. I wonder if perhaps you could give me your opinion on this? As I said, I am not long in this country, I have little knowledge about what is of true value, but I like to think that beauty is universal." She unwrapped the gospel case and placed it on the ebony desk. Her hands were shaking. She willed them to stop. They refused.

Haran studied the box for a long minute.

"You have good taste, for a *m'zungu.* If you like, I will check it against my collection. There is so much that is false around these days, even the expert can be deceived. You know how the master learns to detect the forgery? By studying what is genuine. That is the only way to tell the true from the false. If you will excuse me, please."

He left with the box through a door behind him. Gaby looked at Faraway, who tapped his feet, tapped his fingers nervously.

"Have you got a cigarette?"

"Haran does not smoke, and does not like people who smoke. Anyway, I thought you only smoked after eating."

"And when I get stressed."

He would be opening the box. He would be lifting out the money, the other half of her month's wages. He would be counting the notes. There would be a terminal in there. He would be sending his software familiars out through it into the unseen world to find who is this woman who calls herself Gaby McAslan, what is she, can she be trusted?

Gaby McAslan found herself breathing very quickly and shallowly.

Now he would be examining the box. She did not doubt that he had the expertise he claimed. He would be lifting it into the light and scrutinizing the icons and the quality of its carving and engraving. He would be scratching the wood with his long fingernails to see that the color went all the way through and was not just tourist-curio boot polish. He would be sniffing it to test if it smelled like nine-hundred-year-old wood.

Gaby found she was holding her breath. She released it in a long sigh. Beneath her the fans threw sinister black shadows on the ceiling.

The door at the end of the room opened. Haran returned to his seat. He was empty-handed.

"It is an exceptionally fine piece, Ms. McAslan. You are a very lucky woman to have found such a treasure with your inexperience. If you do not mind, might I keep it for a while? I have a friend who shares my love of African art, I know he would very much like to see your piece. I shall be in contact with you regarding our relationship shortly. I think I can say without any doubt that I look forward to a long and mutually profitable professional patronage. Now, if you will excuse me, I have other matters I must attend to. In the meantime please accept the hospitality of the Cascade Club. I shall instruct the door staff to render you full service anytime you require. A pleasant and good night to you both."

The posseboy who had opened the door closed it behind them. Music and laughter came up the staircase from the club below. You are a bought woman now. You are on the dark side of the street, Gaby McAslan thought. It was no strange thing. She had always been a bought woman. At least Haran's terms on her soul seemed easy.

9

Gaby was working at the cast-iron table in the cool shade of the garden trees when Mrs. Kivebulaya brought the emissary to meet her.

The messenger spoke in shantytown Swahili. It offended his cool to speak English, though it was the lingua franca of the Net. Perhaps he disdained being at the call of a woman. Especially a *m'zungu* woman.

"He has a communication for you from Haran," Mrs. Kivebulaya translated, her professional, spiritual and social sensitivities disgraced by being expected to entertain rude boys and data-gangsters on sanctified premises. "A token of good faith, he says he has been told to tell you. A gift from Haran to mark the start of a new relationship."

Haran's messenger gestured for Mrs. Kivebulaya to take the slip of paper between his fingers and give it to the white woman.

Gaby unfolded the paper. Her optically engineered pupils dilated.

On the paper was the exact location of one Mr. Peter Werther. He was to be found in a New Millennium Traveler camp not thirty miles from this table. Which was a gesture of exceeding goodwill, because for the past five years the world had been of the opinion that Mr. Peter Werther was a knot of rotting skin and bleached hair and grinning bone up among the snows of Kilimanjaro.

10

In Africa there are still roads that bless the driver. The road that runs from Nairobi to Nakuru is one. It climbs up through the affluent dark green suburbs of Nairobi, then the going gets steeper and it begins to wind between Kikuyu shambas of tall yellow maize and sugarcane. People walk along the cracked red edges of it with bundles of cane on their heads, or green-and-yellow cans of margarine and Milo powdered milk. Green and yellow too are the matatus that whine up and down the hairpin bends, so overloaded you wonder that they can move. Up and up it goes and just when you think it will never stop and you will drive straight into the ankle of God it passes through a narrow, heavily wooded pass and the road seems to vanish. There is nothing in front of you but blue air and a thousand feet below the dry, sun-scorched plain of the mighty East African Rift Valley. The road clings to the contours of the hills, descending in a leisurely, African way to the valley floor and the lakes that in season are pink with a million flamingos, the Nyandarua to your right, to your left the sleeping volcanic mounds of Opuru and Longonot. And you are blessed.

On such a road you fold the top down on your SkyNet Vitara and you drive with your elbow on the top of the door and you turn the radio up and you sing and you let the wind blow back your long, red hair. *Thelma and Louise* had been a formative influence on the young Gaby McAslan. Her partner-in-crime was Ute Bonhorst, from the German language section. Gaby had been reluctant to take an accomplice but she needed Ute's German. She needed Ute's silence in return for a half share of an exclusive with one of the hang gliders who had disappeared on Kibo in the Kilimanjaro Event.

They came to the little homemade wooden bus shelter on the very edge and stopped to look at the Rift Valley. Gaby walked to the brink, where the land fell sheer to the Kedong plain. This was a big country, a country not hedged and walled and fielded and bounded and owned as Ireland was. This country was strong and independent and resisted the constraints of humans; it went on and on, over the horizon forever, where their small concerns ended. For the first time Gaby felt she was in Africa. Nairobi had frustrated and baffled and seduced her with its capital city extremes, sophistications, brutalities, but a city is not a country. A city is designed to walk tall in. This land reduced humans and their lives and their cars and their ribbons of dusty road to insignificance, and because you were nothing, you could dare to declare yourself, be that same bright, indivisible atom of being Gaby had felt that night beneath the summer stars on Ballymacormick Point.

Two little boys had set up a stall beside the bus stop. The women bought charcoal-roasted maize and fresh prickly pears. The little boys were too surprised by the sight of white women to haggle over the price. Because she liked them, Gaby gave them each a ten-shilling note, which she knew was more than they made in a week. She hoped they would not get in trouble explaining to their parents where so much money came from.

The Travelers' camp was only a few miles beyond the viewpoint, down a long dirt road that turned off the track to the Safariland Lodge and meandered along the shore of Lake Naivasha. Their wagons were pitched in the shelter of a stand of flame trees. Some were propped up on clinker blocks, wheels removed; a final surrender to the fuel shortages. These would never migrate along the world lines again. A beautiful hand-painted wooden arch stood over the entrance to the settlement. WHAT THE SUN SAID was its name.

What the sun said was *dust.* What the sun said was *flies.* The sun said *heat.* The sun said *melanomas.*

Tents and awnings billowed limply in the slow, hot air. Wind chimes set on ornamental door-posts barely tinkled. Japanese fish kites hung openmouthed, stirring their streamer tails. Stranger fruit hung from the branches of the flame trees: things like cracked leather cocoons bound with steel wire. There were three of them, each about five feet long. They turned slowly anticlockwise to Coriolis force. A lone generator chugged, most of the camp's power came from silent solar panels. All the vans had small steerable dishes on their roofs: the economics of techno-nomadism was that the information revolution had made it not only a desirable lifestyle, but a necessary one. You followed the sun and lived the lifestyle in harmony with the planet until one day the fuel ran out and left you stranded in the heat and drought of Africa's Rift Valley. With the Chaga approaching.

The Kilimanjaro Event had made East Africa the social navel of the planet. International Bright and Beautiful, and those who clung around them hoping that brightness and beauty were contagious, followed the planetary media circus to the plains in the shadow of the mountain. Most had moved on when Africa and things African slipped out of fashion. Some remained. They found room for their humanity to resonate in Africa's great spaces. They made their camps under the big sky and settled into sun-warmed introversion and the evolution of white-boy ethnicity. The men of What the Sun Said were bearded and sat about with their hands dangling loosely over their knees, watching what was watchable. The women, naked to the navel, carried their babies slung at their waists and intimidated Gaby with the firm upturn of their breasts. Children in beads, feathers and zinc oxide war paint on noses and cheekbones came running to greet the visitors. Their skins were tanned hard brown, there were flies around the corners of their eyes and mouths.

"Are you the people come to talk to Peter?" they asked. "We're here to take you to him. Come on." They pulled Gaby and Ute along. Pied Piper in reverse. In one of the big, billowing saffron tents, someone was playing a thumb piano. The children brought the two women to a white awning roped to the side of a dilapidated country bus. *Yee-Ah! Kung Fu!* said the motto painted on the side. Two caricature black men in white judo suits aimed kicks at each other's head.

"Here he is, here he is!" the children clamored. "Peter! They're here! We've got them!"

"Leave the talking to me," Gaby whispered to Ute Bonhorst.

The bus door opened. Peter Werther emerged.

This was what a man come back from the heart of darkness looked like. His face was tanned that dark brown peculiar to Teutons gone native. His hair was blond, long and worn in the community style; shaved at the sides, plaited at the back. Pale stubble made him look younger than Gaby knew him to be. He had the palest eyebrows she had ever seen. He did not affect the white-boy ethnic chic of the Sun-Saiders. He was dressed in a relaxed linen suit over a simple white T-shirt. No jewelry. No tattoos or ritual scarifications or body piercing. His only idiosyncrasy was a leather biker's glove on his left hand.

He greeted them with his right hand. Ute made the introductions in German.

"Gaby McAslan. I know your work," Peter Werther said. His English was comfortable, softly accented with south German. "We get all the on-line services here: SkyNet, CNN Direct, News International On-line. I liked your story about the genitals thief very much."

"I'm hoping to branch out." A swirl of warm wind set the black pods hanging from the trees swaying into Gaby's peripheral vision.

"They are into rebirthing," Peter Werther said, observing Gaby's distraction. "Spiritual metamorphosis."

"There are people in those things?"

"In sensory deprivation. They let them out after three, four days. The thing seems to be that they don't tell you how long they are going to leave you hanging, or even if they are going to come back at all. Face the fear and pass through is the experience. I think that after three days upside down in this heat, you will believe anything you are told about yourself. There are always willing volunteers, and not just from the community.''

Ute had unfolded the camcorder and was videoing the cocoons.

''Background,'' she explained.

''Can we talk?'' Gaby asked Peter Werther. A fly darted at him and abruptly veered away, as if repelled.

''Sure. That is why I have asked you to come here. But private, yes? They are private, personal things I have to tell you. Please come with me.''

Sun-Saiders waved to Peter Werther as he took the two women down to the lakeside onto a wooden jetty that had been built out twenty yards through the reeds into the open water. At the end was a small wooden gazebo. Ute Bonhorst videoed flamingos. Gaby set up her recording equipment on the floor and checked levels. Water sparkled in the gaps between the boards. Peter Werther lit a cigarette.

''Also, this is the only place they will let you smoke,'' he said, offering the pack. Ute did not smoke. Gaby declined. It would be easy to smoke too much on this job. ''I am sure you are wondering, why this place, why these strange people with their strange rituals? Well, they are a good people, it is a good life they lead, but the real reason is simpler. They were the first people I met when I came out of the Chaga. I walked, you see. I was brought to the edge, and told I must leave now, and I just walked north. They do not ask questions, you see. They accept. If I had walked into an army patrol, or a UNECTA base, I do not know what would have become of me, but these people, in their months of travel, gave me the time and space to learn about myself, and what I have been changed into, and what it is I must do. And now I think I know, and I am ready, and these people have let me bring you into their peace and calm because they agree with me that the world needs to hear what I learned, back there.'' Peter Werther smiled. ''I know what you are going to ask. Why am I not dead? After all, UNECTA says no one who goes into the Chaga ever comes out. I am not dead because the Chaga kept me alive. It kept me alive because that is its nature. I could have stayed there forever, in the cloud forests up on the mountain, but it would not let me stay. Someone had to come out and tell the truth about what is in there.

"And what have I seen and experienced?" He put a foot up on the wooden railing and contemplated the pink flamingos and the silver-blue lake and the high dark ridge of the Mau escarpment beyond. "Wonder and horror. Beauty and terror. Paradise, I suppose, but at the same time a . . ." He struggled for a word, spoke briefly in German.

"Insidious," Ute suggested.

"Yes, an insidious hell. Monstrous, wonderful. I could pair off adjectives all day and not have communicated to you anything of what it is truly like in there. It is alien, it cannot be understood; much of it is so strange that it cannot be *seen;* yet we know it, we have always known it, deep in here." He cupped the back of his head with his gloved left hand. The hind brain, the medulla, the brain stem; the roots of primal consciousness.

"The heart of darkness?" Gaby suggested.

"The beginning of all light," Peter Werther corrected. "In there are things that I can only call organic cities, but like no city you are I or anyone would design. Cities of our dreams: miles and miles of pods and clusters and things for which there are no names on avenues that no one has ever walked but me. A million people could be fed and sheltered; and they are waiting for us. We know it, it knows us. Once before, a very long time ago, so long we have forgotten it except in dreams, we met and parted. But it has not forgotten us.

"The lies UNECTA tells! It is not hostile to humanity: it supports life, whatever life comes into contact with it. Symbiosis; that is the way of the Chaga. It feeds and shelters you and you become a part of it. If it was alien, it could not do that; there would be no point of contact between us. That is why I say it knows us, and has known us for a long time.

"It thinks. At night you can hear its dreams in your dreams, like a song that has been sung for a million years. It learns; in the early days they tried to poison it: defoliants, systematic herbicides. The Chaga analyzed and put together counteragents to neutralize them within minutes. It defends itself; fire will not burn it, poison will not kill it. There was talk of dusting it with powdered plutonium waste. The Chaga would have filtered it and made it safe. Not even a nuclear strike would kill it now. As long as one molecule remains, it will grow back again. It's smart. The trees talk. The roots connect, like the cells in your brain. They touch, they share, and they think, but it is not any kind of intelligence we can understand.''

Peter Werther smoked the rest of his cigarctte in the self-conscious silence of a man who has said too much of something personal and unique to him and fears that people think that he is not sane. The screams of playing children came across the water from What the Sun Said. Drums started up. Tribal life for people brought up in the great Western cult of the individual. Peter Werther has been farther into the heart of darkness than any of them would ever dare, Gaby McAslan thought, and so he does not need to play dress-up-and-pretend and stick feathers through his nipples.

''Could you tell us about the Kilimanjaro Event?'' she asked. Ute changed discs on the camcorder. The acrylic wrapper blew around the floor of the wooden gazebo on a wind rising from the north.

''I cannot add much to what the others have said. We had made camp up on Kibo at Elveda Point and were resting: the air is thin up there, it is hard to breathe even when you are not carrying hang gliders. We made radio contact with base camp at the Marangu Gate Hotel and said that we would begin flying the next day. It was just after midnight when the thing came down; all I can remember is a flash and roar and explosion. It is always difficult to describe things like this. Language does not have the words: it is like survivors of air crashes. They have been through the end of the world and all they can say is *boom!* That was what I thought had happened; there had been an air crash on the mountain. Then there was a sudden huge wind that swept away our tents and scattered all our things—that was when we lost Sabine, she went to look for the gliders. She never came back. I think she must have fallen. There are sheer drops along the breach wall. I never found her, afterward. The Chaga would have taken away every trace of her.

''Joachim tried to get in radio contact with base camp and tell them there had been a major accident on the mountain. Lise, Christian and I went down to see if we could find any survivors. The night had been clear, with a good moon, but had quickly clouded up. It can do that, up on the mountain. The wind had risen to gale force. We found where it had plowed up the land and followed it for about a mile downslope. It came in from the northeast, you see?'' He mimed the arc of the package with his gloved hand. ''It had come down on the edge of the Diamond Glacier, about a mile from our camp. There was no fire. If it had been an airplane crash, there would have been a fire, even on the ice fields. You do not think about this at the time; all you think about is finding someone alive.

''When we saw the site, we knew this was no air crash. The crater was about ten feet wide and thirty long. The thing itself was about the size of a bus. You have seen the mock-ups they have done on computer. They are pretty much as we saw it. What I remember is the heat—the thing was still dull red from reentry. I could feel the warmth on my face and hands. I remember having two impressions. The first was of the terrible airline bombing, Lockerbie, do you remember that, or are you too young?''

''I was four,'' Gaby said. ''But I've seen it on nostalgia shows.''

''The other impression was of that old sci-fi book: *The War of the Worlds*? H. G. Wells? I was expecting one end to unscrew and tentacles to come out. Lockerbie and *The War of the Worlds:* that is what I was thinking, standing on the edge of the crater. It looked scary. I know that sounds a funny thing; it was obvious that it had been made—this was not a rock that had fallen out of the sky—but not in the way people would make something. Do you understand this? All the proportions were wrong. They fitted together, but they looked strange. And it was not broken either, like an airplane would have been broken. We knew we were seeing the thing intact, as it was meant to be, and that this was what it was meant to do. It did not look like an accident.''

Across the lake a duster plane was spraying the green circles of sharecrop orchard. Flamingos fled from it, peeling up from the water in a pink wedge of wings.

''The storm was getting up by then; there was nothing else we could do that night. Lise suggested we come back when the weather had cleared. But I know that we all felt, no, we knew, that the storm had come out of the thing in the crater.

''The storm closed in while we were returning to camp. I don't know how we made it. A blizzard, in the tropics. *Unglaublich.* I know now there was more than snow in it, but I now know more about many things. We put our tents up and took shelter. We had no idea it would be so long or terrible. The first day our radio stopped working; we had no contact with our base camp. The second day the strange things started happening. Our tents began to fall apart. A little yellow patch about the size of a pencil point would appear on the waterproof fabric and within minutes grow to the size of my hand. The same happened to our weatherwear; to anything that had plastic in it, which is almost everything in modern mountaineering. Of course, you know what was happening.''

''The spores, the virons, whatever you want to call them, scavenge hydrocarbons to use as building blocks for Chaga-life,'' Gaby said.

''And plants and vegetable proteins too,'' Peter Werther said. ''But never the living flesh of animals, never breathing, moving things. Strange, so? It knows us, you see.'' His gloved hand gripped the wooden railing. Weaver birds were building one of their hanging basket nests under the roof. They came and went with stalks of grass and reed. Humans did not perturb them. They had more important agendas.

''The story is well-known. Lise and Christian and Joachim stayed to wait for Sabine. Because I had the most experience in the mountains, I tried to go down to get help. Their stories end with me walking out into the blizzard and disappearing. That is where mine properly begins.''

He offered cigarettes. This time Gaby took one.

''I was a fool. No experience could have prepared me for what I found out there. It was total whiteout, but at the same time strange shapes were looming out of the snow, like nothing I had ever seen before. Coming out of the ground under my feet, before my eyes. As I watched! In twenty steps I was lost. But I stumbled on, not knowing if my next step would take me over the edge of a drop, my weatherproof clothing rotting and falling apart around me. Rotted through, like . . . what is the word?'' He said something in German.

''Mildew?'' Ute Bonhorst suggested.

''*Ja.* My only protection against the storm was coming apart in my fingers. At that altitude, in such a windchill, you develop hypothermia within minutes. All you want to do is give up and lie down in the snow and let it all stop. That is what you want most of all, for it all just to stop.'' He looked out at the patterns the crop duster wove on the sky. A thin coil of smoke rose from his cigarette. ''That is what I did. It was all I could do, do you understand? I was too cold, too confused, too afraid. I lay down. I went to sleep. And I died. I know it, in here." His gloved hand tapped his breastbone. "I died up there on that mountain. And the mountain brought me back to life.

"There is no time in death. There are no dreams. That is how you know it is death and not sleep. But you do not awake from death, and I awoke. It seemed like an instant, though I have worked out since that I was dead for over a year. When you wake from death, it is all the terrible things about being born again. You are forced from a warm, comfortable womb of flesh into a world that you cannot understand. I woke in darkness, kicking at the bubble of soft skin into which I was curled. It unfolded around me like the petals of a flower, in speeded-up film, *ja*? You have seen pictures of the things they call hand trees. There are thousands of them, millions probably; all pure white. In one of those I came back to life, halfway up the face of a huge reef of Chaga growing out of the mothermass. It must have been half a mile high; the top was always covered in that damn fog that never cleared—the forest would not let me see too far so that I would not try to leave it. It did not want to lose me. Every time I tried to escape, it would bring me back. I would have to fall asleep in the end, and I would wake in a hand tree back where I started, on the side of that damn sky reef. It stole time from me—whole years were lost in sleep. I imagine myself passing through pipes and tunnels and tubes underneath the earth, like the veins and arteries of the Chaga.

"I woke naked except for a few scraps of metal: buckles, a zipper, the remains of my Rolex. You owe me a Rolex, you hear me? Everything had been digested by the Chaga. Even my hair, my eyelashes, eaten by the Chaga. I was naked high on the side of a mountain, but I was not cold. I do not know what it had done to me, but I never needed clothing while I lived with it. I had been changed. And I could breathe the thin air as easily as if I were down on the coast; another change. It did something to my sweat glands; have you noticed how insects never seem to bother me? I am a natural insect repellent. Mosquitoes avoid me: that was one gift the Chaga let me keep.

"It fed me, it sheltered me, it gave me water to drink. There are things like huge flowers up there; when it gets dark they open up and you can shelter inside and they will close around you and protect you. And when storms blew and the rains came, the reef would provide little soft caves—like pores in your skin—where I could curl up and listen to the sound of the wind across the high forest. Sometimes when I fell asleep it would move me to another place, another time. How I knew was that all my hair would disappear again.

"The Chaga is full of ghosts. On the journeys I was allowed to make, I found traces of humans—abandoned game lodges, skeletons of cars and buses. Once I found a cache of old photographs still in silver frames—the glass had preserved them from the Chaga. They became my family, the people in those photographs. I felt that while I had been dead up there in the snows, the world had ended and I was the last man on earth. No, that is not quite right. I felt more like the world had just begun and I was the first man. I was Adam, alone and naked in a new Eden.

"But there are not just the ghosts of the past up there; there are the ghosts of the future. I see you do not understand me; I will try to explain to you how I felt. In places, the Chaga has memorized the shapes of the buildings that once stood there and stored them as, ah . . . ?" He said a German word Gaby could not catch.

"Templates," Ute Bonhorst said.

"Exactly. Templates that time would one day fill in with wood, and brick, and concrete, and in the end, people. Ghosts of things to come. One day I found a tree of human skulls—it had grown from an old Wa-chagga cemetery, but they did not seem to me to be the skulls of the dead, but of the yet-to-be-born, waiting for flesh and skin to grow and thought to fill them. There was a place, high up on the reef—a good two hours' climb—where the Chaga had grown a television tree. It was like a baobab with screens set into the trunk, each tuned to a different channel. It was my eye on the world. From it I learned how long I had been dead and what had happened to those I had left up on Kibo, and what had happened to the world to which they had returned. I learned how deep I was within the forest and what a difficult journey it would be if I were to return to that world and my friends who did not know that I had been brought back from the dead.

"That was the first time the Chaga stole me and took me to someplace else. It had made a mistake in showing me the world beyond. It is not God, you see. It can make mistakes. But it would not let me go. It needed me too badly."

"Needed you?" Uninvited, Gaby took one of Peter Werther's cigarettes. The smoke was normality. The crop duster, circling in the shadow of the Mau escarpment: normality. The children wheeling about on their battered bicycles in the dust and flies of What the Sun Said: normality. They anchored her against the grand insanity of this pale-eyebrowed man's experience of the Chaga.

"I believe that while I slept the Chaga read my DNA," Peter Werther said. "I know that every time I woke, the Chaga had changed in subtle ways. Some of the fruit I normally ate now contained meat that tasted something like the way I smell. The Chaga had spliced my genes into the fruit. It made me eat myself, can you understand that? The flower pods began to absorb my wastes and recycle my water; I shat in the forest, food plants would sprout. At night among the trees I was accompanied by flocks of little bioluminescent balloons keyed to my scent. Through me, the Chaga was programming itself for human habitation. But in another sense, it needed me. It came to me."

"You mean sexually?" Gaby asked.

"It became my lover. That is what I mean. In the big sleeps it had known me as intimately as any one thing may know another. It gave me the chance to know it as intimately as it knew me."

Gaby exhaled smoke in that slow trickling way that people who smoke can say, *I do not want to believe you, but I have to.*

"Ours was a mystical union as much as a physical one. It was more a symbiosis—that is the way of the Chaga, to join with things not of itself and draw them into it. This was the time I began to understand the voice of the Chaga. Do you remember what I said about the song that was a million years old? I believe that my nervous system was adapted to tap into the neural circuitry of the Chaga. I could hear, but I could not understand. It was too fast and too slow at the same time." Peter Werther directed a sentence in German to Ute.

"Sequencing and synthesizing," she said. "You mean, the speed with which the Chaga read and translated DNA and used it to reprogram itself was too fast to be comprehended."

"*Ja.*" The crop duster had drawled away to the north. Rafts of flamingos descended from the wheel of birds to resume feeding in the lake shallows. "As fast as a computer. Maybe faster. Certainly bigger. If you imagine what a computer a hundred miles across could process. But also slower: the intelligence behind it—the mind, the spirit, yes?—works on a different scale of time from us. We are too fast for it; it is a huge, slow, profound vegetable consciousness.''

''Did you ever find any evidence of the intelligence behind the Chaga?'' Gaby did not want to say the word *aliens.* It was not a word for a place as open and filled with light as this. Peter Werther did not have any problem with it.

''Aliens, you mean? No, I never saw anything that made me think there was an intelligence behind the Chaga other than its own. Those cities I found up there; they are not waiting for the alien masters to step from the soil and inhabit them, they are for us, on the day when we learn we cannot run away from the Chaga anymore and come to it as a friend rather than an enemy. We are the aliens. This is the message I was sent out from the Chaga to tell. It knows us, it has known us for a very long time. It is not alien and hostile. It may be unfamiliar, sometimes shocking, but it is ultimately human. It has come from the stars to show us our destiny is out among the stars. That is our rightful place, our destiny. But not as we are now; that is why the Chaga has come, to join with us, and change us into new forms that can live among the stars.''

Ute exchanged glances with Gaby. Peter Werther saw the raised eyebrows.

''Ah, you are thinking, *Another idiot with a mad theory about the Chaga. It has fried his brains, all that hot sun and thin air and years of solitude: he has gone quietly insane.* I can understand that. There are so many people with messages about the Chaga; mine is by no means the maddest. Or the sanest. It was anticipated that I would not be believed—you may even be doubting that I was lost for the five years since the Kilimanjaro Event, that I am Peter Werther at all. Well, I have something you should see.''

He held out his left hand, palm up. With his right hand he removed the leather biker's glove.

''Look closely,'' Peter Werther said.

At first Gaby thought it was an intricate tattoo covering all the upper surfaces of his left hand from fingertips to wrist. Fractal-pattern tattoos had been briefly fashionable among her fellow students in London. Then she thought that it was a strange and terrible birthmark, a complex meander of skin pigments. There was something familiar in the very alienness, like those photographs you see of parts of things in close-up.

"Oh, dear Jesus," Gaby McAslan whispered, seeing.

It was Chaga. The legacy of the alien rain forest was a piece of itself imprinted in the palm of Peter Werther's left hand. Trees, pseudo-corals, mosaic cover: complete, perfect, a million times miniaturized.

Peter Werther slipped off his linen jacket.

Among Gaby's father's library of home-videoed old movies was a tape of *The Illustrated Man.* Five hours a day it had taken to make Rod Steiger up for the role. The most complex skin job in cinema history, but the effect had been breathtaking.

Behold the man, Gaby McAslan. Peter Werther's left arm up to the sleeve of his T-shirt was covered in Chaga. He pulled the white T-shirt off over his head. The mottled infestation stopped at a clearly defined circle halfway across his pectoral—he was in good shape for a late-thirtysomething, Gaby noted in that trivia-gathering way of those who do not want to believe the evidence of their eyes. The Chaga closed across his shoulder, down his scapulars and looped under his arm at the third rib.

"It's growing," he said. Ute Bonhorst mapped the geography of his body minutely with the video camera.

"Doesn't it, ah . . . ?" Gaby wallowed for questions.

"Hurt? No. There is no pain at all. That's the marvelous thing about it, it's quite painless. And you need not worry, it is not infectious. Let us say, no one in What the Sun Said has caught it off me. It is personal to me, my sign, my stigmata."

"How fast?" It repelled Gaby, yet was morbidly attractive. She wanted to touch it, but did not know if she could bear the feel of it beneath her fingertips.

"Oh, very very slow. A few millimeters a day. But it moves in time with its mother, if you understand? To scale. And, like it, this cannot be stopped."

"You've tried?"

"I know."

"How long have you got?"

"It is about nine months since I woke in a flower pod at the very edge of the Chaga. Then it was just a spot in the middle of my palm. So, you can work it out. What do you think? About another year or so? Maybe two? It seems to be avoiding my face: that, I think, will be last to go. It knows how important the face is to us."

"What then?"

Peter Werther smiled.

"Something wonderful, I think. I know that I require less food and water and sleep than before. Even now, I sometimes forget to breathe for several seconds, and have not yet come to any lasting harm."

Ute spoke in German.

"Perhaps," Peter Werther said. "She is asking me if maybe I am becoming, ah . . . ?"

"Photosynthetic."

"*Ja.* And recycling my own water. Becoming a self-sufficient, sealed unit. Perhaps. I do not know. Perhaps I will live forever; whatever, I am not afraid of it. There is nothing to be afraid of; it is not death, it is not disfigurement. It is being changed into a better thing, a fitter thing. I am not the future, but I may be *a* future."

Gaby shook her head in disbelief. Not at what Peter Werther had told her, and whether he could be believed or not, but that she had been given such a gift as this. This was syndication to every on-line newsnet on the planet. This was the center spread of every lumbering folding-paper Gutenberg dinosaur. This was prime-time broad- and narrow-cast news: this was half the industrialized world choking on their microwave TV chow. This was *Time* and *Le Monde* and *Stern.* This was lead lines on magazine covers from stands on Times Square to the Gare du Nord.

This was Gaby McAslan in front of a camera lens.

"They'll never leave you alone once this gets out," she said.

"We can always move. What the Sun Said has been good to me. There is a lot of country up there for us to disappear into."

"They'll find you. They won't give you space like we have. They won't let you say what you want to say, they won't respect your message, or your story, or where you've been, or what you've seen. They'll be asking you how you think the world has changed in the five years you've been away and what you think of the latest fashions and the latest music and the latest supermodel and what the three things are you missed most while you were in the Chaga. They'll do articles on your sex life, they'll run features on the contents of your bloody refrigerator. They'll ask you a million things, but they won't listen to you. They'll make you into a celebrity."

"I know this. But people must be prepared. People must understand. Even one word of mine may be enough. Prophets are never honored in their own countries. Even if they do not listen to what I have to say, it may be enough to see that a man can go into the Chaga and return."

But as what? Gaby thought.

The voices of the children grew louder. They came running along the shore and out onto the wooden jetty, shouting for their brother Peter. Peter Werther hastily pulled on his protecting garments.

"They are my family, my friends. Even if no one else will, they believe me."

The children spilled into the wooden gazebo. The weaver birds fled from their clamoring voices and restless bodies. The children tugged at Peter Werther's sleeves and hands, implored him to come and look at what they were doing.

"Their future too," he said. *"Ja?"*

A great cloud, dark, flat-bottomed, rising to a peak of curdled cumulus ten miles high, edged over the eastern escarpment and cast its reflection into the lake.

11

Gabygram 8
April 24
from: GMcA@136657NAI:EAFTP.

Hi, Reb.

A million thanks for the tapestry. It got here relatively unplundered by Customs and Excise, except for the inevitable wee hole they snip out of the corner so they can stick an endoscope in to sniff for cocaine. It's a beautiful thing; too precious for this place. When I find a more permanent bunk, I'll accord it its due honor. Which, as I've said, may be sooner rather than later. Mrs. K says this is not really the place for me, though she's loved having me—she has a soft spot for Irish girls: apparently I am not the first, which makes me rather suspicious, but I can't go into that here. But she has a friend in the cathedral choir who works in the Kenyatta Hospital who knows someone in the Global Aids Policy Unit who has a lodger who may be moving out.

So, I'm Auntie Gab again? A wee girl. Hannah'll probably stop at two, she's a real "two is enough, three is social irresponsibility'' person. I'm happy, of course, but I warn you, this is what happens when you steal your sister's boyfriend. Actually, Marky and her were made for each other, so they should be thankful to me for having introduced them. Some people like living in a Laura Ashley catalog. Me, when, *if,* I have kids, I want dozens. All over the place. Noisy and dirty and rude and lively.

Very pleased to hear Dad's gallbladder operation was a success. Doctors, what do they know? There's more rest and healing out on the Point than fretting indoors listening to the birds and the wind and wanting to be out there, except that some eejit of a doctor says you're not allowed to. It's good this time of year, the Point; the gorse will just be past its best, the leaves budding. You miss seasons here; whatever changes there are as the planet spins around the sun are too subtle for a white girl like me to notice.

I'm keeping up with United's progress through the Net—we have an office league going, those of us who appreciate the finer points of the Beautiful Game, as opposed to the ethnic cleansing Americans call football. Our very own SkyNet United has, ahem, been doing rather well recently. We *stuffed* the BBC last week: four nil, four nil, four nil, four nil! One of them from the size five of your own dear sister. Tembo would have made a hat trick but for a decidedly dodgy tackle on the edge of the box; the ref was obviously blind, bribed or both, it was a clear-cut penalty. Faraway managed to stop everything that was fired at him, for once, in between showing off his natty new sports gear to his multitude of goal-line groupies. Next fixture is against UNECTA *itself,* that is, when there are enough of our peoples in town to make teams.

So, I'm a celebrity. Local girl makes good. If they're talking about me in the Groomsport Drugstore, I really have arrived. Wish I felt so good about it. Jesus, Reb, SkyNet . . . I get the animations back from the Manga Twins—whom I've never met—E-mail the thing to T.P.'s PDU so it's the first thing he sees when he gets out of the bed in the morning. He creams himself, Reb.

Gaby McAslan is the toast of the Thorn Tree. Even that bitch Abigail Santini shouted me lunch at the Norfolk and managed to do a passable impersonation of being gracious. Pats on the back from Cap'n Bill at head office, even. I tell T.P. the Werther story was worth its weight in cocaine so when is he going to pull me off on-line and put me out in the field as a correspondent?

Fuckpig Nazi bastard asshole. He sits there behind his desk and says to my face, ''Well, I don't know, you're doing so well in on-line it would be a mistake to move you just as you're carving out a niche for yourself,'' and then gives me some shit about wanting me in on-line to cover the *Tolkien* probe when it rendez-vouses with Iapetus at the beginning of next week, because I'm the only one he can trust to do it right. Jesus, Reb, Ute Bonhorst's name is on the copy line, but I made the Werther story, every last bit of it. They don't need a journalist for the *Tolkien* thing. Bastard Dubliner. Never trust a southerner.

On the upside, though, I'm going out on the town with Oksana Telyanina. The Siberian shamaness? She left a message for me on the Thorn Tree. Used to be a regular jungle telegraph back in the Great White Hunter days, now it's mostly wankers on TransAfrica Jeep Safaris with names like Jerome or Letitia telling Rudy and Charlotte they'll meet them in Alex, OK? And one addressed to me. Gaby McAslan. Spelled wrong. Here it is, see? ''Big cocks and vodka, Gaby! Come with me and meet men!'' She writes like a six-year-old. We're going to this place called the Elephant Bar up at Wilson Airfield—she calls it *Weel*son, which is going to remain stuck in my head forever—where the Siberian pilots all hang out, drink vodka, smash glasses and male-bond. They have a strict dress code. Very strict. They won't let you in unless you're wearing shorts. Shades are optional, but if your knees don't show, you're bounced. So, what do you think? T-shirt not too much? Hannah may have got the man, but I kept the T-shirt. At least T-shirts can't get you pregnant.

Gotta dash, Reb. Keep an eye out for my reports on the *Tolkien*–Iapetus flyby. Love to Dad and Paddy and the cats, and Hannah, I suppose, and the sprogs. I'll just close this file and mail it. Love you. Bye now.

12

While Gaby McAslan grubbed around in the smoggy streets of Nairobi, Oksana Telyanina had been halfway around the planet on UNECTA's business. She had also collected a new tattoo, a tiny tree about thc size of a thumbnail on the ball of her right shoulder. It symbolized the soul's search for transcendence and union with the spirit world: the mystical ascent of the apprentice sha-person into a tree to be possessed by the spirit of a totemic animal.

The Elephant Bar's totemic animal was self-evident. There were tusks behind the bar, plastic replicas, not out of ecological sensitivity but because the ivory ones had been sold on the black market during a financial crisis six years earlier, before Sibirsk came and turned the Elephant Bar into little Irkutsk. So now there were not only photographs of elephants, paintings of elephants, posters of elephants, batiks and wall hangings and bamboo screens of elephants, elephant foot stools and tables supported by carved wooden elephants, like Hindu cosmology; there were also icons on the walls, bottles of Stolichnaya on the back bar and little silver pots of caviar all along the counter. At one end a volcanic samovar simmered.

"Story is: elephant walks out of national park, which in those days did not have fence round, like now," Oksana had explained. "Right onto main runway and straight into pissy little Cessna trying to take off. *Boom!* Shredded jumbo for half mile every direction. That is why called Elephant Bar."

The Siberians in shorts and shades and fur hats with the earflaps folded down decided that the women at the table needed their company and sat down with them. Oksana convinced Gaby that it would be a good time to go out onto the airfield and look at the airplanes. Time spent looking at airplanes is time exceedingly well spent.

The air was warm out on the strip. Little night winged things swooped through the soft gloaming. Runway lights were a glowing path to the main tower a mile distant. Fuel trucks nosed among the parked aircraft like hungry piglets. The night smelled of dust and aviation kerosene.

"I thought you were taking me to meet men, not jugfuls of vodka and hormones," Gaby said.

Oksana shrugged. "Not many men in this country at all. Plenty of rides. Few men. If you do get man, you must hold him, hard. I tell you how you keep him forever. Serbski Jeb. That is how. Serbian fucking. You can do it indoors but outside much better. Make sure ground is soft. You get man. You stake him out, yes? So?" She mimed a spread-eagle. "Good and tight. Then you get on top of him and you ride him. Slow. Very slow. When he seems to come, you slow down, stop him. After half hour, forty minutes, he is out of his head. Afraid he is dying, afraid he is not going to die and nothing he can do to stop you. Girl on top. Won't work other way. You always in charge. He'll want more, but careful with it, yes? Not for every day. Holidays, birthdays, New Year; keep it special so he will not get used to it. He's yours forever, I promise.''

"How the hell do you know this?''

"Eight months of snow in Irkutsk. You learn much those long, dark nights by the fire.''

"It's not just fucking, it's everything,'' Gaby said. "I've been here three months and I want something to happen. Something real: not a report of it, or a press release, or even someone who has experienced it himself. The real thing. I want to see the Chaga, Oksana, that's all. I am going out of my head with frustration. I want something to happen.''

"I think maybe your prayer will be answered, Gaby. Something is happening. They have been fuelling up planes all day. Something is coming, very soon, I feel. I do not know what; they will not tell us until the pre-flight briefing, but because of what I am, I can sense things others cannot.''

Oksana fingered a leather amulet on a thong around her neck. "Change is coming. Will be rain by morning. I can smell it. My grandfather had a famous weather nose. I have inherited it.''

They walked under the wings of a stubby, barbaric little jet: T-tail, two big turbofans mounted above the wing roots. It was the same aircraft that was printed on Oksana's faded sleeveless T-shirt. Two black soldiers came around the aircraft's nose. They recognized Oksana and nodded without challenging Gaby. They carried their automatic weapons with the brutal ease peculiar to African soldiers, as if they were bags of vegetables. Oksana placed her hand affectionately on the fuselage. "This is mine. She is not beautiful, but I love her. Do anything, go anywhere for me. Good as any man. Better, maybe. Does not need Serbski Jeb to keep her true to me.''

A Cyrillic word was spray-stenciled under the cockpit windshield.

"What does it say?''

"Is her name. *Dostoinsuvo.* Means 'dignity.' Come, I show you something.'' Oksana opened the hatch. Steps unfolded, alerted by her handprint. Gaby followed her up into the cockpit.

Oksana cleared a mail order catalogue for a Californian New Age store from the vacant co-pilot's seat. *Dostoinsuvo*'s flight deck was a shrine to credit card shamanism. Leather sacks like sun-dried scrotums hung from the cockpit window. The hatch glass had been streakily stained with glass paint to portray images of the Ancestral Tree. Thumbnail icons looked down from between the redundant ceiling switches with the beatific indifference peculiar to Orthodox saints. Color photocopies of mandalas were gunge-tacked to the back of the flight deck door; crystals of various hues and spiritual properties rested in niches in the command board. The bleached skulls of Oksana's totemic animals were glued along the upper edge of the main console, which had been sprayed with green car paint that was peeling under the partial pressurization. Tiny chimes glittered and tinkled in the draft from the air-conditioning vents; the virtual reality helmet was adorned with painted reindeer horns.

"Is like explosion in magic shop, but I love her," Oksana said. "She takes me high, to the places of the spirits, and collects the power of the high places on her wings so I can bring it back to earth. Do not laugh, Gaby. You do not feel it, you do not have the power in your genes."

I am not laughing, Gaby thought. It is the most real thing there is. It is the thing that makes you want to do do so bad you would die if could not do it. But you cannot touch it or hold it for the moment you start to think about what it is you turn away from the thing that produces it and you kill it. You can only find it when you do not seek it, you can only see it when you look away from it. It is pure being. *Dhyana.* It dwells in the cockpit of an An72F at twenty thousand feet as comfortably as in the nested fan-folds of information and video in a complex multimedia news overlay, but it will only come as an uninvited guest.

Oksana slipped her hand into the manipulator glove, flexed it in imagined flight and pointed through the window at the aircraft standing opposite *Dostoinsuvo.* It was unlike any other on Weelson airfield: long, low, lean, mean, wings swept back, nose uplifted to the stars. It seemed to stab the night.

"Is beautiful, no? Beautiful bird," Oksana said. "Tupolev 161. Executive jet variant of old Soviet Blackjack bomber. UNECTA priority transport. Afterburning Kuznetzov turbofans: she will do Mach 2.2 at fifteen thousand feet. Swing wing. Take you anywhere in the world. Of course, they will not let Oksana fly this. For men only. Big macho thing. Penis with wings. But some day, some day, Oksana Mikhailovna will be in captain's chair up there. My ambition, Gaby. See? Both poor unhappy frustrated women. You with Chaga, me with big supersonic dick. But when we are happy, let us not forget this, Gaby? When we have dreams, and men, do not let them come between us, no? Men come, men go, friendship goes on.'' She held out her hands. Moved by the Siberian woman's honest inarticulacy, Gaby clasped them in her own hands. ''Any time you want, any time you need, any time, I will be there. When he is gone—for they all go, in the end—you come to me. I will not go.''

They sealed *Dostoinsuvo* behind them and went back to the Elephant Bar. The Siberians were singing songs from the shows: ''Thumbelina'' in astonishingly close harmony.

13

The rain woke Gaby ten seconds before the PDU on the bedside table paged her, which was ten seconds before Mrs. Kivebulaya knocked and entered with a pot of exceptionally strong coffee.

''You have ten minutes to drink this and get dressed before Jake Aarons gets here,'' she said. ''I think after last night you might need it.''

Gaby screwed her eyes against the white agony of the bedside light. She felt vertiginous, dehydrated, feverish.

''What time is it?''

''Quarter past four.''

Quarter past *four*? Jake *Aarons*? Ten *minutes*?

''All the news agencies are mobilizing,'' Mrs. Kivebulaya said. ''There is something happening, I do not know what. You have just enough time to drink this, put on a face and get out, my dear.''

The rain was so heavy Gaby was soaked through in the few yards between hotel porch and SkyNet Landcruiser. It was only when she had fastened her seat belt and Jake Aarons had driven off that she wondered how Mrs. Kivebulaya knew something big was happening before the news companies.

''You smell like the Tusker brewery,'' Jake Aarons said. He had had no more warning than Gaby, but he was smart, shaved, groomed, professional. Gaby suspected the mental cameras never stopped rolling on his life.

Only the news agencies and the military were abroad in the city this morning. Gaby had never seen so many soldiers. Entire divisions were on the move, rolling in slow, heavy convoys forty, fifty vehicles long through the deserted streets. Military policemen in streaming UN-white raincapes held the civilians up at intersections to let the trucks through. They looked oddly insubstantial, like watery white ghosts, seen from the warmth and instrument glow of the Landcruiser. Uhuru Highway was gridlocked with armored personnel carriers. Something had broken down up by the railway bridge. Jake Aarons smiled at the saturated blue-helmets waving him to standstill with red flashlights and took the 4X4 onto the central reservation. Big all-terrain tires chewed municipal flower beds and lawns to red mud.

"We've got a live one. A biological package. Came down about four hours ago up in the Nyandarua National Park."

"Jesus, Jake . . ."

"They've been tracking it for days, seems. Knew exactly where it was coming down, but the bastards back there"—he nodded in the direction of the Kenyatta Center—"didn't want the press in on it until they'd secured the area. Of course, nothing moves in this burg but we don't hear about it, so the moment the wagons started to roll, we got suspicious and they had to come out with it. If they'd told us before the event, that would have been the biggest story since the Resurrection, but they're flying us up there for nothing, so it's churlish to complain."

Gaby recalled Oksana's premonitions and the heady smell of aviation fuel. Jake took the *keepie-leftie* outside the National Sports Stadium at fifty. Gaby felt the back end begin to aquaplane and grabbed a handhold.

"It missed Mt. Kenya by a hair and came down just west of Treetops. Nyeri's fucked. That's why you can't move for troops. The UN's mobilizing everything it's got for a mass evacuation. They'll never do it, this isn't rounding up a few thousand Wachagga banana growers into resettlement camps. It's one of the most densely populated parts of Kenya up there. In the end, why bother? What it comes down to is the big veto power members don't like the idea of first contact with aliens being in the hands of what they consider a bunch of bloody savages. When John Alien comes walking out of the Chaga, they want the first human he meets to be a big beautiful blond Aryan U.S. or Russian marine with a very big gun. Kenyan politicians are getting fed up with being Uncle Tommed and want UNECTA research resources directed toward human interaction with the Chaga. Your Werther piece gave them ammunition—it isn't an automatic death sentence in there.''

They had left the military machine behind now. The only vehicles on the road were news-company 4X4s, hurtling along the avenue in waves of spray. On either side the townships huddled in the dark beneath the spring rain.

''Nairobi's dead,'' Gaby said, sobering rapidly.

''It's only forty miles north of here. How long's that—three, four years? The Nyandarua Event and the Kilimanjaro Chaga have the city in a pincer.''

Cars were tailed twenty back at the airport entrance while blue-helmets checked accreditations. A white soldier with his head shaved within a millimeter of the bone waved the SkyNet Landcruiser through. Rain fell in strict diagonals through the sodium floods. Staff in UN white with clipboards ran around trying to find the owners of the vehicles that had been abandoned at the edge of the taxiways. CBS. STAR. Tass. UPI. Those were the names on the 4X4s. Jake drove along the perimeter road until he saw SkyNet logos. A blue-beret tried to move him on.

''Fuck off,'' he said under the thunder of a taxiing jet, smiling sweetly.

All of SkyNet East Africa was gathered around the open tailgate of T.P.'s Landcruiser, from where he tried to direct strategy. Gaby nodded to Tembo, fastening the Velcro seal of his waterproof camera cover. Faraway, who could see over any crowd, waved back. Abigail Santini caught Gaby's eye and smiled politically. Antonovs passed slowly, throwing up swaths of sound and spray from their Coanda-effect engines. Gaby had never heard anything so loud.

''Right, we're all here,'' T.P. bellowed. ''Jake, with me and the camera crew. Everyone else, you know what you're doing. When we get down, there'll be transport to meet us. For Christ's sake, don't get split up. What'll you do?''

The ritual reply was lost in the scream of a big Tupolev lifting off into the rain. Women in blue berets and wet combats were already shepherding the non-Anglophone correspondents and their camera teams to a waiting Antonov. Turbofans powered up. Gaby scraped wet hair out of her eyes.

''T.P.! What about me?''

He could not have looked more confused had his car spoken to him.

"Jesus. Gaby. Yes. Important job for you to do. As well as the *Tolkien* flyby, there's a press conference been called down in Kajiado regional HQ. Jake was scheduled to cover it, but with this blowing up, well, it'll have to be an on-liner. You and Ute take a car and cover it for me, will you? The office will patch me through to Nyeri if it's anything cosmos shaking. I'm relying on you, Gaby. What am I doing?"

Abigail Santini was beckoning from the passenger door of the airplane. Both engines were up to speed, the pilot was checking flaps and ailerons.

"You're not taking me."

"Someone has to mind the shop. It's a big thing I'm trusting you with, Gaby. What is it?"

"Fuck you, T. P. Costello!" she shouted, but the words were obliterated by a passing aircraft. "This is not fair."

He turned halfway to the plane to wave bye-bye.

"This is not fucking fair!"

The door closed behind him. The Antonov moved off its stand. There were Cyrillic letters stenciled under the cockpit window. *Dignity.* Slipstream blew Gaby's hair into her face, plastered her wet clothes to her body.

"You owe me for this, Costello."

She watched Oksana turn the Antonov onto the main runway. The aircraft went up very quickly, very suddenly, like a high jumper. She watched it climb until its lights were lost in the rain clouds, then went back to the 4X4 and realized she did not have a clue how to get home again.

14

One and a quarter billion miles distant a voice whispered and something woke to life. You could call it an angel and not be far wrong. It was attenuated, diaphanous. It had golden wings. It flew through unending darkness. It had a fragile beauty, but it was strong; it had come far, flown fast. Like the angels of Yahweh, its only thought was to do the bidding of its master. Like them, it was a messenger.

Six years before the voice had given it a mission and set it on its long, curving course. The voice had spoken again and sent it to sleep. In its sleep it flew on, into the big dark. Now it had come so far that the voice took over an hour to reach it.

NASA space probe *Tolkien* awakened and readied itself for its task. Its obedience had not been diminished by its long flight and sleep. Camera booms were deployed, lenses trained on the object of inquiry. Solar wings of crumpled gold foil unfolded, though so far from the sun, they could only supplement the nuclear batteries. Thruster pods cleared their throats; experiment packages were readied. Twenty different senses were tuned to the still-invisible target. Tight-beam communication dishes sought the distant bright speck of Earth.

Like an angel, the robot had no curiosity and no will. It was not distracted by the titanic beauty of Saturn. Gaudy rings and the eye-catching opal swirls of gas storms the size of continents could not tempt it from its duty. The Iapetus flyby must be done right the first time. Celestial mechanics allowed one shot and one only.

It had flown far, it had flown fast, but events had overtaken it. First the Hyperion Event, for which a new vehicle had been commissioned and tasked six months behind *Tolkien.* Orbital mechanics had been less friendly to it: the relative positions of the planets off whose gravities it caromed like a billion-dollar eight ball meant it would arrive in the Hyperion Gap two years after *Tolkien* rounded Saturn and fell into the great dark. It too had been overtaken: the Kilimanjaro Event had eclipsed both space missions. No need to cross the solar system for a ten-minute peep at the mysterious and alien. The mysterious and alien was approaching across the plains of Africa and the selvas of South America and the rain forests of the Indonesian archipelago at fifty feet every day.

Ten hours from Iapetus, *Tolkien* commenced long-range mapping. Analysts studied the pictures squeezing from their color printers, but the black moon held its secrets close. The NASA scientists had waited six years. A few hours more was nothing. You learned patience in space science. There would be better later. Perilune would bring *Tolkien* within five hundred miles of the satellite's surface at a relative velocity of sixty miles per second. Detail began to resolve at T-3600. Backscatter from Saturn and the light of a sun so distant it was no more than a brilliant star showed the visible surface to have a highly complex, almost fractal structure. At T-2000 the infrared cameras produced their first heat maps of the facing hemisphere. As one wit was to comment, the infrared profile of Iapetus was indistinguishable from that of a pepperoni pizza. Localized hot spots floated on a sea of semiliquid crustal matter overlain with a web of cooler unidentified material. Scattered across the temperature landscape were small, hard, round concentrations of cold. Like black olives.

Whatever the meaning of these structures, Iapetus was a good sixty Kelvins warmer than it should have been.

The high-resolution cameras at T-500 showed new mysteries. The CCD images slid out of image enhancement line by line. The scientists watched. They saw canyons ten miles deep filled with liquid that could not possibly remain in that state in an environment like that of Iapetus. They saw obsidian atolls lift ring walls thousands of feet above the surface of the moon. They saw these atolls bristle with black filaments hundreds of feet long. They saw nets of black tendrils creep laboriously across the granulated black surface. They saw black flowers the size of cities slowly blossom. They saw sheer black surfaces open like wounds and things for which language has no names grow forth. They saw black jellyfish the size of Pacific nation states rise from the hot spots into the wisps of nitrogen atmosphere. They saw slow waves cross oceans of restless black scales. They saw pylons like skyscrapers push from the crusted surface and unfold into sprays of black feathers. They saw the black feathers ripple in a wind that could not exist, and turn toward the distant, unseen sentience of *Tolkien.* Black. All black.

They could not comprehend it, but they knew what they were seeing. They knew where they had seen this before, but they did not dare say.

At T-0 *Tolkien* released its surface impact probes. As Bilbo, Frodo and Sam fell toward Iapetus *Tolkien* spun on its axis and raked the satellite with a fan of single-shot X-ray lasers. Spectrum analyzers read the light from the wounded moon while atmospheric, gravitic and electromagnetic data streamed back from the artillery-shell-sized surface probes. Then *Tolkien* went into occultation behind the moon and the stream of information was temporarily halted. At T-240 the probe emerged from the radio shadow and began to bit-cram full-data download earthward while there was still power in its batteries. Transmission time was twenty-nine hours, seven minutes. On the third planet out from the sun, *Tolkien*'s masters sifted and analyzed and interpreted the information from Saturn and wondered whether to tell humanity what humanity had already guessed. The stuff, the black stuff covering Iapetus. It was Chaga.

Then the voice spoke one final time and *Tolkien* went silent as Saturn's gravity whipped it like a top and spun it out of the solar system. The good and faithful angel fell faster than any human-made object toward the galaxy clusters in Virgo. By the time it felt the tug of another gravitational field, the earth would be a sterile cinder pressed close to a bloated red sun. Any voice that woke *Tolkien* from its Big Sleep would not be human.

15

The sun was high. The day was hot and clear. The sky was cloudless, an intense hot blue that confounds sense of distance. The rain had passed into the hot dry north. The steady wind had sucked the brief rains dry and returned the earth to dust. Today as every day the road was crowded with refugees. Fifty thousand people were moving on it; whole tribes were going north at the speed of a Nissan pickup, or a cattle truck, or a donkey cart, or their own hard, bare feet. Some slapped emaciated cows on with sticks. Some tried to keep their goats from straying under the wheels of vehicles. Stripped, fire-blackened hulks littered the verges, abandoned when they broke down or simply ran out of fuel. The Kajiado road was a fifty-mile wrecking yard. Bands of thin, tall youths in T-shirts advertising fertilizer companies scavenged the wrecks. The little that was left they piled in the backs of only slightly less decrepit pickups. Dark specks in the heat haze that shimmered up from the open lands beyond the road were refugees striking cross-country for the highway. A tall, narrow plume of dust was a vehicle. A wide low plume was livestock. No plume at all was people on foot with all their possessions rolled up in mats carried on their heads.

White military humpies with stars-and-stripes fluttering briskly from their whip antennae hurtled as fast as they could along the road. They had no care for other road users, on foot or hoof or on wheels. They threw the dust of their passage over all equally. Every mile or so an armored personnel carrier was pulled over onto the soft shoulder. Blue-helmets in RayBans watched indolently over the lines of refugees and rested their bare arms on their hideously powerful weapons. Far less frequent were the aid stations of the UNHCR: a couple of Land Rovers and a canvas awning under which old men with big eyes and big teeth looked you in the face and hairless dusty babies fumbled for their mothers' withered teats. If you told them humans had sent machines to the moons of Saturn, they would have laughed painfully and slapped their thin thighs.

It was a fine and beautiful day, and Gaby McAslan was driving down the road south to Kajiado. Ute Bonhorst was beside her. The top was down and the radio on. The radio played a Western rock classic, as it did sometimes between the African music. The two women sang along with it. The music and the big expensive car insulated them from the epic misery of the road. Gaby's was not a profession renowned for its compassion, and Africa had begun to brutalize her.

Past Isinya, a party of young men stood by the side of the road grouped around a dead lion.

Kajiado had grown out of the intersection of the road south to Tanzania with the railroad to the soda flats at Lake Magadi. John Wayne riding high in the saddle would have felt right at home for its high-plains spirit, and for its vernacular architecture. The town's shops and businesses were set back behind wooden boardwalks that followed the slope of the main street in a long shallow flight of steps. At the Masai stores at the top of the town, all things needful to human beings, and many things not, could be bought. A few Masai could still be found lingering on the porch; tall and beautiful and satanically arrogant. The spears they carried had each cost a lion its life. The hot wind from the plains blew their ocher robes up around them, baring their lean thighs, buttocks and genitals. Such was their pride they did not care. At the bottom of the hill was the transit camp. There was no community in southern Kenya that did not have a transit camp attached to it like a mutated Siamese twin. Kajiado's was smaller than most, and shrinking every day. The Chaga was too close. Townsfolk and camp people alike would be dispossessed, soon. The wealthier landowners and professionals had already moved out. Every day a store would board up or shutter down never to open again. Last week Kajiado's only automated teller machine had been yanked out of the wall of the national bank by a rope attached to a

Peugeot matatu. There were no longer enough police to investigate the crime.

UNECTA was the only business in town that was thriving. For a while; then it would have to put up its boards and shutters and go like all the others and leave Kajiado to the Chaga creeping across the railroad tracks and up the sloping main street and in through the door of the Masai stores. Until that time, Southern Regional Headquarters Kajiado was the advance position for UNECTA's administrative arm, coordinating the mobile bases spaced at the four cardinal points around Kilimanjaro.

Unlike Kajiado town, the regional headquarters had been designed to be abandoned. Architecture varied on themes of prefabricated units, inflatable domes and the ubiquitous Kenyan cinder block. It sprawled. Land is cheap when it is going to be taken away from you. The military had built a big expensive base; there was a well-equipped small airport and servicing facilities for the research division's field equipment from Chaga-proof cameras to the tractor units that carried the mobile laboratories.

The guard on the perimeter wire fence checked Gaby's and Ute's identity on a PDU and sent them around the back of Kajiado's only building to exceed two stories; a massive, windowless fifty-foot block marked UNIT 12. It was an object of some significance: it had been painted olive drab and ringed round with razor-wire concertinas. Kajiado Center's conference hall was the disused town cinema. There were still posters for the last picture show, a double bill of *The Ten Commandments* and Jackie Chan in *Streetfight in Old Shanghai*. The interior was a lurid red, which, with the curved roof and walls, made Gaby think of an open mouth. There were cigarette burns on the flip-down seats. Many of the rows were already filled. Gaby knew enough faces to recognize them all as junior staff. The major players were up at Nyandarua getting their faces on the pale blue screen.

A big UNECT*Afrique* horns-and-mountain symbol hung where Charlton Heston had once held up the tablets of stone. On the stage beneath it was a long table with three chairs, three notepads with pens, three carafes of water with glasses upturned over them and twenty microphones parcel-taped to the edge of the table.

Three people entered from the side of the stage and sat down. The murmur in the cinema ceased. On the left sat a Mediterranean woman in a smart suit that would very quickly get sweaty and creased in the stifling heat of the cinema. On the right sat the token Kenyan, who knew it, and said by the bored, distant way he played with his notepad and pen that he was fucked if he was going to answer any questions from the *wazungu.* In the middle sat the man who had come running up to Gaby McAslan at the cash point on Latema Road, kissed her on the mouth and thus saved her from being conned out of five hundred shillings on her first day in Nairobi.

"The one in the middle, who is he?" Gaby whispered.

"Dr. Shepard," Ute Bonhorst answered. "Research director of Tsavo West."

Gaby rested her chin on the back of the empty seat in front of her and closely watched this man pour himself a glass of water, take a sip and look to his associates.

"OK. If everyone's here, we'll make a start," he said. She remembered the Jimmy Stewart Mr. Middle America accent. She remembered the luminous blue eyes. "There will be press releases at the back later with full technical specifications. Can everyone hear me all right? At the back?" Ute Bonhorst shouldered a U-format camcorder with the SkyNet logo on the side. Gaby checked the battery levels on her disc recorder. "Good to see so many of you. Typically, we've been upstaged by the Chaga deciding to pull a PR coup up at Nyeri. And the *Tolkien* probe gave us more than we'd bargained for. So thanks for coming to see the sideshow." There was a murmur of polite laughter. He introduced himself and the people on either side of him. They spoke briefly. Dr. Shepard then outlined the substance of the press conference.

Each of the four ChagaWatch bases fulfilled a different purpose. Ol Tukai, twelve miles to the southeast, specialized in taxonomy and classification. Tinga Tinga, retreating at fifty feet per day over the Engaruka plains toward the Ngorongoro, attempted to unravel the Gordian knot of Chaga symbiotic ecology. South of the mountain, Moshi base moved across the great empty Lossogonoi plateau and studied the climatic and environmental effects of an alien biosphere on East Africa, and East Africa's adaptations to it. And Tsavo West crawled through the great game reserve from which it took its name toward the fragile Nairobi–Mombasa road and rail line and delved into cellular and molecular biology. It was there that the discovery was made, down among the atoms in the country of quantum uncertainty.

There was a bridge between terrestrial and Chaga-life. It was the chemistry of the carbon atom, but the Chaga was not built on the chains and lattices of earthbound carbon forms. Its engineering was that of the sixty-atom sphere of the Buckminsterfullerene molecule; its organic chemistry a three-dimensional architecture of domes, arches, cantilevers, tunnels and latticed skeletons.

"The molecules are immensely complicated, hundreds of atoms in length," Dr. Shepard said, waving the red dot of his laser pointer across the screen, where wire-frame spheres cannoned off each other and convoluted molecular intestines twined and wriggled.

I bet that is the only suit he has, Gaby McAslan thought.

"Locked into hollow cylinders, they become essentially machines for processing atoms. Molecular factories. This is the mechanism by which the Chaga absorbs and transmutes terrestrial carbon—in vegetable form, mostly, but as you all know, it's not averse to the odd juicy complex hydrocarbon or polymer. The fullerene worms break the chemical bonds of terrestrial organic components into the equivalent of short peptide chains—analogies tend toward the biological, for obvious reasons. We're talking, in a sense, about a form of life on a smaller scale than the fundamental units of terrestrial biology; each of these smart molecules is the equivalent of a cell. The fullerene molecules pass the broken-down terrestrial molecules through their guts, for want of a better expression, in the process adding new atoms, realigning molecular bonds; building copies of themselves, imprinting them with information. In a sense, it's a kind of alien DNA, processing basic amino acids and inorganic compounds into the pseudo-proteins of Chaga biochemistry.

"Essentially, the Chaga is one mother of a buckyball jungle."

Gaby wrote that on the back of her hand. Dr. Shepard sat down. The Mediterranean-looking woman stood up. She had a French accent. Gaby did not hear one word she spoke in it. She was watching the way Dr. Shepard sipped his water and inspected his fingernails and doodled on his notepad and folded little scraps of paper into origami frogs and flapping birds. She watched him scan the faces in the auditorium. His Paul Newman blue eyes met hers for an instant and passed.

You don't know me, but I know you, Gaby McAslan thought.

After the token Kenyan had said his few words, Dr. Shepard asked if there were any questions. Gaby was first on her feet.

"OK, at the back, red-haired woman with the interesting T-shirt."

"Gaby McAslan, SkyNet on-line." Ah, maybe you do know me now, or at least wonder whether you might know me, but you are not certain. "From what I understand of fullerenes, they're the dominant molecular form of carbon in deep-space hydrocarbon clouds. Does this astronomical fact have any relation to what *Tolkien* showed us out at Iapetus?"

If the face does not help you remember, will the voice, the accent? She did not know why it was so important for him to remember. But she wanted deeply to impress him.

"As far back as the Kilimanjaro Event, speculative connections were being made between the Chaga and the Iapetus Occultation. It may have been a shock seeing the images that came back from *Tolkien,* but to the scientific community at least, it wasn't a surprise. What our research has proved is that we are encountering a highly adaptive and successful organism, one which, by virtue of its ability to engineer molecules, can create an ecological niche for itself anywhere it can find raw materials. The fullerene worms are quasi-stable and can rapidly switch molecular structures. In nontechnical language, they can reprogram themselves to change with their environment. So, theoretically, there is no objection to them having evolved a form that can colonize the moons of Saturn or, if they can adapt to as inimical an environment as that, anywhere else in the universe, for that matter."

"So the Chaga is not native to the Saturnian System?" Gaby asked, beating a dozen raised hands by not having sat down while Dr. Shepard answered her question.

"Certainly not Iapetus. And we would very much doubt that it originated in or around the Hyperion Gap, either. If we'd an unlimited budget and our own HORUS orbiter, or even a spare SSTO, we'd very much like to send a probe for a sneaky look under Titan's cloud layer, not because it may have evolved there, but because it may have used it as a way station on the way to Iapetus, and ultimately, Earth. There's barroom speculation about Saturn; if not the planet itself, perhaps in the ring system. The planet pumps out a lot of energy, though personally I'm not convinced it's enough to power up so complex and energy heavy a chemistry. Off the record, my private theory is that it does not originate from our solar system.''

Journalists were on their feet, fingers raised. Gaby sneaked in a parting shot.

''Could this have evolved naturally?''

''Are you asking me are the Iapetus and Earth Chagas artifacts of an alien intelligence?''

Their eyes met across a crowded Kajiado cinema.

''Are there aliens in spaceships with lots of windows in them?''

She made him smile. It was a major triumph. He was one of those men whose smiles so utterly transform their faces they seem like two people.

''On the strength of the evidence to hand, I'd give a reluctant no. No UFOs landing on the White House lawn. Well, that kind of depends on where, and whether, the Chaga is going to stop. Have you heard of Von Neumann machines?''

''Machines that move from planet to planet building copies of themselves.''

''The Chaga may be a highly sophisticated Von Neumann machine. Starships the size of molecules. In a sense, what is a living cell but a Von Neumann machine programmed by its own DNA? And we said earlier that the Chaga 'memes,' as we call them, can be thought of as living molecules. As to whether there is a guiding intelligence behind it—I'm blue-skying here—Von Neumann machines can easily outlive the civilization that produces them. The designers of the Chaga—if they exist at all—could have become extinct a million years ago. But is there any reason why our particular brand of behavior and problem solving should be the sole criterion of 'intelligence'? Our intelligence may be so particular to us that we cannot recognize that something truly alien may be 'intelligent.' We're all thinking in terms of little men with big heads and glowing eyes. Anthropomorphic chauvinism. Perhaps the aliens are the Chaga, or have become the Chaga, over aeons of travel. Then again, as you said, the first fullerenes were deduced from the profiles of interstellar molecular clouds, so perhaps the Chaga, or I should say, the Chaga-memes, the fullerene machines, are a form of life that has evolved in interstellar space. But there may be another level of chauvinism: we assume that within any sufficiently complex system, there must be intelligence. That's how God got invented, I suspect. The

Chaga may just be dumb, fecund life, with no more intelligence than the lilies of the field, or a condomful of sperm.

"Thank you for asking that. I enjoyed your question. OK, Jean-Marie Duclos."

Gaby did not hear the French television journalist's question, or any of the questions that followed. She had what she wanted from Dr. Shepard. After the press conference, when the others were filing out and picking up their hard-copy technical releases and blinking in the bright sunlight outside, she came cantering down the steps to the front.

"Can I sound-bite you on 'buckyball jungle'?"

"If you put a little 'TM' superscript after it," Dr. Shepard said. "Or is it an *R* in a circle? You can sound-bite anything you like. I prefer fullerene machine."

Gaby shrugged to say that it was not quite so aurally digestible. Dr. Shepard hesitated as people do when they need to say something that will embarrass them if it is not right.

"Your accent sounds familiar."

"Northern Ireland." She baited the hook. "You saved my ass once."

He must work it out himself.

He worked it out himself.

"The con gang. What was it?"

"Persecuted students trying to escape to Mozambique. They'd got you with the Rwandan refugee one."

"God, yes. And I . . ."

"You kissed me."

He blushed. It was a comfortable, old-fashioned thing to see in a man.

"Gaby McAslan," he said. "You do those 'And Finally' pieces for SkyNet on-line. I liked the one about the bicycle pump fetishists; the guy down in Dar es Salaam who thought he'd go one better and shoved a compressed-air line up his ass and blew his colon out through his navel. You've caught the real spirit of Africa in those stories. Magic realism is plain old day-to-day living here."

"I've moved on a bit since the 'And Finally' pieces."

"The Peter Werther interview. That was quite a coup."

"Thank you." The moment presented itself. "Listen, I'd very much like to do an interview with you; would you have any objections to talking over lunch? There's supposed to be a place that does very good Indian food here, if it hasn't closed up."

"There still is. It does. The Tipsi Café. Regrettably, I'll have to pass on your generous offer; straight after this they're flying me up to the Nyandarua Impact Zone." He glanced at his watch. "In fact, they're holding the plane for me right now. If you want an interview, it's simplest to get in touch directly with Tsavo West." He scribbled a number on the back of Gaby's hand, next to *buckyball jungle.* "Don't wash that. I'll be up in Nairobi for the ambassador's Independence Day Hootenanny, but I don't suppose you'll be there?"

The very rich, the very beautiful, the very glamorous and the very influential were invited to the U.S. ambassador's Fourth of July party. No one less than the rank of station head, or chief correspondent.

"You never know," Gaby said. "Life's full of surprises."

"I reckoned that." Dr. Shepard packed up his stuff in an impact-plastic briefcase and pulled an overnight bag from under the table. "By the way, might I say, it was an ass exceedingly well worth saving."

16

The Tipsi Café was one of those refreshing places that surpass their reputations. The food was wonderful, generous, cheap and served unpretentiously on plastic plates. Everything tasted faintly of charcoal. Over goat sagh, lentils, two vegetable curries, chutneys and chapattis, Gaby picked Ute Bonhorst for everything she knew about Dr. Shepard.

"He's forty-one, comes from Lincoln, Nebraska. His primary degree was at Iowa State in molecular biology; he graduated in 1988, did his doctorate at UCSB in biophysics and the speculative exobiology of interstellar clouds. When UNECTA received its UN charter in 2006, he was immediately head-hunted."

"I don't want his curriculum vitae, tell me about the man." Gaby summoned two more Tuskers.

"You have to call him Shepard. He has a first name, but he never uses it and no one knows what it is. He's divorced—it was a messy affair, I think—he has two boys who come out to stay with him twice a year. Currently he is unattached. Which makes him the most-sought-after male in East Africa. Abigail Santini has been trying to get him into her bed for almost two years without any success. Are you thinking of joining the line?''

''He interests me, that's all.'' From the look she received, Gaby knew Ute did not believe her. She was not sure she believed herself, but this Shepard did seem to be the only truly solid person she had met in Africa. White person. Tembo, Faraway, Mrs. Kivebulaya, even Haran the Sheriff and Dr. Dan sweating with fear in his executive-class seat; these were real, firmly rooted in the landscape, casting dark shadows. The African light was too bright for white people; it shone through them, it bleached them pale and insubstantial. Dr. Shepard stood full in the light and was not annihilated by it. He threw his shadow across the land, his feet were firmly planted in it, like the Masai standing with arrogant nobility outside the stores at the top of the town.

The decision was made while waiting at the crossing for the daily chemical train to pass. In front of the SkyNet Vitara was an open truck. Men were seated in the open back. Seeing white women in an open-top car, an old man reached under his robe and began to masturbate gently, unselfconsciously. The train cleared the crossing. The truck turned left, toward Nairobi. Gaby turned right, toward the Chaga.

''What are you doing?'' Ute Bonhorst said, alarmed.

Gaby pushed the 4X4 into top gear.

''I'm going to see the Chaga. I've been two months in Nairobi working with this thing, living it, eating it, drinking it, sleeping with it, dreaming of it, and now I'm this close I'm not going to let a few miles stop me.''

''We have no clearances.''

''That won't be a problem. Trust me.''

The road south was wide and swept over the low hills of the thorn scrub country. There was not another vehicle. Gaby pressed her right foot to the floor and pushed the Suzuki to its limits. Her long frustration went out of her like a colossal sigh, months deep, and the vacuum it left was filled with the sudden vertigo that comes when you find you have the courage and freedom to do what you most want in the world. She wished this road could go on forever; at the same time she could not wait for it to bring her to her destination.

They ran into the checkpoint five miles south of Ilbisil. Three pig-ugly South African Defense Force APCs were pulled across the road. A black soldier in a blue helmet with green, blue and black ANC flashes on his lapels waved them down.

"Good afternoon, ladies. Could you show me some identification, please?"

He passed the driving licenses and SkyNet accreditations to an officer sitting at a camp table on the verge, eating his lunch. While the officer studied the documents, the soldier walked slowly around the car, looking at trivial things in a vaguely intimidating way, as bored soldiers at checkpoints do.

"Can I ask where you're going?" the soldier asked, growing tired of the game of vague intimidation.

"Oh, south." Gaby waved her hand in the general direction of Tanzania. "We want to have a look at the Chaga."

"Sight-seeing?"

"You could say that."

The officer wiped his mouth with a bush-camouflage napkin and came over to the Vitara. He and the soldier spoke briefly in Xosa.

"Can I see your pass authorizations, please?"

Gaby opened her bag and with one hand folded a thousand-shilling note in the way Faraway had taught her was best for bribing policemen. She slipped it palm down to the South African officer. He glanced at it and passed it back to Gaby.

"That is not a pass authorization." The officer looked up into the sky, then at Gaby. "Excuse me, but could you tell me what time it is?"

"You've got a watch on your wrist," Ute said.

"The officer's may be broken," Gaby said, unfastening her Swatch. "Mine keeps good time, see?" She passed it to the officer.

"Very good time indeed." He slipped the Swatch into a button-down breast pocket. "I would give you a word of advice. For your own safety, we do not recommend that you go any further down this road than the mile-seventy marker post." The officer saluted and smiled beautifully. Gaby put the Vitara into gear, waved and drove off.

"You bribed that officer." Ute Bonhorst's innate Teutonic respect for authority was outraged.

"Certainly did," said Gaby McAslan, child of an ungovernable people.

Beyond the checkpoint the road dipped down into a river

valley and climbed abruptly. At the top of the valley side it swung to the right. The car took hill and bend easily.

And there it was.

Gaby pulled in under a great baobab. She got out of the car and went to the edge of the road where the land fell away to the Amboseli plains. She squatted on her heels and looked at the Chaga. The Zeiss-Leica optomolecules bonded to her corneas darkened.

In her summer on the west coast of the United States she had detoured to the Grand Canyon. The bus had left her at the door of one of the lodges. In the dark, low-beamed interior she had found a sign, quite small, easily overlooked, that read TO CANYON. Prepared for an anticlimax, she had followed it through a small door and found herself on the very brink. Twenty cubic miles of airspace gaped at her feet. She had stood, gripping the rail, for ten minutes, stunned motionless.

The Grand Canyon had confounded all her cynicisms and exceeded all her expectations.

The Chaga did the same. Nothing she had seen or heard or learned about it could prepare her for the physical reality. It was too real, too big. Too close.

She felt as if she were at the edge of an ocean. There was a nearer shore but no farther one. To Gaby under the baobab tree, it went on forever. The difference between the Chaga and the dry acacia scrubland in its path was more than the difference between savannah and rain forest. It was the difference between land and ocean, between sun and moon.

The satellite photographs had shown her the Chaga on the geographical scale, but they could not capture the sense of vastness and inevitability you felt when you stood before it, not looking down with the eyes of God, but out with the eyes of humans. From space it was a dark, insanely patterned roundel painted on to the map of Africa. From a baobab tree two miles from terminum, as the line of advance was formally known, it was as if a window had been opened to an alien planet. If you were to walk down this ridge and through the thornbush and cross that line, you would be transported instantly to some terrible place galaxies away.

When you stood in its path, you understood how completely alien it was to everything you knew. Its colors were alien. They mixed and matched with each other, but they strained the eye.

They did not seem as if they were meant to be lit by a tropical sun and set against the earth-colored landscape of this southern land.

Its shapes were alien. Its skyline could never be mistaken for the canopy of a terrestrial forest. It piled too high, too sharply, too steeply, as if a different gravity applied there. No growing thing was that flat, that wide, that bulbous, that angular, that convoluted. Its line offended the eye. There was something of the coral reef in it, and something of the tropical rain forest and something of the polar bergscape; there was something architectural and something industrial, planned and unconstrainedly chaotic. The Chaga was all these, none of these, more than these. Gaby recalled what Faraway had said on chicken-gizzard night on Tembo's veranda. You could not see it, because there was nothing in it you could recognize. All you could see of it was what reminded you of what you already knew.

Its smells were alien. In her three months Gaby had started to take some of the perfume of her new home into her skin. She smelled faintly of Africa, of earth and wood smoke and leather and shit and sweet-sour sweat. The Chaga was nothing like that. It smelled of half-remembered things; a thousand olfactory triggers that took you back to things that could have no possible connection with it, like days at the seaside, or your first lover's cum, or drinking your first bottle of red wine, or driving a car in January snow. Smell is the play button of memory. But it smelled also of a million more things that were beyond anyone's remembering: alien musks and ketones and esters and complex lipids; the pheromones of the Chaga's long, slow copulation with itself. It smelled of aromatics more exotic than any from the spice gardens of Zanzibar. It smelled of the fruit of Eden. It smelled of the sun-seared rocks of Mercury and the ice floes of Triton. It smelled of the body secretions of the lover of your darkest dreams. It smelled of the birth of stars, the death of galaxies and God's armpits. It smelled of the ocean of unknowing.

Like the sea, it had a tide. The coming in of that tide across the Amboseli plains was too slow to be seen from Gaby's perspective, but she observed the secondary effects of the advance. Terminum was not a sharp demarcation but a zone of transition. Only what was within and without were definite. On the line, Earth and Chaga were superimposed, like some metaphysical derivation of wave-function theory. At the very edge patches of olive, purple and crimson mottled the yellowed grass. As you moved inward the patches merged into a multicolored carpet interrupted by occasional clumps of grass, scrub or trees. Farther still and the first Chaga forms appeared: spires and fingers of pseudo-reef emerged from the mosaic of carpet growth and terrestrial vegetation. A mile beyond terminum only the trees remained, holding their umbrella-rib branches above the squawling mass of Chaga-life. Gaby watched tall acacias sway and fall, undermined by the voracious alien growth. A mile beyond the felling zone only the greatest and oldest baobabs resisted the Chaga. With distance they too were lost, enveloped in swatches of tendrils and stands of pseudo–fan corals. Three miles beyond terminum an abrupt transition took place. The reef growth exploded into smooth columns that rose sheer three hundred feet before unfolding into a dense canopy of burgundy feathers. Only the white palms of the hand trees rose higher, opening begging fingers to the sun.

Gaby could not see what lay beyond the great uplift of forest. It was a bright blur. Nothing more. The Chaga rose gently toward the foothills of Kilimanjaro, forty miles away. The summit of the mountain was hidden by a cap of cloud.

It was still there. It had waited for her. She had been faithful to it, and it had heard, and been faithful to her. Her star. Her Chaga. She felt tears swell and spill down her face. Two, no more. She wiped them away and reached for the visioncam in her bag. She framed Chaga and distant, cloud-hidden mountain in the screen.

''Gaby's videodiary, May fifth, 2008,'' she said. She swallowed down the tremor of emotion in her voice. ''Well, I'm here.''

buckyball jungle

17

The house was older than the country, and very beautiful. A missionary doctor had built it strong and sound as a ship; low, square, with big windows that let light flood into the airy colonial cream-and-mahogany rooms, and wooden shutters to keep out the heat and the dust. The rooms held hidden delights; little cubbyholes in which newspapers from a century ago lay forgotten; niches and locked cupboards that were rumored to contain morphine, or heroin. A deep porch enclosed the house on three sides so that there was sun on it, or shade, according to your taste, at every time of day. There were red brick steps up to it, and a red brick drive that was wide enough to take a span of oxen, which was how the doctor and his family had first come to the house.

After the doctor's children had grown up and gone to the England they had never known but had been taught to think of as home, and the doctor had died alone in his beautiful, strong house, a black bishop came to live there. He had learned his churchmanship in America and owned a washing machine, a color television and VCR, a collection of Johnny Mathis records and a wife who had been told she could best serve God by serving her husband. This she did for twenty-two years, until her husband, who was an outspoken critic of his country's one-party political system, died in a car crash. The police reported the cause as brake failure. The bishop's garage, which had serviced his car the week before, called the police liars. The police called the garage mechanics murderers. Because they were the police, their name stuck.

Now a woman called Miriam Sondhai lived in the house. She was a virologist with the Global AIDS Policy Unit, unraveling the molecular matrix of the HIV 4 virus. It had been the most important work in the world, until the Chaga came. Scientists had deserted to UNECTA in droves, biochemists and virologists foremost among them. Miriam Sondhai had not been seduced. She was a woman of commitment. Her skin was the color of sun-bleached earth, her face was the fine-featured, heart-shape of the Nilo-Hamitic peoples, who are among the most noble and beautiful on Earth. She had the height and grace of a Somali or a Masai, but she was a woman of no tribe, which to an African is to be stateless, homeless, rootless. She had walked with her mother out of the chaos of Somalia, leaving behind a father and two brothers in shallow stone graves.

Now she lived in the house and loved it as it deserved to be loved. But it was too big and expensive for her on her own so now Gaby McAslan was parking her brand-new this-year's-model Nissan all-terrain vehicle on the brick drive that was wide enough to take a team of oxen and putting her clothes in the mahogany closets and her beer in the refrigerator and her precious little things in the missionary doctor's nooks and corners and the eight-foot tapestry of the zodiac her sister had sent her on the living room wall.

After four months in a single room, it was release. Gaby spread her life with wide abandon through the big, light-filled rooms. She turned the morning side of the veranda into an outdoor office. On hot nights she opened the French windows of her bedroom and pushed her bed with its soft ivory linen into the open air. She ran around the place in her underwear or less, she played her music too loud too late, left newspapers and footwear scattered where she had finished with them, blocked her landlady's car with her Nissan ATV, ate voraciously and without regard for whose cupboard the food came from, entertained Oksana and friends with alcohol that was not hers and generally fell in love with the house too.

She did not know how close Miriam Sondhai came to throwing her out in those early weeks. Gaby had never considered that she might be difficult to live with. Self-unknowing being the besetting sin of motherless girls, Gaby blamed it on the lofty aloofness of her host. There was a deliberateness in the woman's intense beauty, as if she had cultivated it to deflect attention from her heart. Even when she went out running in her simple red one-piece in the cool of the evening on the tree-shaded avenues, she displayed that focusedness of purpose. Everything was directed into the beautiful act of putting one foot in front of another. Nothing else mattered. She was as intense and single-minded in her work.

"If we had one tenth of the resources the West is pouring into UNECTA, we could end the HIV 4 epidemic," she insisted. Gaby argued that press coverage of the Chaga focused world attention on the wider issues of Africa. ''HIV 4 is not a wider issue of Africa. It is a central issue of Africa. Twelve million cases in East Africa; twelve million deaths. Two complete holocausts in a single generation. There are villages up north around Mt. Elgon and over into Karamoja in Uganda where there is no one alive over the age of twelve. Entire villages of orphans.'' She would laugh then. She laughed like a Frenchwoman, knowingly and bitterly. ''It is an African problem in that the West does not want to get involved because it sees Slim as a Malthusian check on African population growth. We exceed the carrying capacity of the land, so the angel of death must pass over us and divide the taken from those who are cursed to stay. It is an African problem in that it is African scientists trying to save African people from an African pandemic. It is not a gay plague here, Gaby. It is an everyone plague.''

When she spoke thus in her beautiful, deep whisper of a voice, no one could argue with her. It would be like trying to argue with a Madonna in an icon. When she was beautiful and righteous and untouchable like this, Gaby McAslan would tell herself that all Miriam Sondhai needed was a good hard cock up her. It was because of the frictions, rather than despite them, that the two women became friends. So when the van delivered the dress, Gaby asked Miriam to help her try it on, knowing she would think it decadent.

The dress arrived in a cardboard case with rope handles and folded in yards of tissue paper. Gaby held the sensuous green silk up against her and Miriam Sondhai had softened in admiration. It had come complete with shoes, underwear, hosiery and a clutch bag: Kenya's *watekni* fashion pirates prided themselves that not only were their products faster and cheaper than originals from the Chanel programs they stole, they came with the full range of accessories. The U.S. ambassador's Independence Day Hootenanny demanded nothing less than a dress that would turn every head that looked Gaby McAslan's way. If it did not make people ask, Who is that red-haired woman in that dark green dress? it would be a waste of nearly a month's salary. Given that she was not on the guest list. Given that a junior on-liner had no right to expect to be on the guest list.

Fuck protocol. Networking mattered. Haran would get her there, by the rocket's red glare. He had promised when she asked him, her first returnable favor. What she would say to T. P. Costello, that was something he could not help her with.

Miriam helped her up with the zip and adjusted the waist so that the claw-hammer skirt swung back and the short front piece fell between her thighs to emphasize the long lean lines of her legs. Longness and leanness was what heredity had dealt the McAslan females. They made the most of it. She caught her hair in a bow and flicked it over her left shoulder.

"You look wonderful, for a *m'zungu,*" Miriam said. "I hope you do not come off those heels."

A car hooted in the drive. Gaby frowned at her reflection in the mirror, grabbed her clutch bag and dashed for the taxi. All the way to the ambassador's residence she kept asking herself, What if, what if, what if they do not let you in? Then you get back into this taxi and go to the Elephant Bar and get drunk with Oksana. It will not be the end of the world. Oh no, it bloody won't. So why are you doing it? It will earn you nothing but a world of trouble. Because there are people there it might be good to be remembered by someday. Because where there are people like that, and free alcohol, there are stories, and where there are stories there is news, and where there is news there is Gaby McAslan zooming in on extreme close-up. Networking. You probably won't even have time for a drink, let alone talking to Dr. Shepard from Tsavo West with the Paul Newman blue eyes.

Self-unknowing, Gaby McAslan.

The cars were lined up for a quarter of a mile down the road. Monkey jackets from corporate hospitality had the door-open meet 'n' greet to perfection. Gorgeous frocks and rented tuxes went up the stairs to the double doors.

Do not even think of the theme from *Gone With the Wind,* Gaby McAslan ordered herself. Fiddle-dee-dee to that. The earth is even red, like the strong red earth of Tara.

The meeter 'n' greeter slipped her a thick, gilt-edged invitation card.

"From Haran," he said. Gaby passed him a discreet hundred. He touched gloved forefinger to brow. At the door a frock-coated security person scanned the bar code on the card and checked the on-screen guest list.

"Gabriel Ruth Langdon McAslan," he read. Haran had even got the hated family name right.

"Gaby," she corrected, and swept in. She passed through

the cool, spacious residence with its slow-turning ceiling paddles and went through the French windows onto the patio. Fairy lights and stars-and-stripes bunting were strung between the trees. Garden candles taller than Gaby had been spiked into the grass and attracted knots of people. The first of the evening's bands was opening its set on the staging in front of the shrub azaleas, a handy trio of electric guitar, accordion and sax. Gaby felt sorry for them. It was too early, the guests too sober for their brand of vivacious shamba dance. By tradition, the beer was kept in tin baths of ice; all-American, diplomatic-bagged in from Milwaukee. Gaby lifted a bottle. A waiter appeared and uncapped it with an opener.

"Ms. McAslan!"

"Dr. Dan!"

He shook her hand enthusiastically. Somewhere he had found a tall mint julep.

"How good it is to see you, Ms. McAslan. You have been much in my thoughts since our interesting night together."

"And how was the wedding?"

"Alas, my forebodings were proved right. He was a worthless man. He abandoned my daughter after six nights for a woman wrestler. A Kikuyu woman wrestler, indeed. I fear my chances of getting my cattle back are remote; the rude boy. He has undoubtedly sold them. My daughter is pretending to be distraught, but I think she is secretly relieved. She is one who likes the idea of marriage more than the state of being married. Now she has the chance to do it all again.

"But you, my friend. You have been making a name for yourself. I very much enjoyed the 'And Finally' stories. I could tell you one myself that I have from the very best authority, about a magical condom tattoo that protects the recipient from all known sexually transmitted diseases."

"I've moved away from my source, Dr. Dan, and I'm working on more mainstream, investigative material now."

"Ah yes. The Werther interview. Most illuminating. It is a pity that his disappearance was not considered as newsworthy as his appearance."

"What do you mean? I know he's hiding from the media."

"Is that what they have told you? Peter Werther did not disappear. He was disappeared."

Guests pushed past to the bar, inspired by Dr. Dan's mint

julep. Gaby recognized *Der Spiegel*'s on-line editor. She nodded curtly to him.

"Disappeared by whom?"

Dr. Dan smiled, shrugged.

"UNECTA?"

"Remember where you are, Ms. McAslan."

"The Americans? The ambassador knows about this?" The ambassador was talking by the balustrade with an animated staffer from the French embassy. Mr. Ambassador was a small, impeccably dressed black man; from Georgia, Gaby recalled, which incongruously reinforced the *Gone With the Wind* imagery. His children were running around in their best clothes looking for excuses to set the fireworks off early. His wife stood some paces from him with an expression of diplomatic boredom. She was dressed African style and tended more to the Maya Angelou than the Diana Ross.

"UNECTA, Americans, what's the difference?" Dr. Dan asked.

"What happened?" Gaby wished there had been room in her ludicrous little clutch bag for a PDU, or even an old-fashioned dictation machine.

"They came at night. Helicopters, with night-imaging cameras. They were following in military spy-satellite thermal photographs. Your video footage helped them as well, but you must not blame yourself, please. It is not your fault, you did not finger him—I believe that is the expression? He made himself a target by coming out of the Chaga, for anything that comes out of the Chaga is theirs."

"UN troops?"

"A joint U.S.–Canadian force."

"Jesus. And Peter?"

"I do not know. I am trying to find out. I shall ask for an Inquiry in the National Assembly. Despite the United Nations, this is still our country."

"How do you know this?"

"I have always believed that the wise politician cultivates friendships in unlikely places. I count you my friend, Ms. McAslan; likewise, I count many in the Traveler community. They could not go to the press directly, for they had been threatened that to do so would result in their residency permits being revoked and them being deported from Kenya."

Gaby saw the upward glance of his eyes an instant before the hand fell heavily on her shoulder. She squawked, imagining U.S.–Canadian air cavalry abseiling down from helicopters to take out the Irish woman with the big mouth. Her bottle smashed on the patio. The ambassador looked across, irritated, but the serving staff were already moving to sweep up the debris.

It was worse than U.S.–Canadian air cavalry.

It was T. P. Costello.

"Sorry to butt in on your conversation, Dr. Oloitip, but I need to have a small creative conference with my junior on-line reporter. What do I need?"

"A small creative conference," Gaby said. "With your junior on-liner."

"That's correct."

"We will talk!" Dr. Dan called as T.P. marched her toward the rhododendrons.

"T.P., T.P., listen, I've got something very very hot; listen, T.P., they've vanished Peter Werther."

"Frankly, my dear," T. P. Costello said, "I don't give a damn."

The design of the gardens provided many private places for those whose party quirks precluded spectators. A fat man in a too-small tuxedo came crashing from the shrubs, fumbling at his pants. A woman Gaby knew as a senior editor at ITN fled in the opposite direction, unaware that the back of her skirt had got hitched into the waistband of her panties. T.P. dragged her into the alcove they had so hastily vacated.

"What the hell are you doing here? I cannot turn my back for five minutes but you're hatching some fuckwit scheme or another. What is it with you, woman? What gives?" T.P. shook her hard by the shoulders. Gaby slapped his hands away from her.

"You do not touch me like that, Thomas Pronsias Costello."

He looked at the ground, shamed.

"What is the problem here, T.P.? I'm only doing what any journalist with an ounce of *nous* would have done, making contacts, getting stories, T.P. I've only gate-crashed a party—Jesus, in ancient Baghdad they had entire guilds of licensed gate-crashers—it's not like I raped the ambassador's brown-eyed boy."

T. P. Costello did an unthinkable thing. He sat down on the grass with his head in his hands. All the confidence and competence and ability drained from him like water into a dry riverbed. He seemed on the verge of tears. He patted the ground for Gaby to sit beside him and gallantly swept a handkerchief from his breast pocket and spread it out to protect her lovely dress.

"Ah God," he sighed. His voice shuddered. "Why did you have to come here?"

"I told you, T.P."

"This country. This Chaga-thing."

A new act had taken the stage. A minimal spattering of applause greeted it. Gaby had listened to enough Voice of Kenya radio to recognize one of the most promising new praise singers.

"You're so like her. Not to look at; she was dark; dark hair, dark skin, but like you, she couldn't be said no to. She had to inquire, she had to push it just that little bit too far. She was ambitious, like you. She was writing a book. Oh, it was going to be the first and last word on the Chaga and the people who study it. She never finished it. I've got the material at home. Reams and reams of notes, photocopies, faxes, typescripts. She told me her name once but I've forgotten it. Everyone called her Moon. Langrishe gave her the name. Dr. Peter Langrishe. He was an exobiologist, down at Ol Tukai, before UNECTA went mobile. He was as mad as she was. You know where they met? A place like this. The Irish Embassy St. Paddy's Day ceilidhe. They were insane, both of them. Jesus, Gaby, I met her off the night flight, just like you, I went through the same bloody catechism, just like you. Do you know where she lived?"

"I can guess. The Episcopalian guesthouse. T.P., I'm not her."

"I know. But you do the things she did. You go to the places she went. You say the things she said."

Gaby McAslan said nothing but sat with her knees pulled up to her chin and her arms folded around them.

"You loved her, didn't you?"

"That was the thing. No one loved the right way round. I loved her, but she loved him and he loved the obscene great thing down there. If only everyone had been able to turn around and see the thing that loved them." He grimaced. "She couldn't hold him. I could have told her that—should have told her that. She was down on the coast putting a draft together and word came that he'd gone down in a microlyte crash over Amboseli. But she wouldn't believe he was dead—she had me convinced she would have known if he were: mystical union or crap like that. So she decided to go after him. Last I saw of her was the microlyte I gave her taking off from the Namanga road. I should have taken an ax to the thing. But you never saw what she was like without him. You never saw her depressions, the violent rages, the hours she would spend in her hotel room, staring at the lizards on the wall. I gave her a diary the day she left to search for Langrishe. I made her promise she would get it back to me, somehow. Odds are it's rotting with her in that green hell; but it could have made it back to shore."

"I could find out. At least you would know for certain, T.P."

"And Gaby McAslan would have the story of the decade. *Gone With the Wind* bangs *Out of Africa.* These are real lives, Gaby; real hurts, real histories, real wounds. Tread carefully around them." He shook his head. "You're a good woman, McAslan. It's just you're so like her. What are you like?"

"Moon," Gaby McAslan said.

Sudden fear darkened T.P.'s face.

"Don't say that word. It's too strong a word for a night like this. Do you believe in magic?"

"I know a Siberian pilot who does."

"Speak a name and it will cross heaven and hell to come to you."

"Or silence you."

"Even from the dark heart of the Chaga."

The music ended and there was more applause. Next on stage would be the St. Stephen's Church choir under Tembo's directorship. It was a great honor to be asked to perform at the ambassador's hootenanny. All week Tembo had gone about the office glowing with a modest, Christian pride. Gaby thought his achievement warranted blatant boasting, but wished him hugs, blessings and break-a-legs anyway. She could not understand his religion, but admired the quiet strength of his faith. She left T.P. to go and hear the set.

All the women wore long skirts, white blouses and head scarfs. The men wore blue *kitenges* over black pants and played the instruments: two drums, *kiamba,* sticks and what looked like a piston ring from a truck that you hit with a nine-inch nail. Their four-part harmony was electrifying.

"Up here singing songs of Jesus while down here folk gossip, get drunk and sneak into the shrubbery for a quickie or a snort.''

Gaby had seen him approach but reckoned cool was the way to play it. In his rented suit he looked like Jimmy Stewart in *The Philadelphia Story,* impatient to rip off the stupid, choking bow tie; or Sean Connery—the only James Bond—with his wet suit under his dinner jacket rather than the tux under the black rubber.

''You remember?''

''I remember the T-shirt. And the hair.''

''They wouldn't let me in in a T-shirt with a masturbating nun on the front. The hair tends to go with me. So, how are your buckyballs bouncing?''

''All over the global newsnets, thanks to you.''

''You did say I could. As you can see, I made it here after all.''

''So you did. I like your dress. Suits your hair. And your eyes. Can I get you something to drink?''

They moved between clusters of people on nodding terms with Shepard to one of the gingham-covered tables. The waiter straightened immaculately ironed cuffs.

''I'll have one of those mint thingies, please.''

While he mixed it Gaby pretended to be on nodding terms with people she only knew from photographs.

''So, buckyballs.''

Shepard had a beer. Gaby thought it was very him.

''What do you want me to tell you about them?''

Anything.

''Whatever's new.''

He shook his head, clicked his tongue in disappointment.

''And you were doing so well.''

''No, I'm genuinely interested.'' She tried to adopt a posture she hoped said, *in fullerenes, not you.*

''Well, seeing as you did the best piece from that press conference, I'll let you in to a little secret. We're reinventing organic chemistry from the bottom up. We can analyze and map the basic molecular structure of the Chaga, but to describe anything as complex as its symbiotic biology, or even the associations of fullerene machines that are analogous to terrestrial cells, we've got a long hike to go on that. Damn things evolve so quickly they may always stay two jumps ahead of any containment tactics.''

''That's what you're researching? Ways to kill it?''

They passed close to Jake Aarons holding court in the middle of a group of television journalists. He stood head and shoulders above his peers. He saw Gaby, frowned; saw Gaby with Shepard, looked puzzled; worked something out for himself and grinned impishly.

"I suppose that's what they ultimately want to do. If it had come down back at home, we would have called out the National Guard, cordoned the thing off, evacuated everyone and as like as not quietly nuked it. Not that that would have done any good, in my opinion. *Pax Americana* or not, they can't very well go around nuking other people's territory, but the military can't think in any other terms than enemies, invasion, containment and counterattack. They've been trying napalm down in Ecuador, but that's always been Washington's backyard. Biggest drop since Vietnam. No effect whatsoever: the stuff's as near as possible fireproof. You burn maybe a couple of dozen acres, then the rest starts to super-secrete fire retardants, foams and CO_2. It's back at full climax within a week. This thing *thinks.*"

"I take it you don't subscribe to the military philosophy." The ambassador made his mint juleps mighty strong, or was it the effect of Ozark Mountain bourbon on a sea-level girl at White Highland altitudes?

"Doesn't matter a damn whether I agree with it or not. It won't work."

"Is this on the record?"

"You're recording?"

Trays of chicken wings passed. Shepard scooped a fistful. Gaby ate greedily from her carmine-nailed fingers and wiped them greasily on her glossy, sheer thighs. These mint juleps were a mighty fine drink at this altitude indeed. You saw the glass with those bits of greenery stuck in it like Arab tea and you thought it could not possibly be serious, but then you took your first sip and the mint and the sugar and whiskey fused and it was the best damn drink in the universe to sip when you were gate-crashing the social event of the season in a pirate dress you could barely afford with a boss who thought you were the Sad Lost Girl of his golden years and the only real white man in the country eating chicken wings and talking about buckyballs and napalm while the altitude smeared Vaseline over the lens of your life making everything soft focus and distant so that for a moment you *were* Scarlett O'Hara on the lawns of Tara and what is he saying? why is he looking at me? does he seriously expect an answer? and *whoosh!* the first salvo of fireworks saved her.

There were gasps. There were oohs. There were screams as the rockets detonated high above the ambassador's residence and dropped silver rain. The ambassador's children danced and shouted. A second barrage rose, shedding sparkling stars, and a third. A big *wump* from behind the shrubs provoked more screams as the mortar shot its load half a mile into the Nairobi night. It blew in a deafening multiple orgasm of novas. Car alarms chorused in answer, shocked awake by the pressure wave. A cascade of red, white and blue fell down the sky.

"That was a big one!" Gaby shouted over the din of the lesser lights. "I love fireworks, but I hate the noise. When I was a kid, my dad took me to the Christmas fireworks at Belfast City Hall. They shouldn't have set them off in such a confined space; it was like Sarajevo; rockets shooting all over the place. But beautiful. That's what I love about them, wonderful and frightening at the same time."

"Do you ever think they're like a life?" Shepard shouted. Rockets were zipping up on all sides, setting fire to the sky. "The long, slow rise, the sudden brilliant, brief explosion into glory, the long fall into darkness."

"If you're going to talk depressing, I'm having another mint thingie."

"Are you sure?"

"Probably not. So, what do they call you?"

"They call me Shepard."

"Nothing else?"

"Doctor."

"They call me Gaby." Any more of this mint thingie and she would be flying up like one of the ambassador's rockets and her head would explode in a star-burst of flying red hair. "You know, you could do me an enormous favor."

"A journalist's favor? Can I afford that?"

"I just need you to check something for me. There's a diary, belonged to a woman had an affair with a UNECTA man; Dr. Peter Langrishe."

"I remember him, and her."

"It might still be in Ol Tukai, and I really need it to prove something to someone. Could you . . ."

The big mortar tube boomed and screamed another one skyward. The blast rattled the windows and the beer bottles in their bath of ice. The just-silenced car alarms started up again. Gaby frowned, bent her head to one side, imagining she could hear another noise as the sky rained stars. A sound like a hundred cellular telephones ringing at once.

It was not the effect of altitude and mint thingie. It was a hundred cellular telephones ringing at once. Creeping paralysis seized the party as partygoers pulled phones out of purses, night bags, inside pockets, robes, sporrans. Shepard put his finger in his ear and nodded to the chirping voice of the phone. Guests were already streaming up the patio steps toward cloakroom and cars.

"You'll excuse me if I abandon you in midjulep," he said. "There's a general UNECTA alert in operation. Seems destiny is calling."

"What?" Gaby shouted at his receding back. "What's happening?"

He turned on the bottom step.

"I shouldn't be telling you this."

"Tell me!" Gaby screamed among the beer bottles and the julep glasses and the wing bones of chickens. The fireworks fountained upward, dying unheeded.

"Hyperion's back."

18

Gaby reckoned this was the first time the conference room had been full since SkyNet had set up its East Africa station on Tom M'boya Street. Though it was three-thirty in the morning, every section was represented. The coffeemaker was on overtime too. It smelled threateningly of overheated beans.

Under the big screen, T. P. Costello finished his third cup and pushed it from him across the table, nauseated. He was in a poor state for a live video conference. At some point his solo trip through love and regret had cast him up on the ambassador's bathroom floor, unconscious, a half-drunk mint julep gripped in his fist. His snoring had alerted the domestics. Gaby and Jake Aarons had barely managed to get him to a taxi when the word came through from the head office that UNECTA and NASA would be issuing a joint statement at one-thirty Greenwich Mean Time.

In the front row, Gaby had not had time to change her Chanel-pirate dress. It stank of stale smoke, spilled bourbon, spicy chicken marinade and woman-sweat, but the way the fabric moved around her made her feel a million feet tall. One should be dressed for epochal events.

The SkyNet symbol on the wallscreen dissolved into the NASA logo.

Still have not got rid of that terrible old 1970s typography, Gaby thought. The colophon in turn was replaced by the face of Irwin Lowell, Director of the Huntsville Orbital Astronomy Center. Director Irwin Lowell had sideburns and a bootlace tie. He looked like the photographs of that old science-fiction writer her dad had liked: Isaac Asimov. Gaby had never been able to read more than ten pages of his stuff.

''On behalf of the National Aeronautics and Space Administration, you are most welcome to the Orbital Astronomy Center.'' He talked like he looked, like forty miles of bad road. ''Our findings are largely of a technical nature, so we have extrapolated the following graphic sequence from them which will clarify the nature of the object we have discovered in the Hyperion Gap.''

The sequence opened with a shot of Saturn and its rings. Stock footage, Gaby thought. Bottom of the video vault. Then she noticed that this was not the standard image. A dark line bisected the planet from top to bottom. As Gaby watched, the dark line thickened, but in the absence of any frame of reference she could not judge whether it was millimeters wide or painted down the zero meridian of the second-largest planet in the solar system. Then the point of view moved and the thick black line opened into a huge ellipse and then into a solid disc, mottled with a thousand chaotic colors, rotating around its central axis.

''To give some indication of scale, we've included a schematic of the Unity space station for comparison,'' Irwin Lowell said in his down-home accent.

Gaby peered but could not see it. The resolution clicked up, and clicked up again, and again, and again until the edge of the disc seemed like a straight line against the stars. There it was, silhouetted against a patch of Pantone 141, the web of orbital construction beams and environment modules and solar arrays and manufacturing cores, seeming no bigger on the three-foot screen than a spinning spider.

Reality caught in Gaby McAslan's throat. Everyone knew

the proud boasts. A city in space, a complete community a mile and a half across. Man's first stepping-stone to the stars.

"The object is slightly over twelve hundred miles in diameter," Irwin Lowell said. "Our measurements indicate that it is twenty miles thick at the rim, decreasing to five at the center. This we think is to offset the object's tendency to collapse inward under its own gravitational attraction into a more stable form. The centripetal force generated by the spin, which is one revolution every three-point-five-three hours, also helps maintain gravitational stability. On a related point, the moon Hyperion formerly had a highly erratic axis of rotation; that has been corrected. From its high stability alone, we must conclude that this object could not possibly have formed naturally."

Earth replaced Saturn on the screen. The Indian subcontinent from Cape Comorin to Bombay was obliterated by a featureless gray circle. The lower limb of Sri Lanka protruded from the southeastern quadrant, to the north the great provinces of the old Mogul Empire struggled free. In the shadow of the Hyperion Object lay five hundred million lives, Gaby thought. The gray disc did not look like the presence of a vast, incomprehensible thing, but the absence. Five hundred million people; their mighty, ancient cities; their gods and avatars that were among the first to rule the dreams of humans: taken into the grayness and annihilated. It was like the satellite photographs with which she had adorned her Chaga-shrine; the neat, stamped-out circles of color stuck across the map of the tropics, but more frightening in its blank grayness than the gaudiness of the alien mosaics.

Irwin Lowell reappeared, superimposed over the map. Gaby could tell from his face that he was about to impart an unpalatable truth. Understanding this, she knew what he would say. The Earth map was not a comparison. It was a promise. The thing was moving.

"Our data confirm that at some time in the process of reconfiguring the former moon, a momentum was imparted to the Hyperion Object sufficient to cause it to break free from the Saturnian satellite system." He fingered the metal clasp of his bootlace tie. Scared men who cannot let it be seen that they are scared communicate their fear by such small self-touchings. "Our projections indicate that the object is on a course into the inner solar system." An animated orrery replaced maimed India. The planets slid on their ordained wires. A red rogue line curved inward from the ringed bead of Saturn. It looped around the gravitational field of Jupiter, through the asteroids, past the orbit of red Mars. The blue opal of Earth opened up into its component pair. The red line slipped through the cosmic needle's eye between Earth and moon and was wound into a geostationary skein around the equator. "The calculations are fairly exact. The Hyperion Object will arrive in Earth orbit in slightly over five years. Five years and ninety-eight days, to be exact."

There was murmuring in the conference room on Tom M'boya Street. What brutal things we have become, Gaby thought. So inured to miracles and wonder that we greet several hundred billion tons of reconstituted moon headed down our throats with a ho and a hum. She fiddled with the almanac function of her PDU. Worlds collide on September 27 2013. I wonder if that will be before or after lunch? But they would not do that. They would not sow their Chaga-seed across the planet and let it grow and flower only to smash it all into nothingness with their hammer from the sky. Seize that, Gaby McAslan. Hold it to you. It is the only hope you have. Not just your present, but now your future is in the hands of these Chaga-makers.

A cigarette seemed like a very fine idea. She excused herself and left the room. Irwin Lowell was saying something about mass being missing from the Hyperion Object, which seemed to have been converted directly to momentum by some unknown process. She lit up by the window at the end of the corridor, opened it and leaned out. Day had begun while she had watched the drawings of the things in the sky. Five floors down, Tom M'boya Street was busy with the early-morning traffic. She saw a man in Arab dress pushing a little wooden cart along the edge of the street. It looked like a dog kennel on castors. Gaby knew from experience that if you looked inside it, you would see a crouching woman, veiled and robed, so that only her eyes showed, but they glittered brightly in the darkness. Directly beneath the window, a policeman was trying to break up a fight at a bus stop. A crowd of matatu touts was gathering and taking sides. Gaby exhaled cigarette smoke into the street. Shouting voices rose around her. People died in these street fights. She accepted that, as she accepted the woman with unknown deformities who lived in a box on wheels, or the legless beggar who pushed himself past Miriam Sondhai's house every day on a trolley with a block of wood in each hand. Kenya had brutalized her. Cruelties and sufferings that would have been intolerable in London confronted her at every step, and she ignored them. In this, Tembo and Faraway had succeeded. Gaby McAslan had become African. What they had seen in her as the capacity to learn this was her essential brutality. Looking from the fifth-floor window, she felt more sister to the people on the street than those she had left in the conference room. They were a tough people down there. They were a resourceful people. They had successfully made the jump from Iron Age to Information Age in two generations: they were used to their world ending every couple of decades or so. The Chaga might be eating Africa, but it could not eat Africanness. They begged their alms and cooked their food and fought their fights and caught their matatus because they knew that in the end their Africanness would eat the Chaga.

She finished her cigarette, flicked the butt into the street and went back to the conference.

Irwin Lowell was fingering his bootlace tie again.

"We have pictures just come through image processing from the Chandrasekahr telescope of the moments immediately preceding the advent of the Hyperion Object."

Animation would have rendered it more slickly and realistically, but the grainy CCD images captured the intellectual chill of deep space. Gaby shivered in her gorgeous dress. Cold translucent shapes tumbled slowly against the soft blur of overloaded stars, locking together into fans and arcs of an immense disc. Gaby realized with a shock that the fragile, chiming fans must be tens of miles long. This was engineering on a scale so large the imagination had to step back and back until the perspective made it human-sized.

They were talking now about retasking the *Gaia* spaceprobe, which had been sent out on the heels of *Tolkien* to plumb the mysteries of the Hyperion Gap. NASA was trying to rig together a high-acceleration propulsion unit that would rendezvous with the probe, dock and put it into orbit around the great disc. They had pretty little animated schematics to show how they would do it. All lines and dots and arrows.

I was right to tie my life to the lights in the sky, Gaby McAslan thought. The Ford drivers, the Markys and Hannahs with their beautiful homes and beautiful children could no longer rely on the external universe being too big and remote to touch their internal lives. The universe was coming to them as much as to the man she had seen wheeling his wife in her wooden cart up Tom M'boya Street, or the matatu touts fighting at the bus stop, or the laid-back policeman or the food sellers setting up their sidewalk stalls. But the street people would be ready. They knew intimately that the universe is a place at best indifferent, at worst hostile. They would not flee screaming *the sky is falling! the sky is falling!* when they learned what had happened out at Saturn, what would be happening over their heads in five years. Five years is a long time under the eye of God. Much can happen. They would be ready, and if the sky did fall, they trusted that their arms were strong enough to hold it up.

19

The pink stretch limo had been behind her since she turned out of Miriam Sondhai's drive. It made no attempt to hide; it could not have easily, even among Nairobi's UN and diplomatic plates. Many UNECTA staff lived in Miriam's district, stretch limos in all colors were commonplace, but never so *pink* as this. Gold-tint mirror glass, and a flying-V aerial on the back. Very cyberpunk. And following her. It ran *keepie-lefties* and jumped lights to keep itself in her rearview.

They were still digging up the junction of University Way and Moi Avenue. Bilingual signs thanked drivers for their patience in cooperating with the Ministry of Transport's five-year road-improvement scheme. A five-year plan when in three years there would not be any roads to improve. Gaby suspected the digging paralyzing Nairobi was a cabalistic deal between the city fathers, contractors and a syndicate of newspaper sellers, snack vendors and windscreen washers.

The man with the stop/go sign was letting them through two at a time this morning.

''Bastard!'' Gaby shouted as he flicked his sign to red before she could jump him.

Suddenly there were three men in her ATV. Two in the back, one in the front. They had Afro hairstyles, platform soles, ankle-length leather coats and big smiles.

''Haran begs the pleasure of your company,'' said the one in the front. ''Please follow the limousine.'' He nodded to the road mender, who turned his sign immediately to green for go. The pink Cadillac pulled out and passed. Gaby tucked in behind it. It led her to the Cascade Club. The place had not long closed. It looked weary with all the houselights on, like an aged, aged prostitute who has to go out to the shops and shrinks from the naked sunshine. The air was close and humid, breathed through many sets of lungs. Down in the pit, women were diligently scrubbing mold off the white tiles. It smelled, Gaby thought, *exactly* like the Pirates of the Caribbean in Euro Disney.

The posseboys did not take Gaby up to the glass-floored office but by a circuitous route past staff toilets and storerooms filled with shrink-wrapped pallets of alcohol to a wide covered balcony around a lush courtyard garden of palms, bananas and creeping figs. Higher palm fronds overhung the balcony rail. Waiters in white jackets carrying silver trays attended a number of immaculately laid tables. The patrons were all African or Indian. Haran's table was apart from the others and overlooked an underpowered fountain. A silver coffee set, two cups and a PDU were arranged on the linen cloth. A lift of his finger dismissed the posseboys. Haran rose from his cane chair, lifted the head of his fly whisk and bowed slightly to Gaby.

"Ms. McAslan. A delight to see you again. Please, sit, have some coffee. Esther."

A young black woman moved from where she had been standing behind Haran and pulled a chair out for Gaby. She was dressed in a black leather bikini over a sheer mesh body stocking. Black knuckle-studded biker's gloves matched black biker's boots. Gaby recognized the uniform of Mombi's possegirls. She wore a lot of heavy jewelry, but unusually, no neck chains, only a mismatched choker that seemed to have been woven from strands of iridescent fiber. In place of a pendant, a small printed circuit board with a single red LED eye nuzzled in the hollow of the young woman's throat.

"Smartwire," Haran said. "One of the first benefits of Chaga research, so we are told. Coiled long-chain molecules that contract dramatically under an electrical charge. Not quite dramatic enough to guillotine a head right off, but enough to sever the carotid arteries if I press the button. But Mombi has her own necklace on one of my boys, so everyone's arteries will be staying unsevered, I think." The possegirl poured coffee. Milk was offered, sugar, sweeteners. Gaby waved them away. The coffee was exquisite. She expected no less of Haran.

"So, Gaby, not only are we menaced by the Chaga, we now have this Hyperion Event as well. I understand you have a nickname for it already, what is it, the BDO?"

"The Big Dumb Object," Gaby said, noting the switch to her forename. Haran was like the Chaga, he moved slowly, but inexorably. He reached his points, disclosed his information, changed the landscape of his relationships at his own speed, in his own time and none other. "From the same anonymous NASA wit who named the Iapetus probe after the author of *The Lord of the Rings*. This one is from *The Encyclopedia of Science Fiction*."

"My education must be incomplete," Haran said. "I have read neither of these volumes. Perhaps I should. The times are changing, Gaby, and I must change with them, or history will run me down like a chicken on the highway. There is a time for war, and a time to make peace. There are too many new faces on the street and they have grown up hungry and vicious. Their means are dishonorable: virtual sex parlors, VR-dildonics, videodrugs; their methods distasteful: blackmail, extortion, addiction, kidnapping. They place no value on human life. You can understand, my friend, that they must be shown who is the power in this town if we are to avoid general anarchy. In such times, your oldest enemy is to be more trusted than those who catch at your coattail and call you 'friend, friend.' "

"You're putting out diplomatic feelers?"

"We have exchanged embassies."

"Or hostages."

Haran glanced at the PDU on the tablecloth. UPI NetServe menus scrolled down the screen. The hypertext expansion point blinked on the liquid rollscreen.

"My net is coming apart in my fingers, Gaby. Every day I lose connections. People; my people, who trust me to protect them. Against the police, against my rivals and enemies, like Mombi was once, who would snap them up like a leopard a dog; yes, I can protect them from these, but against the Chaga, against those who serve it . . ." Haran took a flexible minidisc from the breast pocket of his jacket. "Leave us, Esther. This is a private matter between myself and my client."

She had the adolescent scowl nicely. Gaby envied her her firm ass.

The video sequence was appalling. There was no syntax, no narrative. The camera veered from side to side, faces were out of focus, or upside down, or loomed to fill the screen. The soundtrack was shouting and hard breathing and the constant shatter of a hovering helicopter. You saw swooping panoramics of a dusty Kenyan town, you saw jolting images of military vehicles, as if taken by a running man. You saw white soldiers shot from expressionistic angles, you saw sunburned faces beneath blue helmets swim into extreme close-up. You saw lines of people, and armored personnel carriers. You saw town and soldiers and sky whirling madly around, then you heard raised, shouting whiteman voices, heavily accented, and saw something that looked like a zipper, and the dark interior of a sports bag, and heard running footsteps, and heavy breathing, and the sequence ended.

"They took his deck, all his equipment, they took the camcorder on which he shot this secretly, they even took the expensive shoes off his feet," Haran said evenly. "But they did not take the disc, and now I have it, and will make them pay for what they did to one of my posse."

"Who are they?"

"Azeris. Ex-Soviets. It does not matter. They all do it. Especially the ones from the countries that are as poor, or poorer, than this. What they do not keep for themselves, they sell in the Nairobi markets. If you go down to Jogoo Road or Kariokor, you will find it all laid out on the stalls. If they do not have what you want, you can place an order and the soldiers will loot it for you from the next village they evacuate in the name of the United Nations. But you must pay more for this premium service."

"Haran, why are you showing me this?"

The Sheriff laid his fly whisk on the table.

"I am asking you as a favor to expose the ones who did this to my boy. I do not care about the others, but no one, not even the UN, touches one of Haran's. I will not have it said that I cannot protect my own."

"You want me to do a report on institutional corruption in the United Nations forces."

"Listen well, Gaby McAslan. This is what I want. I want the men who did this to my man exposed and humiliated in every nation on Earth. I want their own sisters and mothers to close their doors to them when they go back to their homes; I want their fathers and brothers to turn away and spit when they pass for the shame they have brought their families."

Sip your coffee, Gaby McAslan. Do not let this smooth bastard see the value of this thing he is giving you, for he has the eyes of a Shanghai jade-seller, who sets his price by the dilation of his buyer's pupils. Already, she was listing the Must Knows and the Must Never Knows, the Faithfuls and the Faithlesses. Tembo and Faraway; she would take them; they knew the country, they knew their job, they knew discretion. They would not tell the troll bitch-queen-from-hell Santini, or T.P., who would give it straight to golden-boy Jake. No, she would keep it secret until the moment she rolled it for Thomas Pronsias Costello in his little glass office, and when syndication deals lit up the East African Teleport like a stained glass window, then she would see who was talking junior East African satellite news correspondent. Already she was rehearsing the little doxology: *Gaby McAslan, SkyNet News, Kenya.*

"This does me as much of a favor as it does you," she said.

"Is this not then the most excellent way to do business?" Haran said. "This way, I know I can trust you to do what I ask. I will have one of my boys deliver details of the unit in question and their current location. I presume you will be at the Sondhai woman's for the foreseeable future?"

"For the foreseeable future."

"Good. I have detained you long enough. I would not want to make trouble for you with your employers, when I am in need of their good graces. I am most glad you can do this little favor for me."

He extended a gloved hand. Gaby did not take it.

"Haran. I need to ask a favor in return of you."

"You are aware that what I have asked you to do is in repayment for the favor I did you in the Independence Day thing. This will be a fresh account."

"I am aware of that."

Haran folded his hands in his lap, like a priest awaiting a confession.

"What is it you would ask me?"

"Peter Werther."

"I gave you him as a token of our relationship."

"Dr. Daniel Oloitip says he's disappeared."

"One does well not to pay too much attention to what Dr. Oloitip says."

"He says he hasn't so much disappeared as been disappeared. By the UN. A joint U.S.–Canadian airborne force hit the

What the Sun Said community up at Lake Naivasha and took him."

Haran studied the outspread fingertips of his gloves.

"These are serious allegations Dr. Oloitip is making."

"Haran, I want you to find out if this is true, and if so, where Peter Werther is."

"Are you asking me as a favor?"

He was looking right at her. She had never seen his eyes so clearly. They were like two spheres of lead.

"I am asking you as a favor."

"Finding out and finding where are two favors."

"Then I am asking you as a favor, twice. And I will owe you, twice."

Haran snapped his hands shut. The lemon-yellow leather gloves made a soft, rustling snapping, like a lizard trapping an insect.

"I shall do what I can. I can promise no more than that. You understand that things are not so simple with the UN, or I would not have had to ask you the favor I have. My boys must be discreet if they are not to be discovered. It may be that they will find nothing. But you will still owe me the favor. Two favors."

"Haran, I knew from the moment I met you I would always be owing you."

He smiled. Like his lead eyes, she had never seen him smile before. She wished she had not seen him smile now.

"I shall have one of my boys escort you back to SkyNet. The streets are no longer as safe for visitors as they were, especially for white women. I am afraid there are thieves and con men on every street corner."

Gaby got up from the table. Mombi's handsome envoy had returned with fresh coffee. Haran gently ran his gloved right hand along the possegirl's jawline. Gaby shuddered.

20

''Ten years ago this dusty, rutted dirt road would have been nose to tail with tour buses heading to the game lodges of West Tsavo National Park. Now the only vehicles that move along it are United Nations truck convoys. I counted fifty go past me ten minutes ago. Their dust still hangs in the air. And the place to which they are headed, where once Masai cattle and wild animals existed peacefully together, has turned into something from the Old Testament: an entire nation of refugees.

''In the last census two years ago, the town of Merueshi had a population of three thousand. Today UNHCR estimates there are over one hundred thousand people camped out around Merueshi. In those two years the Chaga has come. Terminum is just two miles to the south of us. Ten minutes' walk, and that, the UN says, is close enough. Everyone, and everything, is to be moved, down to the last cow and goat, the last stick of furniture.

''From fifty miles around, the people have come to Merueshi to be evacuated. Some have their own transport, others were brought in by truck and bus, most have walked carrying all their worldly possessions. Now they wait to be taken north, and they wonder if the UN trucks will reach them before the Chaga does, and if they do make it out of here, what kind of life can they expect in the townships?

''To be forced away from everything you have ever known is hard. What is intolerable is then to have even those few precious things you have managed to salvage taken from you.

''I've come to Merueshi, to the very edge of the Chaga and this scene of near-biblical desolation, to investigate reports of widespread looting and extortion of refugees' property. Not by criminals or gangs of bandits, those certainly exist, or even by profiteers selling space on their own truck trains, but by the very United Nations soldiers who are meant to be protecting them. I have received evidence of black-marketeering in stolen goods by one particular unit of Azerbaijani soldiers under the flag of the United Nations.

''And cut it.''

''We're still running,'' Faraway said behind the camera. ''You can say it if you want to.''

"Oh, all right, then. You can edit this later. I'll give you a mark." Gaby made a chopping motion with her right hand across the camera's field of vision. "Gaby McAslan, SkyNet News, Merueshi, Kenya."

"And we are out."

"Did it look good? Is this sleeveless denim thing all right? No sweat stains under the armpits? If you made my ass look fat, I will hang you by your balls. God, was my nose too shiny?"

Faraway doubled over with laughter.

"You bitch just like Jake. You looked fine. You always look fine to me, Gaby. Mighty fine indeed. Two things, if you please. One, don't swipe at flies with your hand, and two, your hair was blowing across your face. It might be a good idea to shoot it again."

"Jesus, Faraway. That bastard helicopter will come back. I know it. And I'm never as fresh the fourth time."

She could see that Faraway was considering a sexual riposte, but instead he said, "Jake would do it again."

"Fuck Jake."

She knew the look.

"All right. We'll do it again. Got the camp framed? I'll give you a mark."

"One moment please. There seems to be a problem with the white balance."

"I knew it. You haven't the first idea about that camera, have you? We should have waited for Tembo to come back. I don't know why he trusted you with it."

"You trusted him with your Nissan."

"That's different. He has to get the boy. I can't go; the only white woman in fifty miles? What kind of relation is he anyway?"

"Wife's sister-in-law's cousin."

"Blood is much thicker than water in this country."

"But not so thick as money. And remember, I am only doing this because you promised to let me see you with no clothes on. Five minutes. In the middle of my living room."

"You can't possibly hold me to that; come on, it was five o'clock in the morning, I would have promised anything."

Faraway grinned behind the eyepiece as the lens closed in and pulled out into a wide angle.

"You have always known that what I want most in the world

is to undress you and then *fiki-fiki* you as you have never been *fiki-fiki*'d before, Gaby McAslan. Is it red down there too?''

''Shut your gob and we'll go for another take.''

The bastard helicopter came back. It turned high in the air and swooped down low across the camp from its station to the east. Children hid from the hammer of its blades. Women pulled sheets over their heads to protect them from the dust. Lop-eared goats plunged and kicked on their hide tethers; a shit-smeared cow broke loose and careered between the huddles of people. Men in frayed shorts, faded T-shirts and baseball caps with the names of fertilizer companies on the front shooed it away with outspread arms. The helicopter hovered a moment over the refugees, delighting in the chaos it created, then put its nose down and slid up over the low hill where Gaby and Faraway did their fourth take of the news report. Dry brown grass raged and stormed. Dust flew up in a suffocating cloud. Faraway fought with the Velcro closures on the camera hood. Gaby watched her prompt notes fly away from her. Combing her hair from her face, she could clearly see the pilot in the forward cockpit raise a forefinger in an obscene gesture. Gaby screamed curses into the roar of rotors shredding air. The helicopter banked again and slid away north along the line of the road in search of others to intimidate.

''You will have your revenge,'' Faraway said. He was videoing cutaway footage of the camp. ''Here it comes.'' A line of dust moved across the plain: an electric-blue Nissan ATV, driving as fast as the mass of people permitted. ''I am thinking,'' he continued, following it with his lens out of the camp and up the hill, ''that maybe this is a thing worth doing after all. Maybe this will work and we will all be Leonard and Bernstein and have our faces on the television and not behind it.''

''Woodward and Bernstein,'' Gaby corrected. She knew his cool by now. Anything that would earn him fame and face, especially among the easy women he met in Friday-night jit clubs, he would follow with the same phallic determination with which he followed those same women home to their beds. Once vanity got him started, he was kept moving by a deeply uncool, unstreet sentimentality about the world's unfairness. Tembo had required a different tack. Righteousness roused him. He was small, but mighty for justice. As Gaby had unrolled her story Tembo had fetched the equipment her plan required and threw his overnight ready bag into the back of the ATV. His wife had gone about her early-morning tasks with the patient resignation of African women who know that they carry the whole world on their backs.

The first person Gaby had confided in was Miriam Sondhai. She needed the blessing of the sacerdotal woman.

The Somali woman had been slow to answer. It was her way, Gaby had learned. Only when a thing had permeated her like the rain into dry earth, found its level and risen again to the surface, would she speak. That evening after her run, she had come out with a book to sit with Gaby on the side of the veranda that caught the best late sun. Gaby had smoked and worked at her laptop, preparing scripts.

Suddenly Miriam had put down the book and said, "You must do this." The fossil water had risen. Gaby set down her laptop. "You see, they rocketed the hospital for an hour and a half before the troops came in. American Apaches, that was the name of the helicopters. They said the warlords were using it as a headquarters. They were selling the drugs from the pharmacy for arms. Always drugs, for Americans. It is their great Satan. They should fear their own love of weapons, that makes them build things like Apache attack helicopters and antipersonnel rockets. I saw them hit one of the nurses as she ran across the compound looking for cover. The way they work is to explode into thousands of fléchettes. It shredded the skin and flesh from her bones. I was nine years old and I saw a woman turn into a skeleton.

"My father got as many as he could down to the lower levels, but there were many who could not be moved; in traction, or hooked to machinery, or premature babies in incubators. Some of the nurses stayed with them all through the aerial and ground assaults. The ground troops were Pakistanis. They had UN-blue helmets, they had been sent to keep the peace between the tribal factions. They came through every ward, emptied every bed. They pulled people off life-support machines, they tipped babies out of incubators. They went into the theaters and took the operating equipment. They were the ones who looted the pharmacy of all its drugs. Any medical equipment they could move, they took. They loaded it into white army trucks with United Nations painted on the side. They said the trucks were for prisoners, but they were not the kind of truck that could hold people securely. They came knowing what they wanted. They had it all planned. I firmly believe they made up the story about the warlords using my father's hospital as a base as an excuse to loot it, and so the

Americans, because they are so afraid of drugs, would rocket a hospital for an hour.

"We saw it on the satellite news months later. President Zulfikar was pinning medals to the officers who had led the raid. They all looked very clean and very smart and they stood very upright, as Pakistani soldiers do, but what the satellite news did not tell was that the medals were not for service with the UN peacekeeping forces in Somalia, but for their generous donation of ten incubators, three life-support units, two dialysis machines, an X-ray lab and a complete operating theater to the new Benazir Bhutto hospital in Islamabad.

"The hospital did not get the drugs. The soldiers split what they had stolen and sold it to the Americans. Some of the deaths among the UN peacekeepers were from accidental overdoses on medical-grade opiates."

Gaby's cigarette had burned down into a drooping curl of ash.

"This is why you must do it," Miriam Sondhai said. "It is a bad thing when the military is a parasite on its own nation, but it is much worse when someone else's army is parasitical on your nation, and with the blessing of the organization that is supposed to restrain the strong and protect the weak. You must do this, Gaby."

She had her blessing. Hers was holy work. But she wished her motivations were as clean as Miriam's expectations.

Tembo drove the ATV like a maniac. The boy he had brought was tall and thin and dressed in jeans and a T-shirt for a band that had broken up long ago. His hair was shaved so short it looked painted. He radiated that angelic, androgynous beauty peculiar to young African men and women. His name was William. He did not say very much more than that, except that he wanted his money now, thank you.

Gaby drilled him while Tembo wired him with the minicam in the strap of his shoulder bag and fitted the mikes and relay gear. In the back of the ATV, Faraway tuned receivers and monitors and gave encouraging thumbs-up.

"It's simple," Gaby said. "You go in, you walk around, you see anything that looks like soldiers taking *magendo,* you get in close, but not too close. They won't suspect you, there are too many people, but don't attract attention to yourself. If they stop you and want something, offer them a thousand shillings, and if they still want more, give them this portable CD-radio. If they don't get it, you can keep it, and the thousand shillings as well, if you can hold on to it. Now, what's the range of the transmitter?''

''Two hundred feet.'' His voice was soft and sexless too, a man-woman whisper.

''We'll be in the four-by-four, close by at all times. If there's any trouble, we'll pull you out, but I really don't think there will be. Go in, get your stuff, come back, and you'll get your face on satellite television. You'll be a big star, just like Jackie Chan. Jean-Claude Van Damme. A hero.''

Tembo looked at Gaby in a way that said that such was poor currency for the soul of his wife's sister-in-law's cousin.

They dropped the kid half a mile from the town center. He looked back nervously. Tembo waved him on encouragingly. He worked his way into the knots of people. Gaby let him get a hundred yards ahead before following in low gear. For all the people, there were few blue-helmets. A solitary APC passed. The soldier in the front hatch saw a white woman driving and curled his tongue to touch the lower edge of his shades. For the first time the realization of what might happen if something went wrong struck Gaby. She was monstrously isolated—professionally, geographically, racially, sexually. If she fell, there would be no hands to catch her but those of men with guns.

William stopped to talk with some young men he knew sitting on the white stones that marked the forecourt of Merueshi's solitary gas station. Gaby stopped the ATV. In the back Faraway waved his thumbs in the air. The boys' talk was coming through loud and clear. One of the youths pointed into town. William moved on. The 4X4 followed.

The soldiers had set up a processing station in front of the district magistrate's office. A funnel of parked armored cars directed the press of people past a table where a swarthy officer with the thinnest mustache that could possibly call itself such checked names on a PDU. Beyond him were the trucks.

''Go to it, go to it,'' Gaby shouted to her stool pigeon. Unhearing, William melted into the crowd. ''Damn it. Can't see him.'' She stopped the car and peered over the backseat at Faraway's monitors.

''Much meeting and greeting and no *magendo,*'' Faraway said. ''Wait, wait, wait.'' The jerky, wide-angle image of the shoulder-mounted minicam had caught a soldier standing talking with a bearded, barefoot man in shorts. You could see at once that the bearded, barefoot man was at his wit's end. He pleaded with his hands. The soldier caught his eloquent hands, turned them over. The bearded, barefoot man wore a copper bracelet on his left wrist.

"Turn to it, please turn to it," Faraway begged. "Oh, boy, if only you had some lessons in basic camera technique."

"But do not get too interested," Tembo said, mindful of his wife's sister-in-law's cousin's safety.

On the ten-inch monitor they saw the bearded, barefoot man take off the copper bracelet and give it to the soldier. The soldier put it in one of the pockets of his combat pants and handed the bearded, barefoot man a slip of paper. The bearded, barefoot man thanked the soldier effusively with his eloquent hands. He signaled to a thin woman and four children who had been sitting on the earth close by to pick up their things. The soldier led them all away, shouting a path through the crowd. The people pushed in behind them and William's camera caught no more.

"One moment," Faraway said. He wound the disc back frame by frame. "There." In the shuffle, William had been pushed against the soldier and the unit flashes on his uniform had come into sharp focus. The letters were indecipherable, but the regimental badge of a stooping eagle in a blue triangle was unmistakable. Haran's instructions had guided them true.

"Result!" Gaby McAslan yelled, punching the air and forgetting the low roof.

Kid William moved inward. The ATV crawled after him. The camera saw a soldier take a thousand shillings from a distraught pastor and his family. It saw three blue-helmets laugh at a desperate old man offering them the only thing he valued: an aged, aged black bicycle. They saw a boy in combats with an AK47 order a family to spread all their goods on a blanket on the ground and pick through them, taking here a brass-framed mirror, there a wedding ring. The boy soldier was at the most seventeen.

What appalled was the blatancy of it. There was no attempt at concealment or discretion, no implication of shame or misdoing. It was a public market that ended in a slip of paper and the people who received it being taken to the trucks beyond. When a truck was full, it would drive away, the people onboard pressing their hands together in thanksgiving and weeping with joy, and another would come forward to take its place.

The crowds were denser closer to the town center. Bodies squeezed the ATV tight. The heel of Gaby's hand never left the horn. She imagined she could smell sweet-sour fear sweat blowing through the air-conditioning vents. A cute Azeri boy trooper with acne pressed hands and face to the driver's window, licked the glass, rolled his eyes.

"Fuck off," Gaby growled, heart hammering in case he should catch sight of the treachery in the back seat.

"Oh, you beautiful boy!" Faraway exclaimed, snapping his fingers in delight. "He has got an officer! Contact! The officer is asking him if has any money."

"They don't believe in beating about the bush," Gaby said.

"I do," Faraway said, radiantly happy. "I will beat any bush with you, Gaby. William is offering him the thousand shillings. It is right in front of the lens. Tembo, my brother, your wife's sister-in-law's cousin raised smart children. Oh, this is beautiful. They have taken the money, but they think because he has a thousand shillings to give away, he may have more. They are asking to see what else he has. Give them the disc player, William. I wonder, Tembo, was your wife's sister-in-law's cousin ever in Nairobi? Maybe there is some Faraway in him. He is clever and handsome enough. Go on, take it. Made in Japan. Not European Union rubbish. Yes, they like it. That will do them very nicely, thank you, William. Now, just give him the paper, and take him through to the trucks. Why will you not do this? Give him the paper, he has given you all he has, greedy *m'zungu.*"

"I do not like this," Tembo said. "Can we get closer?"

"I'll try," Gaby said. "But these crowds." Do not think of the annihilation of the mob, she told herself as she navigated the ATV closer.

"Oh Jesus Mister Christ," Faraway said.

Gaby glanced at the monitor. The picture was badly broken, as if the shoulder bag were being shaken violently.

"I see them!" Tembo shouted. He was on the edge of his seat with worry. William and the Azeri officer were playing tug-of-war with the bag containing the camera and transmitter. William turned, saw the electric-blue ATV, looked right at the white woman driving it. Gaby could hear his cry for help inside and outside the 4X4.

"Jesus. We're rumbled."

The officer stared at Gaby with a look that passed from recognition to comprehension to hatred in a few muscle twitches. Exactly the look Raymond Burr gave in *Rear Window* when he rumbled Jimmy Stewart. She knew her father's old video collection too well to have forgotten what happened next.

Tembo heaved the big heavy camcorder out of the back, switched it on and brought it to bear on the officer. The officer's hand had been straying to his sidearm. The watching eye of the world kept it safe in its holster. In the moment's diversion William twisted free from the officer and fled through the crowd, leaving behind the shoulder bag with the clever little camera and cleverer little transmitter. Faraway put his hands on his head in despair. It was only partly for the loss of expensive equipment.

Gaby floored the accelerator. People parted before the ATV like the waters before Moses. They passed the stunned officer, they passed the running William. Faraway flung open the rear door, seized William's wrist and pulled him ungently in. The open door flapped wildly on its hinges. Evacuees jumped back.

"Move move move!" Gaby screamed at them. They moved moved moved. It was better than death. She threw the wheel from side to side, dodging by instinct alone. The loom of faces places objects was absurdly like a computer game. Only "game over" is gang rape if you are lucky, a bullet in the back of the head and every vulture for fifty kays around coming to the wake if you are not, she thought. The sweat she could now smell in the car was her own. Fat drops rolled coldly down the sides of her body.

She heard Tembo's cry and spun the wheel without looking. There was a loud bang. The car lurched as it ran over something. In her wing mirror Gaby saw a dog spin across the road. Intestines sprayed from its burst stomach. Gaby wailed. The back door was still swinging and banging. Faraway did not dare risk his fingers trying to catch it.

William pushed his head between the front seats.

"Go right here," he said. "There is an earth road goes west into the valley of the Kiboko, and then south to the Chaga."

"I don't want to be anywhere near the Chaga."

"They will have blocks up on the roads north and east."

Gaby slammed the Nissan into four-wheel drive and swung off the road. The car shook. Speed on the earth road was like driving on corrugated iron. She could barely hold the wheel steady. Now we will see how good the manufacturer's promises are, Gaby thought. Cars with factory-test-to-destruction ratings of five years fell apart after ten months on East Africa's laterite roads. You're a long way from sweet home Yokohama now, little Nissan. God, they can probably see my dust trail from the moon. Why is it the thing you feel worst about is the dog? It was only a poor dumb mutt and if you hadn't burst its guts it would just have been run over by a truck or left to starve in the Chaga or maybe some soldier would have taken pity on it and blasted its brains out with his AK47. So why does thinking about it spinning across the road make you want to cry? Maybe it is not the dog you are crying for, but your brilliant career that got left with tire tracks across its belly in the middle of the Merueshi road.

Faraway stuck his face between the headrests.

"I think it might be a good idea to go a little faster."

"Not without flipping this thing right over."

"I think you should reconsider, because I think hell is coming after us. There are two armored personnel carriers on your tail."

She spared a glance in the rearview. A mile down the tracks were two rising plumes of dust, each with a white speck at its head.

"Oh Jesus," she moaned.

"I know you do not believe in it, but I am praying to God for our deliverance," Tembo said.

"You'll do better than God. You'll get on the cellphone to T. P. Costello and tell him to call the UNHCR or UNECTA or whoever the hell runs this show down here and tell them that we know what's going on and they'd better leave us alone."

The dirt road fought Gaby like it was trying to steal her car. Muscles were knotted up and down her bare arms with the intensity of the struggle.

"I am afraid we are probably out of range of the cell network," William said coolly.

"Well, that is just wonderful," Gaby said. "Just fucking wonderful."

"They do not seem to be gaining on us," Faraway said, peering out of the still-open door and the dust billowing into the ATV. A small herd of Thompson's gazelles scattered in every direction from Gaby's killing wheels.

People paid a lot of money to come to Africa to do driving like this.

Faraway spoke something short and savage in Luo then said

in English, "I regret to inform you that things have just become most serious."

The helicopter came in a hammer of sound so low and loud that everyone in the ATV ducked. The car plunged into a whirlwind of dust thrown up by the rotors. The helicopter turned in the air in front of them and hovered.

"Go south!" William shouted. "To the edge of the Chaga. They will not dare follow us there."

Dare I lead them there? Gaby thought, activating the internal satellite tracker and flicking on the wipers to clear the dust-filmed windscreen.

Lazily, the helicopter drifted after them. It moved effortlessly across the sky, like a cheetah stalking a wounded impala, that the cheetah knows it can run down and kill when it finally tires of playing. Oksana had made sure that Gaby knew the specifications of every aircraft, military and civilian, in the East African theater. Those black insect-things under the stub wings are air-to-surface missiles. That thin black proboscis is a chain gun. Five hundred rounds a minute will shred you and your car and your friends and your story of a lifetime like pissed-on toilet paper. Five hundred rounds a minute, and all you have to bluff them with is to keep driving south, south, south.

The dirt road dissolved into high acacia plain. Flat dark clouds were rolling down from the mothermass anchored to the distant mountain, spreading slowly out across the land that shivered like liquid with heat haze. Between the two ran a line of shadow: the edge of the Chaga. Terminum. Gaby McAslan drove straight into the line of darkness at one hundred miles per hour.

"They are still with us," Faraway shouted from the back. Flirting, the helicopter swept in to harry the little car from the left and the right. It ducked down in front of it in a shatter of engines to try to get the driver to swerve. The driver did not swerve. She drove on to that line of darkness that minute by minute was emerging from the heat dazzle into shapes, silhouettes, seductions. Like a mirage, the Chaga deceived. Its trick was to play with space so that you were always nearer to it than you thought. The darkness Gaby saw lifting out of the heat haze was not terminum. It was the great upthrust of life she had seen and marveled at from the baobab on the Namanga road, that the researchers called the Great Wall. Terminum was elsewhere. Terminum was right in front of them. Terminum was under their wheels.

Gaby slammed to a stop. The helicopter passed raucously overhead and pulled a high-gee turn.

"We lost the APCs a mile back," Faraway reported.

Gaby did not hear him. She stared at the edge of the Chaga, one hundred feet in front of her. One hundred feet. Two days. If she sat in this seat and did not move, the Chaga would come to her, grow around and into and through her and take her to another world. She could step out of this car and walk to it and take off her clothes and lie down in it and feel it press into the skin of her back, like the old Vietnamese torture in which they tied people over bamboo and let it grow through them.

"Gaby."

"The helicopter?" she asked.

"It's standing off about half a mile west of us," Faraway said.

"Go closer," William whispered. "Their guns and rockets can shoot a long way. Get as close as you dare."

As close as she dared was fifty yards. The helicopter held its station, the black nose of its chain gun locked on the beetle-blue ATV.

"Closer," William whispered. Gaby moved the ATV in until she could smell the musky fruity sexy perfume of Chaga through the vents. The helicopter gingerly waltzed a little nearer.

"Do these bastards not give up?" Faraway asked.

"Closer," William ordered a third time, and this time Gaby drove until the pods and bulbs of Chaga-stuff popped beneath her tires and the hexagonal mosaics cracked and spilled orange ichor that blossomed into helixes and coils of living polymer. The helicopter darted in, suddenly swung high in the air so that its rotors looked like the sails of an insane windmill, then spun away and receded across the Chyulu plain and was seen and heard no more.

"Yes!" Faraway shouted. Tembo smiled like a man who knows his prayers have been answered. Gaby leaned forward until her forehead touched the top of the steering wheel and tried to stop her hands from shaking.

"Go west," William said. "We should follow the edge until we come to the Olosinkiran road. They are South Africans over there. We can trust them."

Gaby put her foot on the accelerator.

And the blue Nissan all-terrain vehicle died.

"Oh no," said Gaby McAslan, turning and turning and turning the ignition, pumping and pumping and pumping the gas pedal. The diesel pressure lamp glowed at her. "Oh no no no no no."

Tembo got out and put up the hood. He beckoned to Gaby. Chaga-stuff crackled and burst beneath the soles of her boots. Strange pheromones challenged her.

"I think we have a problem here."

Compressor, fuel lines, cylinder head wore coats of tiny sulfur-yellow flowers, like miniature cauliflower buds. As Gaby watched, not wanting to believe what her eyes were showing her, the plague of flowers spread to the oil pump, oil filter and engine block. Tendrils were rising from the open flower heads on the cylinder block, waving sentiently in the sunlight. In under a minute the engine compartment was a pulp of pseudo-coral and oily metal. A sudden bang, like a shot. The fuel cap had blown off. Yellow fungus dripped from the fuel pipe. The body panels over the fuel tank were bowed out. The tires popped little blue blooms around their rims. Something like crystalline rust was trying to work its way along the paintwork under the protective lacquer. Gaby yelped. The synthetic soles of her heavy-duty boots were blistering. There was man-made stretch fiber in her jodhpurs, in her underwear. It would eat that.

She should have obeyed T.P.'s panties catechism to the letter.

She jumped onto the hood of the ATV to get away from the treacherous earth.

"What is the finance company going to say about this? I only just made the first payment."

"I do not think you are going to get much satisfaction from your insurers," Tembo said ruefully.

They were saying these little things because none of them dared think about the big things. At terminum. Angry Azerbaijanis behind them. Sixty miles of semidesert on either side. No food. No water. No means of communication.

"Shit! The disc!"

Tembo seized the camera and ran as fast as he could out of the Chaga into the virgin savannah. Gaby saw the flexible disc heliograph in the sun, saw Tembo unbutton his pants and then Faraway asked her to please spare his friend's dignity.

"Just pray his digestion is good today," he said.

The camera he brought back was a purulent mass of lichens

and pseudo-fungi. Gaby winced at the SkyNet sticker on the side as responsibility went in and opened up inside her like the Gae Bolga of her childhood legends, the belly spear that unfolded a thousand barbs and tore out your guts. Mrs. Tembo and Sarah and Etambele had waved their father off that morning and Gaby McAslan could not bear the responsibility that they might never be waving him home again. They could die out here, or be vanished by the UN, like Peter Werther, which is worse than dying to those who wait outside. She had put them all into this place and did not have an idea how to get them out.

"Could we walk?" she asked plaintively.

"You tell us where, we will walk," Faraway said. "After all, it is only sixty miles."

"We have no water," Tembo said. "And Gaby would burn before she went ten miles. Also, we have no weapons."

"There are lions?" Gaby asked.

"Leopards are more common around the edges of the Chaga. But the biggest danger is from gangs of bandits who pick over the abandoned villages. We would be safer in the hands of the Azeris than the scavengers."

Gaby wrapped her bare arms around her knees. Her shoulders were already starting to feel hot. The Chaga had risen to ankle height. Terminum was several feet north of them.

"So what do you suggest we do?" Gaby asked plaintively.

Tembo looked at her, the land, the Chaga, the sky.

"I suggest we set fire to the car."

"The hell with that. I worked damn hard for this car."

"It is lost, Gaby. The column of smoke will be visible for a great distance. UNECTA has ChagaWatch balloons every few miles. They would call in an airborne patrol."

"And if the military see it first? Or these scavengers?"

"They are cowards," William said forcefully. "They would not dare go into the Chaga, soldiers or scavengers."

Gaby watched the interior of her car break out into pinhead-sized scarlet blisters.

"Do it," she said. "Torch it." It was only a car. The Chaga could have it. The Chaga could have the clothes on her body and leave her naked and sunburned, as long as the disc Tembo had hidden in his rectum remained inviolate.

The men opened the doors. The red beads had swollen into orange puffballs that burst into clouds of peppery dust as Gaby rummaged in the back for her spare diesel can. The metal had resisted the spores, though the cap had wedged tight around a crust of saffron crystals. Faraway wrenched it off and gave Gaby the honor of liberally anointing her own car with fuel. Before the Chaga could devour the diesel, she lit a length of tattered handkerchief with her cigarette lighter and dropped it on the driver's seat.

The car went up in a satisfying blossom of flame. The refugees started the short walk back to Kenya. By the time they found a place comfortably far from terminum to sit and wait, the ATV was burning nicely in a gobble of fire and carcinogenic black thermoplastic smoke. Gaby watched it burn. Tembo had been right. It was lost to her already, but it is one thing to have it taken from you and another to have to give it away with your own hands.

"How long do you think?" she asked.

Tembo shrugged. The smoke coiled into a neat twister that leaned across the edgelands toward the east.

How much burning is there in one Nissan all-terrain vehicle? Gaby thought, watching the paint blister and flake. She thought about fire, and she thought about fear, and in her extremity she saw the land beyond scared, a calm and watered plain where you can watch twenty-five thousand pounds' worth of car burn with equanimity, even serenity, because you understand that there is no point being scared anymore because it cannot help you.

"Do you want to play a game?" she asked the men. "Kill the time. How about I Spy? I Spy with my little eye, something beginning with . . ." She quested around for a mystery object.

"C," Faraway said, and that was the end of that game.

"All right then, what's the most frightened you've ever been?" Without waiting for the men to agree to her time killer, Gaby told about the time in her first year in London when she had been alone down in a tube station at midnight and a white boy with a Stanley knife had taken her money off her, and her cards, and her disc player, and her expensive shoes, though they neither fitted nor suited him, and then told her he was going to cut long scars that would never heal properly across her cheeks and lips and forehead and breasts if she did not go down on her knees and suck his cock behind the defunct phonecard machine on the westbound platform, and who ran off leaving her things when the last train came in a gust of electricity and hot air. She had gathered up all her things and hidden in the toilet until her stop, when she had dumped the money and the cards and the disc player and the expensive shoes in the trash bin and walked barefoot to her flat. They were polluted now. They were diseased. They would never lose the taint.

"The most scared I have ever been," William whispered, "is going into the town with your camera in my bag. I felt that everyone could see it but had agreed not to tell me. I felt like I had a disease, or another face in the back of my head that was pulling ridiculous expressions and sticking its tongue out at people, but I could never see. When that white officer wanted to look into my bag, I did not know what to do. Every thought flew from my head. It is very frightening when you know that you must do something to save yourself but you cannot think what. But what is strange is that it was the most frightening thing I can remember, but it was also the most exciting, like all the people who could see into me and knew what I was really doing were jealous and wanted to do it too. Does this make sense?"

"It does to me," Gaby said.

"The most scared I ever was was the morning I woke up convinced I had Slim," Faraway said. "I met the woman in a club. She was a strange woman on a strange journey from somewhere to somewhere that went by way of me for a night. She had long ridged scars all over her arms and the backs of her hands. Scarification, you understand? But she was not of a tribe that thinks that sort of thing is beautiful. She had an interest in orifices. She loved to push things into body openings. There was a thing she would do with a champagne bottle. She could uncork one with her lower muscles. For a woman who can do a trick like that, I will buy as much champagne as she wants, provided it is that cheap stuff from India. She liked to do things with the corks, and the wire cages too. Ah! My poor foreskin! And other parts too. But it was worth it, for she made *fiki-fiki* like an animal, like something in heat.

"When I woke in the morning I could not remember very much, but there was a terrible burning pain in my *f'tuba.* And when I pissed, man! I thought I was going to die. It was pissing fire. What had this demon woman done to me? Of course, she was not there to ask. They never are, the women who are real demons. But the pain did not go away, and I thought it was some dreadful disease, maybe even Slim, and that no matter how many bottles of champagne she could uncork with her magic lips, it was not worth the death of the incomparable Faraway. That made me really afraid, so I went to my doctor because I thought that if I did have Slim, then it would be better to know so everyone could have a big party and tell me what a grand fellow I was before I died. So, the doctor looked up my dick with a fiber-optic thing and he falls over laughing, and when he can talk again, he calls in his nurse, and she looks up my dick and falls over laughing, and the next thing I know the room is full of doctors and consultants and nurses and porters and people who just heard a noise going on and wondered what they were missing, all looking up my dick and falling over laughing.

"Do you know what they saw up there that made them fall over laughing? A sliver of red chili pepper. That demon woman! When I was asleep she had cut a tiny little slice of chili and pushed it up my *f'tuba.* Orifices! Devil! It was a week before I could walk straight, let alone piss with pleasure. It is funny now, but at the time, I tell you, my friends, this Faraway was never so frightened. I thought I would die. Really, truly."

"Of course, you have learned nothing from the experience," Tembo said.

Faraway grinned his huge grin. "I have learned never to leave chilies sitting around my home, and that is a very wise lesson for anyone."

"What happened to the strange woman?" Gaby asked.

"I saw her at clubs a few times, dancing with some other man, but she never came near me and I never went near her. Then I heard from a friend of a friend that she had died. She was playing a game in a hotel room with two men and a gun, but I do not know if it was an accident or on purpose. My friend of a friend said he thought there was a video, but the police were keeping it to sell around. But I never saw it. It is sad that her strange journey had to end that way."

"The most frightening moment of my life was caused by a pair of football shorts," Tembo said. Gaby hiccuped with laughter, but Faraway did not and he knew Tembo like a lover. "I was on the St. Matthew's Church in Shikondi's under-eighteen football team, but my parents were poor and could not afford to buy me the team strip all at once. So for doing well in my exams I got the shirt, and for my birthday I got the socks and boots, and when an uncle became a pastor and gave everyone gifts to celebrate the event, I got the shorts. Because they were poor, they bought things that would last: the shorts were the very newest man-made fiber that would never wear out whatever you did to it. This made me think. You could throw these shorts on the rubbish heap and they would never rot away to nothing. They would always be a pair of football shorts. I would grow up, and get work, and marry, if God blessed me, and have children, and the football shorts would not have changed. I would grow old, my children would marry and have children, and if God blessed me, those children would have children, and the blue shorts would not change. I would die, and be buried, and decay to bones and hair and still not one of those artificial fibers would have rotted. And then I stopped thinking about football shorts and thought about me. This would happen. It was not an idea, a maybe, an if. It was a certainty. These football shorts were a measure of my life. This me, that wore football strip and played for St. Matthew's under-eighteen, would one day breathe out and not breathe in again, would go cold and dark inside, would stop thinking and seeing and hearing and feeling, and stop being. It could not be escaped or got around. The most I could hope would be to delay it. I saw this, and it scared me like nothing has ever scared me. And I would have to go alone. No one I knew could go with me, or go before me and come back and tell me what was on the other side. I would go alone, and blind. That is why I found Jesus. Because he was the only one who could go with me, who had been there, and seen what it was like and could tell me what would happen. Because I need someone I can call to in the dark night when my wife and my children are sleeping and the fear of it wakes me up like something very very cold in my heart.''

Tembo looked up and out at the dusty horizon. He stood up. He stared. He shielded his eyes with his hand and peered. Gaby imagined it was Jesus he saw, coming across the dry land toward this borderland between worlds.

''There,'' Tembo said. He pointed to the southeast. ''There! See!''

Gaby stood up and followed the line of his finger and saw the thing he saw. It was a wink of silver in the sky, a tiny heliograph of light that the eye lost as soon as it had found it. The cloud and the plains and the heat haze together destroyed all notions of distance; the thing could have been miles away or hovering at the end of Tembo's finger. But it was growing bigger, and assuming a definite outline. Tembo started to wave his arms. Faraway leaped up and down in an unconscious parody of the Masai jumping dance. The thing was big, the thing was approaching from a very great distance. The thing was near.

Then Gaby knew she had caught too much sun, for the thing coming toward her out of the southeast was nothing other than a classic B-movie sci-fi 1950s McCarthy-paranoia flying saucer. A big white flying saucer, with UNECTA written in blue on its belly.

21

It was when she was sure, absolutely sure, that the metal door was never going to open again that it did and the black woman with the French accent came into the cell with a cup of coffee with UNECT*AFRIQUE*:GO WEST! on the side of it and a pile of clothes. She was not wearing the isolation suit. The stuffs she had sucked out of Gaby in the night had passed their tests.

"Do you have to watch me?" Gaby McAslan asked, naked, sunburned, scratched and scraped and needled and furious with the high and hot anger that is really fear after her night's imprisonment in the decontamination unit at Tsavo West.

The magic of the flying saucer had failed close up. It takes a very strong magic to work at fingertip distance. It had just been a tired old logging dirigible with SIBIRSK shining through the hasty UN-white paint job, with a world-weary crew-woman who had led them up the cargo ramp and then locked them in a windowless cargo bay because she and her comrades were afraid of catching terrible and disgusting Chaga-diseases off these flotsam of the edgelands. And when they had come down a guessed thirty minutes later—no one's watch was working—there had been no more than a glimpse of brilliant sunlight reflecting from the curve of the canopy above them as they were taken by the faceless figures in baggy white medical isolation suits across the landing grid with the mountain-and-crescents symbol of UNECTA painted on it, and down a flight of iron stairs into the fluorescent-lit corridors that smelled of hospital and thrice-breathed air. Gaby McAslan's Tsavo West was a dead white cell with a door that melded into the wall when the woman with the French accent left. Before she went, the woman had explained that Gaby had been exposed to possible contamination by alien organisms; that she and the others, who were in adjacent cells, were undergoing the standard observation and decontamination procedure; that any objects, such as minidiscs, would have to be sterilized before they could be permitted into the Tsavo West biosphere.

All night, as Gaby McAslan sat on her bed with her back to the eye of the lens, her knees hugged to her chest and her hair drawn around her like a cloak, she dreaded about that disc, and what would happen to her if the process of sterilization extended to the footage from Merueshi stored on it. She worried and watched the digits on the clock on the opposite wall click out the length of time UNECTA reckoned it might take for a new and virulent strain of Chaga-meme to melt an Irishwoman into a blob of plastic. One thousand and five clicks, that was how many. And then just as she had forgotten where the memory of the door was, the wall opened and let in air that did not smell of dread and body odor.

"Admit it, you get some lesbo-sado-dominatrix thrill out of locking naked women in cells," Gaby said, pulling on the borrowed underwear, the jeans that belonged to a shorter-legged woman, and the sweatshirt. "Jesus, A. C. Milan. Is this the best you can do?"

"Your friends are in the restaurant down on two," her erstwhile captor said. Gaby almost ran as she followed the woman's directions along the corridor of featureless doors to the external elevator. Open air. The daylight was blinding. The little chain drive at the bottom started to whir. Gaby McAslan was lowered down the face of a six-story office block. She had a chance for a leisurely look at this place to which she had been brought. Across the twenty-yard gap in front of her rose a second, taller unit; a ramshackle affair that looked like dozens of portable cabins piled on top of each other and fastened together with gantries and swaths of power cable. UNECT*Afrique* was painted on its white flank in blue letters thirty feet high. Twenty yards beyond this second pile rose a third, smaller unit that was all heavy engineering plant, solar arrays and satellite dishes. It was connected to the main block by air bridges and walkways and curving umbilical lines, as the main block was to the one down which she was moving. But the most extraordinary feature of this miniature city on the high plains was that each of the units stood on leviathan tracked vehicles, like the monster flatbeds that carried pre-

HOTOL space shuttles from the assembly buildings to the launchpad.

Gaby hit the emergency stop button. The elevator platform jerked to a halt. It was not a trick of the elevator, everything was vibrating. If she focused at a point on the ground, she could just discern the motion, slow as the minute hand of one of her Swatches. The tractors, the units, the moored dirigible, with everything in and on them, were moving backward in perfect synchronization with the advance of the Chaga across the Serengeti plain. Terminum was half an hour's walk across a dry yellow plain littered with the abrupt white stumps of acacias felled to make way for the juggernaut. A group of zebras were cropping the sparse scorched grass. They looked dry and dusty, thirsty for the rains. Everything looked dry and dusty, the plains, Tsavo West, the hazy colors of the Chaga. Waiting for the rains.

The refectory took up a full quarter of Level Two. It was bright and busy and smelled of breakfasts from diverse ethnic backgrounds. Tembo and Faraway were drinking coffee in a small booth under a window with monumental views of the station and the Chaga rising toward the cloud-hidden heights of Kilimanjaro.

"Alas, I have missed my great chance," Faraway said. "An entire night of you without any clothes on. Of course, you know that they only do it so the women can look at Tembo's *f'tuba* and pray and the men look at it and feel envious."

"Ignore my friend," Tembo said gravely. "How are you, Gaby?"

"I feel like everyone in this place has been watching me but isn't going to say."

"It is disconcerting, the first time," Tembo said.

"When you have been into the Chaga as often as we have, they know all about you and you are in and out in under two hours," Faraway said.

"What about the disc, Tembo?"

The small man shook his head.

"They did an internal examination."

"Shit. We have to get that disc before UNECTA looks at it."

"There is more, Gaby. I called my wife last night; UNECTA had already been in touch with her to let her know we were safe and well. They have also been in touch with T. P. Costello. I have been in contact with him; I have done what I can, but he wants very much to talk with you, Gaby."

"Fuck." No discs, no story, no car, no camera. No job, when she got back. Then: "Tembo; where's William?"

"I was hoping you would be able to tell me that, Gaby."

"He's still in decontamination?"

"When I asked, they told me they were carrying out further tests. They will not let me speak to him."

"What could he need testing for that I don't? We were all together all the time; anything he's picked up, we have too."

"Further tests, that is all I know," Tembo said. "Gaby, I am worried for my wife's sister-in-law's cousin."

The black lesbo-sado-dominatrix with the French accent who had released Gaby from solitary confinement came to the booth. Faraway brightened visibly. Flirtation was everywhere.

"Ms. McAslan, the director would like to see you if you are ready. If you will follow me, his office is in the main unit."

The black lesbo-sado-dominatrix with the French accent introduced herself as Celeste and took Gaby up the outside of the unit to a fourth-level walkway and across the gap into corridors marked with black-and-yellow biohazard warnings busy with people in colorful casuals who could not proceed more than a few feet at a time without meeting someone to whom they had to tell something important. Facial hair, baggy shorts and friendship bracelets were de rigueur for the men; the women favored hot pants, halter tops and lots of silver. Gaby expected to see basketball hoops on the laboratory doors.

"There are three hundred staff here at Tsavo," Celeste said, tormentor turned tour guide, leading Gaby up a clattering iron staircase. Gaby practiced the role of Hard-Nosed Journalist with Big Questions That Demanded Answers. She was not convinced. Oh God. T. P. Costello was going to fry her.

The director's office was on the penthouse level. Celeste entered without knocking. There was no receptionist, just a carpeted room filled with collegiate clutter, the inevitable computer equipment, a picture window looking out over the Chaga, a battered leather-topped desk. And:

"You!"

"You."

"You." Hard-Nosed Journalist with Big Questions That Demanded Answers hissed out of her in a whisper.

"Your choice of clichés: 'Fancy seeing you here'; 'What's a

nice girl like you doing in a place like this?' or 'We can't go on meeting this way'?''

''What about: 'You utter utter utter asshole, I have just had the worst night of my life'?''

''I thought they taught you journalists about things like not using the same word more than once in a sentence. Celeste, any chance of you scaring us up some coffee and a bite to eat? If I remember decontam right, Ms. McAslan won't have had too much to eat.'' When the black woman had gone, Dr. Shepard took a more conciliatory tone. ''Decontamination is pretty scary, though. They're a law unto themselves over there. Different division. Luckily, when I found out who they'd gotten hold of, I was able to get one of my team over there to keep an eye on you. I'm genuinely sorry you had a bad experience; but it is necessary. Back in the old days before we got up onto our tracks, there was a contamination incident over at Tinga Tinga. Months of work down the toilet, not to mention a million dollars of equipment. So we have to be cruel to be kind. If it's any consolation, we all have to go through it.''

His apology seemed genuine. Celeste returned with coffee and a microwaved cheese-bacon croissant. Gaby fell on it.

''Oh God, this is the most delicious thing I ever tasted,'' she shrieked. ''Shepard. I need to ask. One of my friends. His name's William Bi. He's still in there.''

''In decontam?''

Gaby nodded. Shepard frowned.

''He shouldn't be. Excuse me a moment.'' He swiveled his peeling leather chair to address the server. His frown deepened. He placed a call on the videophone. While he gave monosyllabic replies to the wheedling whisper on the handset, Gaby drank her coffee and studied his desk. A man's soul is like his desk, she had found. Except when it is like his penis. Shepard's desk looked like the result of much rummaging in Arab markets along the coast. The wood could be ebony. There were worn gold-leaf elephants embossed around the edge of the leather top. It said much about Dr. Shepard—Dr. *M.* Shepard, according to the name sign—that he had had it brought cross-country and maneuvered up in all those vertiginous freight elevators and along the narrow, shiplike corridors and into this office with its God's-eye view of the end of the world. Desk decor heavy on Africana: all fine wood. Probably genuine. Small: they invited you to pick them up and enjoy the feel of their grain against your nerve endings. Half a dozen coffee mugs with sad black salt pans of dried grounds in the bottom. Framed photographs of two boys, grinning, displaying several thousand dollars of orthodontistry. One about twelve, the other nine, ten. Tousle-haired, freckle-faced. All-American kids. Could be the last of an endangered species. A photograph of the younger M. Shepard, in a pink-and-lilac speed-skating suit, with that yearning pose of ready-for-the-off peculiar to speed skaters with twelve inches of steel on each foot. Shame about the color scheme, but check out the thighs. Those were thighs to coat with aerosol chocolate mousse and slowly lick clean. She tried to see if he had kept them in condition.

Dr. Shepard came off the phone.

"They're a bit concerned about some of William's results and want to run further tests."

"What way concerned?"

"I don't know."

"The director of Tsavo West doesn't know?"

"Like I said, they're a different administration. The decontamination and medical facilities report direct to regional headquarters at Kajiado. But I shouldn't worry; it's not unusual for folk in decontam to develop mild viral infections. We just have to make sure it isn't something new from out of the Chaga. They usually clear up after a few days."

"Days."

"I can't think of a better place for him to be."

Gaby helped herself to more coffee from the stainless-steel vacuum jug. No. Don't drink it. Do it. Say it.

"Shepard, there's something else I have to ask you."

In her imagination she saw figures in white isolation suits running along the neon-lit corridors of the decontamination block to hastily convened meetings in midnight conference rooms; the disc shining on the desktop while voices spoke in quick, hushed tones. She saw heads nod, hands shake, voices agree: this could only be satisfactorily ended by flames.

"Would it, by any chance, concern this?"

A click of fingers and the disc was between them, and then on the leather desktop, like a captured sin.

"Have you watched this?" Gaby asked.

"I have." There was not much Paul Newman in Shepard's

eyes, unless it was the Paul Newman in the scene from *The Hustler* where he plays against Minnesota Fats.

"You have to give me that back, it's my property, it's my story. You cover it up, it'll only make it worse when the truth finally gets out. And it will, in the end, believe me. You're either for or against me in this."

Shepard flipped the disc between his fingers.

"What makes you think I'm part of a cover-up conspiracy?"

"You're UNECTA, aren't you?"

"You obviously don't know as much about what's going on in this country as you think. There's little love lost between the military and the research community. The army wants the research division militarized. Because they see us as a gang of fuzzy-minded, subversive, undisciplined anarchists, they would buy expertise from the multinationals, who, if they had corporate souls, would mortgage them to dabble their fingers in the Chaga. I know of a dozen major companies—petrochemical, biotech, molecular engineering, chip design, agricultural—with lawyers on round-the-clock standby to slap patent applications on anything we bring out of there they can reproduce. It's a bigger game than you think."

"You've seen what's on the disc. So what do you think of it?"

"I think it deserves a goddamn Pulitzer Prize, Gaby McAslan. And I think you should bless whatever gods you journalists pray to that it found its way to this office and isn't lying on the desk of some general back in Kajiado. Which is why I'm going to have it squirted to SkyNet, because the longer the one and only copy is in Tsavo, the more the chance that people who will be embarrassed by it will find out what it is and go over my head to get their hands on it. The military have their moles, even here. This will give fresh impetus to the whole debate of why there needs to be an international military presence in this country at all. And when the men in suits next put their heads together to talk about funding, this may be the wild card to take a trick for science rather than institutionalized paranoia."

"I didn't do this as a sucker punch in the UN's internal street fighting," Gaby said. "I did it because it was wrong, and people should see and know it." She was so wide from the truth she could not believe she had just said what she did.

"A principled journalist," Shepard said, not believing her

either. Gaby wished she had not lied to him. She wanted to be Ms. Valiant-for-Truth to him. She also wished he had not told her the dirty things about UNECTA. She wanted him to be a rescuing angel, without ulterior motivations. "Could you give me SkyNet's teleport number?"

She wrote it on a yellow sticky notelet. Shepard turned again to his computer, called up a screenful of icons. The processor accepted the disc and released it a few seconds later. It was sent. It was safe. But it was raw: the tale needed to be well told.

"Shepard, is there anywhere in this place I could borrow a camcorder and a couple of discs for a few hours? I need to get a final report done."

"I think that could be arranged."

Do this, and she might be more than safe. She might be able to win one. But one more thing needed doing first.

"You don't know if anyone here is a Manchester United supporter, and if so, whether they have any gear? I can't make the most important face-to-camera of my career in a sweatshirt with A. C. Milan on the front."

22

Gaby's videodiary: supplemental.
July 26 2008

Not only did Shepard find me a camcorder, he's let me borrow it for the duration of my visit. Tembo and Faraway have gone back on a shuttle flight to sweet-talk T.P. with the report. I'm staying—officially—until William gets out of decontam. Unofficially, because Dr. M. Shepard, Station Director, thought I might like a look at the cutting edge of Chaga research. He's assigned me an empty cabin on Tractor Two, Level Two: there's always someone off-base on R&R or at a conference. At least this woman has something approaching a makeup kit. Borrowing cosmetics is like a starving man stealing food: it's not a sin, it's survival.

I like it. This is a good place. Ironic: it's the nearest inhabited place to the Chaga, but it feels the farthest. I can see terminum from my porthole, but it doesn't feel inevitable the way it does in Nairobi, or immediately threatening, as it did in

Merueshi. It's because this mobile community is one place on Earth the Chaga is not drawing any closer to.

Tsavo West. It's like a New Age pirate ship: not for having a porthole in my cabin, or being asail upon a sea of grass, rigged with gantries and radio masts and satellite-dish crow's nests, or that Tsavo West is aggresively self-contained: the processing plant over on Tractor Three recycles every drop of water, dry sewage waste is processed to the rooftop gardens where apparently they grow killer gene-engineered hemp. It's the people. They have a joyous single-mindedness, like surfing communities; a deeply engraved subtext that informs everything they do. I can understand why the military hates them. There is no formal structure, no imposed discipline, no uniforms—there is no need. Discipline, community, efficiency come from within, from this credo.

So, me hearties, run out the Jolly Roger, set sail for the Chaga, and be thee the governor of Panama's lovely red-haired daughter, ah-har-har-har?

For all the hippy chic, Shepard's got a pretty tight setup. Tractor Two is mostly biochemistry and molecular engineering labs and the equipment is state-of-the-art. A guy with beads woven into his beard showed me the remote handling facility. Custom built. Nothing like it anywhere else. The virtual reality manipulators can take Chaga-stuff apart down to the component molecules and let the operators walk through the atoms. No wonder they're so manic about contamination. The knowledge they have backed up, but they'd never be able to replace the equipment.

Speaking of decontamination, they still won't let me talk to William. The closest I can get to him is a woman's face on the other side of a thick glass panel in a steel door, and she says they are awaiting the results of further tests on the poor kid's viral symptoms. All that stainless steel and blinding white: it's like a Douglas Trumbull movie in there. Tractor One, which is the main ingress/egress port to Tsavo West, is designed to blow free in case of a major incident while the rest sprints away at its top speed of five miles per hour. Tractor One is virtually a city within a city. Up on the other side of the level from the place where they kept me, there is a facility for Away Teams; the ones who actually go into the Chaga and bring samples back. They're totally isolated, like divers on oil-rigs who live in decompression tanks for months on end. I suppose they make their own entertainment, like Oksana on those long, cold Siberian winter nights. One night was enough for me. The thing that impressed me most about Tractor One—and this says a lot about my mind—is that it's the first tee on Tsavo West's one-hole golf course. You drive from the landing grid over to the sundeck on Tractor Two and then it's a five or seven iron to the AstroTurf green on the service platform three-quarters the way up the side of Tractor Three. If you hit it into the Chaga, it's out-of-bounds, but you have to buy everyone a drink. I suppose golf balls in the Chaga is no stranger than golf balls on the moon, though my heart agrees with Mark Twain: golf is a good walk spoiled. Except at Tsavo West it's a good abseil spoiled. Which they do as well, after climb racing each other up the sides of Tractor Two. You can watch them from the rooftop hot tubs. Presumably while toking a jot or two of homegrown weed.

The good ship Tsavo, and all who sail upon her. The ironic thing is that her Captain, the good Dr. Shepard, seems quaintly out of place in all this. All around him things are doing, becoming, while he simply is. That's all. He is. Separate, yet without him, none of this would be. The still center from which all energy emanates.

He's dinnering me tonight; tomorrow I am promised a treat. Something unforgettable. Please, Shepard! I'm too old for all that not being able to sleep at night and finding my food doesn't taste right and I'm not hungry anyway and my mind wandering to visions of his face and discovering whole irreplaceable chunks of my day have vanished. I don't want to let myself fall in love again, I've outgrown that, really, God, I don't want to write him love letters and knit him sweaters and all that stuff in songs because it makes you feel like for a few moments in your whole life you are the most alive thing on this little blue planet.

Oh God. He's here. Already?

23

When she saw the treat in the morning, Gaby McAslan said, ‘‘No way, Shepard. You are not getting me up in that thing. Never.’’

The big two-seater was parked off the main strip in front of the portable cabin that was Tsavo West’s air-traffic control center. The microlyte was a delicate, beautiful insect of spars and wires, spreading its iridescent solar wing to soak in the savannah sun.

‘‘You deserve to see the Chaga as it ought to be seen,’’ Shepard said. ‘‘With the eyes of God.’’ He jumped into the rear seat and fastened the helmet. ‘‘Once-only offer, never to be repeated.’’

‘‘All right, all right,’’ Gaby shouted. Better death than disgrace before Shepard. ‘‘I’m coming.’’

The propeller became a silver blur behind Shepard as Gaby wiggled into the cockpit, fitted safety harness and helmet.

‘‘How long have you been flying?’’ she asked as the microlyte rolled onto the main strip.

‘‘Since yesterday,’’ Shepard said. The engine hum became an irate hornet drone. ‘‘Old joke. I’ve had my license two years. Honest. You’re safe with me.’’

Yes, but not too safe, Gaby thought.

The little aircraft bounced over the rough airstrip and quite unexpectedly was airborne.

‘‘Oh shit,’’ Gaby moaned as she saw directly in front of her a few inches of green and black GRP fuselage and a lot of bright morning sky. Shepard took the microlyte up to a hundred feet.

‘‘Elephant!’’ he said in Gaby’s ear-phone. Twelve of them, moving out of heavy scrub: three bulls with their attendant females and calves, dusted with the red earth of the Serengeti plain. The microlyte’s solar-powered engine was so silent their overpass did not even disturb the white ox-peckers from the elephants’ backs.

‘‘Chaga’s the best thing ever happened to them,’’ he said, circling for a better look. ‘‘Poachers won’t come within twenty miles of terminum. Elephant and rhino numbers have been increasing steadily since the Kilimanjaro Event. Our Away Teams have even found family groups as deep as five miles beyond terminum, on the edge of the Great Wall formation. Paul Orzabal up at Ol Tukai started a study of terrestrial species adapting to the Chaga, but it got dismantled along with the rest of the station.''

They passed over Tsavo West. People in the roof gardens waved. Sunlight glittered from the hot tubs. A Tai Chi class was practicing on the Tractor One landing platform.

''What's this about dismantling Ol Tukai?'' Gaby asked.

''They need a station to monitor the Nyandarua Event but the budget won't run to a new base, so they're airlifting what's airliftable and taking the tractor units north by road, going cross-country along the line of the Ngong hills to avoid Nairobi. Tinga Tinga and Moshi are all being relocated to one hundred and twenty degrees of separation. We began course corrections last night.''

The green and black microlyte crossed terminum. Eddies of warm air spun out from the hidden heart of the Chaga buffeted the wing. Shepard took them down. Gaby gripped the cockpit coaming, telling herself she was too enthralled to be terrified. The fractal tessellations of the mosaic cover bubbled into reefs of pseudo-coral and the open white fingers of the hand trees. The Great Wall rose sheer before them.

''Shepard!'' Gaby shrieked as the microlyte bounced on a rising thermal and hopped over the edge of the Great Wall in a single bound. ''You bastard, don't you ever scare me like that again.''

Shepard chuckled in the way that men do to themselves when they have done something they think impresses a woman.

''There's always an updraft along the edge of the Great Wall,'' he said. ''You can rely on it. All kinds of strange and useful vortices above the Chaga.''

''Strange vortices killed Denys Finch-Hatton at Voi,'' Gaby said.

''Voi's notorious for them. Ask any UNECTA pilot.''

They flew on toward Kilimanjaro over a plateau of dark crimson hexagonal tiles the width of the microlyte's solar wing. Gaby glanced over her shoulder, past Shepard smiling behind his pilot's shades. She could not see the comforting, man-made cubes of Tsavo West. She could not see anything of the human world but a horizon of tarnished gold.

The roof of the Great Wall broke up into chaotic terrain of land reefs and pseudo-corals, piled hundreds of feet high on top of each other, spilling like melted ice cream; strawberry pink, chocolate, honeycomb-pistachio-piña-colada. From this they passed abruptly into a zone where the vegetation was translucent and formed a roof of glittering bubbles. Dark shadows hinted at massive formations far below. The line of transition was exact, as if a circle had been inscribed with compasses on the Chaga.

"The Loolturesh Discontinuity," Shepard said. "It's about five miles wide and goes all the way around the mountain."

"What is it?" Gaby asked.

"We don't know. It's on the edge of our Away Teams' range. But it's expanding outward with the rest of the Chaga. Fifty feet every day."

The outer edge of the discontinuity was as sharply defined as its inner. The land on the far side was a many-colored forest canopy; like flying over a Persian carpet, Gaby thought. A very old and moth-eaten carpet, riddled with holes that permitted intriguing glimpses of another carpet canopy beneath. Analogy, she thought. Our languages do not have the names for what these things are, so we are forced to speak of them in terms of what they seem. The unrolling magic carpet was lifted up and torn in many places by conical mounds pushing through from beneath. Gaby thought of the Devil's Tower, or the inselberg rocks of the sub-Kalahari. The scale and suddenness was about right, but these upswellings were dark red, striped with burnt-orange meanderings like dead Martian watercourses. Shepard banked around the nearest mound. Light glittered at the summit: a single crystal protruded from the peeled-back Chaga-flesh. The crystal was perfectly transparent and the size of a unit at Tsavo West.

"They're an emerging feature," Shepard said. "Within the last six months. Some taxonomist at Ol Tukai christened them 'Crystal Monoliths,' and unfortunately the name's stuck. And before you ask, no, we have absolutely no idea what they are or do."

"Shepard."

"Yes?"

"Shepard, don't talk. You don't have to talk. I don't have to know."

Gaby did not want to hear voices speaking names. Names cut this precious thing of hers into pieces and parts and functions and hypotheses. Dismembered by names, the mystery bled out of it.

To the sound of the electric engine and the wind over the wires, they crossed from the land of the Crystal Monoliths into a land of knife-edged ridges standing above the forest roof that meandered crazily, twining around each other like mating snakes until they fused in a knot of arêtes and canyons. On the far side of this escarpment was a zone unlike any they had yet seen. The microlyte flew above a terrain of ribs and spars and buttresses. Grasping at similes, Gaby thought of the intricate girderwork of the new architecture, or again, microscope photographs of the structure of human bones. Even analogy could not describe this Chaga: it was like *this,* but it was also like *this,* with a seasoning of *that* too, but in the end, none of them.

The cells between the spars and piers were filled with bubbles, some an indistinguishable froth, others large enough to have swallowed the microlyte. Their skins strained painfully against the ribwork. Bubbles were white, skeleton was blue. A Wedgwood landscape. They were flying over an enormous Willow Pattern plate.

The thing was one of those that you see only because you are looking for an instant in the right direction. Gaby saw a dirty white bubble down to her right swell and split. The ripped skin wrinkled back and released a puff of dusty vapor like the smoke of mushroom spores in dry autumns. Things moved in the dust that looked like spindly insect-octopi clinging to silver balloons. They chilled her in a way that the alien landscapes unfolding before her had not. These incomprehensible landscapes were their place. They knew no other. Gaby McAslan was the alien here. Then the wind from off the mountain carried them away. Outcrops of straight-boled trees with domed tops appeared in gaps in the lattice where bubbles had burst and seeded. As the microlyte flew on, the stands of trees joined together into the now-familiar chaos-patterned forest canopy. A few minutes' flight ahead, a wall of pseudo-coral lifted above the canopy of domes. Its top was hidden by the raft of clouds that clung to the mountain. They were on the slopes of Kilimanjaro now.

After long silence, Shepard's voice whispering in Gaby's earphones was a shock.

"That's the Citadel. We think it's where your friend Peter Werther was kept."

"And beyond the Citadel?"

"Beyond the Citadel we cannot go. This thing doesn't have the ceiling."

The microlyte banked across the face of the wall of tubes and pipes and fans. I'm glad the microlyte doesn't have the altitude to penetrate those clouds, Gaby thought. They are the Cloud of Unknowing that hides God, who, like the Chaga, is beyond the power of language to describe. I'm glad that the aliens—if they exist in any form we can recognize—remain hidden in their fortress from the cameras of humans.

She remembered an old sci-fi movie from her father's video library. At the climax, the huge luminous starship of the aliens had floated in across the mountain to meet humanity's representatives. It had touched the earth, and opened its doors. In a glow of light, the aliens had come out. And it had killed the movie. Run a spear into the side of the sense of wonder and let out gasoline and diet Coke. There had been wee ones with oval eyes and no noses, like aliens in abduction magazines, that ran around twittering. Then there was a big long spindly one with arms and legs about eight feet long. He had to bend to get under the door. Gaby McAslan had thought that was most pathetic. They negate gravity, cross entire galaxies in city-sized starships filled with light, and they can't design a door that opens wide enough.

Show us miracles and wonders, but not the little man behind the curtain pulling the levers and shouting into the microphone. If they ever penetrate the mystery up there, I hope there is another behind it, Gaby thought. And another beyond that, and beyond that, so that we never dispel the Cloud of Unknowing.

Shepard had set a different course back to Kenya, one that took them close to a ChagaWatch balloon, many miles lost beyond terminum. Shaggy lilac moss had colonized the bag, so that it looked like some imaginary hairy air monster. The ground cable was crusted with growths like paper wasps' nests, though far larger than any wasp Gaby had ever fled from. As Shepard banked the microlyte around the blimp Gaby noticed flickering activity around the hexagonal cell mouths. Whatever they were, they shone with the iridescence of hummingbirds but moved with the mechanical buzzing dart of insects.

"Good to see Ol' Faithful's still with us," Shepard said. "But I don't think she'll last much longer. The cable goes and they drift away into the Chaga."

"How old is it?" The microlyte went around again.

"About three years. We haven't had a picture out of her in fourteen months, though the caesium batteries are still putting out current. Biggest ecological armageddon since the end of the dinosaurs, but mention radioactivity and it's mass pant-pissing among the environmentalists.''

They swooped away from the lost outpost of the human world. Gaby could make out the brown shore of Africa like a line of islands on the horizon of a dark ocean. Shepard opened up the engine and headed for home.

24

She briefed Shepard on last things in the Mahindra jeep out to the landing field. He would let her know when anything happened with William? Yes. He would corroborate her story if her banks and credit card companies got sniffy about replacing her plastic? Yes. He would write a report for her insurance company? Yes, if she thought it would do any good. He would back her up if the shit hit the fan with T.P.? Yes. He was sure UNECTA would swing behind her and not leave her persona non grata with the United Nations?

''I think you can be pretty sure of that,'' he said as the Mahindra hit a rut and bounced all four wheels in the air. ''In fact, I think I could give you my personal guarantee on it. You see—''

''This is going to be an off-the-record, isn't it? The gazelle, mind the fucking gazelle!''

He minded the fucking gazelle.

''Off the record, I may not be at Tsavo West much longer.''

Her heart lurched. It was nothing to do with Shepard's driving.

''UNECTA is reorganizing its research staff. In the shuffling they've found they need a peripatetic executive director. Superman without the blue panty hose, flying hither and yon, troubleshooting for UNECTA wherever there's trouble that needs shot. It's based at Kenyatta Center, but it's essentially a field job. It's what I want, to be in it, not perched up in that glass penthouse with a desk and twenty tons of paper between me and what's out there. It's the sharp edge of Chaga research, boldly going where no one has gone before.''

''When's the selection panel?''

''A week ago. Modesty should preclude, but I'm the only serious contender. Conrad Laurens, the bouncing Belgian, is the only one more highly qualified, and he can count on European Union backing, but there's a lot of anti-Francophone feeling in the General Council at the moment, and at two hundred twenty pounds, he's going to have trouble fitting into the phone box, let alone leaping out in his Captain UNECTA outfit to save the world. So, do you think you could put up with seeing a bit more of me around?"

When the gods want to destroy you, they answer your prayers.

They drove past work teams armed with chain saws, felling the acacias that stood in the path of Tsavo West's juggernaut retreat. The fellers pushed up their plastic visors and waved to the speeding Mahindra. A white Antonov stood on the shaved strip, feeding from a tanker truck.

"Shepard," Gaby moaned in her five-year-old-with-dental-appointment voice. "Don't send me back, I don't want to go, don't make me go."

He went to file her travel authorizations in the flight center. She seemed to be the only passenger.

"Can I see you again?" she asked plaintively at the foot of the tail ramp. "I mean officially, not serendipitously. Like, um, you know, a date?"

Shepard looked momentarily perplexed. He is going to shrug, Gaby thought. I could not bear it if he shrugs. When they shrug, it means they are saying a thing to please you, not because they want to.

"Sure. I'd like to, very much. I'll be in touch." He did not shrug. "At the very least, I owe you that interview I promised back in Kajiado." The wing-root engines powered up, first left, then right. "Don't forget this." He handed her a transparent Ziploc bag containing what the Chaga had left of her possessions. They consisted of a sleeveless denim top without buttons, a Gossard wonderbra, a pair of gold earrings, a silver Claddagh ring, a steel Parker ball-pen, a packet of Camels and a set of car keys. "Or this."

He handed her a second Ziploc plastic bag. The grand purpose of UNECTA, Gaby thought, seems to be to enclose everything in Ziploc plastic bags. This one contained the stained, dog-eared remains of a notebook bound in Liberty print. Gaby lifted the bag gingerly by the corner, suspicious of contamination. Then she realized what she was seeing.

"Oh my God! You found it."

Shepard shrugged.

"I called in a few markers. Turned up while they were clearing out Ol Tukai prior to the move. They found it in a sealed case in the bottom of a filing cabinet that had been put into storage when Barbara Bazyn moved the security division to Kajiado. God knows how long it's been sitting there. It's a mess, but when you consider what it's been through, it's hardly surprising."

Gaby studied the battered diary.

"So, you came back," she whispered. "You kept your promise to T.P."

"What's T.P. got to do with it?"

"He loved her. He helped her go into the Chaga to find Langrishe. He gave her the diary, made her promise to get it back to him whatever happened. Shepard, you knew them, what were they like?"

"Insane."

"T.P. said that too."

"Obsessed. Intense. Too close to each other to be lovers."

"T.P. said no one loved the right way round."

"T.P. was right. But the diary proves nothing."

"Maybe not. But it gives me a weapon. Everywhere I go in this country I walk in her shadow, and I want to know why, and how, and who. And when I've done that, I want to exorcise her ghost so it won't overshadow me any more." Gaby slipped the diary from its bag, weighed it in her hand. "Thank you Shepard. I owe you. And I'll repay you, some day. What you deserve. I promise."

"I'll think of something," Shepard said, shooing her up the loading ramp of the Antonov. "Now get out of here!" He ran to the safety of the Mahindra.

She was fastening her seat belt as the plane turned into its takeoff run. He was waving at the wrong window, as those who wave to airplanes always do. The engine noise rose to a scream. The little jet dipped its nose, shuddered down the dirt strip and threw itself into the air. The tops of the acacias and the control center and the iridescent vees of the microlytes and the tanker truck and the dusty white Mahindra were falling away and now Tsavo West was just a few lost Lego bricks on the huge burning plain and the Chaga a dark disc curving imperceptibly out of sight.

He is like that, she thought. Most of the men she had passed through her life had been pieces of artifice. Shepard was landscape. He went out into the things around him. He curved imperceptibly out of sight. He was not a product of himself, a man become his own image. He blended into his background, became part of it, drew strength from red earth and heat and empty spaces.

The Antonov leveled off. Gaby lit a cigarette and looked out of the window. She loved to look out of airplane windows. Flying never ceased to astound her. Today a miracle happened. A sign. The clouds around the mountain moved, and grew thin, and broke, and dissolved away, and there, shining in the afternoon sun, great, high and unbelievably white in the sun, and everything that Hemingway had said, but so much more, were the snows of Kilimanjaro.

Then the Antonov banked and she could see them no more. Gaby pulled the Ziploc bag containing the diary out from under her seat and opened it. From the second plastic bag she took her packet of Camels, lit one and settled back to read.

The Liberty print was stained and blotched, the binding boards black with mold. The glue had dissolved, the book was held together by its stitching. It looked like the log of a voyage to hell.

Niamh O'Hanlon, Gaby deciphered from the fly sheet. No wonder she had called herself by another name.

To every book its inscription. I have written my name in black ink inside the cloth cover but the syllables are harsh and clashing in this land of whispered sibilants and strong consonants. How much better the name Langrishe gave me: Moon; generous, looping consonants, vowels like two eyes, two souls looking out of the paper. One half of T.P.'s final gift to me: the journal, cloth-bound and intimate in Liberty print. I treasure it, hug it to me, companion and confessor. T.P.'s other gift to me I treated less kindly: black dragonfly wings shredded by the impact, struts snapped like the bones of birds. Already the Chaga is at work on it, converting the organic plastics into dripping stalactites of black slime. It is over an hour since I lost the beat of the helicopter in the under song of the Chaga: my crash landing must have looked sufficiently convincing for it to abandon the hunt. Forgive me, T.P., but you would understand: skimming across the treetops toward terminum with an Italian Mangusta behind me, expecting to be smashed at any second into nothingness by a thermal imaging Stinger missile, one's options are somewhat limited. Sorry about the microlyte, T.P. But I will be good to the diary, I promise.

Gaby resented this woman she did not know for her intimacy with T. P. Costello. There was another set of footprints, another smear of woman-musk on her Kenya. If she found Shepard's name in these dirty pages crammed tight, tight with frenzied black ink, she would feed the fucking thing to a shredder.

I told Shepard I wanted to lay your ghost, Gaby thought, but now I am the unseen shadow, arriving off the night-flight, following you through the streets of Nairobi, meeting with you, T. P. Costello, Mrs. Kivebulaya, Dr. Peter Langrishe at the Irish Ambassador's party. I come with you to Ol Tukai, I fly with you over the Chaga; I watch you come together and fuck in an Arab bed in a banda on the coast, I feel your jealousies and obsessions that take him in search of these mythical Chaga-builders that he loves more than you; and you, in pursuit of him. I am there when you pitch your tent in the ruins of the old Ol Tukai game lodge, I hear with you the voices coming out of the deep Chaga that you imagine to be Langrishe's, calling you.

I am beginning to wonder if my supplies will be sufficient. I had originally provisioned for twenty days. It may take that long just to reach the lower slopes of the mountain. The riotous Chaga-life confounds my senses of time and distance: I cannot judge how far, how fast I have come. I was so certain then; now my stupidity at thinking I can find one man—who, if I am honest with myself, which I rarely am, may not even be alive—in five thousand square miles of, literally, another world, astounds me. The sense of isolation is colossal.

I saw a vervet monkey today, nervous eyes in the shimmering canopy. A webbed sail of ribs, like some remnant of the time of the dinosaurs, grew from its back. I did not take it for a good omen.

Two thirds down the second cigarette, Gaby decided she did not like this woman. Everything was too much with her: her descriptions, her feelings, her opinions, her experiences, her loving. She was like one of those dreadful Irish woman writers you see on late night talk shows who are terrifyingly articulate and think they have invented sex and no one else can possibly have any feeling or passion of true emotion in their lives. She is dark Gaby thought. Dark side of the moon.

The Wa-Chagga may be the last proud people in the New Africa with my dearly beloved leather jacket I must look like a fetish figure from a sword'n'sorcery fantasy.

Gaby frowned and read again the lines at the bottom of the page and the top of the next. A third time, and they still did not make sense.

. . . the last proud people in the New Africa with my dearly beloved leather jacket I must look like a fetish figure . . .

She held the diary up to the reading lamp. There. So close to the spine you would only notice if you were looking. Two pages had been removed. The cut was very clean and straight. A surgical elision. Wide awake, Gaby fanned the pages against the light. Faults in the lie of the leaves indicated where other sections had been cut away. Toward the end there seemed fewer pages left than removed.

The Sibirsk pilot bing-bonged. Weelson, Nairobi in five. Cyrillic No Smoking/Fasten Seat-belts lit up. The Antonov banked sharply. The who-slashed-it of the missing paper would wait. Right now, Gaby McAslan had to worry about what T. P. Costello was going to say to her.

25

T.P. did not say anything when he met her at Wilson airfield. He did not say anything when they got into the SkyNet Landcruiser, or as he drove into Nairobi. He did not say anything as they turned into Tom M'boya Street, or when he pulled in outside the SkyNet offices. It was when he switched off the car and gave the keys to Gaby that he spoke.

"I'm getting out here."

"What do I do?" Gaby asked plaintively.

"What you do," T. P. Costello said, "is you take this thing home, you go to bed, you sleep for eighteen hours and tomorrow when you are fresh and sharp and bright you put on your most professional clothes and you come here and you report to Jake Aarons and you ask him if there are any assignments for SkyNet Satellite News' new East Africa correspondent. And, because you'll need it, you keep the car. What do you do?"

As T.P. spoke she had lowered her head until it touched the edge of the dashboard. Tears stained the thighs of the borrowed jeans.

"You asshole," she whispered. "You fucking diseased asshole. I thought I was out of here."

"You almost were. You know why you are here and not at the check-in desk at Kenyatta being asked if you want smoking or non-smoking? Because it worked. That's the only reason. Because at this very moment sub-rights are in the middle of the biggest bidding war since the Kilimanjaro Event as casters broad and narrow throw dollars and deutsche marks at you. Because at this moment our dear friend Dr. Dan is on his feet in the House demanding an inquiry into the allegations your report raised while the UN sends in its damage limitation boys to, in their words, 'rotate the third Baku company out of active service,' which in our parlance is the first Ilyushin out of here. Because it's trebles and clean consciences all round at the Thorn Tree. You took the risk. It worked. This time. You see, if you ever, ever do anything like that again without clearing with me, I will bounce you back to bonnie Belfast so quick you'll have friction burns on your beautiful ass. What'll you have?"

"Friction burns. On my ass," Gaby said, still not able to look up.

"That's correct," T.P. said, stepping out of the car. "Oh. I almost forgot. There's no such thing as a free lunch. Your friend Dr. Shepard called while you were in flight. I think you should get whatever contacts you have working on this ASAP. Your stool pigeon William. Seems he's been moved from Tsavo West to Kajiado center for further tests. They're holding him in a special isolation section. Unit Twelve."

She had it. She had it all. She had been faithful to her guiding star and it had honored her with more than she had asked of it. It had put her in front of the camera, but it had also given her a glimpse into its hidden heart that few humans had ever seen, and maybe, if she didn't get stupid and try to play it too cool and wreck things, it had given her the man she wanted. The city, the land, surged with possibility. Something tapped on her window. She looked up. Standing on the Landcruiser's running board was a shaven-headed boy of nine or ten, tapping a forefinger on the glass and holding up for her to buy a model of Space Station Unity he had made out of wire coat hangers and sliced up

Heineken cans. Gaby laughed and sobbed simultaneously and remembered that she had forgotten to tell T.P. about the Moon diary.

26

From glory to glory.

T.P. had begun the great Irish football war chant *Olé, Olé Olé Olé* five minutes before the final whistle. The team was still singing as it headed for the showers.

"One nil, one million nil," T.P. said as he collected his winnings from his UNECTA counterpart.

It had been a memorable victory. Gaby looked forward to postmorteming the goal over much beer when the Manga twins finished editing the video. Seventy-fifth minute. Victor Luthu from Accounts lofts it over UNECTA's dreaded Nigerian midfielder, Kojo Laing. It falls at Gaby McAslan's feet and the left wing opens up before her like the gates of heaven. Into the box and the best cross of her *life* over two defenders and Tembo's head is there, rising, to smack it into the back of the net. She jumped onto Faraway, gaudy as a macaw in his woman-impressing goalkeeper's outfit, wrapped him in freckled arms and legs.

"Hey Kenya! I love this man! I used to think he was a wanker, now I think he is Jesus. They throw everything at him, Faraway stops the lot."

"Want to swap shirts, Gaby?" Faraway said, recovering cool.

Oksana Telyanina ran over and hugged them both. She had been seconded on to Team SkyNet. The Siberians had never enough people in the same place to field a team of their own. In her cut-offs over cycle shorts, borrowed boots and tattoos she was an intimidating left back.

"I near peed my pants!" she shouted. Over her shoulder, beside the corner flag, Gaby glimpsed another person.

Shepard.

"You!" she shrieked, throwing herself on him.

"You look like a horse with that long hair and those tight Lycra shorts," he whispered in her ear. "I would dearly love to pull them down right now and bend you over the substitutes' bench."

"Been thinking about me while I was away?"

"Nothing but."

"So what are you doing up here?"

"Whisking you off on a date. You've got a change of clothes with you?"

"Yes, casual and work. I not only look like a horse, I smell like a horse."

"You'll smell worse where I'm taking you."

She stepped back to give him the sideways quizzical look from under her hair she knew no man could resist.

"You always this insistent?"

"Always."

She went to the changing rooms to pick up her bag. Oksana Telyanina was unlacing her boots.

"You, him, yes?" she asked, making a *fiki-fiki* gesture with her left forefinger penetrating circled right thumb and forefinger.

"I haven't even got to kiss him yet," Gaby said, changing her footwear.

"He is very cute. Man like this, many woman want to baboon. You want to keep him, remember: Serbski Jeb." Oksana mimed pulling a knot tight around a compliant limb. Gaby threw her empty water bottle at her, went out and slung her sports bag into the back of the UNECTA Mahindra in which Shepard was waiting. Shepard placed his palm on her thigh and drove off.

"Where are you taking me?" she asked, not recognizing the trend of the streets.

"Like I said, on a date." Shepard kept his hand firmly on her thigh all the way out of Nairobi, through Keekorok and Olorgesaile and the towns to the west.

"This is some date," Gaby said as the metaled road gave way to red earth.

"Something to celebrate," Shepard said.

"You got the job."

He punched a fist into the air.

"Up, up and away with UNECTA-man! Permanent jet lag. Permanent Montezuma's revenge. Can quote by heart any in-flight magazine in the world. I'll have to buy another suit. There's an Indian tailor down by the City Market can make you anything in twenty-four hours. He might even run to all-enclosing blue suits."

"You'd know about that, speed skater."

"Gaby, I can't wait. I cannot wait for them to ask me to go somewhere and solve something. Sometimes you actually do get what you want in this life."

"I know," Gaby said. "Sometimes, karma takes a holiday and everyone gets what they want rather than what they deserve. The new East Africa Correspondent for SkyNet Satellite News greets the new UNECT*Afrique* Peripatetic Executive Director."

They drove on into the huge west.

"We're going to the Mara," Gaby said.

"There're things I want you to see before they're gone forever," Shepard said.

The red earth road became two tire tracks on a green, watered plain speckled with many trees. The great wildebeest migration had come in the shadow of the rains to this land. They were like a brown river, meandering, breaking into tributaries and backwaters and loops so wide and lazy the migration seemed to stagnate into a swamp of grazing individuals. But they could not stop, any more than a river could refuse the gravity that drew it to the sea. The Mahindra pushed onward across the great plain. Gaby made Shepard stop on the top of a long ridge that commanded a wide green valley filled with animals. She took her visioncam from the sports bag and stood up in the back of the Jeep, panning slowly across the panorama.

"It won't catch it," Shepard said.

"I know," Gaby said in her football socks and shiny shorts and green-and-yellow shirt with MCASLAN 9 on the back and the SkyNet globe on the front. "We never think that all the beauty will go too."

"Changed into another kind of beauty," Shepard said.

"A terrible beauty, as Yeats said," Gaby said.

The camp had been made between two acacias near the bank of a seasonal tributary of the Mara River. There were two tents, a canvas shittery, a safari shower made from an oil drum and a nozzle, a fire, a table with two folding chairs and three Kalashnikov-armed game wardens with a battered Nissan Safari.

"We're in the tent on the right," Shepard said.

" 'We're'?" Gaby queried.

"Well, you're welcome to the one on the left if you'd prefer. The guys won't complain. Evening game drive is at five P.M. Dinner after dark. If you need a shower, ask the guys. They're discreet, which means you won't actually catch them looking at you.''

One of the wardens came with them in the Mahindra as game spotter. The other two went in the other direction in the Nissan, ''to shoot dinner,'' Shepard said. He drove the Jeep himself, following the spotter's directions to plunge headlong into seemingly impenetrable bush or down impossibly steep bluffs.

''You love this, don't you?'' Gaby shouted.

''I was born eighty years too late,'' Shepard shouted back. ''I wish I could have lived in the days of the Union Jack and tiffin at the Norfolk and whiskeys at the Mt. Kenya Safari Club where women weren't allowed in. The days of Lord Aberdare and Baron Von Blixen and White Mischief, when there was just the land and the animals moving upon it, and the scattered tribes and their cattle.''

''But you love the Chaga as well.''

''That's the dilemma. I love them both, but one will not let the other survive.''

The sun had set by the time they returned to the camp under the acacia trees. The night was as clear and infinitely deep as only African nights can be. The wardens had killed successfully and set up a table by the campfire. There was white linen, good crystal and Mozart on a boombox CD player.

''You've put a lot of planning into this,'' Gaby said, showered and dressed in her office uniform of jodhpurs, boots and silk, which was as formal as she could be. ''What would you have done if I'd said no?''

''Kidnapped you,'' Shepard said, in the creased linen suit she had seen on him that first day in Kajiado, which was as formal as he could be. He poured wine. The wardens brought antelope steaks. Afterward there was whiskey. Gaby rolled the cut-glass tumbler between her hands and asked, ''Can I do that interview now?''

''Here? Now? For SkyNet?''

''No.'' She looked at him over the rim of the tumbler, which was another man-trick she had taught herself. ''For me. I want to know who you are, Shepard. I want to know teenybop things: what star sign you are, what your favorite color is, what you like to drink.''

''Taurus. Green: the exact shade of your eyes. Three fingers of Wild Turkey with a little ice and a tablespoon of branch water."

"Favorite music."

"You're listening to it."

"If you were an element, what would you be?"

He paused, momentarily taken aback by Gaby's change of tack.

"You mean hydrogen, helium, lithium?"

"More primitive than that. Earth, air, fire, water."

"Earth."

Yes, you are, Gaby McAslan thought, lighting a cigarette from a candle.

"What color are you?"

"I've already told you that."

"You've told me your favorite color. I'm asking you what color you think you are yourself."

He pondered a moment beneath the slow-turning stars.

"A kind of faded terra-cotta; the exact shade my mother's herb pots used to turn after two summers on the sunny side of the porch."

Yes, you are telling me the truth, thought Gaby McAslan.

"What season are you?"

"This is a funny way to conduct an interview."

"It's the only way to conduct an interview if you want to find anything valuable."

He was silent for the space of three sips of whiskey.

"Fall," he said. "Fall in Nebraska, which is all silver and gold; silver of frost, gold of Halloween pumpkins in backyards and yellow tomatoes on the vine and bare fields of corn stubble and a yellow edge to the horizon under the purple snow clouds that come down from the Dakotas. A fall that is the cold of evenings when you make a fire and your whiskey catches the light and the heat of it, that is just like the line in the song about when the wind comes whistlin' down the plain, and gets into the eaves and you hear the roof shingles rattle, but you're in no hurry to worry about them, not just yet."

My God, Gaby thought, I am about to have sex with a Frank Capra movie. No, that is unfair. You would speak with as much love of the Watchhouse and the Point in its different seasons and moods.

"Wood, fabric, pottery or metal?"

"Pottery."

"Baroque, Classical, Romantic, Modern?"

"Classical. You're not taking this down."

"I am taking this down, where it matters. Circle, square, triangle?"

"A sort of slightly rounded square. Or a slightly squared circle."

"Plains, mountains, forests or islands?"

"Plains. With the aforementioned wind whistlin' down them. And the corn as high as an elephant's eye."

"What kind of car are you?"

"Something pretty much like I drive already. Maybe one of those old British Land Rovers that you could drive forever over any kind of surface in any conditions and it would always forgive you. But with the tail fins, fenders and whitewalls off one of those 1950s cars you used to see in old rock-and-roll movies that looked about the size of Rhode Island. If that makes sense."

Perfect sense. You are getting it now, Shepard. I knew you would. And I am getting you.

"What kind of animal are you?"

He sighed.

"Something big, and wise, that can see a long way across the plain, like a giraffe, but not silly like a giraffe. Not a herd creature. I've never been a team player."

I know that, speed skater.

"But not solitary, like a leopard is solitary. A lion, that's what I am."

"Which sense are you?"

He put down his glass. She had him now. The last question would make it irrevocable. Expectation was a warm whiskey glow inside her.

"Touch," he said, and got up from his folding chair and took her hand very gently and led her to the tent on the right.

"Are we safe?" Gaby asked.

"The wardens keep watch," Shepard said, misunderstanding.

"I warn you, I make horrible loud cat noises."

"Everything makes horrible loud cat noises out here."

"All right, then," she said, and pulled him down on top of her on the groundsheet.

The second time she told him there was something special

she wanted to try. He grinned in the lazy, contented hunting-cat way of sated men who still have an appetite for more. In the tent, there was plenty of rope. Gaby offered a prayer to the totemic spirits of Oksana Telyanina as she quickly tied Shepard to the fly-sheet pegs. He laughed a lot despite the hardness of the ground.

"You won't be doing that in a minute, laddie," Gaby said, swinging herself on top of him and pushing her ginger pubes against his chin. Ten minutes later he was making the horrible loud cat noises. Ten minutes after that he was begging. Ten minutes after that he was in an altered state of consciousness, eyes fixed on the ridgepole, every muscle taut as piano wire. Ten minutes after that Gaby had mercy and let him come. Exhausted, elated, aching; she kissed him on the nipples and curled up beside him, nestling into the warmth and the hardness and smell and comfortable man-ness of him. Nestled there, she fell asleep. She woke in the predawn dark, remembering with horror that Shepard was still tied up.

He was too stiff and sore to take the Mahindra out on the dawn safari. The warden who drove smiled a lot. So did his colleagues as they served the steak-and-champagne breakfast.

Before dinner that evening, Shepard took Gaby out in the Mahindra.

"Something special I want you to see," he said.

The cool had driven the haze and dust back into the earth and in the space between the day and the things that hunt by night, the land unfolded around Gaby. Shepard steered the Mahindra along a wildebeest track older than any of the ways of humans. The migration had been following it for a hundred thousand years. Headlights caught eyes out in the gloaming; stragglers on the primeval way west to the greening plains of the Mara. Gaby had never seen a sun so huge, resting on the edge of the world. Shepard stopped the car in the middle of the great plain.

"Watch and wait," he said.

The twilight deepened into indigo. Summer stars appeared over the plains of Africa in the dark east.

"Did you ever go out at night and look up at the stars and see them very small and close, little dots of light?" Gaby whispered. "And then your perceptions turned inside out and you realized that they were unimaginably huge and distant and it was you who were very small and insignificant, and knowing that was like a sacred thing, that you were tiny, but alive, and they might be huge and magnificent, but they were dead, and because of that you were infinitely greater and more important than they could ever be?''

''Where I come from the sky is like the land; big, exhilarating, endless,'' Shepard said softly. ''In winter, on nights when the wind comes down from Canada that is so cold and dry it freezes the breath in your lungs, the constellations glitter like ice. On nights like that, you can fall into the sky, and keep falling forever between all those ice-cold, frozen stars.''

''That's what I can't forgive the BDO for,'' Gaby said. ''It takes the stars away from us. They aren't distant and numinous, but close, living, intelligent. I don't like the idea of someone else being in our sky, making us small.''

''See over there?'' Shepard pointed. ''Just to the left of Antares. About two degrees.''

''Ophiuchus?''

''You know your way around the sky. That's where they come from. Came down the UNECTA hotline yesterday morning. The gas clouds in Rho Ophiuchi, out on the edge of the Scorpius loop. Since we floated the hypothesis that the Chaga-makers may have evolved in space the orbital telescopes have been analyzing the spectra of deep-space molecular clouds. All the raw material for life is out there; hydrocarbons, amino acids, RNA. It was from deep-space clouds that the first buckyballs were deduced. We've been getting spectra of complex fullerenes from Rho Ophiuchi that are as near as damnit the same as *Tolkien* observed at Iapetus. Only these are about eight hundred light years in toward the center of the galaxy. If we allow the Chaga-makers a generous one-percent light-speed expansion rate, we're looking through our telescopes at a civilization at least one hundred thousand years old, and probably a lot older.''

''Peter Werther told me that this is not the first time we've been in contact with them,'' Gaby said. ''First contact was at the very dawn of humanity, out on these plains about three, four million years ago.''

''They could be all through the Sagittarius arm in that time. God knows how long they have been traveling, how old they are, where they originate from.''

A line of deep red clung to the western horizon under a front of purple cloud. The silence was immense.

''Shepard,'' Gaby whispered. ''You're scaring me.''

"I'm scaring myself," Shepard said. "You're right. The stars aren't ours anymore. They never were. Something got there before us, before we even existed."

"I suppose we could hold hands and whistle *Thus Spake Zarathustra*?" Gaby suggested.

She saw Shepard's face crease to laugh, then he suddenly pressed a forefinger to her lips.

"Shh. They're here. Look."

They came out of the darkness beneath the shade trees. The big lioness came first, head held high, nostrils flared, mouth open, tasting the night. Then came two younger females, moving wide to cover the queen's flanks. Behind them came the cubs. There were nine of them in two litters; some were noticeably larger and more capable than others. They followed the chief lioness in a loose Indian file, foraging two or three steps out of line to sniff a thornbush or wildebeest turd. An old female with sagging jowls and loins brought up the rear.

The pride passed within ten feet of the front of the Mahindra. One of the cubs sat down, stuck its rear leg in the air and licked its crotch. The matriarch looked at the glowing horizon and the 4X4 with its spellbound passengers and moved on. The cubs followed. The lions vanished into the great darkness.

"The Rangers have been watching them," Shepard said. "They told me where to find them. They've lost two, one to hyenas, one that got pushed off the teat. But I think they'll make it now."

"Shepard," Gaby McAslan said. "Thank you. That was a real privilege."

"Wasn't it?" Shepard said. He started the car and drove back along the ancient wildebeest track beneath the huge bright stars of the southern hemisphere.

"Tell me about your children," Gaby asked. "Your cubs."

Their names were Fraser and Aaron. Fraser was thirteen, Aaron just turned eleven. Fraser was the one graced with charisma. The world would always come to his fingertips without him ever having to reach out to it. Aaron would have to work hard for everything he wanted, but in spite of that, or maybe because of it, Aaron was the one whose name the world would know. Fraser would make hearts, break hearts and be happy. Aaron's happiness would always be bought, and so more highly valued. Gaby experienced a stab of jealousy of these others who had a deeper and prior demand on Shepard, from a life and relationship she could neither share nor erase. Seeing her jealousy, for Gaby was not as clever with her feelings as she thought, Shepard said that the boys had been the only good thing to have come out of his marriage.

"We marry young," he said, "the people of the plains states. The winter people. Something deep in the psyche, a need for someone to shelter you from the big sky, a pair of nice warm feet to share your bed. She met me at a skate meet. I was in my soph year at Iowa State, majoring in biochemistry with a minor in biophysics. And speed skating. She had sass: she came right up to me, congratulated me on my win and said I had the cutest thighs she'd ever seen. Also, I had the most visible underwear line she'd ever seen. Also, she'd been a fetishist for guys in tights ever since Christopher Reeve made her believe a man really could fly.

"We got married next spring. It was too soon, we were too young. But how do you know that when you're only twenty? You're not even sure what you are, let alone what you want. But the world forces us to make all the big decisions before we have the wisdom to make them right. Education, career, relationships. What you are to do with the rest of your life. Half your life's big decisions are made before they allow you to do as trivial a thing as vote. You can raise a family, but they won't allow you to buy a drink in a bar.

"We got married in the hot-flush, wet-dream, can't-eat, tear-each-other's-clothes-off stage of love. We never imagined it would change; when it did, we thought it was dying. That's when we decided to have Fraser. Rather, that's when Carling decided to have Fraser. No, that's mean. We did a good thing for a bad reason, and of course it didn't work out the way we'd planned, so we screwed up tighter inside ourselves, scared that all that was holding us together was the kid. We had just moved to UCSB to begin my Ph.D. when Aaron was born. Carling had gotten bored with playing great earth muffin by then and found a job in an architect's office. All the money went straight into child care (but it was better than barf and *Sesame Street*). I had to work nights to get the hardware time, Carling was Ms. Nine-to-Five, so I ended up running all over town in this hulk of a yellow Volvo we called the Pig, getting groceries, picking up from school, dropping off at day care and trying to sleep eat read vacuum and relax in between. Which, I suppose, is great for father-son bonding but not a marriage. Certainly not a marriage. Four hours of overlap leaves a lot of leeway for infidelity. I'm getting mean again. And bitter.''

''She cheated on you?'' A hail of meteorites kindled away to nothing in the sky above the Mara plain. You could see forever in that sky, Gaby thought. Outward and inward. And backward, on these nights that were so still and warm and close you could hear the continent breathing.

''With her boss in the architecture firm. All the clichés. That's what rankled most. It was all the clichés. You imagine that your life partner, your lover, the mother of your children should be able to surprise you even in that. Not her. All the clichés. She kept the kids. She couldn't keep the man, though. I said I wouldn't get mean and bitter, but this still gives great and deeply petty pleasure. All the time she was cheating on me with him, he was cheating on her with a woman he met in a leather club. All the time Carling was standing in front of the judge saying how this man had the lifestyle that would mean the best possible future for her children, he was swinging from Miss Rawhide's ceiling by his balls. I laughed to bust a gut when I heard that.''

''Do you miss the boys?''

''I miss them like I would miss my right arm. When they aren't here, I feel like I'm only partially complete. They come out twice a year, stay for a week at Easter, longer in late summer.''

''Is this a warning?''

''I suppose it is. Not so much about when they're here as when they go.''

''You're presuming a lot about this relationship.''

''When you get to be a divorced forty-something twelve thousand miles from your kids, you learn not to play at relationships. It's a quantum affair. On or off. Everything or nothing. No games, Gaby.''

''I don't play games, Shepard.''

''You do.''

''Not with you.''

''Games players can't stop.''

''Shall we end it here then?'' Gaby asked, temper flaring like a sudden consuming savannah fire.

''That's what I mean Gaby. Games. What do you want?''

''I want you Shepard.''

''I want you too. I want this red-haired green-eyed Celtic fury with her incomprehensible and barbarous accent and her freckled skin that is like a little girl's and her body that is like the wisest, most sinful whore in hell's and her too-quick temper and her pride and her ambition and her recklessness and her childishness and her selfishness and her generosity and her bravery and her exuberance.''

''You men talk the biggest load of oul' shite.''

''But it's guaranteed fresh shite every day.''

The table was laid for dinner back at the camp. The rangers stood by. Gaby ducked into the tent and emerged with a bundle of fabric.

''Present for you. Quid pro quo. Old football tradition; swapping shirts.'' Shepard unfolded the bundle, frowned a moment at the print of the masturbating nun on the front and her confession, now washed almost illegible. He smiled, stood up, unbuttoned his shirt and removed it. Before he could slip on the T-shirt Gaby placed a hand on his chest and drew him, as if it were magnetized, into the tent on the right.

They did not do the Serbian thing that night either, but what they did do was so very good and very long that they almost forgot about the things behind them in the cold past, and the long fingers with which they touched their lives.

27

It cost NASA more to buy off the satellite company whose launch window it appropriated than to charter the HORUS orbiter to lift the propulsion unit to Unity. The hope was to recoup it all and more when the *Gaia* probe went into orbit around the BDO and pictures started to come in. The news services had placed bids already. So the project directors told the financial managers. None of them had ever thought that first contact would be mediated by accountants.

This was the mission plan. The maneuvering unit would rendezvous with *Gaia* out in the marches of Jupiter, hard-dock and fire its engines to swing the probe on to a path that would take it into polar orbit around the Big Dumb Object. The disc's spin would bring every part of its surface under the scrutiny of *Gaia*'s sensors.

Eight hours before launch from Unity a fleet of unmanned USAF single-stage-to-orbit freighters lifted from Edwards Air

Force Base, together with a specialist team in a military shuttle. Revisions had been made to the payload calculations. Extra reaction mass tanks were needed, of a new and more efficient design. None of the multinational crew of Unity believed this as they watched the delta-vee of the USAF shuttle dock with the Interceptor in its assembly orbit, turn its black refractory belly to the stars and disgorge space workers in exo-skeletons and spider-walking Canada arms from its cargo bay. New and more efficient designs; with stars and bars on their sides, that required military specialists to fit?

The USAF shuttle de-orbited with seconds to spare. Safe distancing thrusters burned blue. The *Gaia* Interceptor moved into launch orbit. At fifty miles the main engine lit. The hydrogen flame vanished into the big night. As the interceptor crossed the orbit of Mars it jettisoned the last-minute military fuel tanks and flipped into deceleration mode. This piece of information, alone of all others relating to the flight of the Interceptor, passed through a little known NASA hierarchy directly on to the desk of the President of the United States.

28

Miriam Sondhai told Gaby McAslan that she had a visitor when she returned elemental and glowing to the old missionary house. She was most surprised to find T. P. Costello sitting on the creaking leather sofa, drinking Miriam Sondhai's *chai.* She had been crazily expecting it to be her sister Reb, come out to Kenya on the same whim that carried her through the rest of her life, to see what Gaby had done with the star tapestry.

Gaby's ready bag was on the coffee table.

"Well, now you've finished banging the balls off UNECTA's shiny new peripatetic executive director, maybe SkyNet's new East Africa correspondent wouldn't mind earning her grossly inflated salary," T.P. said.

"You've been through my things," Gaby growled. The bag was badly packed with impractical underwear and few cosmetics. "You've been fondling my panties, T. P. Costello. Probably sniffing them."

"Needs must. I've got a job for you."

"Send Jake. He's senior East African correspondent."

"Jake's sick."

"You don't get sick in this job."

"He's sick," T.P. answered. His face was as fixed and unreadable as a Kabuki mask. "You have ten minutes to get that football gear off, stop yourself smelling like a trapper's jockstrap and look like a professional news woman. Ten minutes, then I'm dragging you as you are to Kenyatta. You've a flight to catch. Your passport's in there too, don't worry. And a tube of factor eight. You're going to need it in the Maldives."

"The Maldives?"

"Foa Mulaku's bubbled up."

"You can tell a man packed this bag," Gaby said, rummaging in it for shower things. "No tampons."

29

Beyond the reef, the bottom fell away and the water changed from the pale green of inshore, where you could see the shadows of the little coral fish cast on the silt, to an ultramarine blue of such transparency that you could look over the rail and imagine the blue-on-blue of the deep water hunters, endlessly seeking, a thousand feet down. The SeaCat passed through the gap in the reef and throttled up. The island dwindled to an edge of coral sand and green palms, then to a line of darkness on the sea, then was lost beneath the horizon. The big catamaran had once ferried holiday makers between the islands of the Seychelles, but UNECTA had chartered it to service its Indian Ocean bases. Now it ferried the world's media. There were three hundred reporters with their knightly entourages on the big catamaran this bright August morning. The bar had never done such good business.

Team SkyNet was on the rear sun-deck, preparing for a satellite link-up with London.

Faraway miked Gaby up, Tembo tried camera angles: "not in direct sunlight, your eyes go dark and viewers will not trust you if they cannot see your eyes." Gaby looked at the birds flocking and diving above the churned wakes. The sea is one thing, she thought. Unitary. Whole. It would be morning over that part of the sea that broke around the Point. Dad would be back from his morning walk, Reb would have the espresso maker bubbling on the Aga. The early satellite news would be on as background to their coffee and Marks and Spencer's brioche. Paddy would be underneath the table thumping his tail to every word that ended in a "y" sound. Suddenly, shockingly, Gaby would burst from the screen in their morning, live with her news of incredible things in exotic locations. It is one thing, the sea, and it is a big thing. Bigger than anything you can bring to it. No human care can match its transcendent unity. Why fear, then, when all things come out of and return to the sea?

"I am patching you in now, Gaby," Faraway said. She nodded. The voice of Jonathan Cusack, *The World This Morning*'s anchorman, was whispering in her ear: "And now we have on the satellite link our new East Africa correspondent, Gaby McAslan."

East Africa correspondent, Gaby McAslan. *Me!* Help me!

Tembo gave her a mark. She brushed hair away from her face. The transmit light went on and Jonathan Cusack said, "So, Gaby, just what is going on out there in the Indian Ocean?"

For a second Gaby thought she was going to throw up live on prime-time.

"Well, Jonathan, I'm on the press boat to East Seven Five, UNECTA's permanent floating observation platform at the Foa Mulaku Object. We should arrive in just over an hour, about one-thirty our time."

"So what will be happening when you get there?" Jonathan Cusack asked nine thousand miles away. Gaby pushed her hair from her face again. Faraway grimaced and made a throat-cutting gesture with his thumb.

"To fill in a little background: Foa Mulaku, or to give it its proper name, the Maldive Ridge Object, was the fourth biological package. It came to rest about six thousand feet down in the waters of the Equatorial Channel. By the time UNECTA located the site, the package had colonized a nine-mile radius of seabed eighty miles to the northeast of the island of Gan. What makes the underwater Chaga-forms so very different from the terrestrial manifestations is that once they've established themselves, they grow upward rather than outward. Foa Mulaku has taken scientists by surprise by coming to its final emergence state much more quickly than predicted—they were originally talking about mid-November, now it's certain that it will come out of the sea sometime in the next few hours."

"Can you give us some idea of what we will be seeing?"

Jonathan Cusack asked. I used to fancy him, Gaby thought. He was my number-one media fantasy figure.

"UNECTA has built a fairly detailed sonar model: Foa Mulaku is a chopped-off cone with its base on the seafloor and its uppermost sections within twenty feet of the surface. The cone is made up of a number of distinct levels piled on top of each other—imagine a giant wedding cake. Over the past month Foa Mulaku has increased its growth rate to forty feet per day, we expect the upper structures to break the surface in the next five hours."

"We'll be going back to the Maldives live as the situation develops, for the meantime, Gaby McAslan, thank you."

She held the smile until Tembo marked her out and the transmission light was extinguished. There was applause and encouraging shouts from the reporters who had ambled out of the bar to watch the baptism of fire. Paul Mulrooney, CNN's Man in Africa, brought her something with rum and ice cubes in it.

"Pissed my pants first live link I did," he said. "Looked straight into the camera and talked about a cholera epidemic in a Rwandan refugee camp with it running down my leg and over my shoes. Thank God they only see you from the waist up."

The course display monitors placed around the passenger areas showed that the SeaCat had passed the halfway point and the journalists began to move to the foredeck for their first glimpse of East Seven Five's gantries. By sea as on land, UNECTA had been forced to buy creatively. A few well-placed bribes had beaten the Indonesian breaking yard's offer on the decommissioned Royal Dutch Shell exploration rig. The submersibles and remote equipment had been beachcombed from the hundred-mile wrecking yard that was the east coast of Scotland after North Sea Oil. Half of East Seven Five's crew were redundant Aberdonian offshore men who mingled uncomfortably in the accommodation blocks with the laid-back researchers from Woods Hole Oceanographic Institution.

As the SeaCat moved in to East Seven Five around a Beriev seaplane refueling from a tanker pontoon, inflatable Gemini craft burst from between the legs of the rig and furiously circled the catamaran.

"Greenpeace protesters," Paul Mulrooney said. "I don't know what they're blaming UNECTA for, they didn't invent the thing." As the rubber boats made a final circle of the catamaran and dashed toward an ancient Greek ferry with a rainbow painted on its bow that was moored a mile west, he shouted, "Go and sail your stupid little boats around Iapetus, or the Rho Ophiuchi gas cloud, if you want someone to protest at."

R. M. Srivapanda, East Seven Five's director, was waiting on the pontoon to receive his guests. He was a dark, patient Tamil wearing one of those round-collared suits that look so well on Indians and so poorly on any other race. The left sleeve was tucked into a pocket: Gaby recalled from T.P.'s rushed airport briefing that he had lost his lower left arm in a close encounter with a boat propeller while diving off Sri Lanka. All he needed was a white Persian cradled in his one good arm and twenty women in red catsuits with machine guns to be a criminal mastermind from a James Bond movie, hell-bent on world domination from his Indian Ocean base. James Bond was waiting up on Level One, in the melee of tripods, satellite dishes and correspondents pouring out of the elevator cages in search of the best locations. He had the smug expression a man would wear if he had license to go anywhere and do anything in the name of UNECTA.

"You!" Gaby yelled.

"Me!" Shepard agreed. He came to her through the tide of news people. Faraway shouted. He found a place with an unparalleled view of the Maldive Ridge Object: a crow's-nest on East Seven Five's main communications mast. Tembo maneuvered himself up, connected up his camera and shot background footage. As Faraway let a hand down to pull Gaby up, Shepard said, quickly and quietly, "Move in with me. I want to sleep with you, wake up with you, breakfast with you, perform acts of personal hygiene with you."

"Jesus, Shepard, you pick your moments," Gaby said as she scrambled up the mast.

"Is that an answer?" Shepard shouted up. But Gaby was already contemplating the thing in the sea. It required a trick of looking to see it, like the pictures that had been fashionable when Gaby had been in her early teens that looked like so much multicolored spaghetti, but if you looked past them, they were supposed to magically resolve into 3-D leaping dolphins or dinosaurs. The trick here was like that, of looking not at the surface but beneath the lap and shiver of the water so that the patterns of light and dark and color joined together and became a picture.

It is not much like a wedding cake, Gaby thought. It is not much like anything other than what it is, what its makers have designed it to be. If it has makers, if those round white brainlike things just beneath the surface are not natural forms, if those deep fissures and meandering blue ridges are not just accidents of evolution, if those spines down there are not something that once had a meaning and function on some world among the gas veils of Rho Ophiuchi, but here, eight hundred light years away, is an empty remnant.

"The dragon in the sea," Tembo said reverently. "It is written in the book of Ezekiel."

It is written in pages far older than those, Gaby thought. It is written in the racial memory, in the same genes that enable babies to swim before they learn the fear of water. The Kraken. The Midgard serpent. The sea gods and mermaids and treacherous she-spirits of the ocean. The thing that lives in the sea.

The public address system whined feedback. A Scottish accent announced seat allocations in the recreation room on Level Three in five minutes. Gaby fought for a place in the line for the woman sitting at a table with a PDU and a box of badges issuing seats on the spotter helicopters. She came to the table and gave the names of her team members to the helicopter woman.

"She won't be needing a seat," a voice said in her ear, and before Gaby could protest that it was *seat* or *job,* Shepard had drawn her aside to a quiet place among the pushed-together pool tables. Journalists awaiting their turn stared.

"I'm probably going to regret this," Shepard said. "Grab your team, come with me."

30

"There is no way I am ever going to fit into this." Gaby McAslan held up the red-and-silver suit with the big black numbers front and back.

"It stretches," Shepard said. He had already pulled his over his swimwear. He ran his thumb up the seals.

"It smells," Gaby said. "Who was the last person inside this?"

"It smells of you. It's made from synthetic skin, the same stuff they graft onto burn victims, with a few chemical tricks we've learned from the Chaga and a color scheme so the helicopters can find you if you fall overboard. The fullerene machines have never touched human flesh, so the perfect material for an isolation suit is skin. Or would you rather another night in decontam?''

''Lois Lane is not the one who puts on the tights in the phone booth,'' Gaby complained as she put the thing on. It did stretch. It was quite comfortable. She would have welcomed a gusset, but presumably men had designed the suits and never gave thought to Visible Sanitary Towel Lines, let alone having the fanny cut off you. They checked suit numbers with the out-lock controller and went down to the jetty.

''Hey! Nineteen!'' Faraway shouted, reading the number on Gaby's chest. He made a yelping noise like a hunting dog in heat.

Tembo was busy in the third boat with a Chaga-protected camera with UNECT*Asie*'s horns-and-yin-yang logo on the side. Faraway wired Gaby as she took her seat.

''We are transmitting back to a satellite link on the rig and they will relay it to London.'' He fitted the plug into her ear and eased her hair back under the protective hood. His touch was very gentle. The other boats had already cast off. In the first was UNECTA's own recording team. In the second was the landing party. Two last crew jumped into the third boat. They frowned at the SkyNet team. Shepard looked at them as if to challenge their right to query him and waved for the off. The helmsman pushed the throttle up. The little surf boat stood up in the water and skidded out from the shadows under East Seven Five into the light.

The sea was dazzling. The speed was brilliant. The sky was full of clucking helicopters. Gaby seized a rail and stood up. She pushed back her hood and let her hair blow out behind her so the faces behind the helicopter windows would see it and know who was down there in Boat Three. Thank you, Shepard. Thank you, God. Thank you, aliens swimming in the molecular clouds of Rho Ophiuchi. Thank you, T. P. Costello, for trusting me not to fuck it up. Thank you, life.

Tembo was videoing the two lead boats. Faraway clambered unhappily over the seats and tapped Gaby.

''I have London on the link.''

She nodded and screwed the phone deeper into her ear. Geostationary static burbled. A studio director in Docklands came on-line to count her in. Instinctively, Tembo turned the camera on her as Jonathan Cusack said: "We're going back live to our reporter at East Seven Five, Gaby McAslan. So, Gaby, exactly where are you?"

And *in.*

"I'm on a landing boat from East Seven Five on my way to Foa Mulaku itself. This rather fetching little number I'm wearing is the latest UNECTA biological isolation suit so we can get close to the object without having to go through decontamination. The scientists who will hopefully be making the landing are in the boat immediately ahead of us: emergence is estimated in"—Shepard had one hand splayed and two fingers of the other upheld—"seven minutes." The lens closed up on her face. Faraway was holding a sign with YOUR NIPPLES ARE SHOWING felt-markered on it. "I'm going to ask one of the crew here what the exact plan is." Out of shot, Shepard was scissoring his hands, eyes wide with panic. Gaby avoided him and sat down beside the helmsman, a sunburned Scotsman with a black "6" on the red front of his suit. Crouching in the bottom of the boat, Faraway handed her a microphone with the SkyNet box on it. Tembo pulled back out to frame them both. Painfully conscious of her nipples, Gaby said, "Excuse me, could you tell the viewers your name?"

"Gordon McAlpine," the helmsman said, watching the other boats throttle back as they came over the emergence zone. He cut his speed to match.

"So, Gordon, could you tell me what's going to be happening?"

"The idea is that we make a visual survey of the surface and pick potential landing sites—we've no real idea of how high it will rise out of the water; some of the locations that look good on the sonar map may prove to be inaccessible. The research teams and the recording crew will go in first; only when it's safe will we run up beside them."

"So a landing is a definite probability."

"Nothing is a definite probability in this business."

Back to the studio, the director whispered.

"Thanks, Gaby," Jonathan Cusack said. "We'll be returning to Foa Mulaku as information comes in, but if I might turn now to our studio guests, Dr. Fergus Dodds of the British Oceanographic Survey, and Lisa Orbach, our resident Chaga expert, for their comments . . ."

Nice one, Gaby, the unknown director said. *Don't go 'way, now.*

She patted Gordon the helmsman on the back. They exchanged thumbs-ups. The boats cut their engines and bobbed on the swelling deep dark water of the Equatorial Channel. The press helicopters wheeled raucously overhead, waiting, waiting.

It is like football, Gaby thought, the most beautiful football, the kind the angels play in the all-seater stadium of heaven, when the keeper throws out the ball and you pick it up and the defenders disappear before you and you're in the box and the goalkeeper is off his line and never has a *prayer.* That kind of beautiful.

A single Scottish voice called out across the face of the waters.

"Thar she blows!"

"Faraway!" Gaby yelled.

"I have them already," the tall Luo said.

Going to you, Gab, said the London director.

"And we're returning to East Seven Five, where Gaby McAslan tells us something is happening," said the unflappable Jonathan Cusack.

"It certainly is," Gaby said without a break. "It's show time."

It had started as a swirling of water, like current around rocks in a shallow river. Now the surface was punctured from below by sharp spines, dozens of them, arranged in rings and rings of rings. When their points were three feet above the surface the spines began to flare gradually outward. The knotted holdfast bases of the crowns of thorns emerged. Now the uppermost folds of the formations that looked like monstrous human brains broke the surface tension. Seawater ran trickling and gurgling through the fissures as the massive white structures loomed ever higher over the flotilla of small craft. The pinnacles of the crowns of thorns were now thirty feet above sea level and still Foa Mulaku pushed itself up from the deep. A structure was becoming evident. This was not an island, but a society of islands: white brain formations surrounded by halos of high thorn coronets, linked to each other by a web of blue-and-red buttresses that were now surfacing, strand by dripping strand.

All this Tembo captured on his Chaga-proof camera and Gaby talked like she had never talked before; talked about things her eyes beheld that she could not comprehend and how they seemed and what they reminded her of and how they made her feel and the nature of the alien and the inadequacy of language to get hold of something for which it had no names and the wonder she felt in the presence of such events, and the fear, and the awe, and all the things the camera could not convey, like the seabirds mobbing around the spires and domes and the way this thing out of the sea smelled and the huge deep noises that came from far down in its roots in the Equatorial Channel, and when she did not know what to talk about next, she just talked anyway because the watching world expected her to say something. And the watching world heard and listened.

The boats started their engines. They moved slowly into the dripping labyrinth of arches and buttresses. The bright water beneath their hulls was brilliant with fish. Foa Mulaku creaked and clicked as it dried in the sun. Emergence had ceased: the thing that lived in the sea had entered a new phase of evolution. The white domes were splitting along their fissures. Objects shaped like tight-balled fists, but the height of two humans, were pushing from the cracks.

"Hand trees," Shepard prompted. Gaby repeated his words to London. The boats probed deeper into the heart of the alien archipelago. Above them, the white fists opened their fingers one by one. Gaby became aware that hers was the only voice speaking in the dripping, creaking basilica of Foa Mulaku and moderated her tone to a reverential whisper. This was a holy place. *A drowned cathedral,* Moon's diary had called the Chaga. This was the place for which those words were properly written. *Sagrada Familia* after the deluge. But it had not drowned. It was risen. Venus on the half shell. The dragon in the sea, wakened.

Gordon the helmsman spun the wheel. "We're going in," he said. The lead boat had already run up onto the shelving apron of the nearest fissure dome. The UNECTA recording boat followed it.

"The Chaganauts are just making sure their faceplates and respirators are secure before landing," Gaby whispered, pleased with her freshly minted neologism. "Just to let you know back in London that if we go ashore, I'll have to put mine up and we'll lose voice contact. They're stepping onto the surface now."

Shepard waved Gordon the helmsman to land.

"They're unloading experimental equipment from the boat," Gaby said. Tembo was lying across the benches with the camera resting on the prow for stability. "As you can see, the UNECTA camera crew has now landed as well. Our own boat is moving in, it looks likely that we'll be making a landing, and I may be allowed to step onto the surface of Foa Mulaku."

Now the studio had gone silent.

"The hand trees." Shepard tapped Gaby on the shoulder. "Look."

Tembo reacted beautifully. He is a hell of a cameraman, Gaby thought. His God has given him a mighty gift.

The white hands were fully open now, but that was not what had excited Shepard's attention. It was that they were all aligned like pieces of a mosaic into a wide, shallow bowl pointed into the southwest quadrant of the sky.

"Look at the angle," Shepard whispered into Gaby's ear through the red-and-silver stretch hood. "I'll just bet that's twenty degrees."

Gaby had set her life by the stars above Ballymacormick Point. She understood immediately.

"The hand trees seem to have formed themselves into what looks like a satellite dish," she told the studio. "As far as I can tell, they're aimed along the ecliptic; in layman's terms, that's the astronomical planc in which the orbits of the planets lie. And we've landed. Gordon has run the nose of the boat up onto the shore. I'm holding off putting on my faceplate for as long as possible so I can keep talking to you. I'm getting signals from the UNECTA personnel who have just gone ashore to stay where I am, but I'm sure that as soon as they make certain it's safe, they'll let me go over." And I am going to have a killer line for that moment, Gaby thought. As great as "one small step for *a* man, a giant leap for mankind." Except I am not going to fuck it up like Armstrong. But Jesus, the first thing the world's going to see is my silver ass going over the side. Boldly going where no woman has gone before and all they are going to remember is my cellulite.

Shepard left the main party to examine where the white brain dome rose from the apron. He had a black "9" on the silver back of his suit. Gaby noted that his thighs did not seem to have lost condition since the photograph on his Arab desk had been taken. He reached a gloved hand to touch the mound. The surface puckered like a face frowning and shot out a polyp of white material. Shepard pulled his hand back. The polyp trembled, creased and folded itself into a hand, the exact double in size and shape of Shepard's. Video cameras swung to bear. Tembo focused in like a sniper. Shepard cautiously brought his hand to within millimeters of the mimic. He opened his fingers, brought them together. The duplicate copied his movements. He cocked a thumb. The Chaga-thing cocked a thumb. He pressed his palm firmly against the alien palm.

And Gaby screamed and tore at her earphones under her hood as the hiss of the satellite link became a roar of noise and pain and Foa Mulaku thundered at the stars.

31

The moped cabdriver thought it was the funniest thing he had ever seen. Three journalists shouting at each other like deaf old fools. He laughed about it all the way to the Addu Reef Hotel, where the foreign scientists had called the conference. When the journalists asked him the fare, he spoke quietly so they would have to ask him again and again. The humor was well worth the tip it cost him.

"Asshole," Gaby McAslan said as she entered the crowded foyer and left her bag with the receptionist. Her ears were still ringing. The doctors on East Seven Five had assured her that no permanent damage had been done when Foa Mulaku sent its message skyward, but not even the Sepultura concert she had sneaked Reb into when she was fifteen, which she had thought was the loudest thing she would hear short of doomsday, had lingered so long in the inner ear.

The Addu Reef Hotel had been designed to look like an ethnic fisher village. It stood on stilts ankle-deep in the lagoon. Its guest rooms, which the richer and quicker news corporations had monopolized, were clustered in little communities at the ends of boardwalks. Ethnic fisher villages did not come with *en suite* bathrooms or fully equipped gymnasiums. Ethnic fisher villages did not have vibrating beds filled with thermostatically controlled fluorescent gel, or glass windows in the floor to watch the fish, or packets of ribbed condoms and leaflets on safe sex in the rattan bedside cabinets. Ethnic fisher villages did not have rattan bedside cabinets.

UNECTA had taken over the nightclub to stage its press conference. The staff had arranged the bar seats in a semicircle and set up a table in front of the deejay's mixing desk. Most of the seats were already taken. Faraway added a SkyNet logo to the thicket of microphones taped to the conference table. Recognizing him, heads turned to seek out Gaby McAslan and bent together to whisper.

"Nice angle, Gaby," Wayne Osborne from Australian Channel Nine said, brushing past her on his way back from the bar with a glass of something amber.

"That's Shepard's line," said a woman with a UPI badge she did not even know. Journalists snickered into their drinks. Gaby found a place in the middle of the back row of seats. Faraway guarded her left flank, Tembo with the tripod her right. Still someone managed to bump into her from behind and drop into her lap a crude cartoon of a kneeling man with an enormous penis fucking a crouching woman dog-fashion. The woman had long hair colored in red ballpen and a talk bubble coming out of her mouth saying, "Gaby McAslan, SkyNet News, with another exclusive."

Tembo snatched the paper away, rolled it into a ball and put it in his mouth. He focused his camera, chewed and swallowed without comment.

The UNECTA team came in. R. M. Srivapanda, just off the seaplane from East Seven Five, took the chair. To his right was a very upright African man in a severe black-and-white suit. Gaby recognized him as Harrison Muthika, press secretary from Nairobi. To Srivapanda's left was an Asian woman who was introduced as Mariko Uchida from UNECT*Asie*'s space sciences division. UNECT*Afrique*'s peripatetic executive director was conspicuously absent.

The press conference opened. Harrison Muthika spoke first.

"I would like to thank you all for coming this evening. I regret the short notice, but once again, the aliens have taken us by surprise. As you are no doubt aware, at seventeen-oh-eight local time the emergent marine object known as Foa Mulaku emitted a phenomenally powerful radio signal."

There were wry chuckles and someone heckled, "Speak up, we can't hear you!"

Harrison Muthika smiled. "This signal spanned the electromagnetic spectrum between the inch and foot bands and lasted for two hours, three minutes and twenty seconds. The power of the signal has been estimated at one hundred and fifty megawatts.''

Murmurs. ''How was the power generated?'' a voice with a French accent shouted. Harrison Muthika held up his hand.

''Please. There will be an opportunity for questions at the end. This enormous burst of radio energy swamped broadcasting in the East African, Indian Ocean and Southeast Asian areas: all communications in those frequencies were silenced. The disruption to cellular networks alone has cost twelve billion dollars in disrupted business, not to mention feedback damage to data-storage systems. Television and navigation systems went down, contact was lost with several thousand ships and aircraft, as well as the failure of air-traffic control throughout the region. It is only by the grace of God that a major air disaster was averted, though we do not yet have a complete picture: outlying sections of the East Pacific net are only now coming back on-line.

''You may be interested to know that the anonymous NASA wit behind the names BDO and *Tolkien* has christened this event 'the Scream.' ''

''It's Carl Sagan, isn't it?'' an American-accented voice shouted.

''I can't confirm that, and I must once again ask you to keep your questions for the end. The transmission has been analyzed and has been shown to consist of one hundred and eighty-seven signals, each carrying a data-transfer code at a rate of one and a quarter megabytes per second.''

Gaby did sums on her PDU. The average whodunit could fit on a floppy disk, about one and a quarter megabytes. One hundred and eighty whodunits per second, times one hundred and twenty-three minutes times sixty seconds, that's seven-three-eight-oh seconds equals one million three hundred and eight thousand and sixty plus an extra five hundred and sixty-one for those last three seconds and that's an entire library of Murders in the Ballroom and Bodies in the Library.

''We were only able to capture the last one hour and five minutes of the transmission,'' Harrison Muthika continued. ''Neural network analysis is still coming through—the code is unlike anything we have yet encountered—but we think we have enough of a recognizable pattern to be able to extrapolate.'' A liquid crystal overhead projector threw an image onto the dance floor video screen. The swoop through the arrayed molecules would not have looked out of place in the psychotropic dance videos that usually played there. Gaby recognized the intertwined spiral staircases at once. Dance to your own DNA. "This is not, of course, what would have been received, it's an approximation by our analysts. The transmitted information consisted of a three-dimension matrix of data expressed in terms of the atomic specifications of its components." Molecules coiled behind Harrison Muthika like serpents mating in a baobob, the tree where man was born. "The DNA model is only a small part of the transmission. The remainder is fragmentary, but if we are correct, it is of enormous significance. It seems to be a complete map of the human genome."

Hands shot up. Harrison Muthika sat down and looked to Mariko Uchida. The UNECT*Asie* woman took the floor.

"You've probably guessed that the target of the transmission was the Hyperion Object, or BDO, as we like to call it. Why the genetic code was transmitted to Saturn space is something we'll probably only find out when the BDO gets here. However, an hour after the end of the Scream, our Miyama orbital telescope took this CCD image of the Hyperion Object."

It looked like any grainy, blurry charge-coupled device photograph to Gaby. The universe as seen through a serial killer's night-vision goggles. An ellipse of gray on darker gray pierced by the burned-out crucifixes of overexposed stars.

"I'll enhance the image," Mariko Uchida said. It was still a light gray shape against a dark background to Gaby, but was there something about the edges? "Here are the images the Miyama telescope took over the subsequent five hours." The picture parade was like a sequence of pages torn from a badly drawn cartoon flicker book. "The object keeps the same face to the sun; we assume that the systems of organization there require energy to operate. I'd call them 'life,' except that they're existing in a pretty hard vacuum. Note the curvature of the rim." The laser pointer jumped from frame to frame as the AV computer flashed up all the images in array. The edge of the disc was folding upward, like flat clay on a potter's wheel being drawn into a wide, shallow bowl. "The increase in curvature is very slight, less than one percent, but when you consider the size of the object and that this happened over a period of five hours, with the BDO about sixty-five light-minutes away, you can begin to imagine the scale of the forces at work here."

She loves them, Gaby thought, these mighty forces. That smile is not part of the architecture now. She loves being dominated by the powers in the sky. She is getting soft and wet on that platform thinking about forces beyond imagining. Whoever is with her will get it good in bed tonight.

"The changes must have started the moment the first signal of the Scream was received from Foa Mulaku. We've had our own extrapolations done of what the BDO might look like when it arrives in Earth space." A sequence showed a creakily animated BDO pucker up around its rim into a conic parabola and stretch. The animation ran twice. The first time the BDO stretched into a great cosmic egg. The second time it rolled into a cylinder five hundred miles long, one hundred and fifty across its flats. "The probabilities for the second, cylindrical form are higher; 58 percent against 39 percent for the ovoid. The other percentages are covered by wild speculations from perfect cubes to space-faring Cadillacs to old men with long white beards. The cylinder model rates higher because it is a well-established format for a deep-space habitat. Given that the axial rotation will increase as the BDO pulls in on itself, like an ice-skater speeding up her spin by drawing in her arms, we estimate that the internal rotational gravity will maximize to point-six of a gee, which seems consistent with an internal planetlike environment. This may just be human chauvinism, however; the Chaga-makers have yet to show any anthropomorphic tendencies; there is no reason why they should need to create a biosphere inside the BDO. However, the content of the Foa Mulaku transmission is significant in this context."

"You think the BDO is being converted into a self-contained Earth-like environment as a kind of alien embassy?" Gaby interrupted. She heard murmuring. She heard whispers and sniggers.

"I do," the Japanese woman said. "I believe the Hyperion Object as we see it is a universal form that has been employed many times before by the Chaga-makers in their migrations and contacts with extraterrestrial environments. There is no evidence that humanity is a particular end point on their journey: they may well have left the mechanisms that turned Iapetus black and produced both the biological packages and the BDO many thousands or even millions of years ago and moved on to other star systems. It is quite possible that the system was programmed to wait until intelligence was highly developed enough to stimulate it, which we have done with our probes to the outer planets."

Peter Werther had said it knows us of old, Gaby thought. Perhaps that is why it transmitted the DNA code and the map of the human genome; to let whatever is out there know that there is still life on Planet Three, and how much the smart apes have changed since last we met.

R. M. Srivapanda was on his feet now. He waved down the raised hands with his one good hand.

"Please, ladies and gentlemen, questions later. There is more." He waited for quiet. "For the one hundred and nine hours prior to emergence, the Maldive Ridge Object has been emitting a series of high-volume, long-time-base, low-amplitude sounds. We have been recording these on hydrophones; phase-shifted and compressed, this is what they sound like."

The nightclub sound system was very good. It played the recording without any hiss or distortion or growl of overload. It must be great to dance to, Gaby thought. The sound started as a high-pitched musical twittering then plummeted in a deafening howl of bass notes that made Gaby think of Portuguese fado singers and Islamic muezzins. The song concluded on a rising note that ascended into the ultrasonic through frequencies that made buzzing ears ache. Gaby remembered the old *National Geographic* floppy disk of whale song she had played nonstop on her bedroom sound system in her teenage "green" phase. Dad had finally threatened to buy dolphin-unfriendly tuna unless she stopped. Whale song. It will talk to them but not to us.

"It has been known for some time that whales use cold currents as wave guides along which song cycles can be directed over several thousand miles. The Maldive Ridge Object seems to be using the midocean drift to the same effect. Tracking of tagged blue whales in the Indian Ocean basin has revealed a strange pattern." He nodded to the technician behind the mixing desk. A map of the ocean basin appeared on the screen, marked with red arrows with tails of varying lengths. The arrowheads were slowly converging on the blue star of Foa Mulaku. "The map only shows the Indian Ocean population, but we have evidence of migrations among *Balaenoptera musculus* pods in the South Atlantic and Pacific. Fragments of Foa Mulaku sound have been appearing in recordings of blue-whale songs as far as Hawaii; the pods are communicating it to each other along the cold current channels. At current estimates, eighty percent of the world's blue-whale population will have moved into the Carlsberg Ridge–Mid-Indian Basin region within three months, and the object is still calling."

"Yes, but what is it saying?" Paul Mulrooney called out. "And why is it saying it to them and not to us?"

R. M. Srivapanda shook his head and pursed his lips.

"At least Greenpeace will have something to do," Wayne Osborne said. "All those whale burgers to protect." The comment did not get as big a laugh as planned.

"Very well. That is all we have to say." R. M. Srivapanda looked at his colleagues. They nodded. "So, are there any questions?"

Three hundred voices clamored at once.

32

She saw the light of the fire and walked toward it along the beach. Crabs scuttled around her feet, always that sufficient second quick enough to avoid destruction. The moon and tide were high. The ocean ran far up the soft coral sand. She climbed over the trunks of slumped palms.

There were four of them sitting around the fire on tube steel and canvas beach chairs up close to the tree line. Marshmallows toasted on sticks over the driftwood embers. One was a dripping blob of blazing goo. Cool boxes held the full bottles; the empties lay careened in the soft sand. Three of the people wore white T-shirts with *Foa Mulaku Sun'n'Surf Club* printed on the front. The fourth had a picture of a masturbating nun.

"Gaby!" Shepard surged to his feet. "Press conference over?"

"Reception said you would be down here," she said coolly. "I was expecting to see you back there." She would be angry with him later when there were no witnesses. She rubbed the palm of her hand against his chin stubble. Purr.

"Come. Sit. Have a beer. Sorry we're out of chairs." He introduced the white T-shirts: Depak Ray, director of UNECT*Asie*'s Kavieng base on New Ireland; Mariella Costas from UNECT*Amérique* headquarters in Quito; Dave Mortensen from UCLA Riverside's nanotechnology unit. "We're blue-skying. What-if-ing. Probing the outer limits. Entering the Twilight Zone. Opening the X-files."

"So, what have you found out in the Twilight Zone?" Gaby asked.

"That maybe the stars are not our destination," Depak Ray said. "Human intelligence evolved as a response to a set of environmental challenges which are specific to the environmental niche we inhabit. Those whales out there swimming toward Foa Mulaku are a different solution to a different set of environmental problems. The Chaga-makers are an interstellar civilization because wherever they come from, their niche demanded that they develop space-faring. We, with our ape's hands and ape's eyes and our ape's brains and our ape's obsessions with individuality and sex, are not evolved to make that jump. If the Chaga-makers were ever individual intelligences like us, they are not now; if we ever match their achievements, neither will we be."

"The Chaga-makers are the Chagas?" Dave Mortensen said.

"Our research at Kavieng seems to support that," Depak Ray said. "For the Eastern Pacific entities—we are trying to have the word *symb* adopted as the official term, 'Chaga' is too specific to Africa—we have found that all the many thousands of seemingly different species are genetically linked to each other. They are all—to borrow a term from physics—isotopes of each other. The symbs are essentially one species with many dependent variants."

"Isogenes?" Dave Mortensen suggested. "Like dogs: cocker spaniels, greyhounds, beagles, borzois."

"That closely related, yes, but the variations are very much more greatly differentiated."

"A clade," Mariella Costas said. "Genetically related to a common ancestor."

"More subtle than that," Depak said. "More like a watermark on paper than a family tree."

The beer and the tiredness were beginning to work on Gaby now. The sand looked soft enough to curl up on and throw over herself like a sheet.

"I can't go for this all-nurturing life-mother goddess thing," Dave Mortensen said. "These people are engineers. They can dismantle the fundamental units of the universe and build anything they damn well like out of them. The Chagas—symbs, whatever—are made things. Technology. Machines."

"I have a problem with such a mechanistic view of the universe," Mariella Costas said. Gaby could not take her eyes off her prominent moustache line. "In my country we believe in community; that in our coming together we become stronger than our sum as individuals. The symbs are like families, communities, clans, tribes if you will. Corporations, perhaps: they have all come together to a common purpose that could not be achieved individually, and, in a sense, they all wear the company uniform: in their genes."

"But if, as the name symb implies, the thing is symbiotic, then it can't be totally self-sufficient," Dave Mortensen was saying now. "Perhaps it needs humanity to be able to move on from this star system."

"The Big Dumb Object seems an effective enough way to propagate the Chaga through the galaxy," Mariella Costas replied.

"Perhaps there are quicker, more efficient ways," the American said. "Wormholes, tachyons, all that spooky stuff at the edges of quantum theory."

"You Americans, you must always have your dreams of the frontier," Depak said. "The place beyond that draws you on. 'The Stars Our Destination': the nobility, no, the *superiority,* of humanity over all possible species, and of *Homo americanus* over all other humans."

This is what it is all about, Gaby thought. UNECT*Afrique/Asie/Amérique.* It is intellectual colonialism. The white boys telling the rest of the world what to think and how to think it. All the poor and the dirty and the overcrowded and the funny-colored. Shovel-wielding Paddies included.

"The Chaga-makers don't need human Big Science," Shepard said. "They've got plenty of their own. Do you know how they made Hyperion disappear? A quantum black hole." Surf fell and crabs scampered up and down the tide line. "JPL did an analysis of gravitational anomalies just before and after the blast. Something with the mass, say, of this island compressed into a singularity smaller than an atomic nucleus. Out in space it's innocuous enough, maybe twinkling a bit in the high gammas as it sucks in the odd stray hydrogen molecule. Feed it with ice satellite, and in point-seven-five of a second it blows in a blast of very hard Hawking radiation and superheated accretion disc plasma. Ninety-percent conversion of mass to energy. Makes comet Shoemaker-Levy's megatonnage look like indoor fireworks."

Gaby thought of Mariko Uchida of UNECT*Asie*'s space sciences division; how excited she had got thinking about the BDO. Slam-dunking micro–black holes was more than soft and hot and wet. It was hog-tied and gagged and crocodile clips on the nipples: total submission to the powers in the sky.

They were debating now about what humanity could hope to offer entities who manipulated the fundamental units of reality. All we can offer the Chaga-makers is what it is to be human. But that is enough. And I think it is what the Chaga-makers have come for.

She flicked off her shoes and went down to the sea. She needed to connect with the reality of water. She walked a little into the tide line, feeling the run and suck of sand under her soles. The surf on the reef was a tremor in the water. Are there sharks out there, under the moon? Gaby thought, come in with the high tide through the gaps in the reef, casting their moon shadows over the soft marl floor of the lagoon? Do they sense me, am I a tickle of electricity along their lateral lines? There had been little sharks in the waters around the Watchhouse, and once she had seen from the Weather Room the silhouette of a great basker off the rocks around the harbor entrance. If they ever stop moving, they die. They need a constant passage of water over their gills or they drown. A drowned fish. Oksana's totemic creature was the wolf. I should have a shark tattooed on the upper slope of my left breast, Gaby thought.

She felt his presence as a vibration in the water before he spoke.

"Too much for you?"

"It seems kind of abstract."

"Everything is, until the BDO gets here."

"Walk with me, Shepard."

He took her hand. No one had done that since she was eighteen. They bred them old-fashioned in the plains states. They walked along the waterline, away from the fire and the people around it and the lights of the hotel standing over the water.

"Shepard, were you avoiding me at the press conference?"

"Of course not, what makes you think that?"

She studied his face by the moonlight.

"I wouldn't like to think that I was an embarrassment to you, professional or otherwise. I wouldn't like to think that you had some reason to be ashamed of me, or regret something you might have done for me. I wouldn't like that at all."

"I'm not ashamed of you. I'm not embarrassed by you."

"So when the shit starts to fly, you'll stand by me? Because it will; this is a dangerous liaison."

She waded into the water, enjoying the heavy lap of it up her thighs, between her legs. She drew Shepard deeper: waist-deep, chest-deep.

"Of course I will."

She pressed herself to him, undid the fastenings of his shorts. Her hands slipped inside his underwear, caressed his balls. He came up instantly hard. She wrapped her arms around his neck, hopped up and twined legs around his waist.

"I'm very glad to hear that. You see, I would hate to share a refrigerator, a microwave, a music system, a shower and a bed with someone I couldn't trust."

"You're—"

"Bags are back at reception."

"I love you, Gaby McAslan."

"I love you, Dr. M-for-Mystery Shepard. Oh!" Like blind deep-sea hunters, his fingers had found their way past the hem of her bleached cutoffs, under the elastic of her panties and onto the tip of her clitoris. He smelled agreeably of sunblock and beer, but she pushed herself as far away from him as her arms would allow because there was one thing she had to ask him, and if she let him have sex with her now she would forget. "Shepard."

"Mm?"

He had his shorts down.

"Ooh. You bastard. That diary."

"Mm?"

"Do you know what happened to it? There are bits missing. Someone has been through it with a very sharp knife and cut whole pages out."

"I gave it to you like I got it from Ol Tukai. If anything happened to it, it was probably there."

"But why bother, Shepard? If the missing pages refer to something UNECTA doesn't want known, why not just lose the diary? Incinerate it, shred it?"

"Do you have to ask this right now? Don't you ever stop being the Investigative Journalist?"

"Seems not, Captain UNECTA," Gaby said and came down on top of him in the moonlit, shark-haunted water.

33

The first time she woke because of the strange bed.

The second time she woke because of the strange room the strange bed was in.

The third time she woke because of the strange dream the strange room made her have in the strange bed.

The fourth time she woke because the videophone was cheeping at four forty-seven in the morning. She could see him in the living room, talking to the handset with his back to her. Gaby had never realized how much hair he had on his ass. She sat up in the double bed and pulled around her the tapestry of stars she had spread as a quilt. He was talking in a low voice. All she could hear were his responses to the inaudible voice of the pixilated blur on the screen.

"Fallen Angel? Where? What's the ETI? What kind of response time? Hold it. I'll be there. Say ten minutes. And the units are already mobile to the site? It actually works. Good. The Tupolev?" She could tell by the way his shoulders moved that he was smiling. "No problem." He folded the screen and came into the bedroom.

"Gab?"

"I'm awake. What's going on?"

He put on a bedside light. It had a leather shade perforated with patterns of African animals. Antelopes and giraffes of light cantered across the walls.

"Something's come up. I have to go."

He was dressing rapidly. He pulled his ready bag from under the bed. Gaby drew the tapestry tighter around her, feeling uncomfortably vulnerable, abandoned naked in an unfamiliar apartment.

"Go where?"

She heard him sigh as he pulled his shirt over his head.

"I can't tell you."

"You can't tell me."

"It's a security issue."

"I though you trusted me. That's what you told me that night on the beach at Addu Atoll."

"I trust you. Please don't ask me about it, I can't answer. This thing, it's not just you, it's everyone."

"How long will you be gone?"

He pulled on bush boots, dashed to the bathroom to get those extra toiletries you always forget to put in your ready bag.

"A couple of days. Maybe a week, depending."

"Depending?"

"You won't catch me out that way."

"Fair game for me to try to find out?"

He was patting his pockets, looking distracted, trying to remember what he might have forgotten. He glanced at his watch.

"Christ. The car'll be here any minute. You do whatever you like, Gab." He swept up his bag and headed for the front door. Gaby followed, swathed in needlepoint zodiac.

"Shepard, haven't you forgotten something?"

He stopped dead.

"Jesus H. Christ! Yes!" When he turned around, he did not kiss her, which was what she had meant. He had the look of a man about to ask a vast favor. "Are you still officially on the leave T.P. gave you for Foa Mulaku?"

"What do you want me to do with it, Shepard?"

He took a deep breath.

"I totally forgot. Totally forgot. I need you to go down to Kenyatta Airport day after tomorrow and meet my kids off the flight from LAX."

"Jesus, Shepard!"

"They always come out this time of year. There's a banda down on the coast, just north of Mombasa, at Kikambala. Take them there; you can get the key from my office. You can do this, Gaby, it'll only be for a couple of days."

"A couple of days?"

"A week at most."

"Shepard . . ."

"Thanks, Gaby. I knew I could trust you."

The door slammed on any comment she might have made.

34

Gaby's videodiary
August 27 2008

I have died and gone to hell.

People think journalism is hard. Journalism is running about getting chased by Azeri soldiers and slapped in isolation units and having to tell the finance company why you set fire to the very expensive 4X4 they lent you the money to buy and being lifted off the street by posseboys and gate-crashing society parties and living under the iron whim of T. P. Costello and flying off at a moment's notice to the end of the world and never getting enough sleep but always having to look good for the cameras and too much coffee and never enough sex and regular mealtimes, what are regular mealtimes? cigarettes are mealtimes. Journalism is wee buns. Parenthood is hard. And long. And thankless. And comes without an off switch, a pause button, a rewind or a volume control.

This is my bedroom at the UNECTA beach house at Kikambala. Outside, the humidity is about ninety-three percent, the temperature in the same figures, the wind is rustling the palms, the surf is crashing on the reef and whatever things creep around in the night are creeping around in the night. Including some seriously big black millipedes with red legs. This is me hiding inside my mosquito nets. Not from mosquitoes. Or seriously big black millipedes with red legs, though if one gets into this room, I'll need institutionalizing. I'm hiding from Shepard's children. They are the spawn of Satan.

I'm just going to have a cigarette.

Where to begin? Rehearsing it in Arrivals at Kenyatta. Hi, you're Fraser and Aaron, right? Your dad's real sorry he can't be here to meet you, so he's asked me to look after you and take you down to Mombasa and make sure you have a lovely time. My name's Gaby. I'm your dad's live-in lover. Went over it and over it and over it as the flight data went from *due* to *landed* to *in terminal* until I had it by heart and they came through the door from Immigration and I couldn't remember a single word. My name: that was about all they got. They've probably worked out what I am.

Adulthood edits out the trivial but significant details of being a kid, like needing to go to the jax all the time and being continuously hungry and the fact that time passes more slowly for children than for adults. I should have made sure they went in the airport. I should have bought them brunch in the cafeteria. I should not have shoved them, jet-lagged, into the Landcruiser and been past the Athi River before they realized what continent they were on, let alone who I was and where I was taking them.

Cigarette two. That bad.

I tried my best. Honest, Shepard. I tried to talk to them, which is not that easy when at any moment some refugee's goat might leap under your wheels, or a refugee's child, or just a refugee. Whatever I said, it was the wrong thing. Good flight? They told me all about how the stewardess had seen they were two boys on their own and taken them up to the flight deck to see the pilots fly the plane. My best friend is a pilot for UNECTA, I say. Her name is Oksana, she flies one of those Antonovs, you know? Really good friend; how about sometime I take you to see her and maybe she'll take us up on a flight and you can see how she flies the plane, wouldn't that be great, no?

Silence.

Overkill.

I try television. I try video games. I try books, comics, movies, music, the environment. I die the death. They've no idea what I'm banging on about. You forget how much of what you thought was your childhood is made up of capitalist product placements and pop-cultural ephemera that don't translate from country to country, let alone generation to generation. Who was it said Britain and America are two nations divided by a common language? It's going to be the longest five hours a girl ever spent in a 4X4.

Down past Kathekani the road comes within a mile of terminum. They're trying to keep the main links to the coast open as long as possible while Kenyan army engineers cut a temporary earth road ten miles to the northeast, but it's mighty hairy. Tourists and sightseers all over the place like ants on a picnic, waiting to see Tsavo West cross the road, and maybe a peek at the Chaga. All the campervans and tents and buses, it's like Ayers Rock, or the Glastonbury festival.

"This is Tsavo West," I say to the kids like I had produced it out of my hat. And it's mighty impressive, looming over the city of tents and campervans and all the people who have come to watch it. "Your dad used to run this place."

"We know," says Fraser. "He was research director."

"We know," says Aaron. "He took us here a lot of times. We know all the people there."

Try then to impress the guys by high-fiving with the SkyNet crew down to report the crossing. Added newsworthiness is provided by a matatu driver trying to avoid the traffic jam on the road and taking a shortcut under the back left track of Tractor One. There are still folk alive in the tangle of metal: they're bringing heavy cutting gear up from Voi by helicopter. Tsavo West has a million dollars of virtual reality manipulator system, but can't pull a casualty out of a wreck.

I'll swear on whatever you like I saw Keanu Reeves in the crowd with this season's babe-on-the-side in mandatory khaki and cute boots. I try to point him out to the boys, but Aaron's looking at the wrong person and Fraser says Keanu Reeves is a nush. I'm not sure whether this is good or bad. I'm certainly not going to do anything so uncool as ask.

After that, I think the only words spoken until Mombasa, when I had to ask them how to get to the Nyali bridge, were, "I need to go to the bathroom." And that several times. Why did God give males bladders the size of peanuts?

Of course they know the turnoff the main road at Kikambala, and which fork of the sand track through the palm trees takes you to the banda. The boys run up the steps like it's Home Sweet Home and I unglue my knickers from the seat to which they've stuck and heave myself into the banda wanting drink smoke bath and ten years of solitary confinement, don't they give you that for child murder? and the boys are in the kitchen looking at me with that dismissive yet accusing curl of the lip children instinctively know crucifies adults with assumed guilt and saying they're hungry where's the food?

The food? I say. The food?

So it's off on foot up the beach for half a mile clambering over fallen palms and saying no politely but firmly to the shell and curio sellers to this place the boys know is called the Kikambala Continental Dining Room where the fish is off the seafood is off the omelettes are off the salad might be off but the steak definitely is and the only thing that's on is the curry which, astonishingly, comes complete with chapattis, chutneys, pilau rice, vegetable sambal, dhall and something so hot I still have the blisters on my gums and is the equivalent of a dollar-fifty per head. I order Cokes, but Fraser says that when they're on vacation Dad treats them like men and they have beer. By now I've learned not to argue with them, so it's Heinekens all round. And they're big enough to put themselves to bed, thank you very much.

Shepard, I need you! I am lighting cigarette number three, hiding in my mosquito nets, talking to this dumb viewcam praying *please, God, tell me what we can do tomorrow?* I cannot take a week of this. Did you do this on purpose, you bastard?

The door opened. Gaby leaped up, stuck her head out of the mosquito net.

"Aaron?"

He was wearing beach shorts, multicolored flip-flops and a most cute little Japanese bamboo-pattern *yukata.*

"Gaby, is there something wrong with us?" He spoke like a miniature Shepard. Inflections, expressions, accent. Jimmy Stewart, the next generation.

"What do you mean?"

"Everything you say sounds angry."

"It what?"

"Like that. It sounds like you're mad at us, or mad at something."

"I'm not angry, Aaron. I like you and Fraser fine. I don't know very much about you yet, but what I do know I like fine. Is it my accent? Does that make me sound angry all the time? It's just the way people talk where I come from, we don't think anything of it because we all sound the same to each other, but yes, I think I see how it could sound harsh and abrupt and you could think I was angry. But I'm not. It's just the way I talk. All right?"

"Okay."

"Look, I haven't started very well, I know. I'm not awfully good at this; guys' stuff, all that. I'm not having a great time either. I want for us all to get on, but it's just I don't know what to do with you. Maybe you could tell me what you like to do, help me a little here."

"Well," Aaron said, "we'd like to swim early. That's one of the things we like to do here. Do you like to swim?"

"I love to swim."

"There's another thing we like to do, but Dad doesn't know about it yet because we're still learning it."

"What's that?"

"Play soccer."

In Gaby McAslan's head, the crowd at Old Trafford rose as one, cheering.

"That's something I like to do very much too."

"For real?"

"For really real. Aaron, there's something you could help me out with."

"What is it?"

Look at him standing there in his flip-flops and *yukata,* Gaby thought, and forgive me the betrayal I am going to ask of him.

"Do you know what your dad's first name is? What the *M* stands for?"

"Yes," Aaron said solemnly, "but you must promise that if I tell you, you'll never tell anyone else as long as you live, not even Dad."

"I promise. Cross my heart."

So he told her what the *M* stood for, and Gaby McAslan kept her promise and never told anyone else as long as she lived.

35

He paid the taxi and followed the sounds of voices toward the sea. They were playing football on the hard sand down by the tide line. Piled T-shirts were goals. From the cover of the trees, Shepard watched them run and shout. After Rutshuru it was like the play of angels. He felt that he had turned his back on a dark, looming continent and the monstrous, incomprehensible things that grew in its heart, and was looking out toward the transcendent, healing sea.

The boys wore only surfing shorts, Gaby was in an olive green thong-back swim suit. She had a smear of fluorescent-blue zinc-oxide cream on the upper slope of each bare cheek. The boys wore the cream like war paint across their nose, eyebrows and tiny nipples. Fraser took the ball off Gaby with a decidedly dirty sliding tackle, turned and blasted it at Aaron in goal. It was still rising as it went past him. As Aaron ran to fetch it, sending white seabirds flapping up before him, Gaby and Fraser did a victory dance, shuffling their feet in the sand and shouting "Ooh, ah, Cantona; say ooh-ah Cantona." Shepard was transfixed by the jigging blue stripes on Gaby's ass.

"Dad!"

Aaron hit him like a well-taken penalty. He had not seen him coming up across the sand. The ball rolled away toward the lapping tide. The others stopped in mid war dance and came running.

"You're back early," Gaby said. "Fallen Angel not take as long as you'd thought?"

Shepard winced, as if inner scabs had torn.

"You could say that." His children clamored for his attention. He scooped them into an embrace. "You seem to be doing all right," he said to Gaby.

"Californians would say I was getting in touch with my inner child. I call it playing."

"Dad!" Aaron shouted. "Gaby taught us a football song!" To the tune of "Stars and Stripes Forever," he piped, "Ryan Giggs, Ryan Giggs, Ryan Giggs; Ryan Giggs, Ryan Giggs, Ryan Gi-igs."

After that it never stopped being good.

In the afternoon they walked out to the reef with masks and flippers. Gaby pretended to be terrified of the boys' stories of sea snakes that came curling around your legs and bit you and you swelled up and went black and your face exploded all in thirty seconds. There was still no food in the banda, so they went again that evening to the Kikambala Continental Dining Room. The Giriama waiter gave them a special table on the veranda, where they could see and hear the sea and drink Heineken and laugh a lot. The boys were too excited to put themselves to bed, and as there was no television or even Voice of Kenya radio, it was decided that everyone was to do their party piece. First of all Shepard sang the Periodic Table to the tune of Gilbert and Sullivan's "I Am the Very Model of a Modern Major-General." After the concluding line about these are all the elements of which we know at Harvard, if there's any more of them they haven't been dis-cah-vered, he added, "actually, there are about thirty, but most of them are just numbers."

"Plus fullerenes," Gaby said.

"They're not elements," Aaron declared.

The boys played the old King of Siam trick on Gaby, where she had to kneel before Aaron while Fraser made her say "O-watanna-Siam" faster and faster until she was saying "Oh what an ass I am," which is a trick everyone knows, but she went along with it anyway. Then Shepard and his sons did a clodhopping soft-shoe shuffle to "In the Mood," to which they forgot the words and ended going dah-da-da da-dada, dah-da-da dadada.

"Your turn," Aaron said to Gaby.

Among the debris of previous residents, most of which had been either alcoholic, narcotic or pornographic, Gaby had found an old Spanish guitar. She had reset it from its odd African suspended tuning. She sat on the wicker sofa, tucked her hair behind her left ear and sang first an old Irish song about nostalgia for places that were now obliterated by farms, junked vehicles, trailer camps and hacienda-style holiday bungalows. Then she sang a song she had always loved about all the lies a man tells a woman and the freedom she finds when she walks away from them. None of the males spoke for some time after she had finished. Then Shepard said, "I didn't know you could do that."

"My dad was of the opinion that every civilized human should be able to cook, draw, play a musical instrument and sing in tune," Gaby said. "Me and the sisters used to make up soul groups. Put on the little black dresses and do the Motown classics to this karaoke tape we had."

"Okay, troops," Shepard declared. "Bed. Fishing boat's coming early."

They went without a murmur.

Later, when the moonlight through the louvered window turned the mosquito net to a pavilion of light, Gaby said, "Shepard, your kids are all right."

"Yeah. They are, aren't they? I know I do it all wrong; it's not all guys together, they shouldn't be drinking beer, and they shouldn't be ogling you in that swimsuit—which they do, believe me. They're just kids, I should let them be kids. Every time I promise myself this time I'll just be Dad and not King of the Wild Frontier and Indiana Jones, but then I see them and they deserve so much, and I want them to have everything that I have, see what I see, touch what I touch, hear what I hear, taste what I taste, feel what I feel."

"Ogle what you ogle."

They lay a time side by side in the big ebony bed that had been brought by dhow from Pemba a hundred years ago.

"Gaby."

"Shepard."

"What do you know about Fallen Angel?"

Gaby leaned out of bed to take a cigarette from the packet on the wicker bedside table.

"It's a plan to capture, isolate and analyze a biological package before it releases its cargo."

"How do you know this?"

She breathed smoke into the glowing apex of the canopy.

"It's a security issue. Between me and my sources. So where did the angel fall?"

"Zaire. Eastern Zaire; place called Rutshuru. We knew one was coming—we'd had the thing on deep-space tracking for several weeks—but not where it was coming to. You never can be sure because of variations in the air-braked descent."

"Except that it's always within plus or minus one and a half degrees latitude," Gaby said.

"We picked a number of locations based on hit probabilities that covered a radius of two flying hours; that way when the package began descent we could get our mobile units to the target. As it was, it came down within half an hour of the base at Kilembe in western Uganda. All our mobile units relocated to Goma, where the UN left an airfield and relief base from the Rwandan civil war. The helicopters were airborne before the thing hit the ground. The Sikorskys picked the thing up before it was even cool. They called me in Nairobi and laid on the Tupolev. I was the only passenger. Mach 1.8, all for myself. A guy could get used to this."

Penis with wings, Oksana had called the supersonic priority transport.

"I got there just as they were bringing the thing in in the inert gas pod. The theory was that the memes, the fullerene machines, whatever the hell you want to call them, would not be able to replicate in a chemically inactive atmosphere. The labs were all set up—the engineers had been busting their buns—floodlights, power, the inflatable domes where the researchers would be working on the capsule. You've seen glove boxes where you put your hand through a wall to work in a biologically hazardous environment. We took it a stage further; we had complete suits connected to the outside by concertina tunnels.

"The team suited up—they were French, a good crew, I knew some of them from Tsavo and Tinga Tinga—and went in. They opened the capsule with a diamond blade cutter—you've seen schematics, you know what the packages look like."

Like things I used to find washed up on the shore, Gaby thought. Egg purses, seed cases, or the recursive chambers and vaults of mollusc shells. But cast up from a deeper and darker sea than the one that breaks around my childhood.

"They took it apart like a medical operation—or defusing a bomb. That may be a better analogy. Each step very slow, very careful, very deliberate, all explained and recorded and documented before they moved on to the next. They spent an hour describing the process of cutting the outer heat skin and peeling it back. Analysis showed it to be a kind of composite polymer wood with certain attributes of a flexible ceramic. Perfect ablation material. As they found it, the carapace was in an early stage of decay; it must become porous to allow the contents to escape.

"Think of an orange—those elongated fluid-filled cells packed into segments—and you'll have some idea of the interior of the package. But red. Dark red, almost crimson. A particularly brutal blood orange. It was getting light by the time they removed the first cell for sampling. Each was about the length of my forefinger and terminated in a complex tangle of light-sensitive fibers."

"Nerve endings?" Gaby asked. "Like a brain, is that what you're implying?"

"Seed and brain cells combined. The pod can program its own contents, change the specifications of the memes to manufacture different forms."

"No Bug-Eyed Monsters saying 'Take me to your leader.' "

"We'd done scans, taken X rays, gamma-flash photographs. The structure was uniform throughout. We weren't expecting any Bug-Eyed Monsters. For which I'm very glad; I was the nearest thing to a leader there.

"I don't know how it happened." A green lizard ran over the wall and clung, head down, under the window ledge. "Maybe the inert atmosphere wasn't as pure as we'd thought, or the engineers rushed the job. First thing I knew that something was wrong was Dominique Ferjac thrashing around in her suit like a fish on a line. She must have sprung a leak, oxygen atmosphere had blown out into the inert chamber and the fullerenes had started to reproduce. The suit was like cheesecloth in seconds. I should have pulled the plug then, but the others wanted to get as many samples as they could inert-bagged and cycled through the lock to the outside. They didn't know it would blow like that. None of us knew it would blow like that. We should have guessed; the thing needs to spread its spores as far and fast as possible. While we got Dominique out of the suit and into the decontam tank, air had been leaking into the inert atmosphere, and when it hit a certain percentage, the capsule went off like a geyser. Like fucking Old Faithful. The bubble went red. It caught the team; we could hear them on the radio shouting for us to get them out, but everything was coming apart around us. The last thing we heard before we lost communications and the bubble collapsed was someone shouting, *'Sauve qui peut, sauve qui peut.'*

"I almost went in there to get them. I was at the seal door on the outer bubble when one of the army officers pulled a gun on me and told me that if I broke the contamination seal he would shoot me on the spot. It was fucking chaos, Gaby. Fucking chaos, I still can't believe everything came apart so fast. Somehow the army got the area cleared before the bubble blew, but we still lost the team, one of the Sikorskys and God knows how much equipment. Have you ever seen a grass fire, Gaby, that moves faster than a man can run?"

"Down on Strangford Lough, the tide is like that across the flats. I once saw it outrun a poor bastard dog." Gaby watched the smoke coil upward from her nostrils. "I can still see the paws, trying to push against the current, and its nose, held up out of the water. I remember its owner, frantic, but there was nothing she could do."

"It moved like that tide," Shepard said. "It moved like fire. Like fire, it consumed what it touched and left everything changed behind it. God alone knows how I made it to the Tupolev—I was last on. Last on. They pulled the door behind me and took off. Twenty seconds after we started to roll, the steps went. It was that close. From the air I could see the whole airfield; it was like one of those satellite photographs in miniature: this circle of hideous color a mile wide stamped on the green hill country."

"You all right, Shepard?"

"I'm all right. Now." He took the cigarette from Gaby's lips and placed it between his own. Gaby's heart kicked with sudden strange eroticism. "I thought I'd given these things up years ago. You never do really quit, do you? As soon as we regrouped back at Kilembe, I sent a skinsuit team back for survivors. We got the team—they're still decontaminating at Kilembe. But Dominique died, Gaby. She's dead. The filtration and pumping system on her tank went down. She suffocated in there, Gaby. Alone. Trapped in the dark. Couldn't do a thing about it."

"You're not to blame, Shepard."

"I was senior officer, and all I did was run around flapping my arms and shouting while Dominique Ferjac died. I didn't know what to do, Gaby. Something happened that I hadn't prepared for and I couldn't make up an answer on the spot."

"Who does know what to do, Shepard? It's an alien world out there, it doesn't obey our rules and laws or follow our management policies or research strategies."

"It doesn't make me feel any better."

"It isn't meant to. It's a token of solidarity from one person up to the eyes in shit to another. Because, as you said, at least it's guaranteed fresh shit every day. And by the way, these things give you cancer." Gaby took back the cigarette, smoked it down to the dog end and stubbed it out on the floor. She rolled against Shepard, moved her hand over his flank in the way he liked so much he could barely stand it. "If that didn't make you feel better, how about this?"

He smiled.

"A little."

"How about this, then?" She did a thing he liked even more that he could just bear.

"Better."

"This?" She moved her mouth down to do the thing he liked so much it almost killed him.

"Best," he moaned, and took her long hair in his hand and pulled her head gently up to look at him. "One last thing. Your friend Peter Werther. He was right. The Chaga has known us for a very long time. In the sample we managed to get out from the Rutshuru package, we found human genes. Or rather, protohuman genes. They differ from ours in a couple of small but significant chromosomes. We've done gene-line analyses and generational backtracking and we think that we have the genes of *Australopi-*

thecus, an ancestor of Homo sapiens that lived and died on the plains of East Africa four to four and a half million years ago."

"Heeeere's Lucy!" Gaby said, laying her head on his belly.

"Heeeere's Gaby," Shepard said, and moved her head back to the place where it pleased him so much.

36

The plane took them away and there were too many chairs at the table and too few pairs of shorts in the washing machine and the rear seat belts in the Mahindra were too neat and too tight and too unused in their housings. He was disconsolate. He had warned her he would be like that, but it did not make it any better for either of them. She was disconsolate too. They had been the best days. Snorkeling on the reef. Fighting over the last chapatti at dinner. Football on the white coral strand at sunset. Haggling for dreadful antiques in the Mombasa markets. Learning the tricks and secrets of tropical fruit. To the Mara. To the SkyNet offices, where Gaby sensed there was something too welcoming and smiling in the faces behind the desks. Especially the women's. Gaby had not brought Shepard and his children as trophies of sexual victory, she was not aware of having fought a war of conquest, but she imagined the whispers running around behind her back like vermin. To the Elephant Bar, on the final night, where Oksana and all the Siberians who could not get drunk stood the boys on a table, drank toasts to them and carried them around the bar on their shoulders, singing "Consider Yourself" from *Oliver.* The Siberians who could not get drunk were very into musicals.

And then they were gone and nothing was good. Gaby and Shepard bickered in Shepard's ugly, under-lived-in apartment like two cats sharing a food bowl until he went to Zaire to try to salvage the Goma debacle and she went to Tom M'boya Street to find that the whispers had mated and bred looks, and mutters, and little gatherings that always broke up when she walked past. There were snide Post-It notes stuck to her videophone; she would return from the toilet to find crude animations of her and Shepard fucking on her terminal screen. No one admitted to these crimes when she stood and accused the room. The women barely acknowledged her, even her first ally, Ute Bonhorst, and most of the men regarded her with polite distaste, like a leper in a candy shop. The Africans treated her as they always had, Jake Aarons was as comradely and at the same time distant as ever, and T. P. Costello held himself above office pettiness. Abigail Santini went out of her way to be friendly. Identifying the source of the infection, Gaby prepared her revenge.

She knew she would find them all at the particular table in the Thorn Tree: T.P., Jake, Mohammed Siriye from Editorial, Abigail. There had to be witnesses. Gaby got a drink from the bar and joined them on the patio. Nods. Greetings.

"Isn't that your ex-housemate over by the jukebox?" Abigail Santini asked. "That Somali woman?"

"Why, so it is," Gaby said. She waved. Miriam Sondhai waved back, feigning surprise.

"Who's that white woman with her? The one in lesbian chic?"

Gaby shrugged and sipped her drink. "Must be a friend." You'll find out soon enough, she thought. When Abigail went to the toilets, Gaby took her bag and came with her. Miriam and Oksana left their table a moment later and followed her in. They were waiting when Abigail came out of the cubicle. It was very quick. Oksana took the right side. Miriam took the left. Gaby bent her over the basins and pulled her head up so she could see both of them in the mirror.

"What you have to understand is that I'm with Shepard because of what he is, not what he can do for me," Gaby said. "I know you may have trouble with this mode of thinking, but you should make the effort. It really can change your outlook on life. Another thing you should understand is that I'm not envious of things I can't have. I know you've been pushing your tits in Shepard's face long before I showed up, but what you don't seem to grasp is that men are intelligent, men can choose, men aren't just dicks with just enough motor system attached to get them to the next pussy. If Shepard had wanted you, it would be your underwear in his laundry basket, but he didn't, and it's mine, and it's going to stay that way. Now, if we've got points one and two, maybe we can push on to point three. You do not go around spreading stories behind people's backs that they're cunt-brained gold diggers who will stop at nothing to sleep their way to a good story. Because everything I have, I got on my own merits, by my own sweat and smarts. I don't owe anyone anything. I see what I want, I take it with my own hand. Last thing to understand: I'm a

Celt, we're a people who prefer direct action to whispering campaigns. If something riles us, we do something about it. And we are people with very, very long memories and very, very short tempers. That's it. Speech is over. Show time."

She took the electric shaver from her bag.

"You would not dare!" Abigail Santini shouted.

"Wouldn't I? I'm T.P.'s green-eyed girl, I'm fireproof."

She clicked the razor on and shaved a beautiful gray-stubbled strip up the back and over the top of Abigail's skull to the forehead. Softly curled black hair fell to the washroom floor. Abigail Santini struggled and swore expressively in Italian, but Miriam and Oksana held her firmly. Gaby admired her handiwork. She had originally intended to shave everything off, but a Union Jack pattern of stripes was more satisfying. Abigail Santini would be forced to shave the rest herself. She pushed her enemy's forehead against the raised rim of the basin and readied her weapon for a second pass from ear to ear.

A gloved hand stayed hers. The back of the glove was studded with Gothic spikes. There were silver rings on the fingers. The hand took the razor from Gaby and switched it off. The ladies' powder room was full of young black women in serious leather.

"Leave us, please," said the leather girl who had stayed Gaby's vengeance. Abigail Santini turned at the door for a parting vow of hatred. A woman in leather pouch and pads over a ribbed bodysuit pushed her ungently out into the bar. The murmur of table chatter ceased immediately.

"I stay with my friend," Oksana said.

"It's all right," Gaby said. "I promise."

Oksana and Miriam left. The possegirls struck poses to match their clothes. Haran entered the women's washroom. With him was the fattest black woman Gaby had ever seen. She wore a voluminous kanga dress printed with scenes from Kenya's political history that made her look larger still. M'zee Jomo Kenyatta, father of the nation, peered from the folds of her matching turban.

"Your peace negotiations have progressed since we last met," Gaby said. Haran smiled thinly and tapped one of the leather girls with his cane. She took up sentry duty outside.

"Mombi and I have reached a position of mutual understanding. At the moment we are engaged in a process of assimilation and rationalization of our operations and clients."

The big woman did not speak. She had the most beautiful eyes. They should not be beautiful, Gaby thought. They should be piggy and cold in rolls of fat.

"Ten drive-by shootings in as many days is assimilation and rationalization?" Gaby asked. Mombi laughed silently but did not speak.

"We kill those who require killing," Haran said. "These rude boys litter the streets; we are only doing the public a service, making the city safe for honest citizens." He perched on the edge of the sink unit and balanced himself with both hands on the knob of his cane. "Concerning our arrangement. I have made some progress in both your requests. It seems that both lines of inquiry lead to the same place."

"Unit Twelve? Peter Werther's in there as well as William?"

"He was taken there directly from the What the Sun Said community. That is our arrangement satisfied. However, knowing you would not be content with confirmation that he has been taken, and where he has been taken to, I have been conducting further inquiries on your behalf into the nature of this Unit Twelve."

"Which you are adding to the account."

Haran smiled. At his signal one of Mombi's possegirls set up a PDU on a washbasin. The screen showed a green-and-white wire-frame CAD animation of an architectural plan. It looked like three of those romantically impractical wheelie space stations from *2001* stacked on top of each other, turning slowly in dark green cyberspace. Gaby bent to the screen, trying to decipher scales and annotations. A tiny box was balanced on top of the central spindle. She knew what it was, and the whole thing leaped into proportion.

"We obtained the schematics for the underground structures from Nairobi Central Planning Department," Haran said. "They are much more amenable to inducement than UNECTA."

"It's incredible."

"The largest piece of civil engineering in Kenya in the past five years. I can show you the construction details and costings. They are impressive."

"How could they keep something this big quiet?"

"It is not so hard when the United Nations runs your country," Mombi said. Her voice was high and musical, another incongruity with her huge body.

"What is it for?" Gaby asked. Whatever price Haran asked of her, it was worth it to bust this secret subterranean citadel wide open.

"That is where we have run into difficulties," Haran said. "It works to different protocols and passwords from the rest of the system. My operatives cannot get direct access to it. Our information is deduced from secondary sources like revenue, accounting, power consumption, logistics. From the engineering specifications, which we obtained from the firms who constructed the unit, we have concluded that it is designed to be a self-contained environment. A comparison of catering costs with wage figures reveals an interesting discrepancy. There are fifty full-time staff on the unit payroll—most of them have medical qualifications, significantly. The amount of consumables passing into the unit system is sufficient for many times that figure."

"How many times?"

"Approximately six times."

Three hundred people, down there under the earth, in those circular corridors, going round and round in artificial light forever. Peter Werther's tan would have faded under the fluorescents. To him it would be just another strange place. To William, who had lived most of his life outdoors, under the sun, without walls—he would wither and despair, thinking that he would never be let out again. What had his experience of the Chaga been that they took him away and shut him up in these curving corridors?

"Who are these people?" Gaby asked.

"We do not know. UNECTA keeps no lists. This place does not exist, remember."

"How can we get them out?"

"You cannot," Haran said. "No one has ever come out. How can you get people out who are not officially in?"

"Only one thing comes out," Mombi said. "Blood. Every three weeks, a consignment of two hundred and eighty-three samples is sent by courier to the Kenyatta National Hospital Department of Hematology."

"We know this by the shipping documents," Haran said. "One of my posse members has a relative who works in the hospital reception."

This is how it gets done in Kenya, Gaby thought. By a relative of a friend, or a friend of a relative. They had information networking in this land long before the worldweb spun its silk lines across the globe. Blood. Two hundred and eighty-three drops.

"Which section?"

"The GAPU HIV 4 Research Section," Mombi said. Haran laughed. Gaby had never heard him laugh before. It was like the bark of some feral animal scavenging along the lanes and hovels of the townships.

"For so many months, you were living in the same house as the answer to your mystery," he said. "You moved too soon."

"Haran's man has gone through the records," Mombi said. "The GAPU Hematology Unit has been processing samples for twenty-seven months."

"They are testing them for HIV 4?"

"It seems that this is so. As my partner has said, it is difficult to penetrate the security of these organizations. We have reached the limits of what we can find out. Now you are uniquely placed to learn the truth. When you do, I hope that you will share it with me, for unlike my friend Haran, I am a woman who loves her country."

Haran laughed again and pushed his cane forward. At the sign, the *watekni* moved from their positions to the door to cover the withdrawal through the Thorn Tree bar. Mombi inclined her head to Gaby as she swept out. Haran paused a moment.

"Most uniquely placed, Gaby. The truth may be closer even than Miriam Sondhai. If UNECTA's peripatetic executive director does not know what is happening in his own organization, who does?"

He touched the tip of his cane to his planter's hat and Gaby was alone in the women's room.

T.P. was at the table by the street. The others had all left. He did not look like a happy owl.

"I can't have this, you know."

"T.P., T.P., listen, it's a conspiracy—"

"Heard it before, Gaby. Journalists report the news. They do not become the news. It's not professional. I don't care who started it, but I will not have the press community thinking I'm running some kind of female mud-wrestling stable. This is a disciplinary matter, Gaby. I'll overlook entertaining heavily armed *watekni* in the ladies' jax. But you do not try to turn the senior on-line editor into Sinead O'Connor."

"Fuck, T.P.—"

"I'm prepared to let it ride this once, provided you donate a month's wages to a refugee aid charity of your choice."

"Jesus. T.P."

"And I want to see the receipt. A written apology wouldn't go amiss either. You're dangerous, Gaby. Not just to yourself—that's par for the course for a reporter out here—but to everyone who comes into contact with you."

"Trust me, T.P."

He left some shillings. "I can't. That's the trouble."

37

In the anonymous hired Toyota pickup, Gaby McAslan watched the figure in the red one-piece turn out of the gateway and run along the grass verge. Fifty-five minutes. She waited until the woman turned on to Ondaatje Avenue and got out of the truck.

God, what if she has got a new code for the alarm? Gaby McAslan thought as she walked down the brick drive to the front door.

Three. Eight. Four. Four. Two. Seven. Four. Nine.

And pray.

And *turn.*

The door opened with the silence of aged mahogany on well-oiled hinges. It was in here. Miriam Sondhai was the icon of many virtues, but not the Madonna of memory. Her attention was turned to loftier things than the numbers that define modern life. She got her cash card swallowed every week. As she jogged across the Dental Hospital car park toward Mandela Highway, she would have the door code tucked into the tongue pocket of her running shoes. Gaby's entire scheme rested on the theory that Miriam was similarly lax with her passwords to the Global Aids Policy Unit system.

She would be on the long straight run into Nairobi now, against the flow of traffic. Fifty minutes. Gaby's favorite scene in her father's Hitchcock collection had always been the one where Grace Kelly in the gorgeous frock searches the murderer's apartment while Jimmy Stewart watches helplessly from his rear window. It is one thing watching, and quite another doing, she realized.

Where to look? The Filofax on the table. Too obvious. She

had a bad memory but she was not stupid. Same for the PDU. The handbag, hanging from the teak-and-antelope-horn coatrack.

All truth is in the handbag.

She would be past the new Sirikwa Hotel now, waiting at the *keepie-leftie* for a gap in the traffic. Forty-five minutes.

Lip gloss. Small change. Stamps. Card for the hospital car park. Keys. Other people's things. An envelope with a Somali stamp, franked Mogadishu. Silver propelling pencil. Paracetamol. Madonnas do not need paracetamol, or feminine hygiene products. A little flat address book, corners reinforced with Scotch tape. On the cover a brown man with kohl and a curling black mustache groped under the dress of a brown woman with kohl and no mustache. *Indian Erotic Art Birthday Book.*

Madonnas certainly do not have *Indian Erotic Art Birthday Books*.

She took the book to the coffee table, flicked through the pages of exquisite Tantric couplings and anniversaries. *Don't Forget* above a miniature of a green-skinned woman having her vulva licked by a man with his little fingers crooked in a spiritual attitude. Underneath, long codes of letters and digits.

Thirty-six minutes. She would be coming up on the big intersection at the bottom of University Road.

Gaby pulled up the PDU's rollscreen and hooked it to its frame. The liquid-crystal-impregnated plastic blinked start-up icons at her. She stroked the touch panel and opened up the directory. The call connection to the Kenyatta Hospital was made in seconds. A cigarette would be desperately good, Gaby thought. For a fatal instant she almost succumbed. She clicked for the Global Aids Policy Unit. Password queries interrogated her. She typed in the first of the codes in the birthday book. She went straight through to the virology department. Jesus, Miriam, take more care. It's a sharp-toothed world that you're running through in your red Lycra suit. Another interrogative. Try the next on the list.

Invalid password.

Number three, then.

Invalid password.

Sweaty-palms moment. Three strikes and you are out. Dare she run the risk that the next code on the list would be wrong too and alert the firewall defenses? Fuck it. She'd faced down Azeri BTR-60s and Hart assault helicopters. HBP37-FFONLHJC162XC.

No wonder she wrote them down.

The rollscreen filled with icons. Miriam's workspace volumes pulsed hot. The answer could be in them, or it could be in any of the other hundreds of nested files. Up to now it had all been balls and adrenaline. Now came the work, to the metronome footfalls of Miriam Sondhai on the streets of Nairobi.

Gaby pulled down a find menu and typed in BLOOD AND/OR SAMPLES. TWENTY-TWO FILES FOUND, the PDU told her. She picked the first from the pop-up menu. It was a database of cell culture samples from an ongoing experiment into the relationship between the HIV 4 virus and the nuclear material of helper T-cells.

File two. Monthly staff blood-test results. Joseph Isangere; confirmed antibody reaction. Jesus.

File three: blood types and organ-donor registrations.

File four: a locked file on the results of staff blood-and-urine tests for drug use. They'll let you know someone has caught the terrible thing they work with, but it's top secret if they toke a little sensimilla of an evening to get the damned viruses and the things they do out of their minds.

Twenty-three minutes. Miriam Sondhai would be on Uhuru Highway, beating along the earth sidewalks past the bus queues and the matatu touts, the city on her left, the bleached, dismembered park on her right: liquid and beautiful as Gaby had seen her that first morning from T.P.'s Landcruiser.

File five. Open sesame.

HIV 4 test referrals. Promising. It was a hell of a database. Fifteen thousand entries. Gaby set up search parameters for KAJIADO, UNECTA, UNIT 12. She held her breath as the command FIND ANY went through to the hospital. Do not think about how long it will take to come through the cell net onto the PDU, she told herself. Do not think that at the end of Uhuru Highway, Miriam Sondhai is on the way back. Do not think that there may be a hundred watchdogs set to bark at the scent of any of these parameters you have set.

The search failed on KAJIADO and UNIT 12, but on UNECTA it threw three hundred names at her. Some had been found under UNECTA as accommodation address or employer. The majority—two hundred and eighty-three—cited UNECTA as source of referral.

"Result," she whispered. Seventeen minutes. Ticking clock, pounding feet, heaving breath, hammering heart. She could copy the data onto the disks she had brought and be safely back at Shepard's before Miriam Sondhai stripped down for her shower. But if they were the wrong records, she would have to break into the hospital system again.

Check your source before you commit, Gaby. A thousand hacks in the welfare line will tell you impatience was their downfall.

She displayed the list of names.

Naomi Rukavindi, formerly of Moshi in Kilimanjaro district of Tanzania; you will do for a start. There was a bad Photo Me image of a startled-looking woman with nice hair and grinning teeth, there were statistics of age and physiology, several entry points that could be opened by password and sheets of antibody counts and lymphocyte activity curves and immune response deviations. At the top of the screen a number indicated that this was page 36 of 36. Three-weekly samples, Mombi had said. One hundred and eight weeks. Over two years monitoring the progress of a disease that killed in six months. Gaby clicked up FIND FIRST and on a hunch spread it beside page 36. The counts and the ratios and the histograms and the curves matched exactly. She scrolled through the file, graph after graph. There was no discrepancy.

"You should be dead, Mrs. Naomi Rukavindi," Gaby whispered.

She sampled other UNECTA referrals. The first file was forty-eight pages, the shortest three. None of them showed any deterioration in condition. Not one had died of the killer HIV 4.

The face at the top of that most recent three-page file belonged to William Bi, wife's sister-in-law's nephew to Tembo.

She glanced at her new watch.

Five minutes.

Christ.

She unwrapped the disk she had brought, carefully stuffing the cellophane wrapper into her bag as the PDU formatted it. COPY FILE, she commanded, and watched the sands run through the digital hourglass while she imagined Miriam Sondhai coming up Nkrumah Avenue past the chain-link fence around the primary school. What if the traffic has been light? What if she has not been held up at the junction of the *keepie-leftie*? At any moment she might hear the pad of running soles on red brick.

The copy completed. She checked the hard disk for fingerprints before shutting down. And don't forget the rollscreen. Jesus, the thing's still warm. She was out the door when she saw the *Indian Erotic Art Birthday Book* on the coffee table.

Had the handbag been open or closed? Knowing Miriam, she bet on closed. The mahogany door shut heavily. She was halfway to the car when she remembered to reset the alarm. The *armed* light winked at her.

Plus one minute. Into extra time. She got into the hired pickup, started it, and as she glanced into the rearview to move off, she saw Miriam Sondhai come around the corner of Nyrere Avenue. Go. Go. Go. She glanced into her mirror again at the turn into Ondaatje Avenue and saw Miriam swing off the footpath into her drive.

Five cigarettes and a quarter of a bottle of Shepard's sacramental Wild Turkey stopped her hands shaking enough to load the disk into her PDU and open up the stolen database. The icon unfolded in a list view. Fifteen thousand HIV 4 referrals, arranged alphabetically, starting with Aa, ending with Zy.

Aa being for Aarons. Jake H.

38

She heard the first shot as she was jangling the wind chimes outside the front door.

Jake Aarons had a very beautiful front door. He had swapped it for his 4X4 with a Makonde carver down on the border between Tanzania and Mozambique. It was seven feet high and seven feet wide and he had brought it all the way back to Nairobi on the top of a matatu. Jake was very happy about the deal. A new 4X4 was easily bought. No one in Nairobi had as beautiful a door. But he was not answering it this morning.

There was a second shot. Gaby gave up jangling and went around the side of the house. She found Jake Aarons standing knee-deep in the pool in the quadrangle between the house's two wings. He was dressed only in a pair of shorts with a red maple leaf on the left flank. In his left hand was a bottle of tequila, in his right a revolver. On the pool edge stood a full-length mirror. Gaby watched Jake take a long pull from the bottle, raise the gun at the mirror and blow a hole through the reflection of his own head. There were two other holes in the mirror; at groin and chest height.

"Jake."

He whirled, dropped the bottle, brought the gun to bear on the bridge of Gaby's nose.

"Jesus, Jake!"

The tequila bottle bobbed twice and went down. Jake lowered the weapon with a sigh.

"He's gone, Gaby. The bastard left me. Took my money, took all my fucking money, the little bitch. He packed his things and went and took my money."

He grimaced like a silent scream and sat on the flagstone edge of the pool. The hand holding the gun dangled between his legs.

"How did you find out, Gaby?"

"Jake, I'm so sorry."

"No, I'm sorry. What you are is well placed for a good career move. Over to our chief East Africa correspondent, Gaby McAslan. Rush around with commiserations and sympathy and brown-nose rich old uncle with the legacy." He brought the gun out and aimed it again at Gaby. It seemed too heavy for him to hold. "Unwise to contemplate blackmailing a man with a gun and absolutely nothing to lose by using it."

"What kind of person do you take me for, Jake?"

"The most terrible of persons: the ignorant manipulator. You play with lives, you can't help it. You are irresistibly drawn to those who are in a position to advance you. You don't know this, of course, and it's your complete innocence that makes you ultimately unrefusable. That poor bastard Shepard you're banging; have you any idea the conflict of loyalties you're costing him? Of course you don't, you haven't the first idea what a monster you are, honey, and because I'm a terminal old fruit who can say absolutely anything he likes, you're going to have to listen to it and learn by it."

"Hold on. T.P. doesn't know about this?"

He laughed.

"Oh, I have given myself away, haven't I? Nobody knows save thee, me, the hospital and that fucking faithless bastard who said he'd stay with me always and hightailed it with his dick between his legs when he found out that Ol' Bwana Jake had gone down with the Scourge."

Gaby cried out and covered her ears as Jake emptied the remaining chambers into the mirror. Birds rose from their roosts on the terra-cotta roof tiles with a clap of wings.

"Do you want to know the irony of it? You probably don't, but you're going to hear it anyway. It didn't even start as four. It started as a dose of three I reckon I picked up from some emergency dental work I had to get done over in Uganda a couple of years ago. Safe sex? I wrote the book on it. The condom kid, that's me. Safe dentistry? They don't tell you about that one. But what the hell, if you can afford the AZT, the interferon and the anitbody transfusions, you won't even get turned down for life insurance with a dose of three. The hospital keeps an eye on you and every other month or so takes a blood sample to make sure the HIV 3 virus hasn't mutated into the HIV 4 variant. And everything was fine, until last month."

"Foa Mulaku." She had got the story because T.P. said Jake was sick. "T.P. did know about the HIV 3."

"T.P.'s known all along about the three. You misjudge him, Gaby. He may be the last honorable man in broadcast journalism. The hospital called me in: anomalous antibody proteins in my samples. You're dead from the moment they say 'anomalous antibody proteins,' but you can't stop yourself hoping. You look for signs and wonders, like rainbows, or counting birds on power lines or monkeys on trees, or adding up bus numbers to see if they come to anything but thirteen; anything that seems like a promise of a yes. You bribe Jesus with prayers and candles; Allah too, if he'll do the job. Even the Hindu gods down at the temple: just give me a sign. And then the letter arrives asking you to come see Dr. Singh and they might as well tell you in the letter it's four, you're dead, because then at least you could work it out in your own private coming-to-terms and not having to go through sessions with a Personal Trauma Counselor sitting with her hands folded and that fucking cow-looking-over-a-gate expression that is supposed to radiate empathy and understanding. Jesus Christ!

"And then the person you turn to for real empathy and understanding, because of all the times he's told you he loves you, he cares for you, he'll always be there for you, he'll always help you and sustain you and empower you and carry you when the road gets too hard for you and all that Jonathan Livingston Seagull personal-development shit, leaves you three lines on a sheet of file paper on the kitchen table saying he's sorry, so sorry, but his life path is calling him on. Life path! Takes five thousand dollars of my money to help him down his yellow-brick life path!''

Jake threw the gun at a glossy starling standing on the paving, staring at him with its head inclined. It leaped away into the sky with a squawk.

''So, how did you find out?'' Jake asked.

''I got into the Global Aids Policy Unit database.''

''Not legally you didn't. Who hacked it for you? Haran?''

He is in control here, Gaby thought. His sickness has given him mastery over guilt and sympathy and he knows he can make me do whatever he wants.

''How long have you known about Haran?''

''We all make deals with the devil. What's he charging you?''

''An eye for an eye. But Haran didn't do the GAPU files. I did it myself. Stole the passwords from Miriam Sondhai.''

Jake Aarons pursed his lips and nodded. It was a combination of gestures Gaby could read well; his professional curiosity was stirring. He could not stop it any more than a kleptomaniac could stop stealing.

''Stay there.'' He went into the house, wrapped himself in a bathrobe and boiled a kettle in his blue-and-yellow kitchen. It looked like the kitchen of a man who eats out a lot.

''Tea? Earl Grey? Tequila's piss. Tea is thinkin' drinkin'.'' He brought a tray with pot and cups to the side of the pool and invited Gaby to dangle her feet in the water beside him. ''Now talk. Talk to me of things newsworthy, because it stops me having to think about all the things these little chips of protein in my blood are taking away from me.'' He poured two bowls. The set was Japanese, decorated under the glaze with Buddhist prayers. Gaby kicked off her boots and told him about the blood samples from UNECTA, and about the vanished William Bi and Peter Werther and the place they had been vanished to. She did not tell him that the HIV 4 victims were alive long after the virus should have killed them. She did not want to give Jake a shot at a salvation she was not sure she believed in herself.

Jake savored his tea.

''I think we are like the Trans-Canadian Railroad builders

who started at either coast and met up in the middle," he said. "Answer this: what's the great UN lie about the Chaga?"

"Anyone who goes deep never returns."

"Now listen to a story," Jake said. "Back in the early days, before the UN effort found its feet and most of the evacuation and containment strategies were left to the national governments, the Tanzanians set up camps at Moshi on the southern side of the mountain to take the Wa-chagga people who had been cleared from the higher slopes. There was a common belief then that the growth would stop when it reached the bottom of the mountain. Of course, it didn't, so not only did the Tanzanians have several tens of thousands of Wa-chagga to evacuate from the resettlement camps, they also had eighty thousand residents of Moshi and God knows how many from the surrounding district. It's no surprise that in the chaos they managed to lose a couple of hundred Wa-chagga. In fact, it's a miracle they didn't lose more. Officially, everyone from the camps is present and correct, but a little *magendo* buys a lot of truth. When you find out that half a tribe has gotten lost, you get to thinking about what else may have disappeared as well."

"Or been disappeared." Not one word of this conversation was going according to Gaby's game plan. We have roles to play, she thought. You are the embittered dying man seeking reconciliation with the world, I am the offerer of comfort, sympathy, solidarity and trawling for a career move. You should not be talking to me about lost tribes. You should not have that I-spy-story glint in your eyes.

"Thank God the UN and WHO keep records of those they process into their camps, or I would never have found the pattern. What I found out about Unit Twelve is that everyone who gets disappeared there has been in contact with the Chaga. And now you tell me that they all have HIV 4. What's the connection?"

Still Gaby did not tell him what she suspected about that place.

"I got curious about where this lost tribe went when they slipped out of Moshi camp," Jake continued. "They went back to their ancestral lands. To Kilimanjaro. Into the Chaga. In deep. And they're still there. The Tactical safari squads have had contact with their far patrols. They're living, deep in there, and they're thriving. The Chaga is looking after them. And I'm going in there to find them and prove that the UN has been lying to us about what it is really like in there.''

"How?''

"Like you said, we all make our deals with the devil. I didn't fancy the *watekni*'s terms on my soul. I like simple cash transactions. So do the Tacticals.''

"Jesus, Jake.''

"Posterity will show who was wise and who was not, Gaby. The posses are finished. Every day the Chaga snips a little bit more off them. The Tacticals aren't interested in information as commodity. They're not interested in commodity at all. They're interested in their future. They know the Chaga will disinherit all current vested interests. All but theirs.''

Jake Aarons poured more tea.

"Civil war?''

"In the end, yes. But not a Rwandan-style tribal slaughter fest. Nor even Somali warlordism. When it comes, and it's coming sooner than the government thinks; it'll be a war for and against the Chaga. To stay, or to be let go. The future and the past. While the politicians are starting to question the United Nations' article of faith on indefinite evacuation, out in the townships there are powerful factions—my own Black Simba cartel among them—in favor of mass migration into the Chaga. Their safari squads bring more than goodies back from beyond terminum. The fact that they go back and forth so readily already proves UNECTA's obsession about decontamination is a lie.''

It's a blind to check for HIV 4, Gaby thought.

"You're taking me, Jake,'' she said aloud.

"I detect steel in your voice, Gaby. This time that red-haired Celtic charisma is just going to have to fail you. My plans are made, they have been for months. If anything, the Slim diagnosis just gave me the impetus to take my courage in both hands and do it. Strangely enough, those plans don't include you.''

"I'll tell T.P.''

Jake went into the house and returned with a cellphone.

"Tell T.P. that his chief East Africa correspondent has Slim? I'll tell him myself.'' He punched in the first eight digits of T. P. Costello's direct line. "He ought to know.''

"I'll tell him about your little expedition into the heart of darkness.''

Jake's finger hovered over the final number.

"Old newshounds never die, he'll say. He wouldn't refuse his most faithful reporter and best buddy the chance to ride into pissed old hacks' Valhalla, least of all with the story of the decade attached. Your move."

The words came in a rush, like starlings from a shaken tree.

"I'll tell Shepard."

Jake stared at Gaby for many moments. He lifted his finger from the button and set the cellphone on the tray next to the Japanese teapot.

"You would too, you bitch. So, Jake, went the day well? Sure; I look for support from the man who tells me he'd lay down his life for me because I find out I've six months to live, and three of them as an incontinent, incompetent, gaga skeleton hooked into a life-support unit and he runs off with five thousand dollars. Then my business colleague blackmails me. Best of days, world."

"You'll have my complete silence. The exclusive will be yours, I don't want any credit. I just want to go in there, Jake. That's all I've ever wanted."

"And the words *Chief East Africa Correspondent* under your face on the ten o'clock news."

In time you will stop feeling guilty about what you have done, Gaby told herself. It will be just another lump of pink scar tissue from the bad you have had to do to make good. She picked up the cellphone.

"So, do I call Shepard?"

"I'll call for you tomorrow, about eight," Jake said. "I'll introduce you to the team, I'll put your case, but the decision about whether you go or not is theirs. Whatever they decide, you will keep silent. If you betray the Black Simbas, not all the favors in Haran's bag will save you from them. You understand me?"

"I understand you."

"Tomorrow. Eight."

39

Gaby's text diary
Day One

I write this diary sitting against the great baobab that is all that remains of the world I understand.

Camp One is five miles within terminum at the foot of the sudden lift of forest called the Great Wall in a zone of transition where terrestrial life is dismantled and incorporated into Chaga-life. The chaotic terrain of land corals and rotting acacias makes it a good place to hide from the spy satellites, Moran, our leader, says. Tomorrow we will go in under the canopy. That is, if it doesn't come to us first. The Great Wall is on the move. We are camped among beige barrel-shaped objects like straw mushrooms three times my height. Every so often one will split and extrude a slender dark red bole. You can see them grow before your eyes. Some go up fifty, a hundred feet without any sign of stopping. I wish I could have brought the visioncam. So much more easy to show than describe, but Jake guards the Chaga-proofed camera's limited stack of pre-loaded discs jealously.

If I've learned anything from Moon's diary—which I carry with me in my pack—it's the importance of knowing where to start. So I won't begin with the lies I told Shepard about the reporting jobs or the surreptitious gathering of my gear—the canvas back pack, the hand-tooled all-leather boots, the metal canisters for water, toiletries, sun-block, cigarettes—even the Chaga-proof steel toothbrush; or the meeting above the shop on Kamukunji Street where I was introduced to Moran and M'zee and Sugardaddy and Rose and Bushbaby. And the dog.

I'll begin with the firefight, because it marks a definitive transition from the familiar to the alien. We've been walking south toward terminum from the place where the Black Simba's humpy dropped us. M'zee, who, as his name suggests, is the oldest and most experienced in our team, sees a plume of dust south of us that is moving against the general direction of the willy-willys that blow across the Amboseli plain. M'zee glasses it and confirms: a scavenger patrol in a recycled 4X4 they've fitted with a heavy machine gun. We're pinned between it and the spy satellite coming over the horizon in ten minutes. On Moran's orders, we take cover in a dry gulch under our thermal profile quilts. These are amazing pieces of military technology: they draw body heat from the inside and redistribute it to match the average profile of the environment outside. You're effectively infrared invisible. My chief concern is not scavengers or satellites but finding a scorpion creeping over me. I wait. I sweat. I dread. Then I hear the helicopters and freeze. The satellite is up, has spotted the scavengers and alerted the military. The air cav come right over the top of us, hover and move off into the south. A few moments later there is a distant stutter of heavy-machine-gun fire, the turbine shriek of helicopters taking evasive action and then the snapping, staccato rattle of Gatling fire. I feel the ground shake to a dull explosion, and no more gunfire. The helicopters pass over us once again and swing away into the west.

When the satellite is down below the horizon, we roll up our thermal quilts and move quickly before ground troops come in to secure the area. I know from experience how far a column of smoke is visible in this country. Our course takes us close by the wreck: Jake begs a photo opportunity. Moran agrees, sends Sugardaddy with us for protection. Sugardaddy does not expect survivors, but death in the bush attracts a dangerous wake. I take shots of the smoldering shell of blackened steel and the corpses scattered on the charred ground. I've never seen a killed human being before. The fire has burned the upper parts to the bones; the parts in contact with the ground are intact, down to the scraps of blue denim and cotton T-shirt. Jake says that is the way bodies burn in war. When a jackal more courageous than its packmates darts in to tear at one of the bodies, I scream, "Kill it, just kill the fucking thing, can't you?" Sugardaddy calmly lifts his Kalashnikov and blows the bastard thing into the bush in a shatter of bone and gut.

Moran is angry that Sugardaddy has risked security with a shot, but Sugardaddy is a Luo, like Faraway, and like Faraway, satanically vain. Calling on the respect due his age and experience, M'zee keeps the peace between the two men, but the day will soon come when Sugardaddy and Moran will fight to the death, like pack animals. We are all jackals, out here.

We were on such high alert watching for the dust trails of soldiers coming to investigate that I only noticed we had crossed terminum when I felt a crawling sensation on my left wrist like I used to get when I was a kid and the cats slept on the bed and I imagined their fleas were creeping all over me. My new Swatch was breaking out in orange pimples. I had been so careful about everything else and forgotten about the plastic watch. I dropped it to the hexagon cover just as the strap rotted into rags and drips of digested polyethylene. My last connection with the human world was broken: time. There is no time in here; no history, no future, only the eternal now. Present, and presence: the sensation of the Great Wall at my back is that of an almost sentient mystery, crawling toward me on a billion red millipede legs.

40

Gaby's text diary
Day Two

Time for a line while they get the boats ready.

All morning we have marched through the Great Wall. If the edgelands taxed my powers of description, the Great Wall staggers me. The slender red trunks rise for five, six hundred feet before dividing and redividing into hundreds of branchlets, each of which supports a single enormous hexagonal leaf. These leaves all lie in a horizontal plane, so that they form a more or less continuous surface; the impression is not of being in a forest, but among the pillars that hold up the roof of the world.

Ecclesiastical . . . like being in a drowned cathedral, my forerunner described this place in her diary. I hate to have to use another's analogy—especially hers—but it best conveys the feel of this place. The roof leaves are translucent and color the light that falls through them in a cyclorama of ancient lights, interspersed by edges of white where the sun shines through the gaps between plates. About thirty, forty feet from the ground, the trunks split into enormous aerial roots and buttresses, so that we walk through an architecture of vaults and arches and piers. There's incense in this cathedral: cinnamon and mold and coal tar and something I cannot identify but which must be powerfully pheromonal because it's given the boys stiffies and my nipples are so hard they're rubbing against my vest. And you imagine that in the stirring of the leaves in the wind and the creak and sway of the trunks you hear God walking in the woods of his new Eden.

Things move up in the canopy; some so fast you cannot be sure you have seen them, some so slow you cannot be certain they are moving at all. A long way off, something is twittering. Nothing earthborn ever made a noise like that.

How do I feel, moving through this cathedrallike place? Spooky; exalted. Unbelieving, as if it has all been painted by Hollywood set designers and will fall down with a crash when the wind blows strong enough. Wishing it to be real, hoping to glimpse again that thing I saw gliding between the smooth trunks that looked the size of a microlyte, but at the same time impatient to see what novelty the God of the Chaga will reveal to me.

We move like small, fierce vermin through this colossal landscape. As befits El Macho Honcho, Moran goes first, his trusted deputy M'zee behind him; next comes Bushbaby, then the other woman, Rose, who has not cracked one word to me since we started, then Jake, me, and bringing up the rear, Sugardaddy. Seven of us. I'm sorry. Once it got into my head, it just wouldn't go away. How could you resist the temptation to sing ''Heigh-ho, heigh-ho''?

Not forgetting the dog. Which is a shit-brown mongrel that you see hundreds of sniffing around in the townships and pissing on things and being driven off with stones. But out here, its pariah nose triumphs where man-made navigation devices fail. It's led us straight to the cache where they have buried the canvas boats. That is because he isn't any old pariah, Bushbaby says proudly. He's been bred to this work. By the silent Rose, her cousin. She breeds and handles Chaga-hounds. None better, she says. I believe her. While the boys snap the boats together, I sit and moan and groan and try to ease my blisters and nipple rub from this damn horny perfume. My collarbones are rasped raw. Rose reaches up to this thing that looks like a red honeycomb growing on the root buttress under which we are sheltering. She squeezes a brightly colored blob from one of the cells. She offers it to me and for the first time speaks.

''For you,'' Bushbaby translates from Kalenjin. ''Eat it. It will make you feel better. It is quite safe. It is forest food. Anything that is red in the Chaga will always be edible.''

Better death than nushing out, as Fraser and Aaron Shepard would say. I pop the thing in my mouth. It is the size of a finger banana, the texture of a jungle slug and tastes of cinnamon, whiskey and leaf mold. Two minutes later a glow starts in my belly.

As I write this I feel I can march straight up the trunk of one of these roof trees carrying everyone on one hand. Plus the dog. I feel good, da-na da-na da-na da. It grows all over the Chaga, this stuff. The market potential of this stuff would be incredible, if I could get some out. Doesn't keep, Bushbaby tells me. Like the manna of the Israelites. Didn't their holy food come down from heaven too?

But I notice a thing about Rose. When she gives me the forest food, I see that the little finger of each hand has been crudely amputated.

Moving out now. More when I get the chance.

Later

Moon can't have come this way. I can't find any reference in her diary to these swamps and waterways that meander through this incredible, terrifying terrain. But she wrote years ago: the Amboseli swamps would have been outside terminum. The ruins of the old Ol Tukai game lodge she describes must be days ahead of us. When you are in the Chaga, you forget that as you move inward through it, it moves outward past you.

There is a sky again. The ceiling of the Great Wall has broken up into isolated roof trees (how hard it is to give names to things, to describe them as they are, not how they seem!) rising sheer out of what Moon describes elsewhere *drained coral reef.* Yes, but on the mountainous scale: the finger corals are hundreds of feet high, the brain corals the size of houses. Hand trees almost as tall as the parasol sequoias, miniature Foa Mulakus, all stilt legs and horns. Most of what we pass through I can only describe by listing their mundane counterparts. Cornucopias. Organ pipes. Mug trees. Barnacles. Bubbles. Lightbulbs. Pom-poms. Frozen chickens (really! About the size of a truck, and exactly that morbid shade of factory-farm chicken skin). Cathedrals. Mixer taps. Windmills. Cheese graters. Panty hose. Watch springs. Candelabras. Scramble nets. We follow the narrow twining watercourse through a Disneyland of kitchen paraphernalia. FX by Hieronymus Bosch. Our boats are eerily silent, driven by truck-battery-powered engines. We hardly leave a crease on the water as we move between the overhanging pipes and frills. Jake is in the lead boat with Moran and M'zee. Mere women and dogs follow, with the untrustworthy Sugardaddy's hand on the tiller.

We are in a state of armed vigilance. Hippos are public enemy number one. They could easily capsize these snap-together canvas assault boats. Bushbaby and Rose have Uzis: the only satisfactory way to stop a hippopotamus is to put the maximum number of shells into it in the minimum amount of time. Personally, I'd feel much happier with something with the firepower of half a regiment rather than this fifty-caliber Magnum they've given me, even with the dandy little Chaga-proofed laser sight that I mustn't use too often because we can't change the power pack. Go ahead, hippo, make my day. Did I fire five shots, or did I fire six?

Some of the birds I've seen hunting in the shallow water seem to be carrying strange parasites like autonomous, mutated body organs.

About ten minutes ago Rose, through Bushbaby, asked if she could braid my hair for me. I've been admiring hers since I met her at the pickup point: plaited and wrapped with threads, string and wax, strung with tiny Indian bells and amber beads. Bushbaby says they've both been admiring my hair for as long. They can't get over the color. Rose unpacks her threads and wires and beads from her pack, sits behind me and sets to work. She lifts my hair. I grasp her hand, turn to face her.

''Posse?'' I ask, holding up the maimed hand.

She nods her head. ''Mombi.''

You see the pink Cadillacs and the zoot suits and the girls cute and pouting in nylon and leather. You never see the deputies and the law they enforce. For the first infringement, the left little finger. For the second, the right little finger. To keyboard users, this maiming is symbolic as well as functional.

They lose their patience when it comes to the third offense.

I kiss the back of Rose's hand, never taking my eyes off her.

She's doing a fabulous job on my hair. The beads swing and click at every move of my head. It's more than just a pastime or sign of personal affection. It's a ritual. A marking. I'm one of the tribe now.

Moran is shouting back from the lead boat. We'll camp tonight at the remains of Ol Tukai Lodge where this snow-watered swampland runs out of Lake Amboseli and we enter the Loolturesh Discontinuity. I am back in her footsteps again: Moon, Niamh O'Hanlon, my Arne Saknussen.

Later

Moran says he thinks there is somebody else out there.

Day Three

M'zee agrees. We are not alone in here. It's not the Wa-chagga: their country is on the far side of the discontinuity. UNECTA explorers are a possibility. The Black Simbas have no quarrel with them, but UNECTA reports to the military, with whom all the Tacticals are unilaterally at war, so contact is best avoided. The only thing the Tacticals hate more than the military are their cartel rivals. A lot of wealth and power crosses terminum into the camps, some are realizing later than others, so they send combat teams to follow the safari squads to their source, kill everything that breathes and claim what they find for their cartel. They're scary. The Wa-chagga nation have a treaty with the Black Simba Cartel, they will protect us from claim jumpers. But they are a day away across Lake Amboseli in open canvas boats and the first and last you will know about claim jumpers is the itch of a laser sight on your forehead and nothing ever again. Fabulous. *Apocalypse Now* in the Loolturesh Discontinuity.

There are things scarier than claim jumpers. Obi-men. Forest wanderers. People who have found their way into the Chaga, become trapped by it and changed.

"Changed?" I ask.

No one answers.

Jake is with us in the women's boat today. He wants footage of the lake crossing and feels he should direct the shots so we don't waste space on our limited supply of discs. He's never been this deep. Lake Amboseli had once been seasonal, fed by subterranean springs drawing snowmelt from the mountain, evaporating in the heat of the dry season. Now it is permanent, sealed under the transparent roof of the Loolturesh Discontinuity. The roof is made of balloons fifty feet in diameter, stuck together somehow, moored about three hundred feet up on lines and gnarled holdfasts gripping the floor of the lake. Thousands, probably millions, of balloons, as clear as glass. Shot: a receding perspective of the still waters of Lake Amboseli with infinite regress of vertical lines. Steering through the holdfasts makes slow passage, especially when you do not know what you'll find around the next knot of cables and roots.

There are things moving in the balloon canopy; things that cling to the curved undersurfaces feeding off the occasional veils of translucent blue moss; and other things that float like animate zeppelins, steering themselves between the cables by languid ripplings of gossamer tail membranes. Jake has to tell me to stop shooting. But they're there, they're real. I have them.

Monkeys have colonized this vertical landscape. They run up and down the cables, fingering morsels out of the crevices between the plaited strands, cramming their faces as they watch us pass beneath. Many of them carry elegantly obscene deformities: antlers of green coral, mottlings of green-and-purple mold, extra sets of red arms and hands.

Changed.

She saw this, I remember. She noted this. But she draws no conclusions about whether these are prenatal deformities or the Chaga somehow manipulating the flesh of the grown animal. No conclusions that I have read. Maybe they, like so much, are in the vanished pages.

This landscape breeds paranoia.

Jake. I am learning not to treat him as a folio of clichés. He is more alive here, with death so strong inside him, than I have ever seen him before. He manages to maintain his sartorial crispness—God knows how, I look like Jana of the Jungle after a heavy night. Even his sweat rings are precisely circular. His spirit is strong, but I fear that his body is beginning to betray him. He tires easily. His sleep is troubled—several times a night he will cry out loud enough to wake the camp. Jake tells me he hears voices in his sleep. Mutterings in his hind brain, like someone talking in another room, loud enough for the voice to be heard but not the words it is speaking.

She wrote about spirit voices, calling her deeper into the heartlands. She imagined them to be lost, crazy Langrishe's. Did she ever find him? Is he still out there in all those thousands of square miles of the alien?

Later

Camp three. Well into the weird now. I should do that doo-de-doo-doo, doo-de-doo-doo from *The Twilight Zone* except everything up here does it naturally.

Up here.

Ha-ha.

We're on the far side of the discontinuity, in the land of the Crystal Monoliths. The Land of the Wa-chagga. We hope it was their turds Dog found close by the landing where we stashed the boats. Fresh turds. About an hour or two old. Nothing lasts too long here. If they aren't Wa-chagga, they mean that the ones who were following us are no longer following us. They're in front of us.

Beyond the discontinuity the terrain changes as abruptly as those old Tarzan movies where Johnny Weissmuller runs from Sahara sand straight into tropical jungle. The Crystal Monolith zone isn't just one Chaga. It's a whole department store of them, stacked on top of each other. Each level is a separate biosphere with its own unique flora and fauna.

The way forward is up.

Dog's unfailing nose leads us to the climb: a hundred or so steel pitons hammered into the main column of what looks like a Fassbinderesque *Fitzcarraldo* fantasy of an oil refinery lost in Amazonia. Sugardaddy unpacks a couple of hundred feet of old-fashioned hemp mountaineering rope and body harnesses and goes up the pitch. It's beautiful. Rock dancing. He hauls up Dog, who swings slowly in his harness, like a canine Foucault pendulum.

The only thing holding me to these steel pitons is the determination that I am not going to be hauled up like a side of meat. Don't look down, they say. I have no problem with that. Rose comes up after me with almost as much style as Sugardaddy, her Uzi dangling under her ass.

There's an old American slave expression I can't get out of my head: the Way in the Air. We are pilgrims on that Way, toward holy Zion; *Ngaje N'gai,* the House of God in Masai. Up here, you see that it is not so much a level as a web of spans, buttresses and branches. Imagine the organic equivalent of an L.A. freeway interchange and you've something of it. The branches are as wide as freeways. Where the spans join, you could host a full-size Cup Final with all the supporters and car parking. It's easy to be blasé: most of what surrounds you is empty space. Get careless and it's four hundred feet straight down. Dog goes snuffling along the thinnest tendrils with heart-stopping nonchalance.

Only a little light filters down through the higher levels. I stop a moment to savor a rare beam of sunlight on my face.

Looking up it, I see a handful of blue sky scratched by a jet contrail. This level is Monkeyland, with a few tribes of chimps (is that the proper collective noun?) thrown in. The chimps seem to rule the roost and have absolutely no fear of humans. They hoot at us from their enclaves high on the trunks, throw shit at us. Some of the bigger chimps carry the thighbones of large animals.

Are chimps supposed to do that?

M'zee smelled the storm coming before the first gusts drew spooky sobbings and moanings from the tier forest. We made it to a flange and set up camp three as the gale hit us. A big wind in the Chaga is a mighty scary thing. Everything moves. Everything tosses and sways and creaks and groans, and every moment you think, Oh Jesus, it's all going to fall apart, we are all going to die. You look for something strong and secure to hold on to, but everything is moving with you. And the wind really howls, like it is after your soul, and if it can't get that, your body will do. It would have blown us in our little thermal quilts clean off the level and into four hundred feet of screaming death were we not buttoned up. Bushbaby, Rose, me and Dog, who is lying proudly licking his erection, are bundled up in something like a cross between a secret cave and a sleeping bag that opened in a tree trunk when Moran licked it. Inside, it's a spongy tube lit by bioluminescent patches that stretches as you push at it until there's enough room for three women (in somewhat close proximity) and a dog. Bushbaby showed me the teat in the floor you can suck for a supply of nutrient sap. Tastes like piña colada, she says. I'm not that desperate. Yet. Above the slit door through which we squeezed like birth in reverse is a tennis-ball-sized bud that Rose stroked to seal the membrane against the rising storm. The same trick will open it. All a tad parturitional for my liking. Peter Werther, the Chaga Adam, spoke of being sheltered in things like these. Who then was the Eve from which the Chaga learned womb magic?

Some unseen mechanism keeps us supplied with fresh air, otherwise we should all smother from a combination of sweaty unwashed woman and dog dick. Enough for today. Bushbaby says Rose is wondering what I'm always writing writing writing at. I'm wondering too.

She woke and remembered how she knew this moment. It was the memory of winter storm nights in the Watchhouse when the rain rattled the bedroom windows and the wind gibbered under the eaves and you curled up in your duvet, cuddled by cats, enjoying being so warm and safe and enclosed. You would wake in the hourless hours the clock did not measure to find the storm passed, and in the huge silence behind it, you would creep downstairs and into the porch to stand and lose yourself in the tremendous stillness lying across the land.

Not even Dog twitched as Gaby slipped through the door lips into the cool, clean air from the high country. The only sound in the tier forest was the patter of raindrops dripping from level to level to level, running down to earth. The slow rain glittered as it fell; the night forest shone with ten thousand bioluminescent lights. Gaby felt she had been set to walk among the stars. Exalted. Chosen. Invulnerable. She walked out along a high-arching bridge, drawn irresistibly into the mystic. At its far end the arch joined with others in a tangled boss of cords, tubes and organ pipes. In a covert between two human-sized racks of panpipes, Gaby did a thing she had not done since she was ten years old, in the secret places of the Point known only to herself. She took off her clothes. She laid them in a neatly folded stack, found footholds in the pipes and climbed until she came to another arch. She found a safe roost at the edge and sat with her feet hanging over the star-filled abyss. She listened to the drip of water through the tier forest. She felt the Chaga on her skin.

She could disappear here. This arch would lead to another, and that to yet another, and take her far beyond any hope of return to the human world. Eden again. Return to animal awareness; the eternal Now before the Fall armed humanity with consciousness and care. Beyond money, beyond power and telecom and tax bills, beyond mortgages and bank loans and pensions and insurance. Beyond the day-to-day drudge of pushing the boulder of living in a society up the asymptotic slope of Mt. Entropy. Freedom without a bar code. She did not wonder the Western industrials wanted it ring-fenced. The Chaga's Grace Abounding was the denial of consumer capitalism. But it is an insidious Eden where everything may be had by reaching out to take. It is the determination to push that boulder of hopes and dreams through the relentless material world that makes you human. If you were to get up from this place and walk in there and never come back, the Gaby McAslan that you have made yourself become would evaporate.

She shivered, suddenly cold and naked. It was beautiful out there, but it was the beauty of the serpent of Eden. She got up from her pitch, climbed down through the *vox humana* and *vox angelica* and put on her clothes. As she crossed back to camp three she saw a figure seated on the edge of the drop, in the same position, legs over abyss, in which she had sat.

She froze.

"You too?" Jake Aarons's voice said. "It is sacred, isn't it?"

"And scary," Gaby said. She sat cross-legged beside him, a little back from the brink. "It's beautiful, it's awe inspiring, it's the closest I've come to a religious experience, and it's the end of everything it means to be human."

"Or a gate into new ways of being human," Jake said. "What the Chaga says to me is, now you don't need to compete for resources, now all the rules of supply and demand are torn up: there is enough here for everyone, so now you can experiment with new ways of living, new ways of interacting, new societies and structures and sociologies, knowing that you have permission to fail. Screw it up and it won't cost you and your children your lives. Like America was, back in the pioneer days when all the religious communities came over from Europe because there was space for them to follow their beliefs without interference. Continual experiment."

"Or stagnation."

"Pessimist."

"Fuzzy-minded pinko."

Jake laughed. It sounded very loud in the silent tier forest.

"I have to be optimistic, don't I? But it's more than wishful thinking. What I'm going to say will sound to you like classic schizophrenia paranoia, but the voices, the ones inside, I know whose they are."

"Don't tell me it's God, Jake."

"Hell no. It's the voice of the Chaga." He held up his hands, begging time to explain. "Don't 'Jesus, Jake!' yet. You believed Peter Werther when he said he could hear the Chaga thinking to itself. Look at this place, what is it? A web of nodes and connections, a neural network, for Christ's sake, on the macro- and micro-scales. Everything connects in here. Everything thinks. Do you know what the latest theory about the Crystal Monoliths is? They're the Chaga's primary memory storage system. Bevabytes of information stored holographically in a crystalline matrix. Hard drives the size of skyscrapers. Somehow I'm plugged into the system too. I'm the *watekni* on-line cyberpunk fantasy. Direct neural connection to the data-net.''

''Jesus, Jake.''

''Don't try to tell me it's all a fantasy of a sick man who will make any deal with any devil to beat the Big Four, Gaby.''

''I'm not going to, Jake.'' Now. She had to tell him now. She took a deep breath. ''Jake, do you remember the day I came to your place, when I learned about you from the hospital files. I learned something else. All those people in Unit Twelve, all the HIV 4 sufferers who have been exposed to the Chaga: Jake, they're all still alive. They should have died years ago—you told me, the thing kills in six months, tops—but these people are still alive. There's something in here, in this place, this jungle, that stops HIV 4. That's why you hear your voices; it's working its way into you.''

Jake looked at Gaby. She could not read his expression. He got up from his high place and walked away through the dripping forest. Gaby called his name but he did not look back.

41

Gaby's diary
Day Four

Contact.

M'zee has the senses of a hunting animal. We are on the high paths, moving through a thickening fog. M'zee stops, looks up, raises a finger and circles it. The Black Simbas unsling their weapons. Safety catches click off. We are not alone. M'zee takes point with the heavy machine gun they call *m'toto:* the Baby. Moran covers his right flank, Sugardaddy his left. I am behind Moran, Jake behind Sugardaddy, with orders if anything happens to get down, stay down, keep out of fields of fire and shoot anything that comes at us. Bushbaby and Rose back-mark. Rose lets Dog off his leash to run ahead.

Every few seconds we turn and check that the faces beside and behind us are the ones we saw last time. The fog grows thicker. My shorts and top are silver with dew, but I can feel the sweat running down my sides. My saturated pack feels like it weighs eighty tons. My blisters are bleeding into my boots. My calves are wrenched with cramp from yesterday's climb. At any moment two hands may reach out of the fog and take my head off with a monofilament garrote. I have never felt more afraid. I have never felt more alive.

When I used to go out with Private Pete the Soldier, I would parade my offended Political Correctness when he hoped that his unit would get transferred to Bosnia because he wanted to see some action. I understand him now. It was the only expression in his limited emotional vocabulary for the thrill of being alive. My God. This place is turning me into a War Bore.

M'zee holds up a hand. Dog is standing five feet in front of him, hackles raised, lip curled.

I am in cover before Moran can wave us down. I roll into a water-filled channel where two strands of branch twine over each other. Something oozes from under my thighs. I don't think about it.

M'zee and Moran go forward. Dog trots after them. They disappear into fog. I lie in the cold water listening for gunfire. It doesn't come. I grow chilled. It must come. It doesn't. It feels like hours, down in the cold ditch. A rustle of movement. I roll onto my back, grabbing for the Magnum.

"If I were your enemy, you would be dead now," Bushbaby says. "Get up. We are moving."

On Jake's signal I unholster the camcorder and follow him in.

We find them in a small amphitheater of dwarf hand trees. The men have been crucified on the white fingers of the hand trees. The women have been hung by their heels. The bodies have been stripped. All have been killed by a single bullet in the head. The bodies have been mutilated. The men's penises have been cut off and stuffed in the women's mouths. The Chaga has started to claim the corpses. The men hang like images from medieval plague crosses: high-relief crucifixes half-fused into the flesh of the hand trees. Gaping mouths, eyes staring out of the melt of flesh and forest. The women's trailing fingers have elongated into tendrils that weave seamlessly into the web of cables and branch fibers.

Flies and things like green thistledown rise in clouds as Moran examines the dead. He finds a tattoo on the ball of the first woman's shoulder: an outline of a cube, the sign of Sheikh Mohammed Obeid's Children of the Hajji cartel. He reckons they have been dead for four or five hours. It looks like they were surprised setting up an ambush for us. They were undoubtedly killed after they were strung up.

My berserker adrenaline burn has gone cold in my blood. War sickens me. There is nothing glorious about it, nothing noble. Just cruel and sad. This is a terrible place to speak your last word, think your last thought, breathe your last breath and know absolutely that the last thing you will see is the figure standing over you with the gun.

I keep thinking back to a boy in my class at uni. We were never friends, our social circles did not intersect. I only got to know him by the manner of his death. He had the worst death I can imagine. He was into cave diving; which is insane at the best of times, let alone the suicidal solo dive he made against all advice into the flooded tunnels under the Marble Arch cave system. He didn't even learn when the piece of grit jammed a valve and blew all his air supply away and he only just made it back to atmosphere. He was certain there was an undiscovered major cavern at the end of the narrow tunnel he had been squeezing through when he got into trouble. He went down the next day to find that cavern. He never came back. They reckon the same thing happened again, but he was too far along the pipe to make it back. He died alone, under miles of rock, in the cold and the dark, knowing his air was bubbling away, knowing that he wouldn't make it, knowing that the last, the very last thing he would ever see would be his headlamp beam shining on limestone tunnel.

The body's still down there. It's too dangerous to recover it. In water that cold, that far from light, it could remain intact just about forever, floating trapped under those miles of rock.

I had nightmares for weeks after I heard how he had died. It's the scariest story I know, because it's true.

I think of those three men and two women, dying alone, helpless, where no one will ever find them, where no one will ever know, and a shaft of ice drives deep into my soul.

Before we leave them, M'zee pauses to rip out a tremendous fingers-in-mouth whistle and yell "Wa-chagga!" at the top of his voice. As we advance, he repeats the call. Eventually I distinguish an answering whistle out of the forest soundtrack of unearthly whoopings and chimings and twitterings. M'zee returns a long monotone blast; a complex twitter replies. We've given the passwords and crossed the firewall. What wrong note, what incorrect response, did those poor bastards back there give?

The Wa-chagga await us in a large natural atrium encircled by curtain walls of woven tendrils drooping enormous folded flower buds. They number nine: six men, three women. But for the color of their combat pants, which are Chaga purples, crimsons, lilacs, they are indistinguishable from the Black Simbas. I am a little disappointed, I had been expecting Noble Savages. One of the women's T-shirts has a picture of the Brazilian international striker Arcangeles printed on it.

They all look very young. They all carry very big guns. They all have red-green things looped around the backs of their heads, with one tendril that goes into the ear and another that brushes the upper lip. They are a combined defense patrol/trading mission, like the armed merchant adventurers of the age of the navigators. They are all the Tacticals are permitted to see of the Wa-chagga nation and its organic towns scattered across the foothills of Kilimanjaro. I pull the camera out to video this historic moment.

Everything goes horribly quiet.

A Wa-Chagga boy with the straight-bobbed dreadlocks suddenly exclaims, "I know who you are!" His English is almost accentless. "You are from television: Jake Aarons, SkyNet News! And you are Gaby McAslan. You did all those funny end-of-the-news stories."

And we are deluged with hands wanting to be shaken and smiling faces and voices welcoming us and asking for an autograph and will they get on the satellite news?

Later, Mr. Natty-Dread, whose name is Lucius, an economics graduate from the University of Dar es Salaam, shows me how it is that we are such big stars among the Wa-chagga. It may have been designed as a Daewoo microvision, but then someone ripped off the casing and half the electronics and shoved in a slab of Danish blue cheese with half a pound of *fettuccine verde* and not only is it somehow working, it can pick up pictures from as far away as Zimbabwe. Organic circuitry, Lucius says. The Chaga can analyze any electronic circuit board and synthesize a smaller and more efficient organic equivalent. The thing runs on nuts. Nuts particular to a certain plant; peel them and you have a handful of five-volt batteries. The headsets I noticed are more of the same: organic two-way radios, though most of the time they're switched to Voice of Kenya. Lucius lets me try his. He has it tuned to the pirates along the north Tanzanian coast, who do radical dance music.

Black Simbas and Wa-chagga sit down to trade. The weapons are swiftly agreed upon; Sugardaddy, the Black Simbas' chief negotiator, takes an order for ammunition. The computer software, sealed in metal cases, is taken after animated bargaining in Swahili between Sugardaddy and Lucius, who seems to be a boy of some authority. The cigarettes are set aside while their merits are weighed. The flasks of Coca-Cola concentrate provoke great excitement. Sugardaddy personifies superior aloofness while fingers are dipped in the flask and sucked to make sure this is the real thing. If any people are experts on cola, it is Africans. Words are exchanged, hands slapped; all the cigarettes are accepted and the deal is sealed. The Coke, I learn, is a once-only trade; after the Chaga picks its molecules and synthesizes it, the forest will be raining Coca-Cola. Will it do diet too, I wonder?

In return Sugardaddy gets two steel vacuum flasks. In the first vacuum flask is a powerful all-purpose antibiotic that will kill even penicillin-immune bacteria. In the second is a cure for cholera. The Chaga synthesized both. Lucius tells me that none of his people have been sick since they escaped from the camps and returned to the mountain.

"You cannot get sick," he says. "Not with counteragents to every disease blowing on the wind. You take them in by the million with every breath."

Including, it seems, something that stops HIV 4 dead in its tracks.

Later

I rather think Lucius is trying to come on to me.

The rest of the men are sprawled around the microvision watching women's kick-boxing relayed from Bangkok and drinking native beer. They mutter doubtless obscene comments at the screen and laugh. The women are sitting in a ring by themselves, talking in Swahili and laughing and clicking their fingers. I sit apart to write, and Lucius comes and sits himself down beside me.

"They are crass, boorish men," he says, looking at the

group around the television. "You are like me; you are intelligent, sensitive, educated."

I ask him how intelligent, sensitive, educated college boy becomes gun-toting, camouflage-wearing, freedom fighter.

"Loyalties are long and strong in Africa," he says. "When I heard what was happening to my family's farms up on Kilimanjaro, I could not stay away, not while I might have some power to help them. I could do nothing against the Chaga, but when my people escaped from the camp at Moshi, I went with them, because I knew they would need all manner of abilities to rebuild the nation.

"We found the Chaga at the minimum level of habitability. We were not wise to its ways, we did not trust it to feed and shelter us. Some died—the young, the very old, the vulnerable—and from their bodies the Chaga learned the needs of humans and grew them. From their flesh came the meat we eat, from their blood the water we drink, from their skin our shelters, from their bones our towns and settlements, from their spirits the light and the heat and the electricity that powers them. I say it like religious scripture. It is almost a prayer among us. You are thinking we have made the Chaga our God? Yes, in an African sense; gods who are petty, and practical, and ask you questions like, Lucius, which would you rather have, a perfect soul or a new Series 8 BMW? and do not get upset when you say a BMW. The Chaga gives us both: it weaves outside things into itself and makes them more than they are. And in doing itself, it makes itself more. Outside the Chaga is life. Inside the Chaga is life times life. Life squared."

I press him on what he means by the Chaga making things more than they are. It echoes Jake, when he said on the night of the storm about the Chaga being the gateway into new ways of being human. Lucius is evasive. It is getting late, he says. The others are calling him. No, they are not. What they are doing is peering in tense concentration at the Asian Babes All-Action Topless bout. But at least I won't have to stop him trying to chat me up. Jake takes his place beside me. Topless All-Action Asian Babes hold limited appeal for him, I suppose. Getting bitchy, Gaby. Hot news. While the guys' brains have been befuddled by oiled Asian titties bouncing in extreme close-up, he's been working on them to let us visit one of their settlements. They would not agree to that under any circumstances, but he did wheedle the promise out of them to take us deeper into the Chaga to see something that they will not specify but they think will interest us greatly.

"When do we go?" I ask.

"First thing in the morning. Lucius will guide us."

The women are talking among themselves with great animation, laughing and hiding their faces behind their hands. They must be talking about sex.

Day Five

We made our farewells in the early mist. Rose, Bushbaby, M'zee and Dog are staying to conclude business with the Wa-chagga.

We ascend steadily for about an hour. There are ways between the levels; swooping catenaries of plaited piping that anchor tiers to piers like the cables of a suspension bridge. Lucius runs up them with the cocky ease of one of those spidermen who build the Manhattan skyline. He's trying to impress me. What it makes me want to do, encumbered by ordnance and acrophobia, clawing for every finger- and toe-hold, is knee him in the nuts. The canopy thins, the light grows brighter. Lucius educates me in Chaga-lore: anything red will always be edible, orange is water, blue electricity, white information. Green and yellow are heat and cold; black is drugs, both pharmaceutical and recreational.

We come across a moment of lost history tangled up in the cables between worlds: the overgrown skeletons of three helicopters, trapped like insects in a web and sucked transparent. Jake rubs away the crust of pseudo-lichens and discovers Tanzanian army markings. The cockpits are a writhe of tendrils and yellow spines: I imagine picked-clean skulls, greenly grinning. Or do I imagine?

Upward. By noon break I want to lie down and die and let the Chaga grow over me like that lost helicopter squadron and suck my soul up into the Crystal Monoliths that I can just begin to glimpse through the forest roof. At least Lucius can clear up a mystery before I die. I ask him if he or his people ever encountered a white woman traveling inward alone, three, four years ago. Yes, he has. She was . . . Irish, like me? Yes, but not red, like you. She was dark, in complexion and spirit. A woman like this you remember. She ran into one of the foraging parties from Rongai village. They brought her in—this was when Webuyé was chief, before the new regime moved for a more reclusive policy toward strangers in the forest. She asked everyone if they had seen a white man pass that way some months before. She would not stay for more than one night before she must move on inward, in search of her man.

There is another way, Lucius says, in which I am like her. We both spend hours writing in journals.

I know, I say, taking the Liberty book from my pack. This is that diary. I lay it on the cable between us. Lucius looks at it suspiciously: does it say anything about the Wa-chagga, and Rongai village? he asks.

All references to humans living in the Chaga have been cut out, I tell him. With a sharp knife.

The Wa-chagga did not do this, he says, flipping through the yellow pages.

I ask him if he knows if Moon ever found the man she was searching for. Yes, Lucius says. He was in the patrol that met her, many months later, wandering in the chaotic terrain at the foot of the Citadel. She had been near exhaustion, and deeply mistrustful. She had asked the Wa-chagga to take her to Nanjara settlement, where the people had been kind to her before, and then toward terminum. She would not speak about what she had experienced up in the high country beyond the Citadel, but it was clear that it had changed her.

After she had collected her things from Nanjara, the Wa-chagga patrol took her through the tier forest to Lake Amboseli, where they would give her into the protection of a tactical squad, but she had broken away then and fled into the fastnesses of the discontinuity.

So, T.P. This is how it ends. Paranoia and disillusion on the white mountain, and a love that was not strong nor so deathless as Moon thought. Those who love too big lose too big. If it's any consolation, Langrishe couldn't keep her either. Funny. Sad. Terrifying: how it all keeps coming back to that one word: changed.

I'm frightened for Jake.

Upward.

I hadn't thought we were so high. All of a sudden we come up through the canopy on to the top of the forest. I can see. I have a horizon. I can feel sun on my skin. I have a landscape once again.

The Crystal Monoliths rise over me, as high above me as I

am above the deep root forest. Their facets sparkle sun diamonds across the canopy. Before me, the web of branches and spars runs between the splayed fingers of the ridge country I glimpsed that morning Shepard took me up in the microlyte. Beyond the canyonlands, clouds rip softly on the upper ramparts of the Citadel.

The canyon country looks easy walking. It lies. The ridges are made of a porous, crumbly substance that sinks under your boots and disintegrates between clutching fingers. It took an hour to make it onto the nearest ridge top, whereupon Lucius told us with sadistic pleasure that our way lay across the forest valleys between.

Bastard.

If it's tough on me, it's hell on Jake. We have to stop every ten minutes for him to rest. He still hasn't spoken to me about what I told him on the night of the big storm. I'm not pissing you Jake. I wouldn't. Not you.

Lucius promises we'll be there before nightfall. We're not. It's nightfall by the time we start on the final valley traverse, close to midnight before he tells us we can stop, we've arrived.

At first I can't see there is anything to have arrived at. Then after a time listening to the night sounds of the Chaga, I realize it's a seeing trick, like Foa Mulaku before it came to the surface. I begin to make out a pattern among the biolights in the branches, like a luminous join-the-dots picture. Suddenly they resolve and I realize I am standing on the edge of a colossal drop looking across at walkways, staircases, rooms, gantries, houses, platforms built into an island of Chaga rising out of the deep dark root country.

Someone has built a town in the tree-tops.

42

His name was Henning Bork. He was from the University of Uppsala. With Dr. Ruth Premadass, Dr. Yves Montagnard and his sister, Dr. Astrid Montagnard, he was all that remained of the UNECTA expeditionary dirigible *Tungus*. They had constructed and lived and continued their work in this arboreal settlement they called Treetops for five years. They had also produced Hubert, age four. *Looks four, acts four hundred,* Gaby described the child in her diary. This was what happened when boffins mated;

(Yves Montagnard was the father, but Gaby's hypotheses about the mother either flew in the face of the evidence—Ruth Premadass was a very dark Tamil—or contravened the fundamental taboo of almost every human society.)

Could explain why he was such a mutant, Gaby thought.

New faces were a novelty in Treetops. Resurrecting social niceties, Henning Bork hosted a dinner party for all his guests. They sat around a long narrow wooden table on a balcony overlooking the big drop that was Treetops' main defense. The food for the meal all came from the Chaga. Some of it Gaby could not tell from its terrestrial original; some of it tasted of *this* but with the texture of *that,* and some of it was unlike anything in her experience but, after the shock of unfamiliarity, was very good to eat indeed. Dr. Premadass handed around a dessert fruit that looked like turd-on-the-cob and tasted *exactly* of lazy summer evenings when you do not have to go to work the next day.

"This could be as big as chocolate if the food combines ever got their hands on it," Jake Aarons said.

"We discover a new food crop every week," Astrid Montagnard the botanist said. "We have cataloged over two hundred Chaga-staples that could have a major impact on global nutrition. This is many times the number that were introduced into the Old World from the Americas."

"The Chaga synthesizes foodstuffs from the human DNA template," the Frenchman at the opposite end of the long table said. He was a molecular biologist. "Nothing you find out there will ever be poisonous, or even mildly harmful. The better it knows us, the more finely tuned to our needs its provisions for us will be. I am sure our Black Simba guests have been approached by representatives of biotechnology corporations to smuggle samples through the security cordon."

"We have taken samples, yes," Moran said. "But I have heard that they cannot make them grow."

"Of course they cannot," Yves Montagnard said forcefully. "It cannot be separated from the Chaga. It is all one thing, one system. Every part needs every other part; it is a true symbiosis. Maybe they can splice the genes into a terrestrial species and get some hybrid that will grow in a field, but that is the complete antithesis of what the Chaga is about. They want another agribusiness product; out there is the end of agriculture. The end of the slavery of the plow. The end of markets and subsidies and surpluses that mean grain mountain here, famine there. Everything may be had here just by taking. It is the return of the hunter-gatherer society, which is the best-nourished, healthiest and most culturally adventurous on earth.''

''You must excuse Yves,'' Henning Bork said. ''This place reinforces idealisms but takes away people on whom one can vent them.''

Ruth Premadass brought coffee, or what the Chaga passed for coffee. The wind gusted, stirring the hovering globes of bioluminescence, swaying the branches of the big tree that upheld the community. Gaby gripped the table as the decking shifted. Dr. Premadass poured Chaga-coffee without spilling a drop.

''Do not worry,'' Henning Bork said. ''We built it to stand far worse than this. And it has stood far far worse than we ever expected. The Chaga has grown into it, made it strong.''

''How does it come to be here at all?'' Gaby said, asking the question that the guests most wanted answered.

Henning Bork pressed his palms together as if he had been eagerly anticipating this opportunity to practice the art of after-dinner storytelling.

''The last flight of the *Tungus*. This is the tale.''

The Sibirsk airship *Tungus* had been sent out from Ol Tukai Lodge early in the second year of the Chaga's expansion, when the mass of alien life began to differentiate into separate zones and speculations about it being a product of alien design began to solidify. Aerial photography had shown complex formations developing far beyond the reach of UNECTA's foot expeditions. The Chaga-makers themselves might inhabit them. Aliens had been big that year.

The idea had first been used in the Brazilian selvas in the 1980s. It was very simple. A lighter-than-air transport flew in a large, lightweight folding raft, set it down on the top of the forest canopy and quickly unfolded it to distribute its weight over as large a surface area as possible. Scientists used the raft in the tree-tops as a secure base from which to study the attic ecology. When they were done, they could pack up the raft, call in the LTA and float on to another location. Now with Western can-do and Eastern wealth, UNECTA planned to do it bigger and better. The lifting power of the Siberian logging dirigibles could transport an entire research laboratory onto the roof of the Chaga. Regularly resupplied by airship, it could remain there indefinitely, a scientific community in the canopy.

Tungus lifted from Ol Tukai with a crew of two and four scientists equipped with accommodation, plant and supplies for five weeks, bound for a predetermined location on the northern slopes of Kilimanjaro. The airship crossed terminum and was never heard from again.

"We did not know that the envelope of Chaga-spores reached so high above the canopy," Henning Bork told his dinner guests. "We lost the first gas cell fifty feet up as we were coming in to land. We were heavily laden. When the second blew, we knew we could not make it back. Captain Kosirev was trying to soft-land the airship on the canopy when we lost all lift and came down.

"It was by sheer grace that no one was killed or badly injured," the Swede continued. "It was obvious that the ship could not be made airworthy again. Nor could we signal for help; the radio had been consumed by the Chaga. Of course, we did not know then that the Chaga reconstitutes what it consumes; the radio, and our experimental and analytical equipment as well."

"So you could call for assistance now," Jake Aarons interrupted.

"Yes," Henning Bork said. "But we do not wish to. We have a self-contained, self-sustaining research community; we are constantly making new discoveries, delving deeper into the secrets of the Chaga. There is always something more to discover. This Treetops of ours is on the very edge of the Chaga's major zone of morphological experimentation; the sector beyond this ridge country that we call the Breeding Pit. You should see it: it is the evolution engine of the Chaga; the place where all its stored genetic information is made flesh and varied. You could observe for a hundred years and never see the same thing twice. We have an observation platform up there; I will take you there tomorrow to witness it for yourselves. Maybe then you will understand why we do not wish to leave. Why should we go back to the outside world only to have all this taken from us and given to someone else?"

"Professional possessiveness?" Gaby said. That is not the reason, she thought. There is some other thing that keeps them clinging to this raft of tents and platforms in the tree-tops, and they have made a compact between themselves to keep it from us.

"You continue your mission by other means," Jake said. "You seem well set up here; electricity, heat, food, water. But what happened to the dirigible crew?"

"That is a bad thing," Henning Bork said. Gaby saw him look at his colleagues in the way that people do who need to get their stories straight. "A very bad thing. They tried to go back. They could not live here, they did not find in this place the intellectual excitement that ties us to it. They provisioned themselves with what we could spare from the wreckage of *Tungus;* which, as you can see, we efficiently recycled, and set off across the canopy. This was a long time ago, before we programmed in the defenses. The Chaga was less, shall we say, busy then."

"The Chaga was smaller too," Moran said, sensing the insult and returning it.

"But much more dangerous," Astrid Montagnard said. Hubert was seated in her lap. He stared at Gaby. The brat never seemed to blink. "Strange, alien, dangerous. Now the Chaga is developing toward human norms, but then, in those early days, everything was being tried. Everything."

"They didn't come back," Gaby said.

"Yes," Henning Bork said. "We do not know what became of them."

"The Wa-chagga know nothing about them," Lucius said.

"But they could still be alive out there," Jake Aarons said. Gaby understood the reason behind the question.

"They could," Henning Bork said.

"The forest sustains you and the Wa-chagga," Jake continued. "It could also sustain them, couldn't it? Could it do more than that? Could it somehow adapt them to live more closely with it? Enter into a kind of symbiotic relationship with them, change them? You said that this Breeding Pit was the Chaga's engine of evolution, where life is varied. Human life, human flesh?"

"What are you driving at, Mr. Aarons?" Henning Bork asked. The wind shook the great tree again. It felt wet and cold on Gaby's skin, like secrecy.

"Organic circuitry," she said, shifting the conversation from delicate subjects, like any civilized houseguest. "Organic television?"

"Yes," Henning Bork said.

"Organic satellite television?"

"This too."

"You can get SkyNet Sports? There's a match I'd really hate to miss."

43

One nil (Gaby stormed at her diary). Tragic. The Dagenham Girl Pipers could have put up a better defense. Bizarre, watching Alan Jeffers's halftime analysis on a television that looks like a head of melting broccoli in what used to be the control cabin of a Sibirsk airship but is now part of a Lost Boys fantasy treehouse in the deepest darkest depths of the Chaga.

The room they've given me is a tent of poles and blimp skin about fifty feet down-trunk from the main center, right on the edge of what they call the Moat. The view in the morning should be memorable, if I'm still around to enjoy it. The wind is getting up; the whole place flaps and sways like a ship in a hurricane. Full sail ahead for the heart of darkness, me hearties! A ship cast adrift in the tree-tops; like something out of your favorite childhood story. A ragged crew of bourgeoisie marooned on a desert isle, playing out their genteel rituals. Too few faces too often seen, I sense an almost incestuous introversion. Perhaps literally. They tell much; they keep more secret, but they've grown naive at secrecy from too much intimacy. They make mistakes, they are clumsy with their misdirections. This room, for example. Why do I get the feeling I'm hot-bunking in someone else's space? Someone who isn't accounted for by Treetops' crew manifest, spooky Hubert included. Something not kosher here.

There was a polite cough from outside the door curtain. Gaby put down her pencil, closed the diary. The curtain rolled up on its drawstring.

"Got a moment?" Jake Aarons asked. He came in anyway. "I think I have a sane explanation for the voices."

"Not the voice of the Chaga."

"Yes, the voice of the Chaga. But not mystically or magically or divinely. Scientifically. The Chaga can synthesize organic circuits; you've watched goddamn organic satellite television soccer. If it can build out there, why not in here?" He tapped his forehead with a finger. "What's this stuff in here but the cellular circuitry for an organic computer? From the moment I crossed terminum, the Chaga's been building an organic modem in my head out of my own protein, molecule by molecule, cell by cell, strand by strand. Networking me into this immense data storage and processing system. That's why it's getting louder and clearer: the connections are spreading. It's not just voices now, Gab. It's visions—pictures, images, like snapshot memories; glimpses for the briefest second of the utmost clarity, then gone.''

''Pictures of what, Jake?''

''Other lives, Gab. Other worlds. Other ways of being. And of this world as well. Peter Werther was right. They've been here before. At the very start of humanity, and the very start of it all. Those things we have recorded in the Burgess Shale; the incredible diversity of life in the Precambrian, like never before or since . . .''

''They did it?''

Jake shrugged. The wind billowed the fragile room. Gaby was very conscious of the great gulf beneath her.

''Jake, why don't we all hear the voices and see the visions? Why is it just you?''

He grimaced painfully.

''I have a theory about that too. I'll not mince words. This circuitry, this organic modem growing in my head, it's a mutation. Something is causing the cells of my body to grow in such a way as to receive electromagnetic signals from the Chaga, and trigger my own neurons in response. Something is reprogramming the DNA in those cells to grow that way. Now, that is a very difficult thing to do in a developed organism. Easy enough in the sex cells of your parents so that the offspring will express the mutation, but to get into all the necessary cells, and change their programming, then switch it on . . . that's difficult.

''Unless something is already present in the body, in the cells, in the DNA, that acts as a host. A vector. A mole on the inside of the genetic firewall to open the way for the DNA hackers.''

''The HIV 4 virus.''

Jake grimaced again.

''Every day during the desert campaign in World War Two, Field Marshal Montgomery would study a photograph of Erwin Rommel he kept on his desk. Not say a word, just look at it. Know your enemy, was Montgomery's motto. It won him the desert war. I know my enemy, Gab. I've studied all his strategies and tactics; his surprise offensives, his tactical retreats and regroupings. He's tough—tougher than me—but I know how he works. I know what his weapons are, and on what terrain he likes to fight—right down in the chromosomes, street fighting in the DNA strands—and what camouflage he uses to outfox my immune system. But maybe I have overestimated him; maybe he isn't the undercover death squad, maybe he's just the Trojan horse that gets taken into the city and opens the gates to let in the real invading army. And, maybe, it isn't an invading, destroying army out there, but foreign industrialists and investors. Maybe they don't want to put everyone to the sword, but set up a shop here, a factory there, a resort someplace else, do a little urban renewal, stick in some new infrastructure, and by the time they've finished, you're a little colonial outpost of some biochemical superpower."

"I'm getting a little lost in analogy, Jake. You think the HIV 4 virus is some kind of catalyst that allows the Chaga mutagenic agents to work on developed cells?"

"Catalyst," Jake said. "That's exactly the word. That doesn't react in the process. It fits, Gab: all the secrecy around Unit Twelve and the HIV 4 victims who should have been dead years ago. All exposed to the Chaga. All entered into some kind of symbiotic relationship that stops the HIV 4 virus from developing into AIDS."

"You were fishing from Henning Bork at dinner."

"He didn't deny it."

"Jesus, Jake, you said you had a sane explanation." The hovering biolights flared up at Gaby's raised voice. "You know what this implies about HIV 4?"

"It's a made thing." Jake nodded. "I've thought of that. It certainly predates humanity, maybe most of life on Earth. It's the Chaga-makers' engine of variation, and a hideously effective one: only those infected individuals who expose themselves to the mutagenic agents survive. Maybe it wasn't an asteroid impact that eradicated the dinosaurs, or habitat depletion; maybe they had progressed into an evolutionary dead end and the Chaga-makers undertook a little winnowing."

"Jurassic AIDS?"

"Maybe. Maybe the SIVs and HIV 1, 2 and 3 are degenerate variants of the original virus. Given the virus's ability to switch sections of genetic material, maybe there are millions of variants of the HIV 4 virus. Scientists have always had a chicken-and-egg problem with viruses. Maybe they all came from someplace else.''

''Lots of maybes, Jake.''

''Are you telling me that I believe it because I want to believe it? You were the one handed me this magic bullet in the first place.''

The wind gusted up from below, bringing with it the chiming calls of unseen, unimaginable creatures. The balloon-silk walls flapped and swelled. The captive light globes gusted around the little fabric room, casting sudden strange shadows.

Hubert climbed like an animal. Gaby's heart almost stopped when she saw him go straight up the bole on the edge of the moat. ''He's born to it,'' Henning Bork assured her. That sentence means more than it says, Gaby thought. As they moved through the high canopy toward the escarpment where the Treetoppers maintained their watch post, Gaby could feel the child, up there in the dense overgrowth, stalking the slow, clumsy adults. Hidden eyes, watching. The disturbing thing was that even when the boy was back with them, she could still feel them, watching. An hour up the valley in which Treetops rested brought the small expedition to the observatory. It was a cupola of spars and silk scavenged from the wreck of the *Tungus,* perched on the scarp where it fell sheer to the Breeding Pit below. Henning Bork, Yves Montagnard, Jake Aarons and Gaby McAslan fitted into it like segments of an orange. Gaby tried to unsling the camcorder without injuring anyone.

''Where's Hubert vanished to now?'' Jake asked.

''He'll be playing somewhere,'' Yves Montagnard said. Gaby thought she would not be so unconcerned if it were her flesh and blood playing around such sheer drops and pitfalls. But Jake had found her something to video.

She remembered the land beneath her from the microlyte flight. She had thought it looked like a Willow Pattern plate. Now she was on the very edge of it and it did not look like that at all. She slowly swung the camera across the spars and swelling spheres and thought it looked like something flayed and festering, all blue veins and gas-bloated, suppurating flesh straining at skeletal ribs. It looked fleshy and obscene and intimate, like a laparoscopy of a cancerous ovary.

At the limit of her zoom, at the foot of the Citadel, a bubble burst in a spurt of milky liquid and powder. Something darted from it, too far and fast for the camera to follow. She panned up the dark green rampart of the Citadel, to the clouds that hung over Kilimanjaro. Peter Werther had been brought there and set down, ass-naked as Adam in Eden. He had walked away from Eden, and the price of it was a disinfected white suite deep under Kajiado Center, and multinational doctors measuring the advance of his own private Chaga across his body. *Anything that comes out of it is theirs,* Dr. Dan had said. She looked at Jake, talking excitedly with Henning Bork. He fulfilled their criteria. They would claim him. They would take him down into their circular corridors and locked doors and never let him see the light of day again. She looked at Jake and feared for him. But he was not stupid. Many things, some sins, but never stupid. He knew all this as well as she, and he had made his decision.

He wasn't coming back.

"Some of the larger bubbles contain whole ecosystems in miniature," Henning Bork was saying, scanning the Breeding Pit with binoculars. "Like little—what is the word?—dioramas, of life on other planets. Of course, it is one of our many frustrations that we cannot reach them in time to sample them; they only last a day or so before they are reabsorbed. Before we ran out of disc space, we videoed many hours footage of these dioramas. Frequently we cannot comprehend what we are seeing. Sometimes we cannot recognize it as living at all. Occasionally we have seen things so alien as to be horrifying. Ah! Luck is with us!"

He pointed over the rail. Gaby followed in onto a huge bubble a mile to the west. The skin was painfully distended against the hoops of blue ribbing. Gaby thought incongruously of sex toys an old partner of hers had liked to sport. The bubble rippled, as if kicked from inside, and split. White dust sprayed from the rent. The skin tore in a dozen places and collapsed. Behind the camera, Gaby now thought of ancient newsreel footage of the destruction of the *Hindenburg*. But cold. Without fire.

Even at highest magnification, Gaby could not tell if the thing inside the bubble was natural or artificial, organic or inorganic. City, forest; forest, machine. It looked like a city, or a forest, or a handful of stone fingers. Each was the height of a small skyscraper: the proportions of the Breeding Pit could have reduced Manhattan to a toy town in a plastic snowstorm. City,

Gaby decided on the basis of the regular geometric patterns on the sides of the stone pillars. They were in the shape of three-dimensional fractals of ever-diminishing tetrahedrons. Terra-cotta red. Some of the larger formations were fifty feet in diameter, stubbled with smaller arrays of tetrahedrons. Gaby cursed the camera's lack of resolution: the surfaces of the tetrahedron formations seemed in motion.

"You're right." Henning Bork answered her puzzled frown. "It's a living fractal. Each generation of tetrahedrons grows out of the surface of its parent. Some are in the process of sporing—when the tetrahedrons reach the molecular level, they leave the parent body and migrate across the rock surface to a new seeding zone. This is a diorama we have recorded several times before. We believe it is a kind of living clay that uses chemical energy to reproduce itself from the minerals of its parent rock. A parasitic living clay, perhaps. There is evidence that terrestrial clays were a matrix for early forms of RNA molecules. Perhaps this is the end point of a different geological RNA-based evolution."

A warning flashed in Gaby's viewfinder. *Disc change. Last disc.*

"The Chaga's reconstruction of a living clay it encountered somewhere on its travels," Yves Montagnard added.

"Buckyball golems," Jake whispered.

Hubert rejoined the little expedition on the trek back to Treetops. Whatever he had found out along the escarpment ridge, it had made him remember what it was to be a boy. But in her diary that night Gaby still made insidious comparisons with Fraser and Aaron Shepard. It was not just that they were Shepard's kids and they had been part of one of the great times of her life. Hubert was too much a child of his environment. His strangeness seemed almost genetic. Gaby closed her diary and tried to sleep but found herself continually waking with a powerful sensation of not being alone in her little canvas cell. Each time the only presence was her own. She would force herself back into sleep and dream of things that had watched her unseen in the Chaga canopy, followed her back to Treetops and come flapping across the air moat to smother her with flopping skin wings.

She woke with a cry.

In the room. It was *in the room.*

At the sound of her voice the bioluminescents woke and

filled the fabric cube with a green glow. By their light, something moved. Gaby rolled out of her hammock onto the spongy floor and grabbed her Magnum from her pack. The red seed of the laser sight wove across the billowing walls and came to rest on the forehead of a four-year-old white girl with hair as black as the night outside. Her face was as thin as famine.

"Light!" Gaby shouted. The bioluminescents brightened. Crouching on the floor, Gaby and the girl stared at each other, tied by a thread of laser. Then the girl gave a cry, ran to the window and, before Gaby could catch her or stop her or warn her, dived out into four hundred feet of moat. Gaby screamed and lunged for the window. By the dim light from the tier forest she saw a thing very like a very large, very pale bat ghost across the gulf. It flew on webs of skin stretched between wrists and ankles. Gaby saw it light on a branch and turn a dark-eyed, black-haired smiling face to her.

44

They were arguing again in their private patois of French, English and Russian. Gaby banged a plate hard on the table. It broke cleanly along across the middle. They all looked at her.

"Your daughter?" she demanded.

Nothing slept soundly in Treetops. Gaby's cries had roused the colony in less than a minute. Fearing assault, Lucius and the Black Simbas had armed themselves. There had been potentially fatal misrecognitions as the hives of bioluminescents warmed up. Order had inhered at the center, on the bridge, around the Scandinavian calm of Henning Bork. He had given Gaby the floor to tell what she had seen. Then the arguing had started.

"My daughter, yes," Yves Montagnard said. "Hubert's twin. Little Nicole."

"If you're Papa, then who the hell is Mama?" Jake asked.

"Never mind whose baby or whose twin," Gaby interrupted, "she's fucking Batwoman. I saw her fly, for God's sake. Peter fucking Pan."

"That is the nature of her change," Henning Bork said. "That is why we hid her from you. But she is a wild thing, and very curious. She would not be hidden."

"She's not living in the jungle on her own, not at her age,"

Jake said. "Someone else is out there. You lied to us about the crew of the *Tungus*." All investigative journalists are frustrated master detectives, Gaby thought.

"Only half lied," Ruth Premadass said. "Ludmilla is Nicole's and Hubert's mother. She was the airship's copilot. When we learned outsiders were coming, we had her take Nicole up to the Breeding Pit Observatory."

"I thought my room felt lived in," Gaby said. "No wonder Hubert was so keen to come up to the observatory with us, and go running off into the trees."

"But the captain," Jake insisted. "What was his name? Kosirev? Did you tell the truth about him? That he tried to make it back, and got lost?"

"We did. It is true. But it is worse than lost," Henning Bork said. "Changed."

Gaby saw Jake follow his curiosity to the brink of disclosing undisclosable things about himself. Careful, friend.

"Like Nicole, do you mean?"

"No." Henning Bork sighed. "How can I say it? A new body, I suppose. A symbiote, a parasite? We do not have the language for what the Chaga is doing to flesh."

"Obi-men," Sugardaddy said. "That is what you are trying to say. I have seen them, but briefly. They move fast, for such huge things, and so silently. It is as if they command the forest to let them pass, and to close behind them and conceal their tracks."

"What have you seen?" Jake asked.

Sugardaddy shook his head like an old man who finds the world has surpassed his extraordinary stories.

"So many things that they could not all be from the same creature. Hair. Skin. Organs in transparent sacks. Great clawed feet, thighs bigger and stronger than an ostrich's, but the finest, thinnest fingers. More like hair than fingers. The faces; I remember those best. You see the faces, in those folds of flesh. . . ." He shook his head again.

"Yet they are all the same creature," Henning Bork said. "We call them orthobodies. They seem to be symbiotic organisms that can take the human body into them and mesh with the nervous, digestive and cardiovascular systems. They seem to enhance human faculties in many ways: improved health and immunity from disease, great strength and speed, extended sensory range, the ability to interact with the Chaga environment."

"I have seen them walk free," Sugardaddy said. "They opened up like a woman's thing, and the people inside walked out, like they were being born. I say that because they were connected to those things by birth cords. This is what happened to your captain?"

"Does this happen to everyone who is lost in the Chaga?" Jake asked. You are scared, Gaby thought. You are right to be scared, if this is the price of your deliverance. No wonder UNECTA keeps those poor bastards locked up where no one can see them.

"Not everyone," Yves Montagnard said. "The Chaga is the place of perpetual change and transformation, but the changes take many forms. For some it is attracting an orthobody—it seems that the attraction is essentially sexual between human and symbiote, the merging voluntary, almost an act of love. For others it is to be changed in the womb, by changing the genes of the parents, like Nicole and Hubert—oh yes, my son is changed, but it is not an outward change like Nicole's gliding membranes. And some are changed in their own bodies by the symbiosis of Chaga virons with terrestrial infective viruses."

"HIV 4," Gaby said.

"Utilizing retroviruses as carrier bodies to insert molecular information into genes had been a trend in genetic engineering research long before the Kilimanjaro Event," Ruth Premadass said. "When Ol Tukai's taxonomists noticed mutations occurring in fully differentiated monkeys that had adapted to the Chaga environment, it seemed a fruitful line of inquiry. I was on the team set up at Kajiado Center to investigate relationships between Chaga virons and genetically hypervariable retroviruses. Just before the *Tungus* mission, we made the breakthrough into the SIVs—Simian Immunodeficiency Viruses—and were hypothesizing similar interactions with the human immunodeficiency viruses."

"The Chaga is an engine of evolution," Yves Montagnard said in his Big Ideas voice. "It has come to move us forward as a species, perhaps as many species. Our technology has brought us to an evolutionary dead end. Biotechnology allows us to evolve in the directions in which we wish to be evolved: taller, stronger, healthier, higher IQ, more beautiful. We imagine this will be the future humanity. Absurd. If a tribe of *Australopithecus* had sat down to design the next evolutionary breakthrough, they would have planned something that could run faster, see further, smell better, have sharper nails to grub out insects and roots. They would not have planned talking, thinking, toolmaking Homo sapiens.

"Out there is an environment as alien to us as Paris would be to *Australopithecus,* an environment that changes to demand new responses from us, that can generate a thousand habitat niches. We do not know what we will need to expand into the universe, so the Chaga gives us the gift to diverge into a thousand, ten thousand, a million subspecies; a million seeds of humanity cast into the dark."

" 'And say which seed will grow, and which will not,' " Jake quoted.

"Yes," the Frenchman said fiercely. "And maybe, because there is enough room out there, all the seeds will grow. Transhumanity. Post-humanity. Pan-humanity. Any of these, all of these. On these East African plains, humanity was born; it must be more than cosmic coincidence that it is on these same plains that the new humanity, the thing that comes after us that we cannot see, will arise."

Gaby thought of the legend of the tree where man was born, and all the races of Earth returning to that ancestral baobab with its roots in earth and its branches among the stars to be dissolved in its hoarded waters and made anew. Sweet, seductive Big Ideas. How long their legs are, how easily they stride over us. Look, they are already over the horizon while we plow our way through the mud. How many centuries has it taken us to learn to see that people whose skin is a different color from ours are as human as we, and now you are asking us to hug these winged children and hybrid obi-men and changelings to us. Things we may not even recognize as human we must call brother and sister.

"I am an uneducated workingman," Moran said unexpectedly. "I do not understand these things well. I do not know about *Australopithecus* and evolution and what you call transhumanity, post-humanity. All I know are my people, my home, my cartel, my family. I know my country. I know my children. I know this." He drew a long-bladed guerrilla knife from the leather sheath on his thigh. The blade was beautiful. He was a man who could care for an edge. Moran set the knife on the commons table. "Tell me what this means to me. Tell me what this means for my family, my children, my nation."

For the first time Gaby felt some measure of admiration for Moran. He was African. He could stare into the headlights of Big Ideas, Big Science, Big Dumb Objects without being dazzled and ask the only question that had any meaning: *what have you done for me lately?*

"Be thankful for the children you have now," Lucius said quietly. "If you believe in a god, pray for the ones yet to be born, that you may learn to love them as you love the ones that are already yours."

"The mutations are happening to you too," Jake Aarons said. "Just like here. That's why you didn't want to take us to your town."

"Yes," Lucius said. "This is what these ideas you barely understand mean for your family, your children, your nation, Moran. Learn from us, that they will not destroy you as they are destroying the Wa-chagga nation by setting us against each other. In my town, Kamwanga, and in Nanjara and Usarangei and Mrao; Ngaseni and Marangu Gate too, we say that change is the nature of the Chaga, but it is never harmful or destructive, and these children who are born different because of it are to be cherished and valued just like those who are normal. It is no sin or shame or sign of the disfavor of God or the anger of the spirits. It is the way of this place."

"But that is not the case among the other settlements."

"They take the changed children as soon as they are born and expose them."

"Jesus," Gaby whispered.

"Institutionalized infanticide," Jake said.

"Yes," Lucius said grimly. "It is destroying the Wa-chagga nation. We are abominations to each other. People from Kibongo will not speak to people from Usarangei; the people of Marangu and Marangu Gate are enemies because of this. Soon I fear we will kill each other."

"The children," Gaby said.

"We have asked the councils of the towns who oppose us in this to let us take the changed children, but they fear that we are breeding an army of monsters to annihilate them. So we follow the men who leave the children in the forest. If we cannot bribe them, we wait until they have gone and take the baby. But we do not save them all. We cannot save them all. We trust that the Chaga is as kind to them as to all others who have to rely on it for their lives. But it is a hope, nothing more. Of the ones we save, and of our own, there are many that do not survive. They are too deeply changed. You would tell me that they are victims of evolution, Mr. Montagnard; that they are variants that do not adapt and are weeded out. I cannot be that sanguine.''

The blimp-cloth curtain that hung across the doorway twitched aside. Moran and Sugardaddy drew weapons.

''You do not need to do that,'' the figure in the door said. It spoke in a woman's voice, heavily accented with Slavic. ''We are no danger to you, unless you are of the party that thinks that children are abominations of God.'' A small sandy-haired white woman dressed in cutoff combat pants and a tattered T-shirt entered the long room. A child clung to her legs; a girl child, white, naked, agonizingly thin. She had the luminous eyes in a filthy face that turn favela urchins into angels. The child stared at the alien bodies in the common room and pressed closer to her mother. Flaps of skin were stretched taut between wrists and ankles. Follicles puckered into gooseflesh.

''You scared Nicole. She came to see why she had to be taken away from her home and came rushing back to me to tell me that a strange woman had pulled a gun on her. You do not need to hurt her, she will not hurt you. Why should you want to hurt her? Because she is different from you? So I have brought her back here for you to see that she is not a monster or a freak or an example of evolution in action or the first generation of the new humanity,'' the Russian woman said. ''She is just a little girl, and Hubert is just a little boy, and they find themselves in a strange world with new and frightening abilities and they are trying to find out how it all works and how they can live in it. They do not contemplate the mysteries of the universe or solve the grand unified field equations. They sulk. They fight each other. They have tantrums. They do not like to go to bed, and they spit out their food and will not eat what we have made for them. Just a boy and girl. So, the girl can glide on her wing membranes; so, the boy can link with the thoughts of the Chaga and in his dreams pass his consciousness into animals and birds and the creatures that the forest has made; but they are not offenses against God or Allah or the holy church. Nicole will say hello to you, but first you men must put your weapons away, because they are frightening my daughter.''

45

They left Treetops the next morning. Gaby was dazed from lack of sleep and too much wonder. Her sense of disbelief was gorged, like a snake that has swallowed a goat. The progress through the canopy to the rendezvous point with M'zee, Bushbaby and Rose was slow. Jake constantly fell behind and the party would have to wait while someone went back to bring him along. Moran was growing impatient with the delays and halts. The next time it happened, Gaby volunteered to be the one who went back. She found Jake several minutes down the branch, seated in a dip of cable that swept up to anchor points at the base of one of the Crystal Monoliths.

"I reckon you've got ten, fifteen minutes clear before they start to look for us," Gaby said.

Jake Aarons smiled his sophisticated Thorn Tree bar smile.

"What will you tell them?"

"That I never found you."

He thought about the implications of the lie for a few moments.

"Yes, that should do it. I don't like you having to lie to them; they're good people."

"Moran is a jerk."

Jake laughed.

"Got a cigarette?"

Gaby did.

"I didn't know you smoked."

"At theatrically appropriate moments I do."

He was not a comfortable smoker, but he seemed to enjoy the Camel.

"Traditional last request," he said.

"For a while I thought you'd chickened out of doing it," Gaby said.

"For a while I had. They spooked me with that orthobody stuff. That's worse than dying, that. Like a walking iron lung made out of meat. Rather take my chances with UNECTA and Unit Twelve than that. What convinced me was that kid, Hubert. He was born with it, I caught it, but we're both the same in here. We hear it. We see through its eyes. We dream its dreams. We share the same circuitry, in here, and so maybe it isn't some desperate old faggot's final fantasy to wave in the face of death like a karmic press card. I know that if I stop to look at it too closely, it's insane, what I'm planning to do. But we're humans, Gab, we can adapt to anything. We can triumph anywhere. They wrote operas in Auschwitz, for Christ's sake. Yves Montagnard was wrong. There is only one way to be human in here. What we wear over it doesn't matter.'' Jake glanced at his steel Rolex. ''Couple of minutes before the natives get restless. When it really comes down to it, Gab, what matters is that I'll be in it. I won't be watching, I won't be an outsider looking in, recording, reporting, commenting. I'll be in it. I'll be a part of whatever story is being told here. All the rest of the world can do is watch: watch the Chaga, watch the BDO, watch the stars, watch the screen to see the television news watching it too. But I will be what is being watched. I will commit T.P.'s cardinal sin. I will not report the news, I will be the news. And if you don't understand what a mighty, mighty temptation that is, you're no bred-in-the-bone journalist.''

Jake exhaled the last of Gaby's cigarette and carefully crushed the stub under his heel.

''T.P. should know, though. I know it's a heap of shit to hang on you, but tell him, Gab. Tell him everything. And Tembo too, because he's a good man and I can trust him not to shoot his mouth off to some woman like Faraway would. Tell them. No one else. Oh yes. One last thing I owe you, Gab. That diary Shepard gave you. Haven't you guessed?''

''Humans living in the Chaga. Moon met the Wa-Chagga.''

''Gaby, Gaby, Gaby.'' No one could ever do the look of professional disappointment like Jake Aarons, that was not disappointed in your limitations, but in your failure to live up to your talent. ''It's not what, or why; it's who. Who would give you an obviously maimed diary, which you were bound to investigate, when it would have been so much easier to deny it ever existed?''

''Shepard?''

''He's a man. I'm a man. We do it with different targets, but down here we're all the same.'' He clutched his groin. The gesture was disturbingly undignified. ''Where dick takes over, mind leaves off. He was so mad keen to get you into his bed he sure didn't care about the consequences. Hell, he probably couldn't even see there would be consequences through the fog of testosterone."

"Shepard."

"Time to go, I think." Jake stood up, offered Gaby a hand. Just like that, the last good-bye. These things are best done quickly. They say short, sharp pain is better than years of nagging numbness.

"Jake."

"Don't say anything, because even one word might make me not do it, and I wouldn't want to hate you for that for the rest of my life. Don't say anything, don't try to follow me, don't call out my name, don't look at me. Just kneel down and close your eyes." She surprised herself by doing what he asked. "You'll know when you can open them again." She felt his fingers lightly touch her eyelids in blessing. *Someplace wonderful* was a breath against her cheekbone.

She opened her eyes. He was gone. She screamed his name ten times. The Chaga did not answer. She cried a time for him, but not too long, for she must get back to the Black Simbas before they came to look for her.

46

They came down through the roof of the singing forest. The men had not believed Gaby's story about being unable to find Jake and fearing he had fallen any more than she did, but they were male and proud and would not allow themselves to recognize that a woman would dare to lie to them. Gaby blindly followed Sugardaddy through the tier forest. Her inner viewfinder framed an immaculate Jake Aarons climbing the final ridge to stand a moment to look upon the distant ramparts of the Citadel and steel himself for the descent to the mad lands below. The tension and guilt mounted to near sexual intensities. She would turn around and go after him. She would find him. It would be easy, because it was meant to be. Several times this happened. Each time, the kick inside was less brutal, and in the end she knew that she could live with him gone. It was a kind of dying. That was the way to feel it. Life is made up of a million small dyings and rebirths. She turned that thought over and over in her head as she came down the swooping cable.

That was how they were able to take her so completely unawares.

Branches rustled. Something enormous dropped out of the sky onto her and knocked her down, knocked the breath out of her, knocked all sense and seeing out of her. The something rolled her onto her back. She gasped, choked, fought for breath, waved her hands. Found herself looking up the barrel of an assault rifle at a white man in Chaga camouflage fatigues with a blue helmet bearing a map-of-the-world logo Gaby reckoned was important but right now could not work out why.

"Fuck, a white bitch," the white man with the gun said. He had a South African accent. He seized Gaby by one hand and pulled her to her knees. While she coughed and spat he wrenched her arms behind her.

"Hey!" she shouted as she felt steel links lock around her wrists. The South African with the gun pulled her to her feet. She saw three black men trying to cuff a struggling, kicking Moran. Lucius was already immobilized, Sugardaddy writhed on the path, clutching his stomach. A blue helmet stood over him, legs apart, weapon held high, butt downward.

"What are you doing?" Gaby screamed as the soldier wrenched her arms painfully behind her. "Who the hell do you think you are?"

"The U-fucking-Nited Nations, lady," the white soldier said. "And we don't think it, we know it."

There were more UN troops at the rendezvous point. M'zee, Bushbaby and Rose were prisoners, together with a Wa-chagga woman who had been left by the trading party to wait for Lucius. The South Africans had jumped them two days ago, Bushbaby told Gaby. They were a new and dangerous thing in the Chaga, a United Nations deep patrol, hunting and eliminating guerrilla and subversive elements breaking their interdict. They had found the remains of the slaughtered safari squad. They had found handy culprits. There would be charges of murder in addition to security violations when the dirigible got them back on the other side of terminum. Bushbaby said she was sorry. She was so sorry. She had been left in charge, but they had been too fast. Too well trained. They had been all over them before she could get her hand to her gun. Moran listened to her pleas, then spat in her face and kicked her as hard as he could between the breasts. The UN soldiers dragged him away. He did not resist them, but stared at

Bushbaby while the black officer called in the airship. All the time that the drone of fans emerged from the forest chatter, he glared at Bushbaby as if he could stare her dead. Rose sat on the ground with her knees pulled up against her chest, rocking slowly, weeping silently.

They had shot the dog.

47

She stood in the shaft of sunlight as the door from the transfer unit sealed. A voice warned to keep away from the sides. The floor lurched and the circular platform began to descend. Gaby kept staring at the high skylight. An edge of gray cloud lay across the plane of blue. The October rains were coming. The gray concrete shaft changed color, to green, to yellow, to blue, to white as the platform moved down it. The same voice that had warned about getting too close to the shaft sides informed the detainees that they were in the Zone White preliminary decontamination area. The platform stopped at Zone White Level Three. This deep, the skylight was a tiny square of light. Gaby looked up the shaft of light, let it play warm on her face.

The containment seal opened and people in white isolation suits came to take her out of the light. The room into which they led Gaby, the Black Simbas and Lucius and the Wa-chagga woman was white and blindingly lit from no apparent source. Behind a long glass window a number of people in civilian dress wearing UNECTA badges sat at a desk. A white man donned a headset, tapped the microphone a couple of times to test it was working properly and told the detainees to place their equipment on the long white table to the right. The isolation-suited figures that had brought them in opened the packs and tipped the contents onto the long white table. They sorted through the piles of possessions, bagging items of interest, dropping the remainder through a slot in the wall that Gaby knew went down to flames. She watched her thermal quilt go through the slot in the wall. She watched her spare clothes, her toiletries, her pack go down to the flames.

The searcher lifted her diary.

"Don't you touch that; that's mine, my diary, you've no right to it! Give it back to me!" she shouted.

The faceless figure in the isolation suit inclined its head quizzically and dropped the diary into a bag. It found the other diary, Moon's diary. Gaby said nothing as it was bagged and sealed. Jake's camcorder had been taken back on the airship, with the weapons. Now she had nothing to make people believe her.

"Undress, please," said the man behind the glass. He had a Middle American accent. He looked a little and sounded a lot like Shepard. Gaby fixed her eyes on him as she took off her Chaga-proof boots and dropped the cropped cotton top, the purple-and-red Chaga camouflage pants, her bra, her panties. She kept staring at him as the people in the white suits bundled up her clothes with everyone else's and dumped them down the slot in the wall. The man whom she thought of as the anti-Shepard could not meet her eyes.

"Proceed into the next section, please," he ordered.

Gaby did not take her eyes off him as she walked through the sliding door. That was how she missed seeing Moran leap on Bushbaby and slam her against the metal door frame. But she heard the soft splintering crack of skull on white-painted steel. And she saw Rose run at Moran, her fingers curled into claws. And she saw the milling bodies, flesh and white fabric; she heard the voices yelling in Swahili, Kalenjin and English. She saw the five white suits pull Moran away and hold him. She saw five more take Bushbaby away on the trauma cart. She saw Bushbaby spasm like she was having an epileptic fit. And she saw the glossy splash and trickle of blood on the door frame that the white-suits quickly wiped away.

In the next zone they sat Gaby in a chair and cut away all the threads and wires and beads and plaits that Rose had woven into her hair. They cut carelessly, hacking off the bangs of hair that Gaby had not cut in seven years. She looked at the coils of red hair on the white floor and knew that she could survive this. Whatever lay behind the next door could be no greater violation than this.

In the same room were a number of tiled cubicles. The voice of the anti-Shepard told her to cover the lighted panels with her feet and hands. As she stood spread-eagled two white-suits worked over her with high-pressure needle sprays. Through the steam and spray she stared at the camera on the wall with which the man with Shepard's voice was monitoring her. She could cry here. No one would see. Tears would only be more water on her body. She should cry. But she would not while that man looked at her through the eyes of the lens.

Warm air vents dried her body and the shaggy mess of her hair. She was given a white paper robe and moved on to the next zone. The words UNIT 12: ZONE WHITE were printed in blue on the back of the robe. The paper rubbed her raw skin.

In the next zone was the birthing chair.

There was a greater violation than the cutting off of her hair.

She struggled, but they strapped her arms into the cuffs and her feet into the stirrups. Then they did the things with the dilators and the rubber gloves and the endoscope and the lubricating jelly.

"You don't need to do this," she kept telling the doctor who had his fist in her vagina. "There is no medical reason for this. You just want to humiliate me because we fucked the UN up the ass."

Then the doctor did something that made her gasp and tear at the leather straps. He had not needed to do that thing either.

They took her to the next sector, which was a dead-white room with a white table and two white chairs in it. Gaby was placed on one chair. After a time the door slid open and the man she called the anti-Shepard entered and sat across the table from her. He was dressed in a beige linen Nehru suit. The badge clipped to his breast pocket identified him as RUSSEL SHULER, with ACCESS ALL LEVELS.

Gaby placed her hands on the white table and stared at the space between them. After the birthing chair, she could not look Russel Shuler in the eyes. She could not look anyone in the eyes.

"Interview commenced twenty-eighteen, October second, 2008," he said to the air. "Preliminary debriefing of Ms. Gaby McAslan."

Gaby looked up.

"Have you got a cigarette?"

"I'm sorry. Smoking isn't permitted in this unit."

"In that case I want to see the European Union ambassador. My treatment here contravenes the UN's own charter on human rights."

The man called Russel Shuler sighed and asked her to tell him everything that had happened to her in the Chaga.

"You shot Rose's dog," Gaby said. "How is Bushbaby?"

Russel Shuler frowned, then identified the street name.

"Ah. Yes. Her. I'm sorry to have to tell you this, but she died in theater."

Gaby closed her eyes and imagined turning the table over, picking up the white chair and smashing blindly about her until everything was in as many pieces as she was.

"We'll be charging the man, the one who calls himself Moran, with murder, of course."

"Get me the EU ambassador," Gaby McAslan said quietly.

The man sighed, which was the signal for two big men in medical whites to come and take Gaby down the curving white corridor to a windowless white room with a steel toilet in one corner, a hygiene cubicle in the other, a bed as far away from the toilet as possible, a television screen on one wall and a television camera on the other. The door sealed seamlessly into the wall, as had that other door in that other white room in Tsavo West.

"I want Shepard, get me Shepard," Gaby screamed until she could barely force the words from her vocal cords. Then she tore off the paper robe, ripped it into shreds and stuffed them down the steel john. She made a nest out of the bedding, folded herself into a fetal position in the middle of it and cried herself into dreams of running down curving white corridors after the ever-retreating figures of Bushbaby and Dog until they came to a brink and fell into simmering magma and Gaby could do nothing to save them because her head had been shaved and her hands tied with her hair.

She woke with a cry. The door was open.

"Shepard?" she said.

Three figures were silhouetted against the white corridor. They wore surgical scrubs. Between them was a birthing chair on castors.

"You don't need to do this," Gaby said as they put their machines into her and sucked their syringes of fluid out of her. "You don't have to do this. You have no right to do this. No right. No right. No right."

There was something in the needle they had given her, for she slept without dreams after that, and when she next woke, it was because the door had opened again and it was Shepard standing there. Her heart leaped. She lived again. The joy burned through the sleep and the chemicals, and in the clarity she saw that it was not Shepard, but his evil twin, come with a white sweatshirt and a pair of white drawstring pants because he was not brave enough to sit across a table from a naked woman.

This was the pattern of time in Unit 12. Door opening and either Russel Shuler or the birthing chair; door closing; numb, fetal sleep; well-prepared food that could have been dog shit for all that Gaby tasted of it, fiddling with the television controls, staring at twenty-year-old reruns on Voice of Kenya of *Remington Steele* or *Oprah Winfrey*. From time to time she realized that behind that screen should be news channels: CNNs, SkyNets, Foxes. Instead she found herself looking forward to the Venus de Milo beauty-cream ad. One fix was enough to have her rocking back and forth for hours in her nest of quilts, quietly singing "Venus de Milo, Venus de Beauty." It made her stop wanting a cigarette. She wanted a cigarette more than she wanted out of this white room with its shower cubicle and steel pissoir and camera eye watching her rocking gently in her nest, singing. Sometimes she thought that whatever they gave her in the needle must be very good, that she worried so little about wanting out of Unit 12. It was life. She would adapt. She was doing very well already. Russel told her so in his debriefing sessions. But a cigarette would be perfect.

And then she would wake in the dim night light and feel the full weight of Unit 12 press down on her and she would know that the stuff had worn off, because she could recall where and what and who she was, and what had been done to her, and how long it would go on for, because they had absolute power here. Then she would beat her fists bloody on the place where the door had disappeared until the white scrubs came, and she would wake wondering what she had done to her hands that they were bandaged, but not too worried, because it was almost time for *Santa Barbara.*

And she woke.

And there were two silhouettes in the door.

"Ms. McAslan?" said the nearer of the dark figures. Gaby frowned in her nest of quilts. The figure spoke with a Kenyan accent. "May I come in?"

Gaby nodded. The figure entered. He was a tall, very black black man in a pale brown suit. His tie was very neatly knotted. He carried a briefcase. He set the case on Gaby's bed. She backed away from it into the corner.

"My name is Johnson Ambani," he said. "I am a lawyer. I

am very happy to find you in passably good health, Ms. McAslan. Could you please sign this document?'' He spread two pages on his briefcase and marked where she should sign with black *X*s. He offered Gaby his stainless-steel ballpen. She stared at it as if she had been offered a snake.

''What am I signing?''

''Documents seconding you as consultant to the National Assembly Ministerial Special Inquiry into human rights violations on Kenyan and foreign nationals by the United Nations,'' said the second figure, a big, broad black man. In silhouette his earlobes were loops of stretched flesh.

''Dr. Dan?'' Gaby said in a voice she had not used since she was six.

''In person, Ms. McAslan,'' Dr. Daniel Oloitip said. ''Now, if you would have the world see what is being hidden in this place, you will sign the papers Mr. Ambani, my legal adviser, has prepared for you.''

Questions could wait. Not long, for they were very huge questions, even under the chemical smog in her head, but long enough to scribble *Gaby McAslan* at the black *X*s without reading the print. Johnson Ambani fastened a plastic badge on Gaby's soiled white sweatshirt. It had her SkyNet pass photograph on it and read NATIONAL ASSEMBLY MINISTERIAL COMMISSION OF INQUIRY: SPECIAL CONSULTANT.

Her hair was long and beautiful in the photograph.

''Dr. Dan,'' she said. ''Could someone get me a cigarette?''

48

The curving white corridor was full of black men and women in dull suits. They followed Dr. Dan like the tide the moon as he swept past all the white doors that were identical but for the numbers on them. Barefoot and vertiginous from the tranquilizers, Gaby kept at Dr. Dan's shoulder by momentum alone.

''Things move slowly in this country, and they go by devious routes, but they get there,'' the big politician said. ''Two years I have been pressing for a government inquiry into this place, but all happens in God's time.''

''You knew?'' Her brain had been lagged with roof insulation.

"About what the UN is doing here? Something. We all have our sources; I would not wish to compromise mine so close to its center. You!" He turned, pointed at whatever one of the UNECTA followers-on in white fell beneath his finger. "Fetch Ms. McAslan a cup of very strong black coffee. You were my trump card, Ms. McAslan. My finger of God. When I found out that the UN was detaining a Western journalist in contravention of the Kenyan Constitution, and the UN's own convention on human rights, it was very easy to swing the international media behind me. They are all up there, behind the wire, howling for you, Ms. McAslan."

The Unit 12 staffer brought the coffee. Gaby tried to sip it as Dr. Dan wheeled his political circus on down the corridor.

"They wouldn't let me see any television news. You don't know what it's been like down here, Dr. Dan."

"You are the lead story on all the channels. Even then, Mohammed al-Nur tried to invoke UN immunity and dismissed my writ of habeas corpus." The Egyptian chief secretary was a leading advocate of the United Nation's suzerainty over national government. "However, for a good Muslim, Mr. al-Nur shows a regrettable interest in women having sex with dogs."

"Allegedly," Johnson Ambani said.

"Allegedly. But I am still sure that he would not like the video we made of him in the room in the Hilton with the Giriama woman and the Doberman to find its way into the hands of the prurient and corrupt Western press. I am told it was quite a technical challenge getting him, the woman and Doberman in focus at the same time."

Gaby suppressed a guffaw. Not even Unit 12 Zone White was sealed and aseptic enough to keep out the infectious bizarreness of everyday African life.

"They made a bad mistake in trying to disappear you, Ms. McAslan. But it would have been a worse mistake to let you go, having seen what you have seen."

"The camera!" Gaby shrieked. The strong black coffee had burned away the dope like the sun the morning mist. "They took my camera; it's all on it, everything, about Jake and the Treetoppers and the Wa-chagga and the Breeding Pit. Everything."

Dr. Dan nodded to Johnson Ambani, who opened his briefcase and took out another paper.

"This is an authorization to sequester material evidence," he explained as Dr. Dan signed it without reading. He gave the paper to one of the women lawyers in the entourage. "Could you take this to Administration and have them find and give you Ms. McAslan's camera?" She ran off, ungainly in tight skirt and heels.

"And the diaries," Gaby shouted after her. "Mine and the Moon diary, they've got them both."

"That is already taken care of, Ms. McAslan," the lawyer Ambani said. He went into his magic briefcase again and produced two plastic bags stamped with biohazard symbols and UNECTA's crescents and mountain. "We found these with the rest of your personal possessions."

Russel Shuler the anti-Shepard was waiting at the top of a wide ramp that curved down to the zone below White Level Three.

"Turnabout is fair play, Russ," Gaby said, tapping the badge on her dirty sweatshirt. "This time I get to do the debriefing."

"It's too big for you," Russel Shuler said to her. "It's too big for anyone. We're not ready for it yet. Believe me, I am not the enemy here."

The Zone White workers remained up above as Russel Shuler led the delegation down the ramp. The wall color changed to red halfway down.

"Zone Red is our maximum isolation and observation area," Russel Shuler said. "While I understand that all parts of this complex are to be made open to you and that my staff here are to render you every possible assistance, I must advise you to consider hard the implications of making public what you see here."

"Dr. Dan," Gaby whispered as Russel Shuler led them along the musky, moldy-smelling red corridor. "Shuler's right. The Chaga, it changes people. Not just mentally or emotionally: physically. It uses the HIV virus as a vector into cells to reprogram the genes. It can change living tissue."

Warm air spiraling up from deep in the coil of tunnels rattled the inquirers' identity badges.

"Nevertheless, they are our people down here, whatever changes have been done to them," Dr. Dan said. "Whatever they look like, whatever they have become, we shall see what is to be seen."

Russel Shuler circled the politicians and lawyers around him outside a door that had been painted, Gaby thought, exactly the color of hell.

"Ladies and gentlemen, you are now on Zone Red Level One. This is the area in which we hold those HIV-altered patients whose adaptations are largely neurological. In many cases, their faculties and abilities seem quite superhuman; in almost all, they are impossible to explain or quantify."

He opened the hell-colored door.

The room was furnished as lavishly as a luxury hotel. A radiantly beautiful Nilo-Hamitic woman was sitting cross-legged on the king-size bed, cats-cradling with the laces of her training shoes. She smiled to her visitors but did not speak.

"Sarai is a manipulator of probabilities," Russel Shuler said. "We've tested her using electron-tunneling quantum-effect experiments; somehow—God knows how—she can affect quantum world-line collapse so that the outcome is always in her favor."

"Excuse me, but I do not understand," Dr. Dan said.

"Put crudely, in quantum theory, if you flip a coin, it is not either heads or tails, but a state of both heads and tails until the act of observing the face of the coin collapses those possibilities into a single certainty. Either heads or tails. What Sarai does is make sure that it is always the side she calls. The outcome is always in her favor."

"She makes her own luck," Dr. Dan said.

"Like us coming to this place now," the assemblyperson for Nanyuki said.

"Everything serves her purposes," Russel Shuler said.

Sarai smiled powerfully and folded her cat's cradle inside out.

In the next room a very thin man was sleeping in fetal position. The rise and fall of his chest was so slow and shallow Gaby doubted for a time that he was breathing at all.

"He goes into sleep at the start of the October rains," Russel Shuler said. "He wakes again at the start of the March rains. His metabolism slows to a crawl. Like hibernation, except that in low-energy sleep the aging process is suspended. From our point of view, his life span is greatly expanded."

From his own point of view, it is as short and fragile as any of ours, Gaby thought. Too few sleeps and wakings.

She read the name on the next room.

''Here,'' she said to Russel Shuler. ''I want to see who is in here.''

William Bi was the name on the door.

''Please excuse me,'' a voice called over a rhythmic creaking. ''I will not stop because you won't be staying very long, and if I stop I will not come third.''

William Bi sat on an exercise bike, pumping the pedals hard. He was dressed in stained red sweatshorts and cropped sweatshirt. On a flat wallscreen a garishly animated cyclist raced across a poster-color road toward an ever-receding horizon.

''Hello, Gaby,'' William said, without taking his eyes off the screen or breaking his rhythm. He was as thin and young and androgynously beautiful as Gaby remembered when the dirigible lifted them from the burning Nissan ATV on Chaga's edge. ''I thought I'd be running into you here.''

''William, I'm sorry. I never meant this to happen.''

''Sarai is the only one can make happen what she wants to happen. But I can see what she makes happen, so I am content.''

''William's time sense has been altered,'' said Russel Shuler. ''He lives in a longer present moment than we do. What we perceive as the present is about six seconds. William's present is about three and a half minutes, both forward and back, with limited pre- and post-cognition up to about half an hour.''

''I think you should call the maintenance people,'' William said, leaning over the handlebars of the exercise bike. He had overtaken the first computer cyclist and was coming up on the rear wheel of another. ''The air-conditioning plant is going to give you trouble again in about ten minutes.''

Russel Shuler took an intercom from inside his Nehru jacket and made a call.

''He's almost always right,'' he said, when he had finished talking to the engineers. ''We've had to stop members of staff getting racing tips off him, or lottery numbers.''

''He can see into the future and the past?'' one of the assemblypersons asked. ''All at once?''

''Simultaneously, yes. I don't think our short-time-frame minds can ever properly conceive what it must be like. Perhaps a state of permanent déjà vu for both the past and the future.''

''She will not thank you for it,'' William said abruptly, pumping hard at the pedals. Sweat rolled down his forehead.

"The diary. Reminds her too much of things she would like to forget."

He passed the animated cyclist and crossed the finish line. As he had predicted, he was third.

At the top of the next down ramp, Russel Shuler said to the commissioners, "Down on Zone Red Level Two are the moderate physical adaptations. You may find some of them disturbing, but please do not display any negative emotion in front of the patients. Many of them are experiencing great difficulty in coming to terms with what the Chaga has done to their bodies."

The color of the walls in Red Level Two was several shades deeper than the corridor above; blood rather than sheer hell.

In the first room, a woman reclined on a wooden beach lounger under a ceiling of dazzling white light. She was naked but for a polka-dot bikini bottom. Her hair, her eyes, her skin were dark green. Russel Shuler told the inquiry that she was a photosynthete. Her skin and circulatory system had been infected with complex molecules that bonded to the cells and enabled them to draw food and energy directly from sunlight, like plants. The full-spectrum tubes in the ceiling approximated normal African daylight. In the dark she would wither and shiver and die.

The woman turned her back to the National Assembly Commission of Inquiry and picked up the copy of *Viva!* she had set down on the floor.

Dr. Dan picked the next door at random. Behind it they found a middle-aged woman on a chair with a monkey grooming itself on her shoulder and her hands on her knees. At her feet a cat sat licking its crotch. A bird bobbed on top of the dressing-table mirror. The dressing-table top was smeared with white bird shit. The woman had no eyes. Blank skin covered her eye sockets. She had no ears. Her skull was a smooth curve of flesh. Yet when the people came into her suite, she turned her head toward them, as if seeing and hearing, and welcomed them warmly.

"It's the animals," she told them. "I see through their eyes, hear through their ears." She lifted the monkey onto her lap. "But they have such short little spans of attention."

Russel Shuler explained that the woman had neurological grafts into the nervous systems of her animals. She could switch her point of view between them and was learning to multiplex: cat sight, monkey smell, bird hearing.

"I've seen this one," Gaby said. "In the Chaga. Hubert, the

Treetoppers' kid; he can share his consciousness with other creatures in the forest."

"Indeed?" Russel Shuler said.

"I must look out for him," the woman with the animal eyes said.

"What is it all for?" a woman lawyer asked as they hurried onward down the corridor past doors they did not have time to look behind toward the ramp to Zone Red Level Three. "What is the reason for these transformations?"

"Evolution, ma'am," Russel Shuler said. "Just ways of being human. No more reason for it than the eyes on butterflies' wings or a peacock's tail. Every reason and no reason. It works. It's right for its place and time."

He addressed the inquiry in general.

"Before we go down to the third and final level, I must warn you that this is where the most radically changed are housed. What you see may provoke repugnance, shock, even fear. Remember that they are human. They will not harm you, they are not dangerous. They are just people; experiments in ways of being human. If any of you don't want to come with us down to Level Three, you can get straight up to the reception area by going a couple of hundred yards back along this corridor and taking the service elevator. I'll give you a few seconds to make up your minds."

Mine is made up, Gaby McAslan thought. I have found only one name on my list of the disappeared. The other two are down that ramp, whatever they have become, and so I will not go back.

Russel Shuler waited his few seconds. No one turned back.

"Okay," Russel Shuler said. "One final thing. If you have anything plastic that you particularly value, you'd be advised to leave it here. In some cases, the alterations have spread beyond the individual to the environment."

"What does that mean?" Dr. Dan said, unfastening his badge and digital watch.

"You'll find out."

They went down, leaving a small pile of identity badges, watches and pens behind them.

The first door opened onto an antechamber into which the commissioners fitted with much jostling. In the facing wall was a long curtained window and an airlock door. Russel Shuler picked up a microphone plugged into a socket underneath the window.

"The temperature and CO_2 levels are too high for human tolerance in there," he said. "But I'll get Kighoma to say hello to you." He spoke into the microphone in good Swahili. "Pray this is one variation that doesn't take," he said as he drew back the curtains.

The room beyond was quite conventional. The young man who waved from the chair in which he was reading a football magazine was not. His skin was such a flat black that he seemed to have no facial features. His hair was bone white. His eyes were milky, as if afflicted with cataracts. His nose was very large and broad, his chest wide and deep. While Russel Shuler and assem-blypersons spoke with him in Swahili, Gaby observed him more closely. The dead black skin was thick and waxy; hairless, almost poreless. The milkiness of the eyes was caused by a membrane like a cat's third eyelid that flickered back and forth between blinkings.

"Superb adaptation to water retention," Russel Shuler said, observing Gaby observing. "The third eyelid holds in tears for recycling and keeps out dust particles and potential allergens. He doesn't sweat, his urine is highly concentrated. He adjusts to the temperature of the environment. That skin also protects him from ultraviolet radiation and prevents ingress by airborne particles. Likewise, the nose filters and sinus mucus membranes."

"He's a man for the end of the world," Gaby said. "Termi-nal humanity for a polluted, radiation-burned, greenhouse Earth. He can survive there, and live, and thrive. Jesus Christ."

"Yes, Mr. Shuler, you are right, we should pray," Dr. Dan said. "Pray very hard."

Kighoma waved good-bye and went back to his football magazine.

Russel Shuler paused before opening the door of the next room.

"You may find this one particularly disturbing. We keep the lighting low; he seems to prefer it that way, though he is adapted to wide fluctuations in light levels, as you'll find out. It's safest just to stand and let your eyes adapt. You may feel something move past you very close and very fast. Don't be alarmed; Juma likes to play with his abilities, and he's a bit of a practical joker. If you can, try not to flinch out of the way; his margins of error are very narrow."

The dark room felt full of unseen dimensions, like a cinema

where the projector has broken down and everyone is afraid to move. It was big enough to keep its own little winds: Gaby felt air currents stir the fine hairs on her arm. She sensed massive objects poised overhead. Someone coughed. The big chamber returned odd echoes. Gaby relaxed her eyes and let them unfocus; an old astronomer's trick her father had taught her. The masses she had sensed above her were rectangular shelves and blocks, piled on top of each other like the mother of all overhang climbing walls. Walls, blocks, ceiling were covered with steel rungs. The center of the room was filled from floor to roof with girders and pylons. These too were covered in handholds. Postindustrial jungle gym, Gaby thought. At the same moment she saw something flip over the edge of a cube just under the ceiling, go down the wall at such speed it was more like a fall, dash past her and hurtle up one of the central pylons to flop onto the top of the cube opposite. A black face looked down at the people below.

Hands. The thing had seemed all hands. Too many hands.

Russel Shuler called in Swahili. The face frowned, nodded from side to side: maybe yes, maybe no. Then it flipped over the precipice, swung with dizzying speed down the wall, leaped to a girder and hung there.

There were cries. There were gasps. Johnson Ambani crossed himself.

The thing had looked all hands because it was all hands.

The boy could not have been more than eighteen. Apart from a complete lack of hair, he was quite normal down to the base of his rib cage. It was below there that the changes had been worked on him. He had no lower torso, no legs, no feet. In place of these was an extra pair of shoulders, arms and hands. He gripped the rungs with his upper and lower right hands. He was dressed in a blue-ribbed high-neck bodysuit that allowed all his hands to move freely. Russel Shuler asked him in Swahili if he would come down and meet the commission of inquiry. He stood on all four hands on the floor. Gaby thought of a sleek black animal, and feared she was being racist or sexist or change-ist. The boy heaved himself onto his lower arms and stood upright, shifting his weight from hand to hand. He stood as tall as Gaby's shoulder. He extended an upper hand in greeting to one of the legal aides. The woman danced away, then remembered her position and gingerly took it.

"Please," the boy said in faltering English. "I am so bored.

Can you make him make them take me up there? I want to be up there. It is where I am meant to be. I am learning myself English. It is what they talk up there."

"Up there?" Gaby asked, and understood in the same breath. "Christ."

"Unity space station," Russel Shuler said. "We've approached NASA about transferring him. Juma is adapted for life in free fall. His legs and hips began to atrophy soon after we took him into quarantine—like gangrene. We had to amputate. At the same time as the lower arms started to grow, the internal organs were reconfiguring themselves. The things that have been done to the boy's body are terrifying. He's a tough kid."

"Please," Juma said again, to all the assemblypersons. "I am so bored."

Gaby could not shake out of her head the image of the legless beggar who had pushed himself on his trolley past Miriam Sondhai's house with wooden blocks strapped to his hands.

"Let him go," Dr. Dan said with vehemence in his soft deep voice. "Let them all go. This is no place for them. You have no right to keep them here like animals. Even my cattle are more free and respected than these people."

And as the Masai bleed their cattle, the UN bleed their herd for their HIV-infected blood, Gaby thought.

"Where would they go?" Russel Shuler said. "Back to their people? Back to the townships and camps? Their own mothers wouldn't recognize them as human, let alone once having been their children. How long do you think they would last, even the ones that don't need special environments? How long before some Islamic fundamentalist mullah or apocalyptic Christian evangelical preacher condemns them as abominations of Satan and starts the purges? Your National Assembly Commission of Inquiry may have already sown the seeds of that holocaust. All those newsmen camped out there are going to want to know what you found down here. Maybe it's safer if the world doesn't find out."

"If not now, then when?" Gaby said. "Time's against you. Time's against all of us, because that big green machine down there is getting closer and we are all running out of options."

"Please," Juma called from the high ledges among which he had taken refuge from the arguing. "This is not my place. I am so bored. Take me up there."

Russel Shuler passed the next doors. He stopped the party by a curtain of heavy plastic strips that hung across the corridor.

"You'll remember what I said back on Level Two about the alterations having spread to the environment. That area is beyond this curtain. There's still a chance to go back if you want to."

He stepped through the hanging strips. All the commissioners followed.

The smell was almost physical in impact. It was not that it was vile or fetid; it was that its complex esters and ketones punched deep into the hind brain and touched awake memories that had slept for decades. Gaby recalled the baobab on the curve of the Namanga road where she had first seen the Chaga, and the fragments of memory its perfume had stirred in her. Spicy sexy sweaty seductive magical mysterious Chaga-perfume. There was Chaga growing down here, deep under the earth. A bluish glow, like television light, shone from around the curve of the corridor. Russel Shuler led his guests toward it.

Gaby cried aloud. It was every child's dream of Jules Verne's giant mushroom forest at the center of the earth. The corridor was overarched by ribs of pseudo-coral from which hung bioluminescent fruit and clusters of red honeycomb. Fingers of damp yellow sponge dripped from the ceiling; stumps of the same material reached toward them from the floor. Organic stalactites and stalagmites. The floor beneath Gaby's bare feet seemed to be glazed, fused bone.

"It's expanding," Russel Shuler said. "About fifty inches per day. We have a month and a half before we abandon this level. Eventually it'll take over the whole facility. You were right, Ms. McAslan. Time is not on our side."

He placed his hand on an orangelike extrusion from a puckered mouth of muscle in the corridor wall. The lips opened with a sigh.

"It's all right, it won't eat you," he said.

The room beyond was huge. UNECTA had never designed it this size. You could comfortably fit the SkyNet offices on Tom M'boya Street under this roof.

"It's been working on the rock," Russel Shuler explained as Gaby followed the fluted columns and cables up and up to the ceiling of bioluminescent balloons. "Thank God it hasn't hit any vital systems yet." From the roof Gaby scanned down the piles of slumped spheres (profiteroles, she imagined) and the fifty-foot-high multiheaded florets (broccoli, she thought) and the fingers of the ubiquitous land corals to the white man with long blond hair and a pale beard and liquid blue eyes standing at their feet (Peter Werther, she knew). Dressed in surfer shorts.

"Good afternoon," he said in his soft south German accent. "I've been expecting you. Would anyone have a cigarette?"

"Peter Werther," Gaby McAslan whispered.

"Gaby McAslan." Peter Werther warmly shook Gaby's and then the hands of all the commissioners.

"Peter," Gaby said cautiously. "When I interviewed you back at What the Sun Said, you had a mark, a sign of your time in the Chaga. A piece of it growing over your body. It isn't there anymore."

"Tell her," Russel Shuler said.

"It is still growing on my body," Peter Werther said. "It will never stop growing on my body. You see, this"—he touched himself lightly on the chest and bowed shortly—"is not my body. This is only an extension of my body. Peter Werther is this room, and the next room, and the one beyond that, and the corridor from which you have entered, and the molecule machines working their way through the solid rock toward the light and the air. This is no more my body than that land coral, or this light balloon, and no less. They are all aspects of me, grown out of me. My body, my mind, my personality, are all around you.

"Are you sure you don't have a cigarette?"

Gaby realized she had there and then quit smoking.

"We couldn't decontaminate him," Russel Shuler said. "Not without killing him. We'd been observing him on Zone White for ten days when the thing started to run wild."

"You asked me how long, do you remember? Back at Lake Naivasha," Peter Werther said to Gaby. "Not long. Twelve hours, until my skin was completely covered."

"We took him down to Red Three, where we had a clean medical unit." Russel Shuler took up the story. "He was comatose by then. Vital signs were going mad. It was like that thing was playing games with his physiology, testing to the edge of destruction."

"Russel refuses to believe me when I say that I was not in a coma," Peter Werther said. "I was dead. Again. Like I died up there on Kibo in the snow when the Kilimanjaro package came down. The Chaga brought me back then, it brought me back again. I have died and lived twice, and now I am quite sure I will not die a third time.''

''They came out of the soft orifices first,'' Russel Shuler continued. ''Eyes, nose, mouth, anus: the seeding tendrils. Then the spore fibers burst through the skin, everywhere. We had to evacuate. He was starting to absorb the bed and the monitoring equipment.''

''Something wonderful, that is what I told you.'' The conversation was between Peter Werther and Gaby. Russel Shuler, the commission of inquiry, were distant spectators. ''Is this not wonderful? How can I begin to tell you what it is like to return to consciousness not as a man, but as a forest, a mind spread through many parts, many bodies at once? I do not think it can be told, only experienced. But I missed the sensation of being a body, of being able to move and relate my senses to direct action. So I built this body that you see, the body I remember and like best. But I have other bodies that I have built with special abilities for special purposes. They are not human bodies, these other Peter Werthers. Come with me. I shall show you this underworld I have become. Virgil to your Dante.''

Gaby thought of old Big Bwana White Hunter movies as Peter Werther—she could not think of him as an extension of the environment—led the commission through his private jungle to a mouth door between balloon cables.

The second chamber was bigger than the first, and filled with dense fan vegetation. When Gaby glimpsed eyes peeping between the fronds, she asked Peter Werther if these were the other selves he had told her about.

''No, they are people. Victims of this place,'' Peter Werther said.

''Arboreal adaptations,'' Russel Shuler said. ''The most common form. There are so many of them they're nearly a tribe.''

The parted fronds closed. Gaby heard movements, rustling in the coral canopy.

There were seven of them; three men, two women, two children. They were as agonizingly thin as winged Nicole Montagnard. Ribs visible under T-shirts. Faces of three decades of televised famine. Gaby could not bear to look at their collarbones. But they were not lethargic, painful, exhausted of life like the starved. They were healthy, energetic, quick of mind and body, right and fit. The adaptation had given them very long forearms, very long fingers, very long feet, very long curled skin tails. Holes had been cut in the backs of their football shorts to accommodate the prehensile tails. Some wore theirs coiled around their legs. The women favored looping theirs over their arms. The children bound themselves close to their mothers with their tails.

Tree people. Monkey people. A hundred childhood racist clichés bubbled up in Gaby's mind. She tried to prick them with reason. Changed. Ways of being human. Old prejudices burst hard.

They had appointed the man who spoke English as the head of their small tribe. The changes had left enough of his face to identify him as Masai.

"Dr. Daniel Oloitip." He exchanged greetings with Dr. Dan in Masai. "You are my assembly member. My elected representative. I voted for you in the last election. I am very glad to see you here, but I am wondering—we are all wondering—what are you going to do about us? When are you going to set us free?"

"Soon," Dr. Dan said. He looked at Russel Shuler before continuing. "Soon you will all be set free from here, to go back to your people, your families, your homes."

The man laughed. It was the contemptuous laugh of the proud Masai.

"My family will not know me, my people will not accept me, my home has been taken away by the Chaga. So we must go to the Chaga. That is freedom for us. Where else is there?"

Peter Werther took the commissioners by another sphincter door into the main corridor, and from there into a new Chaga chamber. This was the smallest of the rooms Peter Werther had excavated from the underpinnings of Unit 12. It was just big enough to take the ghost of a house. Gaby could think of no other likeness. The memory of a house, fleshed out of Chaga-stuff. Ghost walls of foam. Ghost floors of yielding sponge. Ghost windows of translucent yellow gauze that rippled in the air currents that blew through this underworld. Ghost door of hanging moss. Ghost curtains of creeper, ghost lights of bioluminescent bulbs. Ghost furnishings: chairs, tables, beds, grown from soft green coral.

And in the middle of the green ghost of a house sat the angel of media. This angel was a white woman wearing a white sleeveless vest and red-and-purple Chaga camouflage pants, kneeling on a meditation stool grown from the floor. Her wings were spread wide. They touched the soft walls of the ghost room. They were not feathered like the wings of Jehovah's angels; these were sheets of iridescent gossamer, like a dragonfly's wings, and they were full of faces. Faces of movie personalities. Faces of media celebrities. Faces of sports stars. Faces of actors in advertisements for Diet Coke and tampons. Faces of people from Africa and South America and the Pacific Rim and Europe. Faces of foreign correspondents and satellite news reporters. Gaby saw Jake Aarons's face. Old photograph; sharp smile, sharper suit. Gaby saw her own face appear for a moment and fade into CNN's European link man. Like the photograph in the badge she had left at the top of the ramp, her hair was long and shiny and beautiful. The angel wings flexed slowly, billowing in the media wind. The woman's eyes were closed. Her chest rose and fell slowly, as if in contemplation. She had black, naturally curling hair that fell to her shoulders.

She opened her eyes.

"Well, lookee here," she said. She had a Dublin accent. You can take the girl out of Barrytown, but not Barrytown out of the girl.

"Moon," Gaby McAslan breathed.

The woman rose from her stool. Her wings folded and furled into a place on her back Gaby could not see.

"You are Gaby McAslan," Moon said. She sounded disappointed. "I know who you are. I've been watching you. Following you. I know all about you."

"I know who you are," Gaby said. "I've been following you, so long, so closely. I know all about you. This is how I know it." She held out the ruined Liberty print diary in its transparent, UNECTA-stamped sack. "T.P. sends his love."

49

The October rains had come. From horizon to horizon the sky was a plane of gray cloud. The red dust of Kajiado had turned to watery mud. Gaby splashed barefoot through it to Dr. Dan's government Landcruiser. UNECTA had been unable to spare the women any footwear, but had lent them yellow plastic rain sheets. Gaby wrapped the camera with the last testament of Jake Aarons stored on its discs in hers. Moon draped hers over the thing on her back that the long lenses at the wire were not allowed to see. All the way up in the elevator, all the way through the legal wranglings in Reception, Gaby had stared in nauseated fascination at the thing that pulsed and glowed in the small of Moon's back where she had cut the white vest top away.

Once when she had been a kid walking the dogs on the Point, she had come across the body of a drowned sheep that had washed up in a gully. It had been a long time in the sea; the wool had all fallen out, the body was swollen, eyes eaten out by crabs. It was not that it was dead that had scared Gaby, it was that it looked so alien. She had come back day after day to look at the rotting, disgusting, fascinating thing until the high tide took it out again.

The thing on Moon's back was dreadful and wonderful in the same way. Through the transparent flesh Gaby could see how it clung to the woman with a hundred red millipede legs, pushing neural connectors into her spinal cord, alien as a drowned sheep, feeling its way into places no lover ever could. It was an ally with astonishing capabilities: the furled wings were sheets of organic circuitry powered by light. They carried Moon through the planetary telecommunications networks: they could receive hundreds of terrestrial and satellite channels simultaneously, decode them and filter selected information into her consciousness. Television dreaming.

The two women got into the backseat, dripping on the upholstery. Gaby combed back her savaged hair with her fingers. It would grow. It would be right again. She had the pictures. They would make everything right again.

"We go," Dr. Dan said to Johnson Ambani, who doubled as driver. The government Landcruiser drove away from the olive monolith of Unit 12. Kenyan flags stirred damply on the wing pennons. A second Landcruiser fell in behind. In it were Lucius and the Wa-chagga woman. They had no place either in this nation, among these people. They were going south too, back to the Chaga. The Black Simbas had already been returned to Nairobi, except for Moran, who had been remanded in prison charged with Bushbaby's murder. If convicted, he could be hanged. Gaby's horror of ritual execution struggled with her anger at Bushbaby's death. Nobody had needed to die.

She hated the stupidity of killing. She hated the fragility of human lives. She hated death.

The media was waiting outside the wire. Hundreds of them, waiting in the red mud and the rain. Cameras, boom mikes, long lenses. Some had stepladders pushed up against the wire. Dr. Dan had played the ace of trumps. Vanish a black African HIV 4 victim and it is another entry in the WHO's databases. Vanish a white female European television journalist and the news vans are ten deep on the football pitch on the other side of the road. Gaby grimaced as she remembered T.P.'s cardinal sin: she was the newsperson who had become the news. As the government cars approached, a few cameras flashed. A stampede began toward the gate. Blue helmets opened the gate a crack and pushed through to hold the reporters back.

"Keep driving," Dr. Dan said. "Do not stop. If you run one down, I will vouch for you."

Johnson Ambani did his best to obey his client but the reporters overwhelmed the blue helmets and poured in around the Landcruiser. Lenses were shoved against the windows. Flashes bounced around inside the car. Voices clamored, hands thrust microphones and disc recorders. *Ms. McAslan, Dr. Oloitip, who what do you when will you how did you can you will you?* Gaby glimpsed a SkyNet logo in the wall of technology and Faraway head and shoulders above the press. T.P. She saw T.P. She pressed her palms to the glass and shouted his name. Johnson Ambani inched forward until he had enough space to floor the accelerator. A few diehards ran after the Landcruiser. They must be freelances, Gaby thought. The car bounced over the railroad tracks at speed and turned left onto the Namanga road. The second Landcruiser emerged from the scrimmage and followed.

"Moon," Gaby said. Time and space were running out. "I need to know. The story the diary doesn't tell. Your story, yours and Langrishe's."

"You don't stop, do you?" Moon said. "Professional unto the last. You get the exclusive."

"This is for me, and me alone. I need to know how the story ends. You owe me this. I can guess some of the bits that were cut out of the diary, but I don't know how it ended. I don't know if you ever found Langrishe."

Moon looked at the rain falling on the high savannah for a time. She could not sit straight in the seat because of the thing on her back.

"Yeah, I suppose I do owe you. Found Langrishe? I suppose so. Found something that used to be Dr. Peter Langrishe."

"Changed."

Moon laughed.

"Most definitely. But not like those poor bastards in Unit Twelve. It wasn't disease-engendered. Like this thing of mine, it was something the forest grew. Up there in the Citadel, there are things like bodies in search of souls. And when they join, they join forever. Can you understand what I am telling you?"

"Obi-men. Orthobodies. Langrishe went into one of those?"

"This a story or an interview? Yes. He hid it from me at first, when he came to me out of the cloud forest up on the mountain. He would come to me by night, or hide himself in the fog; never let me see him too closely. Just the voice, ranting on and on about evolution, about how he had found the aliens, how the Chaga was their tool for expanding humanity into a truly galactic species. He was right, he had found his aliens; they were him. He was them.

"He showed me what he had done to himself. He thought he was glorious. Magnificent. I saw an abomination. A travesty. The denial of all my love for him; that he would do such a thing so lightly, without thought for anything but himself. All I had ever been was a donkey to nod at his theories on 'the alien' and a pair of ever-open thighs. Do you know what it is like to be betrayed by the thing that is the sum purpose of your life?"

I am learning, Gaby McAslan thought.

"I wanted to run from the sad, sick thing, back to my world, my people, my life. But I couldn't leave him, not like that. I still loved him. You can hate the sin but love the sinner. He was a monster, but many women have loved monsters. Monsters on the outside and monsters on the inside.

"He wanted me to become like him. I wouldn't do it. He used all the old emotional blackmails: we could share a deeper love in new bodies, he could not love me fully in my baseline form. New humanity, same old bitchy tricks. He had an orthobody prepared for me; showed it to me, did everything short of physical force to make me go into it. When I refused absolutely, he drifted away from me. He turned to others like him; I went to live among the Wa-chagga at Nanjara village. I needed human faces, human voices. But I needed Langrishe too—I couldn't leave him. Everything that I had loved was still there, intact, enclosed in that alien body. What's the psychologists' term? Approach-avoidance conflict? So when the foragers went out from Nanjara into the high forest, I went with them, to meet with Langrishe.''

''Why?'' Gaby asked.

''The ones back at Unit Twelve all asked that same question. To have sex with him,'' Moon said. ''Sex was all we had left. He could walk out of the orthobody—the thing had him on an umbilicus. Twenty feet of freedom. Freedom enough for a fuck. And all the ones at Unit Twelve had that same disgusted expression, darlin'.

''Then he trapped me. It was easy for him to do—the orthobody's nervous system was an extension of the forest, he could manipulate the Chaga almost any way he wanted. That was how he had always been able to find me. We fucked, I slept like I always did afterward, and the next thing I knew I woke up in some Citadel wall bolt-hole bare-ass naked, completely hairless, two months of my life erased and something not at all nice hooked into the base of my spine.

''He had the audacity to be furious. It was not what he planned for me. The Chaga had subverted him, diverted me away from the orthobody into which he had schemed to implant me. I knew then that I had been catastrophically wrong, so wrong I could not see how wrong I was. There was nothing left of Langrishe inside that atrocity, except obsession. That was all there had ever been, the need to sacrifice everything, even me, to his lust for the alien.

''I knew I had to escape from the Chaga entirely; he would always be able to find me, defeat me, bring me to him. In time he would change my body as he wished. A hunting party from Kamwanga found me at the foot of the Citadel. I persuaded them to take me to Nanjara, where I knew the people. I needed supplies, yes, but I needed evidence even more. I needed the diary. From Nanjara, the foraging party took me outward: they were headed to a meeting with a Tactical safari squad, for an extra cut on the deal they could smuggle me through the UN military cordon around terminum. They didn't understand that I wanted to be found by the military. I wanted to be taken to a UNECTA base. I wanted to be debriefed on what was going on up there in the Citadel. I wanted them to read my diary, then see the evidence growing in the middle of my back and cut it off me with scalpels.

''I left them before the rendezvous point, made my own way

to terminum and through to the outside world. Of course I got spotted and picked up by an airborne patrol. They took me to Ol Tukai, the base where Langrishe had worked. While I was bound up with his new incarnation up on the mountain, it had found itself a set of tracks, got up on them and gone mobile. I gave them the diary. I told them the things I had seen in the heart of the Chaga. I showed the thing on my back. They did tests. They did scans. They drafted reports and told me that the thing was unlike any other living organism they had ever encountered and that it would be an offense against science to do what I wanted and cut it out of me. There was a medical facility they wanted to send me to, where there were scientists who would look into the thing more closely and see if there was any way of removing it without killing it and leaving me hemiplegic."

Moon laughed again.

The Landcruiser had stopped at an army checkpoint. Johnson Ambani sighed and took the last piece of paper from his briefcase and gave it to a barely deferential soldier, dripping and miserable. He had North African looks, bored and bad-tempered in October rains. The soldier saluted and told Johnson Ambani how far south he could safely drive.

The government car moved on, toward terminum.

"You had to get away from Langrishe, but now you have to go back," Gaby said. "After all that he did to you, after all he would do to you."

"Not anymore," Moon said. "I learned things about myself in Unit Twelve. It's very good for that. They give you a lot of time for self-discovery. Years of it. About all there is to do, self-discovery. I learned to love this thing on my back. I have to. It's not me, but it's part of me. Like an eternal pregnancy; a piece of something separate but intimately connected; something that needs me. Like Langrishe needs me. That was why he wanted to change me: so that he would not have to make his journey into what he is becoming alone. It scares him; I realized that, down in Unit Twelve. He isn't sure he can cope with what he is being made into. He needs me, he needs the solidity of a love that doesn't have to be exactly as he is, but will walk with him wherever he goes. He needs me to anchor his humanity, to tell him he is still human, still capable of being loved."

"And do you love him?" Gaby asked.

The Landcruiser crunched onto the stony verge. The road

here ran in a long straight slope down into the valley of a seasonal river now boiling in spate. On the far side it climbed as long and as straight up to the top of the valley. Halfway up that road lay terminum.

The second government car pulled into the opposite verge. Lucius and the Wa-chagga woman got out and stood in the rain. Sheets of water streamed down the cracked black top. The river was red with eroded earth.

"Thank you," Moon said to Dr. Daniel Oloitip. "I will always remember this." They shook hands over the back of the seat.

"No doubt we will meet again someday," Dr. Dan said. "The future seems to insist on it."

Moon and Gaby got out of the car. Gaby held out the diary to her. Raindrops crackled on the plastic seal. Moon closed Gaby's hand on the book and pushed it against her chest.

"Give it back to T.P. I promised him I would get it back to him. I don't need it anymore. A new story's starting; what happens, how it unfolds, is for no one but me to say." Moon peeled off the UNECTA plastic raincape and let it fall to the ground. Rain plastered her thin vest to her shoulders and breasts.

The Wa-chagga had given their thanks and farewells and were halfway to the bridge. Moon sighed, lifted a hand in farewell and followed. Gaby watched her walk down to the river. She had gone a few yards when she paused as if struck by an afterthought, and turned.

"Tell T.P. I'm sorry. He's lost out again. He can give up on me now," she shouted. The gray rain streamed down her face. "Gaby McAslan. Even if we had known each other longer, we wouldn't have been friends, I think."

"You're probably right," Gaby shouted back. But she watched the woman go down to the bridge and wade through the red floodwaters and climb the long straight slope on the far side into terminum, where Gaby could not see her anymore.

50

T. P. Costello stopped the big SkyNet 4X4 outside the ugly house in the university district. It was late, dark. Even the reporters had gone home. Gaby could not see any house lights, but the Mahindra was in the drive beside her Landcruiser.

"Go on. You need sleep. The edit can wait."

"Don't want to," Gaby said. "He'll be there."

"You have to face him some time."

"When I can look at a chair on castors without wanting to throw up or knife someone, that's time."

"That bad."

"Worse. He left me there, T.P. He left me to fucking rot."

"Soonest done, best mended."

"That's a load of fucking shite, and you know it, Thomas Pronsias Costello."

T.P. rested his wrists on top of the steering wheel and pursed his lips. Gaby knew that it was not because she had affronted him. He was trying to find a way for him to go into that house with her and face whatever must be faced. You stand by your friends, Gaby thought. You do not leave them in hell when it is in your power to save them. But this is not your fight, now. This is mine alone.

"Why the hell couldn't Jake tell me he had HIV 4?" T.P. said after silence.

"Because you can't stop yourself picking up other's shit," Gaby said gently. "You did it with Moon, and she still left you. You just go on martyring yourself for people you care about."

"Ugly little habit. It's a crashing cliché, but I can't really believe he's gone."

"He's not dead," Gaby said.

"I know that. Not dead but translated? Transfigured? What's the religious expression? But it is death, of a kind. The Chaga, I mean. It's there, it can't be stopped, it draws closer every second of every day, it's the end of all we recognize and understand. We can look at it and contemplate it when it's far away, but when it starts to creep up on our lives and homes and work, when it starts to take things that mean something to us, it scares the living shit out of us. Go, get out of here. If the hacks come back and give you grief, call me. I know a policeman or two owe me more than they owe anyone else.''

''T.P.'' She held out the Moon diary to him. ''She said I should give it back to you.''

''Hell no. Complete the circle? I wouldn't give her the satisfaction. I don't want the fucking thing. You take it. Do what you like with it. Shred it. Burn it. Wipe your ass on it. Gaby!'' She had been about to slam the door. ''One thing. Go easy on Shepard. He's only a man.''

The electronic lock yielded to her touch. She went into the dark living room and set the diary on the coffee table. She went back into the hall and up the stairs. The bedroom was dark.

''Shepard?'' she said into the darkness. ''I want to talk to you.'' No answer. He must be hiding from her up in Zaire or down in Tsavo. That would be good. A night, a day or two all of her own to get a perspective on what she felt, then she could see him without wanting to tear his eyes out. She went downstairs again to make herself a drink. She flicked on the living room light.

Shepard was sitting in the ugly low-backed leather armchair. His feet were flat on the floor. His hands were flat on the armrests.

''Christ!''

''Gaby.''

Surprise became shock became anger, vomiting upward like black bile. She could not stop it. She did not want to.

''You fucker,'' she said. ''Do you know what I have been through? Do you know what they did to me? Of course you know. You're all in it together. You're all one big happy family. UNECTA looks after its own, doesn't it? Like the fucking Masons; huddling together, keeping your little fucking secrets from nasty nosy bitches. Well, it's out now. You thought you could keep it all quiet, keep that nasty nosy bitch locked away where no one could ever hear her. Do you know what they did to me down there? They fed me drugs. They turned my head inside out; then they strapped me into a chair and fist-fucked me. Did you laugh when they told you? Did you tell them it was no more than the bitch deserved? Do her good? Because I sure as hell didn't see you breaking your balls to bust me out of there, Shepard. You let them have me. You let them do it all to me. You would have let me rot in there. So why didn't you do anything? Cost you your peripatetic executiveship? The red-haired bitch an embarrassment to you now? Was that what they told you? On your way up the ladder, make sure you lose the Irish bitch? Asks too many favors. Asking too big a favor, was it, for the man who purports to love her to stop his good buddies ramming their rubber-gloved hands up the place he used to ram himself? Or did they beg you for a piece of the action too?

"Okay. Okay. Maybe you had an excuse. Maybe it wasn't that you wouldn't; you couldn't. Maybe you were over in Zaire or the Mountains of the fucking Moon and you only found out when you got back and the whole thing was blown. But you still lied to me. You deceived me. You made me think I could trust you, and then like every other man, every other fucking man I have ever known, you betrayed me."

Gaby picked up the diary from the coffee table. Seeing him sitting there, immobile, emotionless, she wanted to smash that passionless face with it until blood flowed and bone cracked or he made some acknowledgment of her fury.

"Give it to me just as you found it? The fuck you did. I know, Shepard. The dumb Irish girlie worked it out. So what did you do with the missing pages? Stuffed them into some little trinket box under the floorboards in case this scene ever happened and you needed them to placate the Valkyrie? Or did you actually have the balls to burn them? No. No." She strode across the room and back. She stabbed at him with an accusing finger. "You wouldn't do that. Couldn't do that. Not Mr. UNECTA Shepard. Those pages are filed neatly away somewhere in case UNECTA ever needs them. Jesus, you gutless bastard. Did you think I wouldn't work it out? Do you think that little of me? Or were you just blinded by this?" She grabbed her crotch, pumped it savagely back and forth. "You lied to me. Okay. Men do that. I should have learned by now. My fault for being naive and hopeful and expecting too much of five inches of erectile tissue. But what makes you an unforgivable bastard is that you thought I was a whore. You thought if you gave me this"—she held up the diary—"I'd give you this." She rubbed her hand between her thighs. "And you kept paying and getting what you thought was your for-value-received until one day the market bulled and the price got too high and you let the whore go. Isn't that it? Of course it is, that's why you aren't saying anything. That's why you won't look at me. Because you're scared. Because I'm right.

Because you can't face the truth. Well, come on, Shepard. Say something. Let's hear it. Or am I not even worth a pathetic half-hearted excuse? Come on, Shepard. I'm waiting. What have you to say to me?"

"There was a fax waiting for me when I got out of the disciplinary hearing," Shepard said very quietly. He did not move in his chair. He did not look at Gaby. He did not look away from her. He did not register anything in his field of vision. "It was from home. From my folks in Lincoln.

"There was a car crash. In Santa Barbara. Carling was driving. Fraser is dead. Aaron is critical in intensive care. The car crossed the center line—the police don't know how yet—and hit an oncoming tanker. Carling always was a shit driver. She died instantly. Fraser was the front-seat passenger. He always had to ride up front. Privilege of being oldest. They cut him out, but he was dead by the time they got him to the hospital. Aaron suffered massive internal injuries. His back is broken. He may not live. If he does, it's certain he will be paralyzed from the waist down. One of my sons is dead along with my ex-wife; the other is crippled. That is what happened to me today."

To Gaby it was as if he had got out of his ugly leather chair, crossed the room and driven his fist wrist-deep into her belly. She could not breathe. She could not see. The world ceased to exist. She found herself standing against the wall, head thrown back.

"Oh dear Jesus, Shepard."

"Perhaps I could have borne it, perhaps in time I could look at the world around me again and see something good and rich, if there had been someone I could trust to hold me if I put my weight on her. Someone I put my life, my career, my personal and professional integrity on the line for, someone I made a dumb mistake for, once, that grew to devour me. Someone for whom I was prepared to crucify myself before the UNECTA General Council to save her from the consequences of her impetuosity, and when the General Council said no, compromised security by leaking the information to someone in a position to do something with it. But I'm stupid; you've told me that, you must be right. The world isn't like that, is it? I lean, my support seems sound, I trust it with my full weight, and it snaps and I fall." He stood up. The movement was as slow and precise as a piece of Japanese drama. "I'm going out now."

"Shepard!" Gaby screamed.

The living room door closed.

"Shepard!" she screamed again.

The front door closed.

"Shepard!" A third time.

The Mahindra's door closed. She heard the engine start and saw the headlights swing across the curtains. Gaby threw her head back and howled like a dying animal.

Finished.

51

Ring.

Come on.

Ring ring.

Answer it.

Ring ring ring. I know you're there, it's three-thirty in the morning, where else are you going to be?

The mahogany door opened.

"Who the hell are you?" Gaby asked the tall young black woman standing in the hall dressed in a hastily wrapped kimono.

"I live here," the woman said. "Who the hell are you?"

Miriam Sondhai appeared behind her.

"It's all right. I will take care of this."

The young woman moved behind Miriam Sondhai but did not leave. She suspiciously studied Gaby with her arms full of crumpled star tapestry.

"Miriam, it's all over with Shepard. I can't live with him anymore, can I stay here?"

"No."

Gaby's foot had been over the threshold.

"What?"

"No, you cannot come into my house," Miriam Sondhai said. "It is not open to those who abuse its trust. I know what you did, Gaby McAslan. You are not so clever as you think, nor I so stupid. My PDU logs outgoing and incoming calls. I know I am forgetful, but not so much as not to know when I go out running. You covered up too well; if you had made it a break-in, I would never have suspected, but there was only one person who knew the alarm codes. Why did you have to deceive me? Why did you not ask me for this information?"

''Would you have given it to me?''

''So, because you are on the side of truth and right and good, that excuses it, does it?''

''Miriam, I'm sorry.''

''No, you are not. You would do it again if you had to. You would break into my house, hunt through all my private, personal things, abuse the trust I have put in you. Even now you think you can turn up on my doorstep and imagine that it is all right for you to ask me for help because you think I do not know what you did.

''Everything I entrusted to you, you abused. So, I will give you one last trust, and then I will not be afraid that you may abuse it, because there will be nothing more of me you can take. Listen, Gaby McAslan.

''When I was eight my mother's mother came up from Chisimaio to mind me while my mother was at a conference in Cairo. I was happy to see her; I loved my grandmother. I was excited when she hired a taxi and took me into town. I thought we would go shopping. But we did not drive to the markets, or the streets where the foreigners bought things with dollars and deutsche marks. She took me to a house in the suburbs beside an Islamic school. It was the house of the teaching mullah. My grandmother introduced me to him, told me he was a very holy man and that I must do whatever he said.

''He took me into the kitchen and made me sit on the table. Then he made me pull up my skirt and he took a razor blade and cut off my clitoris. My grandmother kept saying that this was right, it was a good thing, now men would want me and I would make a good wife and bear many children. But it would not stop bleeding in the taxi, or in the house. My grandmother was scared, but she did not dare take me to the hospital because my father would learn what she had done while I had been entrusted to her care. She wrapped sheets around me to stop the bleeding, but it would not stop and she got really frightened and ran away. The cook found me when she came in to make the dinner and took me to my father's hospital. He called my mother; she came back on the first flight from Cairo to comfort me, but what is cut away can never be put back. Female circumcision had been the way in my mother's family; her mother had done it to her, and she had sworn that it would never happen to her daughter. But she had been betrayed by the person she trusted. She never saw or spoke to her mother after that. On her dying bed, the old woman called for my mother to forgive her, but she would not come to see her. My grandmother died unforgiven.''

The young woman put a hand on Miriam's shoulder.

''I was a child; I loved my grandmother. I trusted her. She took me to a man who mutilated me with a razor blade on a kitchen table. What you have done to me is no different, Gaby McAslan.''

Miriam Sondhai turned away. The housemate looked at Gaby as if she were something that had died in the porch. She closed the heavy mahogany door on her.

''Fuck you, Ms. Pure and Perfect!'' Gaby shouted. ''And your fucking lesbian girlfriend too! You're not going to get very far with her with no fucking clitoris! I don't need you! I don't need any of you!''

She blared the car horn peevishly all the way down the drive and along Nkrumah Avenue. It left a high-pitched echo in her head; the sound of it all coming apart. She had always thought it would all come apart with a rending crash, or an avalanche thunder, not this constant hiss of everything being destroyed atom by atom. She pushed the Landcruiser faster, faster along Nairobi's boulevards, trying to outrun it, but you cannot drive faster than what is in your inner ear.

She cried aloud and spun the wheel. The Landcruiser shuddered. She kicked in four-wheel drive and went up and over the central strip on to the other roadway. When it comes apart, down in the molecules, you need magic to put it back together. You need the person who told you she would be there when it all came down.

The house was a prefabricated hut set in a long row of identical temporary housing that had inevitably become permanent. Gaby could not decipher the Cyrillic name boards, but the bunches of dried herbs and sets of wind chimes hanging from the guttering identified the bungalow. Contrail-streaked dawn was filling up the land as she tentatively knocked on the door.

''Oksana, it's finished.''

''Gaby. Oh my God. Come in come in come in.''

She made tea with big whacks of vodka in it. She let Gaby rant and swear and cry and spill it out on her coir matting. She let her wear herself out with the telling of it, and then put her to bed with a sleeping pill. A timeless time later Gaby awoke, as the troubled wake in defiance of all chemical assistance, hoping that it was reality that was the dream and that she had woken into the way things were truly meant to be. But it was not, because it never is and never can be.

52

Dogs will bark in the night before an earthquake.

Sometimes, just before your world is hit by lightning, you are allowed to hear the rumble of the approaching storm.

It was in the face of Joshua the doorman.

It was in the faces of the people in the elevator—more assiduously avoiding eye contact than usual.

It was in the Germans by the window and the Scandinavians in Gloom Corner and the Eng. Langs. in the middle.

It was in Tembo and Faraway looking up from their desk. It was in Abigail Santini's certain smile as she brushed past. It was most of all in T. P. Costello's looking up scared and guilty in his glass cubicle.

Because you can hear the coming thunder does not mean you can avoid the blast, any more than the barking dogs can stop your house falling into the chasm.

"Gaby." T.P. came into the newsroom. "A wee word in my office."

They all followed her with their eyes. T.P. closed the door and perched on the edge of his untidy desk.

"T.P., if it's about that report, I'm sorry if I screwed up your syndication deals, but yesterday didn't feature for me. To be honest, Shepard and me had a big fight. Totally honest, Shepard and me are finished. I've been staying with Oksana; that's why you couldn't get in touch with me. I can do the voice-over today; hell, I'd love to, give me something to take my mind off things." She saw T.P. was fidgeting with and repeatedly glancing at a piece of paper on his desktop. "T.P., what is that that's so interesting?"

"It's a fax from UNECTA Administration Headquarters. It concerns you."

And then the storm breaks, and it is not thunder at all, but that entropic inner-ear whine of molecules breaking apart and whirling away.

"I'm sorry, Gab. My hands are tied. I can't fight this, not without putting everything at risk."

"What is happening, T.P.? Tell me."

"They want you out. Forty-eight hours to leave UNECT*Afrique*'s field of operations."

And when the silent lightning strikes, it goes straight and sharp through the heart and nothing survives.

"Oh Jesus, T.P."

"They're getting their revenge for the Unit Twelve exposé. The UN need a sacrificial goat to show the brownnosers in the National Assembly they still have balls. Dr. Dan's swimming for his life in the political feeding frenzy and you're a soft target. *M'zungu.* Filthy hack. Woman. Persona non grata. Of course, it's voiced in the most diplomatic language, but the iron fist is that they may have to 'reevaluate their position vis à vis the international media presence.' In plain English, either you walk or every news network gets its UN accreditation rescinded, UNECTA puts on the great stone face, and they end up squabbling for the odd press release and maybe a conference for Ramadan, Yom Kippur and Christmas. My hands are tied, Gaby. I can't be the man who sinks the entire East African operation."

"My God. I knew I hurt Shepard bad, but I never had him down for a vindictive bastard."

"Shepard resigned as executive peripatetic secretary yesterday. Word on the inside is he jumped before he was pushed: an internal inquiry reported that while he couldn't be directly connected to your investigation into Unit Twelve, his relationship with you made him a significant security risk. In fact, he had already committed several breaches of protocol and privilege."

Gaby closed her eyes.

"Can't you bargain with these people, T.P.? I can't lose this now, not like this."

"I've been haggling like a Moore Street fishwife," T.P. said. "This is their best offer. They wanted you not just out of Kenya, but out of SkyNet. But for the fact that our beloved proprietor, Cap'n Bill, gets wet every time he sees you on-screen and wants to suck your toes, you'd be finished as a journalist, here or anywhere. What would you be?"

Finished, T.P. But I already know this.

"What am I going to do?" she said.

"Well, for a start, you've got forty-eight hours, so earn what I pay you. Give two fingers to UNECT*Afrique.* Finish that report.

Give all those interviews I have so painstakingly lined up for you. Clear your desk and walk out of this building with a 'fuck you, honey' look on your face like the billion-dollar babe you are."

"T.P., you talk the biggest load of oul' shite."

But she did what he said. She finished her final report, and though it didn't change anything or make anything any easier, she managed to feel about a couple of hundred thousand dollars as she tucked the cardboard box of desk impedimenta under her arm, and that was currency enough to look Abigail Santini in the eye.

"Gaby!"

Faraway was standing up at his workstation. He smiled the famous Faraway smile and drummed his hands on the desktop. Tembo stood up and joined the rhythm. And the whole office rose and thundered hands on desks, banged chairs, rattled files, disk boxes, thumped books. In his glass cubicle, T. P. Costello raised a triumphant fist.

They hung out the windows and whistled and cheered as she walked down Tom M'boya Street to the car park.

Gaby gave an interview an hour at the Elephant Bar. It was a political choice of venue. The Thorn Tree was the journalists' bar. The interviewers were all media people who had never noticed her before Unit 12 but were now her best friends and greatest admirers and most fervent supporters.

Between the interviews, she called Shepard. Each time she got his answering machine. When she was satisfied that he had gone back to the U.S. to bury his son and ex-wife, she drove over to get the rest of her things. There were not many. She packed them quietly. She was glad to be out of the house. It felt as if the dying had taken wings and crossed the ocean and come to roost there.

The Siberians threw her a party in the Elephant Bar that night. Many SkyNetters came, though T.P.'s official farewell lunch was scheduled for the next day at the Norfolk Hotel. The dress code had been relaxed this once, but most guests enthusiastically observed the see-knees rule. The Siberian pilots performed "There Is Nothing Like a Dame" from *South Pacific* in Gaby's honor, complete with the acrobatic dancing marines. Then they carried Gaby on their shoulders around the bar and across the airfield singing "Bloody Gaby Is the Girl We Love."

"I knew I would lose him," Gaby said to Oksana after the singers had gone back into the bar to drink much more and left them out on the strip with the airplanes. "I can't allow myself to keep things. I was the kid who had to take all her Christmas presents apart on Boxing Day because I'd got bored with them doing just what they were meant to do, and then couldn't put them back together again."

"You are a bird who flies in straight lines," Oksana said. "You pick your destination, you spot your landmarks, you fly straight toward them. Me, I go in circles, because that is how the world goes. Things come close, things move apart again. This way nothing is ever lost. You will come back to this country. No one who comes here ever leaves it, in here." She touched the place where her breast had been tattooed with the totemic mask of the wolf. "And you will find Shepard again, because you have never really left him, in here."

Aircraft lights moved in the big dark over the city. Gaby thought about the time on the coast, with the kids. The circles had been closest then, and therefore all they could do after that was move apart. But some journeys end, she thought.

She saw Fraser taking the ball off her in a sliding tackle and turning to blast it over the goal line. She tried to imagine his journey ended. She tried to imagine him dead. Something tore within. She saw Aaron coming out of the sea in his mask and snorkel, flapping over the sand in his yellow flippers. He would be in a wheelchair forever. If he lived. The thing inside tore a little more. When it tore all the way, all the things that had fallen apart inside would spill out and she would be a long long time picking them up and trying to put them back in their places. If she was careful, it would hold until she was out of this place, away from these people she did not want to shame with the nakedness of her despair.

At T.P.'s valedictory lunch, Gaby discovered more prominent friends and ardent admirers of the type who wait until the afternoon your plane leaves to tell you so. Regret was expressed about her hair, a beacon in the news community.

"It's growing right back," Gaby said. But she saw how Abigail Santini smiled at her.

Dr. Dan had been invited but sent his regrets that he would not be able to attend through his lawyer Johnson Ambani. He had been subpoenaed to appear before a ministerial committee to answer accusations that he had exceeded the remit of his inquiry.

"I thought I was in the shit," Gaby said. "Shouldn't you be helping him with your magic briefcase?"

"This battle he insists on fighting himself," said Johnson Ambani.

The Norfolk's Indian food was outstanding, the beer wonderful. Faraway propositioned Gaby behind a mound of samosas and the sewn-up thing inside tore a little more because she understood for the first time that all Faraway's jokes and innuendos and double and single entendres had been constructed to conceal the truth that he was crazy about her.

He and Tembo came with T.P. to the airport.

"Why do the bookstalls sell so many novels about terrorist hijackings and air crashes?" Tembo asked. Then he said, "Go with God, Gaby McAslan. I will pray to Jesus that you return safely, and come back to us. I know this will happen. Jesus' blood never failed me yet."

Faraway said nothing but hugged her and turned away so she would not have to see anything as uncool as emotion on his face.

"Be clever, my girl, and let who will be good," T.P. said. "What'll you do?"

She did not answer, because just then the ground-side stewardess called for the final passengers for the flight to London Heathrow to proceed immediately through passport control.

The booking computer had been kind. It had given her a row of three seats all to herself. She looked out of the window as her plane climbed. The 747-400 banked and she glimpsed the Nyandarua Chaga through rents in the rain clouds. From ascent altitude, it was a huge many-colored carpet laid over the hills and valleys of the White Highlands. Gaby watched it until the veils of high alto cirrus closed over it and she could see the places with the oldest names in the world no more. She drank and slept the rest of the eight hours to Heathrow.

She came through London immigration in the dawn hours and booked a shuttle ticket to Belfast. There was nothing in London for her to go home to. There was everything in Ireland. She bought people alcoholic presents and waited in the cafeteria for her flight to be called, drinking grapefruit juice. She watched the aircraft come in to land and thought about the shaman called Oksana Mikhailovna Telyanina and her plane called *Dignity.*

The commuter flight was a third full. She gave herself a window seat and watched for landmarks as the feeder jet followed the line of the coast into the city at the head of the lough. It crossed the narrow finger of the Ards peninsula, turned above Donaghadee—she recognized the Copeland Islands, and the lighthouse on its stone pier. She saw the Watchhouse on its little headland by the harbor, and the autumn brown of the Point.

Her father met her at the airport. He had bought a new car: a Land Rover 4X4. Paddy the black dog was in the back. Sonya was in the front. More than cars had changed. Gaby pleaded tiredness as her reason for having little to say on the drive home.

Reb and Hannah and a slightly sheepish Marky were at the house to greet the returning heroine. Hannah's oldest, in her very best junior Laura Ashley frock, stared aghast at her auntie Gaby. The new baby cried because Paddy started to bark.

After the lunch, Gaby begged time alone, and pulled on her Africa boots and a weatherproof coat and went out onto the Point. She walked the way she had walked the night she thought the stars had called her name. They too moved in circles, but their orbits were slower and grander and more subtle than human lifetimes could sense. She stood at the edge of the land looking out to sea. The wind stirred the fields of winter barley behind her. She had forgotten how cold this land was. It penetrated all her layered tropical-weight clothing. The sea was choppy, breaking in frantic little white folds of foam, constantly reabsorbing itself. She picked a flat stone from the shore and skimmed it out to sea. Two, three, four bounces. She skimmed another one. Three, four, five. Six was her personal record. She did not beat it, or even equal it, today.

Hannah and Marky had gone home by the time Gaby returned from the Point, but Hannah came back to the Watchhouse that evening: sisters together. Hannah was wearing a little black dress. Gaby knew the significance. The alcoholic presents were drunk. The sisters reminisced and embarrassed their father in front of Sonya about his inevitable shortcomings as a parent. Then Hannah got the tape out, and the microphones, and Reb whisked Gaby upstairs into the spare black body and mini that fitted and no more. Dad and Sonya shouted impatience as Gaby dashed on makeup. There was a round of applause as the soul sisters took their mikes and their positions.

''Wait for it,'' Reb said, and Gaby smiled as the introduction played, because it was the one to the song that said when you feel that you can't go on, all you had to do was reach out and someone would be there. She pushed out a hip, lifted one arm, two, three, four, and *in.*

finis africae

53

On the south side of the sky it is February 9, high summer as the *Gaia* probe goes into a highly eccentric pole-to-pole orbit of the Big Dumb Object and is captured by the object's small intrinsic gravity, a moon of an ex-moon. In the months since the Scream, the Big Dumb Object has rolled from a twelve-hundred-mile diameter disc into a hollow parabolic cup three hundred miles deep, open to space at the forward end. The artifact is spinning at a rate of one revolution every twelve minutes. The mathematics of maintaining an orbit around an object that is constantly changing shape have never been performed before, but the Flight Control crew are confident in their computers and *Gaia*'s reserves of reaction mass.

The highest point of the probe's course, over the middle section of the elongated cup-shaped object, is fifty miles. Closest approach, over the open end, is two and a half miles. In astronomical terms, that is a French kiss.

The thing devours comparatives, shrivels superlatives. *Gaia*'s first full frontal of the interior cavity, shot from thirty miles out, shows the largest enclosed space ever beheld by humanity. It is like looking into a pit one hundred and fifty miles wide and three hundred deep. You could drop all seven of Dante's circles of hell, and all the other hells of the great hell describers, into that pit and never see them again.

The rim of the cavity is ringed with a forest of stalagmites (some argue stalactites) nine miles deep. Each stalagmite, or stalactite, is twelve miles high. Like teeth, a junior data processor at Gaia Control comments in the coffee line. After that no one ever looks at the BDO without seeing a planet-eater, heading earthward, jaws wide open.

Spectroscopic analysis reveals a thin CO_2 atmosphere clinging to the inside of the cylinder. As far as the cameras can see into the interior cavity, it is carpeted with the characteristic coralline forms of climax Chaga: an entire geography, an undiscovered country. Later passes confirm early glimpses of objects in the zero-gee vacuum of the BDO's spin axis. They are two hundred miles down-shaft. Computer enhancement shows them to be spherical, slightly under three hundred feet in diameter and bearing a strong resemblance to the delicately beautiful glass shells of terrestrial microscopic diatoms. The objects are in motion. One after another, they are accelerating along the BDO's axis. On February 18 the first leaves the BDO's open mouth. An hour later the second object emerges. Three hundred and twenty-seven such diatoms are launched from the BDO in the next thirteen days. One comes within a hundred feet of *Gaia.* In astronomical terms, that is more than just a French kiss. That is deep throat. The ejected objects move to a position one hundred thousand miles ahead of the Big Dumb Object and scatter into a disc three thousand miles across. The namer of names at NASA christens it the Swarm. Their purpose becomes apparent when Asteroid M113C, an erratic orbiter whose return leg from beyond Jupiter would have brought it within three thousand miles of the Big Dumb Object, suddenly disappears. *Gaia*'s sensors, at the extreme limit of their range, disclose the presence of fifteen smaller bodies occupying M113C's orbit. In gross defiance of celestial mechanics, they are all moving out of that orbit to rendezvous with the Swarm.

In Washington, the disappearance of M113C hangs questions over those last-minute improved-design fuel tanks that had been flown up to *Gaia* and jettisoned around the orbit of Mars. Operation Defend Freedom may be nothing more than a gesture of defiance.

As the Big Dumb Object approaches Earth's picket-line, it rolls into a cylinder three hundred miles by fifty broad. The dark end—the remote explorers have devised their own terminology—is sealed. On its far side is a terrifying icescape of bergs and floes the size of Balkan nations and icicles tens of miles long: the BDO's fuel store; mass directly converted to energy and momentum.

At the other end—the bright end—the encircling teeth have fused together into a solid ring. The hole at its center is dwindling. Estimated time to closure is one hundred and five days. *Gaia*'s keyhole on the world within shrinks, frustrating the exomorphologists and the xenobiologists: fascinating changes are taking place inside the cylinder. Atmospheric pressure is twenty times that when *Gaia* went into orbit: O_2 production is increasing exponentially. Annular mountain ranges have appeared, each sixty miles apart. They are growing upward at one hundred feet a day. In time they will divide the inner chamber into five segments.

On December 28, an order is transmitted from the office of the president of the United States of America to Mars space. The jettisoned fuel tanks blow off their outer casings, revealing small thrust maneuvering systems. A carefully controlled burn takes them out of Mars space into an intercept course with the Big Dumb Object. Balanced on top of the propulsion units are five megaton MIRV warheads. They are aimed to fly straight into the open mouth of the Big Dumb Object, arm themselves and detonate simultaneously against the rotating shield wall of the dark end.

The new name for the nuclear assault on the BDO is Operation Eye of Needle.

Between 02:30 and 17:08 of March 16, the United States of America fights and loses its first interplanetary war. In an expensively commissioned battle suite under the Pentagon, the Joint Chiefs of Staff and the chief executive of NASA watch the numbered icons on the big Matsui wall screen disappear one by one as the Swarm senses, intercepts and destroys the missiles. At 16:03 the president is called at his golf club and told the news. No damage has been inflicted on the enemy. Friendly casualties are one hundred percent.

On April 23, *Gaia* completes its forty-one-thousandth orbit of the Big Dumb Object and the aperture in the bright end closes, sealing in its wonders and horrors and secrets.

54

The house stood by the edge of the water. It was tall and straight, with a red tile roof and peeling white walls. Palm trees closed it in on three sides, on the fourth shaved grass in the English lawn style ran down to steps beside the inlet. The windows of the white house had shutters that would not close because they had been painted to the walls. The higher windows had balconies that the house's guests had been instructed not to use because they were rusted through. From the high windows on the water side you could see all the way up Kilindini Harbor to Port Reitz. This was the view the woman was looking at this morning, from the very highest window, just under the red roof tiles. Her arms were bare, and folded on the sill, and she was resting her chin on them. She was watching the Likoni ferry, which crossed the harbor to the south mainland only a hundred feet from the house. The ferry was a big ugly bathtub of a thing, puffing black diesel smoke as it swung across the narrow water. It ran its ramp onto the concrete landing place. Even before it had come to a halt, people and vehicles were swarming off the ferry onto the steep road up to the city. The woman watched an overloaded bus growl along behind a huge wooden pushcart laden with margarine cans. The men were having difficulty shoving the cart up the slope and were asking passers-by to help them. The woman could hear the bus's angry horn blaring. Meanwhile the ticket sellers were dancing between the vehicles waiting to board the ferry. They danced so swaggeringly and cleverly that the woman reckoned that despite the apparent impossibility of the task, no fare ever went uncollected by them. The first vehicles were rolling down the slope as the last trucks were coming off in spurts of diesel smoke.

On the other side of the water the passengers were already tailed all the way up the road. As the ferry made the four-hundred-yard crossing, the woman saw a convoy of white military vehicles come over the brow of the hill. Sandwiched between them were black Mercedes limousines with tinted windows: state cars from the South Coast hotels the government had requisitioned. The convoy swung onto the wrong side of the road and drove past the waiting passengers and nimble fare collectors to the water's edge. Soldiers with blue helmets got out of the military vehicles to hold back the people on the road and to channel the traffic coming off the ferry into a single line. The convoy was first onto the ferry. From the high window the woman watched them cross the water and escort the black government Mercedes up the hill and out of sight.

Then she looked beyond the ferry, into Kilindini Harbor, with the stacks and cracking towers of the oil refinery behind. She looked at the refugee hulks careened along the shore, and the aprons of rafts and pontoons and boats surrounding them that had reduced the harbor to a single narrow channel. It would not be long before the boat towns closed on either side and you would be able to walk from Mombasa to Kilindini. A haze of blue wood smoke hung over the floating town of the boat people. The trees that once had come down to the waterside on Kilindini shore had long since been hacked down and carried away for fuel. The woman had heard that the boat people were walking as far as Diani in search of firewood. She had also heard of some boat people exacting a wood tax from those who had to cross their boats to reach their own. She had also heard that the police were shooting anyone trying to cut firewood around the government hotels.

They would take the best beaches for themselves, the woman thought. And the best rooms, and leave her a top-floor room in a guest house with no elevator, no air-conditioning, plumbing that functioned only erratically, a ceiling fan that did not function ever, lizards on the walls, balconies that would drop you sixty feet to the ground if you stepped on them, shutters that would not shut out the light and the heat when you wanted to sleep in the siesta time, and the best view in all Mombasa.

''It's good to be back,'' Gaby McAslan said. She turned from the window to the man on the bed. The man on the bed smiled. He was comfortably sprawled in the casual exhibitionism of a man who has just had sex, looking at the woman.

''It is good to have you back,'' Faraway said. ''At least, I am glad to have had the chance to find out that it is red down there too.''

Gaby sat on the bed beside him and kissed him. He held the kiss, moved her hand toward his swelling penis.

''Things to do, Faraway. Got to go down to Diani Beach and grease a few palms to get this security clearance. Three days wasted, sitting around on my ass, while Nairobi vanishes.''

''I would not say wasted,'' Faraway said. ''And it was not always your ass you were sitting on. Come on, I want to do this thing again.'' He picked up the Walkman headphones and the pair of black tights. Static hissed through the Walkman earphones; the radio had been tuned to white noise. ''Devil! When you put the phones on and blindfold me so that I cannot see, cannot hear, only feel, only touch, it is like I am nothing but an enormous penis. Miles and miles of *f'tuba.*''

''That's what it's meant to do. Tactile enhancement through sensory deprivation.''

"Where do you learn such tricks?" Faraway folded his hands behind his head and watched her dress.

"Do I have to be taught them?"

"I always said you were a devil woman. You have corrupted my soul. I am damned."

"You are an idle bastard. Station managers are meant to have clearances sorted out in advance."

"Deputy station manager. I was promoted beyond my competence. I tried to warn them, but it is the curse of bureaucracies. Listen, woman; while you are buying drinks for civil servants in beach bars, this idle bastard will be trying to arrange transport for us to Nairobi, liaising with the new regional headquarters in Zanzibar, and explaining to T. P. Costello why his special assignment reporter is still stuck in Mombasa. Such hard work deserves a reward, if not an apology. Tonight." He held up the black tights and the Walkman headphones. Gaby hit him with a pillow. She took his car keys.

In the line for the ferry she realized that the slit on the sarong skirt showed far too much thigh to the ticket boys, the lace-up boots were clearly the work of a frustrated foot fetishist, but the animal-skin-print fashion tickled the primeval hunter-gatherer in the back of her brain. Faraway had assured her it was this season's style as he outfitted her in the dollar shops along Moi Avenue with replacements for the heavy winter clothing she had brought from her cold northern civil war. Faraway's idea of fashion was something that allowed him to look at women's legs. Gaby slid the dark glasses up her nose as she drove down onto the ferry. Not even time for an eye job. Actually, she thought, the shades were cooler.

Hot-climate clothes. Hot-climate car. Hot-climate music on the radio, that sounded good, that sounded right. It had never sounded like that anywhere else she had heard Kenyan music. Tropical fruits had been like that too; when you got over laughing at the price, you found they never tasted as good as they had when you bought them from Kariokor Market or a wooden stall by a roadside bus stop. And the fabrics and the fashions and the furnishings only looked right under equatorial light. But even the wrongness of those things had been enough to bring her back to the place where they were right. Smells especially. Wood smoke. Charcoal. Shit and diesel. Tropical fruit. Dry earth, cow dung.

Blacktop after rain. Night-blooming flowers. Instant Africa. You never leave it, because it never leaves you. Africa is in the heart. That is why you have sex with Faraway. He has always been the faithful one, the one who sent funny, rude letters and presents on your birthday that found you wherever in the world you had been sent. He was the one who came all the way to London on the chance that it might be more than just friendship, but London had not been the place for that, nor Ireland, where you took him to show him to the people and places you drew your power from—he had complained all the time about how cold it was, how cold. However special, those had not been the places. This was. The heat made it right. The light made it right. The smells and sights and sensuousness of the ancient Arab island city made it right. Kenya was the place where friends could transform into lovers, with no regrets.

She hoped.

The road south was a ten-mile parking lot of UN military hardware. Soldiers whistled and cheered at the white woman in the open-top car speeding past. She knew better than to make obscene gestures at them. What Faraway had heard about them shooting foragers was evidently a rumor. Everywhere were women with bundles of firewood on their heads. Maybe the men thought the soldiers would not shoot women. Maybe no one shot anyone, but the men had told the women that story anyway because they were lazy. The hotel signs on the left side of the road all carried addenda: MINISTRY OF AGRICULTURE, LIVESTOCK AND MARKETING under the GOLDEN BEACH HOTEL; MINISTRY OF FINANCE riveted over the DIANI REEF HOTEL board; MINISTRY OF EDUCATION swinging under the TRADE WINDS sign. Gaby dodged scooter couriers with cardboard boxes of state documents perched perilously on the back. The Kenyan government had not been in its new home long enough to set up a computer network, and the word around town was that it was already looking for a place to move to when Mombasa fell. It would all fall in the end. SkyNet could relocate to Zanzibar, but a government cannot run out of nation to govern.

Gaby turned in at the sign for the Jadini Beach Hotel. A plastic shingle informed her that it was in fact the Ministry of Foreign Affairs. At a checkpoint hastily assembled from an oil drum filled with sand and a bent metal pole on a pivot, Gaby showed her press card and asked where to go for an application for a Form DF108. The policemen directed her along a road that went around the back of the tennis courts, past the water-sports store and the pool chlorination plant to the staff accommodation block where the department that handled DF108 applications was housed.

There was another checkpoint behind the tennis courts. Gaby showed the man her press card. The man refused to swing up his bent metal pole and let her pass. Access to this department for foreigners required a form DF108.

"I am trying to get an application for a DF108. I can't unless you let me in."

"I am sorry. I cannot let you in without a DF108. Have you tried your consular office?"

"They sent me here."

"This is most irregular."

"Will this make it regular?" She held up two hundred-shilling notes.

"Attempting to bribe a government official is a serious offense," the man said.

"Look, you stupid man, all I need is two minutes. If you won't let me past, then you go and get me one."

"Desert my post in the time of my country's need?"

"If you say 'it's more than my job's worth,' you can add assaulting a government official to your charge sheet," Gaby McAslan said. A black Mercedes came crunching down the sand road and stopped at the other side of the barrier. The driver sounded his horn.

"You will have to go away and apply through proper channels," the government official said. "Do not waste my time." The government car sounded its horn again. The official lifted his pole and saluted as the Mercedes came through. Gaby considered darting through the gap, but the pole came down so fast it bounced on its welded pivot. The black car stopped alongside the SkyNet RAV. A mirrored window hummed down. A big sweaty black face looked out.

"You should be impressed that in these corrupt times there are still people conscientious about their jobs, Ms. McAslan," the man said.

"Dr. Dan!"

The politician summoned the government official.

"The *m'zungu* is with me," Dr. Dan said. Gaby thought she heard the official say, "Yes, minister." The Mercedes turned among the palm trees. Gaby followed it through the barrier. The official was saluting again.

"I thought you were dead," Gaby said. The tables around the pool had all been occupied by men in suits with PDUs and cases of papers, but the presence of Dr. Dan cleared any number of civil servants and brought waiters swarming. "Politically or actually."

"Whiskey, yes?" Dr. Dan signed the bar chitty. The glasses were etched with the coat of arms of the Republic of Kenya. "I almost was. Both ways. When they could not kill me politically, they tried other means. It has a long and honorable history in our country. But I do not die so easily. This much"—he held thumb and forefinger an inch apart—"is as good as a million miles. But now we have a new president and a new order. And a new foreign minister." He stirred his drink with his plastic giraffe. The years have been soft to him, Gaby thought. He is bigger, slower, heavier, but it is the weight of wisdom and power and slow-stalking cunning.

"Foreign minister," she said. "That's how T.P. was able to get me back into the country after four and a half years in the wilderness."

"I could not help you when you needed me last. It was the least I could do—I do not know why there has been a problem with the DF108. But there will be no problem now. I have thought much about you, over the years."

"I've thought about this place every single day I was covering those wars. One bloody stupid little ethnic slaughter fest after another. Freeze the ass off you in Siberia this time of year. Mother Russia's fucked, but won't lie back and submit to the inevitable."

"Mother Kenya too."

"What's it like up in Nairobi?"

"They say it is well established in the northern suburbs. The Tacticals are coming out of their townships to fight each other and the security forces. The UN pretend they are implementing an evacuation plan, but there are too many people, and there is no law, no order, and not everyone wants to be evacuated anyway."

"Are they really letting them go?"

A group of secretaries were cooling their legs in the pool as they ate their lunches. They kicked up the water, laughing.

"They say a thousand a day pass through the Westlands gate alone," Dr. Dan said. "Of course, they cannot control entry to it any more than they could ever control any other part of it. Who knows how many tens of thousands cross terminum unauthorized? They tattoo them, did you know that? The UN soldiers on the gates have tattoo guns. They are instant, painless, so I am told. Once you are marked and pass through the gate, you may not return on pain of being shot."

"What symbol do they use?"

"A letter *E,* on the back of the hand. It stands for 'Exile.' It should have been a *C.*"

"For 'Chaga'?"

"For 'Citizen.' "

"They need you, Dr. Dan," Gaby said. "They need your vision and bloody-mindedness to build a proper nation."

"Thank you, Ms. McAslan. Do you recall when we first met, on the night flight from London, that I regretted that the Chaga would not give us time to build a nation? Five years on I can see that the Chaga is giving us the time, and the space, and the resources, to build the Kenya we should have built. A fine nation, an African nation; that is not some continuation of Western colonialism in another form, with Western legal and political and educational systems, Western values and morals. In the Chaga we can find African solutions to African problems—maybe we will find out in there that what we thought were our problems are those we have been given by the West. We can do a frightening thing: we can build a new Africa that does not owe the West anything, that does not need what the West has to sell us, that has resources and capabilities the West can only envy." Dr. Dan looked out across the pool and the palms that led down to the beach, and to the gray hulls of the warships beyond the white water of the reef. "Those gunboats, that they say are there to protect us; they are no different from those letter *E*s the United Nations tattoos on the hands of the exiles. They are afraid of us. They are afraid of what we could become, when the nations of the New Africa become the most powerful on earth. You asked me for my vision; I have shown it to you. I hope you are content with what you see. Ah!'' A civil servant in a Hawaiian shirt and creased chino pants gave Dr. Dan an envelope. ''Excellent. Thank you.'' He handed the envelope to Gaby.

''Your DF108.''

''You don't know what this means, Dr. Dan.''

''A friend for the new nation, I hope. Oh. I almost forgot to mention. An old friend of yours has come back to Kenya.''

''Oksana Telyanina?''

Dr. Dan frowned, not recognizing the name.

''No. Dr. Shepard.''

55

She flew up on an early flight in a cavernous Antonov heavy-lifter. Faraway was with her. They were the only civilians. Their seats were in the middle of the center block, far from the windows. She would not be able to see the Chaga. Gaby tried instead to get some of the soldiers to talk about their anticipation of the withdrawal from Nairobi, but they were young and this was their first time out of their mother countries and they had been intimidated by their non-commissioned officers into suspicion of journalists. Gaby ended up sleeping most of the flight on Faraway's shoulder. The white-boy soldiers wondered what a white woman was doing with a black man. The black-boy soldiers wondered why a black man did not find his own kind good enough for him.

T. P. Costello was waiting in arrivals, like that first time when everything was fresh and clean and thrilling and could not go wrong. He did not seem to Gaby to have changed his clothes in four and a half years. Within those clothes, his flesh had softened and slumped, his chin descended, his hairline ascended. But irredeemably a boiled owl.

''What the hell kept you?'' he asked, because he knew she knew it was expected of him. ''The UN's announced its withdrawal from Nairobi. Three days and it's open city.''

Everything that points backward points forward. Old Landcruiser in the car park. New fluorescent-orange zebra stripes.

''People with big guns kept mistaking the SkyNet globe for the UN logo,'' T.P. explained.

Old catechism, new rubric. T.P. handed Gaby a sleeveless

jacket the same color as the car's stripes. ''Color-of-the-day for the press corps. Don't look at it like that, these have saved the lives of several folk you know.'' He took a canvas bag from a pocket and dropped it into Gaby's hand. She almost let it slip through her fingers; it was extraordinarily heavy.

''What have you got in here?''

''Krugerrands. You'll need negotiables. Forget dollars, forget deutsche marks, forget yen; gold is the only universally convertible currency on the streets. And something to keep it, and you, safe.''

He handed her a .45 revolver. Gaby's little frozen wars had taught her how to handle weapons, though she detested their feel against her skin. She broke the piece. It was loaded.

''These are Black Rhinos.''

''You put them down, you don't want them getting back up again.''

''Where am I supposed to keep this? In my handbag?''

In the backseat, Faraway laughed priapically, thinking of suggestions.

''Goes without saying that you can't get accommodation in this burg for love nor money,'' T.P. said, following the directions of the MPs with white gloves toward the exit checkpoint. ''Even your old friend Mrs. Kivebulaya's guesthouse is like a sardine tin.''

''Gaby will be staying with me,'' Faraway said. T.P. greeted the disclosure in purse-lipped silence as the soldiers waved the Landcruiser through onto the city road.

In four and a half years since she last drove along this road, the squatter towns had grown to enclose the airport on all sides. Cardboard shacks slumped against the perimeter wire, used the backs of warehouses and hangars as lean-to walls. The pall of eternal blue wood smoke hung over the plastic roofs, interspersed by the occasional dense plume where a shanty was burning. The women carried their burdens of sticks and plastic basins of washing on their heads. The men sat on their heels and watched the women work. The children with flies around their eyes and their fingers in their mouths looked at the airplanes taking off over their heads. Everything was the same, but it was different. The spirit had changed. The people in the alleys, or sitting by the side of the road selling their piles of Sprite cans and karma bracelets seemed listless and apathetic. The life had gone out of them, leaving them transparent and desiccated. Gaby understood. They were the tidewater people; the flotsam left beached now the others had all gone out on the waters; to the coast, to the new transit camps in the east and far north, to the Chaga. Of those who remained, some were too scared to go. Some were too poor to go. Some did not wish to go, but would wait with what they had until the Chaga came and made them decide where to go. They would not wait long. Gaby saw the hostile skyline of coral fingers and land trees rising in isolated stands above the shanty rooftops. A mile to the north, a copse of Loolturesh balloons hovered over the encircling slums.

For some, this was enough to overcome their fear or their poverty or their inertia. By car, by bus, by truck, by matatu, by moped taxi or oxcart or handcart or donkey, by bicycle, by foot, they would take their things and their lives onto the road. The outbound lanes of the airport highway were a slow procession of the dispossessed, fifty feet wide, ten miles long, grinding along between lines of guarding soldiers.

"Hm?"

"I said, have you heard that Shepard's back?" T.P. asked.

"I've heard." She wanted it to sound like it meant no more to her than the return of some other journalist she respected but knew only through his work. She wanted it to sound like that to Faraway. Shepard had never written to her, never tried to contact her, to give her a chance to explain or apologize or say can we start again. So why did her heart kick her every time she heard his name and thought of him back in this dying city? Because she loved him. She did not love Faraway. She had given him sex for his loyalty and friendship and goodness, but not love. They had all been right, all the ones who had said she was a monster. "So, what's he been doing?"

"Over in Uganda and Zaire mostly, getting his hands dirty. UNECTA didn't want to lose him, so they demoted him to fronting a transterminum research team working out of Kilembe. Getting a lot of respect; most of those patent new-gene food staples the agribusiness corporations have cut from Chaga sources come out of work done by Shepard's team. Then last week they find his replacement as UNECT*Afrique* peripatetic executive, Conrad Laurens the Bouncing Belgian, dead in a bedroom in the Intercontinental with three Chinese babes. So Shepard gets called back to help with the great Going Out of Business Sale. They've gutted what's left of Ol Tukai—the thing ran out of fuel, so they left it beached in the middle of a drive-in cinema. Chaga's taking the thing to pieces now.''

The Landcruiser slammed into an emergency brake. T.P.'s knuckles were white on the wheel. Both feet were flat to the floor. He threw the wheel and missed by inches the UN truck that had stopped dead in the middle of the highway. Gaby untangled herself from the back of T.P.'s seat, opened her mouth to yell at him and saw it.

It was coming in across the shantytown from the north, far off the glide path of any aircraft, and low, very low. Too low for safety. It was big, and it was coming fast. If it did not hit the road, it would not be by much. If the truck had not stopped, it would have been hit. The thing passed overhead in a rush of air. It seemed to hang over the Landcruiser. Gaby could feel the cool shadow of its wings. There was something of the bat in it, and something of the hang glider, or microlyte, she thought, but also the predatory streamlines of a multirole combat aircraft.

God, but it was big.

The people on the far side of the highway threw themselves flat as the thing seemed to dive at them. It puffed gas. Its wings warped. For all its size, it was as light as a leaf. It lifted up above the shanties at the edge of the road, gained a few hundred feet of altitude and banked.

The sudden hammer of helicopter rotors was almost shocking. The machine came up from behind a ridge to the south of the road: a Hind B assault helicopter. It scraped the tin-can chimney tops, pulled a high-gee turn and went after the intruder.

Everyone was standing up now, watching the helicopter close with the flying thing. There was a burst of chain-gun fire and everyone cheered. Another, more cheering. A third and the great bat-glider-jet came apart in a dozen spinning pieces that smashed into the shantytown. Gaby saw shards of wing and tail and streamlined fuselage go cartwheeling up into the air together with sheets of corrugated metal and pieces of wood and shredded plastic.

But the squatter-town people on the highway were cheering

like it was a carnival, or the pope had come. Gaby got out of the car and looked toward the crash site, shading her eyes with her hands. The helicopter wheeled in triumph and came across the airport road in a storm of dust and turbine roar.

"I didn't think they'd be that big," she said.

"Do a hell of a lot of damage when they hit, but it's only the poor of the parish, so the UN doesn't worry," T.P. said, standing beside her. Soldiers were running up the shantytown dirt streets, fanning out in a search pattern. "Their job is to keep the access to the airport open, that's all. That's the closest one's got in weeks. They're losing their touch, but at least the helicopter downed it before the payload became active. They're like crop dusters, spraying Chaga-spores all over the damn place.

"You think the doodlebugs are impressive, you should see the Hatching Towers. Dozens of the things, up on the edge of terminum, about three hundred feet high. The doodlebugs grow in pods at the top. They hatch, stretch their wings—just like butterflies, I can show you the footage—and then drop off the tit and glide away. The Kenyan army—what hasn't deserted yet—is up there blasting away at them with artillery. Of course the Chaga grows them back as fast as they blow them away, but they're at least slowing them up. The helicopters usually get what's left. I'm surprised they let one get this close to the airport. One hit there and the whole UN program is fucked."

"Where did it learn to build a thing like that?" Gaby said.

"From us. Where do you think?" T.P. restarted the car. Gaby looked long at the isolated plantations of alien Chaga growing out of the human landscape. Biological packages. Winged seeds, like the paired helicopters of the sycamore, sent spinning in their hundreds by the equinoctial gales. Beautiful weeds; her father had called sycamores. They pushed everything else out; took the place over.

And that greatest winged seed of all, the Big Dumb Object, was only three months from Earth.

"I'll drop you at Faraway's," T.P. said, dodging the military traffic as he headed for the golden towers of Nairobi. "If you can make it, we'll be at the Thorn Tree. There are folk there looking forward to seeing you again. Otherwise, UN Press Center, tomorrow at eight-thirty. Jesus, it's good to have you back, Gaby. What is it?''

She did not answer. She was getting used to the weight and feeling of a gun in her hand.

56

Tembo greeted Gaby with unrestrained Christian joy and showed her videoprints of his new daughter, aged ten months. Her name meant After-the-Rains. Gaby said it was one of the most beautiful names she had ever heard for a child, but she had been born under the bitter star of the dispossessed. She had already lost one home, and the temporary prefab she had been rehoused in was five days from terminum. You could see the land corals and fan trees from the front door; two streets away. When they got to one street away, Tembo and his family would leave. He did not know where for. He hoped it would be Zanzibar. That was why he had come to the UN press conference in the Kenyatta Center Conference Hall; because today General Sir Patrick Lilley, Supreme Commander East Africa Land Forces, passed out the exit visas to Kenyan nationals.

T. P. Costello had reserved a block of seats halfway down the center aisle.

''Missed you at the Thorn Tree last night,'' he said to Gaby.

''Better things to do,'' she said, unable to hide the grin.

''Tell me you're not banging Faraway.''

''I'm banging Faraway. And for your information, he bangs exceedingly loud, and long.''

''Slut.''

She did not tell him about the sensory deprivation thing with the blindfold and the white noise, because he would have misunderstood. It was partly for the totality of skin on skin. The rest of it was to shut out the constantly hovering helicopters and the bursts of gunfire from the streets and the distant thud of the artillery up in the northern bourgeois districts futilely shelling the edge of the Chaga. To shut it out and forget that Shepard was out there on those streets she did not know anymore. To pretend, in the silence and the blindness, that this body under her was any body, this skin any skin, any color she wished.

The conference hall fell silent. A tall, sandy-haired white

man in desert camouflage fatigues had taken the place behind the lectern. He studied his notes, pushed his glasses up his nose and surveyed the rows of news people. Gaby thought of wire-haired fox terriers. General Sir Patrick Lilley. Sandhurst class of '85. Active service in Bosnia, Somalia, Rwanda, Iraq, Peru, Pakistan. Do you think the world has forgotten that off-the-record, on-the-camera comment about leaving the bloody wogs to sort it out for themselves? Not the people in those burned-out villages and bombed-out towns, whom you refused to protect because it might mean your little-boy soldiers being shot at. Not the people in this hall, this country. We are all wogs; and we sort it out for ourselves. When I go onto those streets, it will not be with your blue-helmeted nannies. It will be with people I and the street respect. It will be with the Black Simbas.

"Good morning, ladies and gentlemen," General Sir Patrick Lilley said. "Nice to see so many familiar faces. Before we get on to the allocations, the usual update." He talks like the Last Englishman, Gaby thought. "Terminum of the Nyandarua symb is officially fixed today as a line-of-latitude map reference one degree twelve minutes twenty-three seconds south. Program your GPS locaters accordingly. The usual caveats about wandering onto the wrong side apply.

"Users of the Nairobi LocalNet of the East African teleport have been experiencing transmission breaks and data-errors. We have discovered that this has been caused by the intrusion of symb organic circuitry into the optical-fiber network. The Nyandarua symb seems to be integrating itself with the East African teleport. We are unable to predict the long-term consequences of this; should it pose a threat to security, we will have to seek government approval to isolate the Nairobi LocalNet. For the meantime I'm afraid we'll all just have to tolerate the interruptions and dropouts."

Gaby wondered his beret did not slide off his head at such an angle. Hat pins, that's your secret, isn't it, Sir Paddy?

"Now, to the chief business of this press conference. I will be calling the agencies that have filed for exit visas in alphabetical order. Would those called please have their documents certified by my aide." Who was a fox-terrier bitch. Gaby studied the faces of those who waited to hear their names called by General Sir Paddy. All were black. Most had the look of terrified resignation to the inevitable Gaby had once seen on a wildebeest pulled down by the nose and disemboweled by a pack of hyenas.

General Sir Paddy called SkyNet down, section by section. Gaby watched T.P. collect his way out of Kenya. She heard a name she did not recognize and was most surprised to see Faraway go cantering down the steps. Then she heard her own name and went down to pick up the papers and the plastic badge with her photograph in it from the fox-terrier bitch. General Sir Paddy was into Transworld Television by the time Gaby had regained her seat. It was only there, seeing the hands clutching their visas and identity badges that she realized.

"Where's Tembo's? What about Tembo?" Nobody could look at her. She yelled down at the podium. "What the fuck about Tembo?" General Sir Paddy paused in his reading of the names to frown at this loud, ill-mannered rebellious Irishwoman.

"T.P., you have to do something. He's got a wife and kids, for God's sake. He's like family, like my favorite uncle. You owe him, T.P."

"There's nothing I can do, Gaby. My hands are tied on this one. Believe me, this guts me as much as it does you."

"I've heard that before, T.P." She made to go down to confront General Sir Lilley on his podium. T. P. Costello grasped and spun her around with unguessed strength.

"Get on Sir Paddy's tits, and you fuck it up for all of us. We walk a very fine line here."

"Four and a half years, and you're still feeding me the same brownnose shit," Gaby said. "When are you ever going to realize that we don't need these people? Faraway, Tembo, I need you. And your family, Tembo. And the keys to the Landcruiser, T.P."

"Where are you taking them? It?"

"To get on the tits of whatever agency decides these things, until they give me the result I want."

57

The UNHCR sent her to the OAU offices. The OAU sent her to the UNHCR, but she told them the UNHCR had sent her here, so they suggested she try the IRC. The IRC said it could not do this thing and sent her to the EU embassy. The EU embassy looked at her as if she were dog shit on the mat and told her to go to the Kenyan Ministry of Foreign Affairs Office on Harambee Avenue. This was a purely internal affair, Harambee Avenue decided, and sent her to the Home Affairs and National Heritage Office on Moi Avenue, where seven hundred Rastafarian pilgrims in red, gold and green who had come to join the great exodus to the Holy Mt. Zion in Africa were camped with their children and the goats they purchased from refugees glad to part with them for hard currency. Harassed UNHCR staff in white-and-blue bulletproof vests were trying to move them onto the buses that would take them up to the Westlands Gate to be processed through. The hard-currency goats cropped the sparse grass central reservations and nibbled the tips of the smog-blighted yuccas.

As this process was going to take some time and little After-the-Rains had started to cry and Gaby's temper was fraying, Tembo suggested a shortcut through service alleys that would take them out at the other end of Moi Avenue. There were dead bodies in the alleys behind Nairobi's golden towers. They were swollen and waxy with gas and rot. Gaby could not avoid driving over some. She made herself listen to After-the-Rains and not the crack and pop of bursting flesh.

It was as bad as the Rastafarians outside the Home Affairs Office. Five hundred people were trying to push through the revolving doors. Policemen shaded themselves under the thorn trees, unable to take effective action. On Faraway's suggestion, Gaby turned out microphone, camera and camera crew.

"Could you help us get in there?"

The policemen eagerly gave up their lounging and cleared a path to the door. They managed to do it smiling to the camera. This was a pity; the camera was not running.

They fought their way to a counter clerk who sent them to a superior who referred them to an executive officer on the fifth floor in an office with a desk, a chair, a PDU and eighty cardboard document boxes, who said that all press accreditation was being handled by the UN and sent them to East Africa Command Headquarters on Chiromo Road.

There was not a shop left open on all of Haile Selassie Avenue. Those that had not been looted and burned out were shuttered. In the expensive shops, that sold watches and jewelry and other negotiables, the steel security curtains had been smashed in by ram raiders. The back end of a Suzuki 4X4 projected from the front of Sharma and Sons Discount Jewelers. Traders had set up pitches on the sidewalks: a trestle table spread with CDs and disc players; a plastic fertilizer sack split and opened on the ground on which bottles of Volvic mineral water were piled in little ziggurats. A man with a rifle at his side sold car batteries from the porch of the Christian Publishing Office. In the back row of seats, the children were crying. Mrs. Tembo held them in her arms.

"Hush now, babies," she said. "Don't cry, don't cry."

Gaby's identity card and DF108 were inspected at five different checkpoints on the approach to East Africa Military Command. The soldiers turned out all the passengers to take up the seats to make sure they were not carrying explosives before they would open the barrier to the visitors' car park. Gaby left Faraway as a deterrent to thieves and marched Tembo, Mrs. Tembo, Sarah, Etambele and After-the-Rains into the reception area and demanded to see someone with the authority to issue an exit visa to SkyNet's most valuable news gatherer and his family. After forty minutes an adjutant was sufficiently underbusy to come and tell the civilians that they were in the wrong section of East Africa Military Command. This was East Africa Military Strategic Command. They needed East Africa Military Logistics Command, which had taken over the Church Army Training Center on Jogoo Road.

Landhries Road had been sealed off with a barricade of wrecked cars where a doodlebug had come down on the country bus station. Detour signs hand-painted on the rusted doors directed traffic along Pumwani Road. The slums had grown bigger in four and a half years; down to and over the Nairobi River. Slums never grow any smaller. They are bad when they are lived in, but worse in decay. Many of the shanties had collapsed or slumped into the river, which was a swamp of plastic, scrap metal, wood and dead things.

There was a roadblock up at the top of Kericho Road. Two

Nissan pickups with antiaircraft guns bolted into the truck bodies—*picknis,* as they were known on the streets—were parked nose to nose, restricting the traffic to a single line past men carrying automatic weapons. Incongruously, they were dressed in red-and-purple Chaga combats under football managers' coats. The cartel banners drooping from the *pickni*'s whip aerials sported the black-and-white fuller sphere of a football on a green field. Football, buckyball, Gaby thought. She knew them: the Soca Boys, one of the smaller Tactical cartels that had remained fiercely nonaligned while the others forged alliances and brokered power blocs. A show of strength; a message to the Premier Division managers that the Soca Boys could be valuable players to have on-side when the final play-offs came.

The Tacticals waved through a pickup hidden under a pile of firewood. Gaby fished out a couple of Krugerrands. The Landcruiser crawled closer. A smoke-belching municipal bus went through the checkpoint. Gaby had not thought they were still running.

"Hide your guns," Gaby hissed. "You in the back, look scared."

"That is not difficult," Mrs. Tembo said.

A Soca Boy in a Grampus 11 coat came to the open window.

"Hello, *m'zungu,*" he said. "That is a mighty colorful car you are driving. Would you like to put my face on television, newslady?"

The helicopter came in from nowhere across the shanties, hard and fast: a big Hokum gunship with UN painted on the side. At the sight of it, the Soca Boys ran for their vehicles. The helicopter turned in the air. The *picknis* drove off at speed. The helicopter tried to follow them through the warren of cinderblock project housing. Minutes later Gaby passed a convoy of UN armored vehicles coming at speed up Leman Road. In two days they would be gone from this city, but for those two days they still ruled the street and they admitted no challengers.

"Isn't that where you led the choir?" Gaby asked as they passed a big red-brick church with a red tin roof.

"St. Stephen's, yes," Tembo said. "But no one is singing there anymore."

The United Nations East Africa Military Logistics Command Headquarters, formerly the Church Army Training Center, was directly opposite St. Stephen's Church. Once again, identifications and authorizations were inspected, and Gaby marched the family into the reception area and refused to move them until she saw whoever was in charge of exit visas. She had to wait only thirty-five minutes this time for an aide to talk to her, Tembo and Faraway. They waited another thirty-five while the aide referred the application to his superior, and another thirty-five while the superior checked with the people down in reception and decided if he could talk to these civilians. Tembo's wife and children sat on plastic chairs under the window of the temporary building that was the reception area and ate vending-machine sandwiches and chocolate. Faraway looked out the window, drinking coffee. He is one of those men, Gaby thought, who unconsciously relax into postures that look good to women.

The superior said that he could not vet an application for an emergency visa on Gaby's authority alone. Faraway negotiated in his capacity as deputy station manager. The officer was still not convinced. Faraway called T.P. on his cellphone and gave it to the officer. Gaby looked out of the window at the soldiers sitting by the side of Jogoo Road. She saw a man in Islamic dress come up the road pushing something that looked like a dog kennel on wheels. Gaby remembered this man, this machine. There would be a veiled woman hidden inside, with only her eyes catching the light. Some of the soldiers offered the man money. He refused to accept any of it. Gaby watched him pass up the road. He is part of the Kenya that was, she thought, that I loved but cannot find anymore, for it has turned alien and ugly, like a rotting slum, or a woman hidden in a wooden hutch.

Faraway had his PDU on the desk. Hardcopy documents were squeezing forth. The officer took them across the compound past the chapel to the accommodation block where the work was done. Tembo looked from Faraway to his wife to his children. Some of the military who came and went through the reception area squatted down to talk to Tembo's beautiful daughters.

The robed man with the wooden hutch on wheels was coming down Jogoo Road again. Gaby watched him pass again the soldiers sunning themselves. They did not offer him any money this time. He passed out of sight.

The officer was coming back across the compound now. He looked out of breath. His white face was red. He seated himself behind the counter and put two forms in front of Faraway for him to sign.

Gaby saw all the things that happened next as separate, discrete edits of experience.

She saw the beggar man in Arab dress come running up the road as fast as he could. He did not have the trolley with him.

She saw the soldiers at the side of the road get to their feet as he ran past.

She saw Faraway turn from the reception desk with his biggest smile and a piece of paper in either hand.

She saw the white light, and the fireball inside the white light.

She heard the explosion. She heard it like it had blown into every cell of her body and shaken its death noise out of them.

She saw the window of the reception cabin fly inward in a million stinging insects of glass. She saw Tembo throw wife and children down as the glass passed over their heads. She saw Faraway dive for the floor, tuck himself into a ball, arms wrapped over head. She saw the reception staff take cover behind their desks and counter as the glass rained down on them.

She seemed to be the only one standing, like the domed building in Hiroshima that was directly under Fat Boy.

Gaby could take in every detail in a flicker of an eyelid. The man in Arab dress was lying facedown in the middle of Jogoo Road. The bomb had gone off a hundred yards farther down. There was nothing left of the wooden trolley that had carried it. Three trucks were burning; one of the refugee buses was overturned. The bodies of the soldiers were scattered like chaff. Over everything hung a huge silence and slowness. Then the sound rushed into the still place after the bomb and there were screaming men and burning vehicles and yelling people.

"Come on!" Gaby shouted to her team. "We've got work to do."

Faraway jammed the emergency visa into Mrs. Tembo's hands and ran after Gaby.

It was like she was a neutrino. She moved through the destroyed vehicles and the knots of shocked people without interacting with them, without being deflected by their confusion and suffering from her purpose. Soldiers pulled comrades from the tangled wrecks of vehicles, dragged shattered bodies away from pools of burning fuel. Gaby passed by. Scraps of meat and seared cloth were scraped into a gutter. Gaby sent the eye of the lens over them and moved on. Troopers comforted their screaming friends. A man sitting beside a soldier with no face shouted and shouted and shouted for a doctor to help his buddy. Combat medics triaged victims. Sirens wailed in the distance: ambulances, fire engines, fast approaching. In the middle of it all Gaby sent her camera eye probing. No one noticed her. The fire engines foamed down the burning vehicles. Ambulances civilian and military moved between the army trucks and disgorged trauma teams. Still no one saw Gaby and Faraway and Tembo. It was only when the military police came to seal the area that people saw there was a news team among them, filming the worst moment of their lives. Two white-helmets rounded up Gaby and Faraway and Tembo and pushed them beyond the edge of the cordon.

"Fucking ghouls," one of the MPs said.

Gaby did not hear him. She had seen a UN Jeep arrive at the center of the destruction. A man jumped out and was saluted by a soldier, who escorted him through the wreckage and the bodies.

Gaby knew that man.

"Shepard!" she shouted. "Shepard!"

But she could not make him hear her over the sound of the sirens and the dying.

58

"So, I must find out on the satellite news that Gaby McAslan is back in Nairobi," Oksana Telyanina said. The samovars still bubbled in the Elephant Bar, but a boxing ring stood where the fire pit had once burned. Framed signed photographs of woman kick boxers competed for wall space with the icons and photographs of Russian aircraft alongside mandalas and neo-pagan posters. There was serious money in unlicensed kick boxing, the Siberian woman had told Gaby. And the Elephant Bar had become the Last Chance Saloon for subcultures from all over the planet who had decided that the Chaga was their best future. Their paisley-patterned buses and dead trans-Saharan Land Rovers were piled five high in the yard across the road. Changes; even for Oksana Telyanina. Better English. Shorter hair: a quarter of an inch all over. More tattoos: her totemic tree of enlightenment had sprouted branches across her upper torso; tangling a hundred tiny iconic tattoos in its twigs. Brutal animal-print fashions that seemed to Gaby to symbolize the easy weapons and sacramental violence of Nairobi before the fall.

"Do they know who did it yet?" Oksana asked. They were at a table on the veranda, overlooking the rows of An72Fs. These and a few army helicopters on the far side of the field were all that were left; since Kenyatta had been closed to commercial traffic, all the big jets had moved there.

"The Americans are trying to tell us it was some Islamic fundamentalist group, but with them it's always either Islamic fundamentalists or drugs. I was there, I saw it; it was some Tactical cartel showing its rivals the UN can't push it around. They're getting bolder, stronger. More savage. Fifteen dead, last count."

"If you want to stay at my house, you know where the key is," Oksana said. "At least you will be safe, this is a protected area."

"Until the UN leave. Thanks, but I'm with someone else."

"Who?"

"Faraway."

Oksana tried to look wise, which is not easily done when you have only a quarter of an inch of blond stubble on your head. For a moment Gaby thought that she might be one of the kick-boxing women in the ring tonight.

"And is he as good as the reputation he puts out about himself?"

"He's keen, he's clever, he'll try anything, he's got great stamina but he lacks, ah, finesse."

Oksana spluttered in her beer.

"Candidate for Serbski Jeb?"

Gaby suppressed a shiver. The bondage game had gone sour for her after the birthing chair in Unit 12. Be blind, be deaf, be reduced to taste, smell, touch, but be free. She would not take or give control in sex again.

"He's in love with me enough."

"But you're not with him."

"He deserves it, but I'm not in love with him at all. It's a bad habit I've picked up, sleeping with friends. I convince myself that they understand, but they always take it the wrong way and hurt gets done. It's not love, I try to tell them; it's touching. It's feeling good with another. It's wanting to wake up in the morning with another body in the bed. It's needing something to touch me, otherwise nothing will ever touch me again. Look at me; I'm heading for thirty. I've got gray hairs, my metabolism's shot to hell—once I did all my best work on a diet of alcohol, nicotine and chocolate, now I even look at food and it teleports itself into my belly—it's a toss-up which hits the ground first, my tits or my ass, and my lifestyle won't let me settle, let alone have anything approaching an adult relationship. So I sleep with my friends, because I can trust them and need their bodies beside me in the morning, and they all fall in love with me and come apart when they find me in bed with some other friend.

"I want to have a grown-up's relationship of edginess and compromise and having to sacrifice to get things in return you never asked for and hoping that it'll still be there beside me in the morning to touch when the hair has all gone gray and the tits have hit the ground. I want to have things demanded of me. I want to have to work at loving. I want to stop being free."

"You want Shepard," Oksana said. A girl waiter in boxing gear brought more beer. It was not Tusker, you could not get any of the good Kenyan beers anymore, but it was cold, and at least you could imagine an elephant sauntering across the runway. "Big cocks and vodka!"

Gaby returned the toast.

"I saw him today at the bombing. He didn't see me. It was like four and a half years rolled up and disappeared. I want him, I've never stopped wanting him, but I'm scared that if I find him, he won't accept my apology, or me."

"It is all circles, like I told you last time we met in this place," Oksana said. "If it is taken from us, it will be returned to us sometime. But to find your way back, you must first set out."

"Do you get this stuff off the insides of Christmas crackers?" Gaby said meanly. Then, knowing she had been hurtful, she said, "You told me you had the gift of seeing into hearts. Look into my heart; tell me how it all fits together in there because I don't know anymore."

Oksana pulled her chair around to the other side of the table, leaned forward and looked into Gaby's eyes. The Siberian woman's eyes were blue; Lake Baikal blue, that is the deepest blue in the world, and in a blink that was not a blink Gaby saw the ten thousand years of tundra ice that lay behind them and empowered them. It was no shit. It had never been shit. The power was real.

"You want me to do it for you," Oksana said. A helicopter

lifted from the far side of the airfield and passed noisily over the bar. "I cannot be the one who lays the way. You want him to forgive you, but you fear he will not, or cannot, because it is the hope that he will, and can love you again, that is the star that has guided your life. You have changed stars, Gaby, and you do not know that yet. You are still following the old star, and it leads you away. To follow this new star is to take the risk that it will fail, and your strength and trust with it. You see me and you wonder if I am another one of these people who cannot help be drawn to you and love you, and you are afraid of these people because you cannot stop yourself loving them a little. Even Faraway, whom you say you do not love; you fear hurting him. You love him. You love me, but you are afraid of how I might reply to that. You must not be afraid of me. I love you, purely, and impurely, but my place is at your side and not underneath you and whatever you decide I will honor."

"I don't deserve you, Oksana," Gaby said. "I don't deserve Faraway, any of you."

"We do not always get what we deserve. You see that?" Oksana pointed at the dark horizon away from the glow of the city. Gaby understood; she was pointing to a dim star among the constellations of the southern hemisphere: the BDO, three months from Earth. "If anything means that we do not get what we deserve, that does. The Chaga out there does. It is ours, if we have the courage to go into it, and take hold of it. Come on. It's getting cold out here, and they have just started the first bout."

Inside the bar, the spectators were ten deep around the ring. A Giriama woman with scarification ridges beaded across her chin and brows was kicking the living shit out of a hauntingly beautiful Indian girl with long black hair tied back in a ponytail. The men cheered and howled and laid their dollars and deutsche marks and Krugerrands down.

59

She was cruising south of terminum in the shadow of the hatching towers with Faraway in a Black Simba *pickni.* The Black Simbas had lent Gaby a driver, a bodyguard and a tail-gunner. The tail-gunner stood in the back, sweeping the avenues of middle-class villas with the swivel-mounted heavy machine gun. He called himself Cool K and wore expensive wraparound shades. The bodyguard was called Missaluba. She resented having to mind the *m'zungu* woman and her tame black cock. She wanted to be in the action up at Parklands. The driver was called Mojo. He drove frighteningly fast, because he had been told he was too old for the fighting up at Parklands.

It was day Minus One. The Kenyan army had fallen back in the night to positions among the Ngara and Northern Ring roads, defending the downtown district. The United Nations was a ribbon of white and blue stretched for ten miles along the airport road. This was the first day for many weeks that you did not hear the helicopters hovering over you. They were all gone to guard the link to the airport. The northern suburbs had been abandoned and the Tacticals were dividing it up between themselves. *Picknis* chased each other along the tree-shaded avenues. The white plaster rendering of doctors' and accountants' bungalows was chipped away by bullets. Heavy armor maneuvered through the gardens, bringing down trees, crushing children's slides and climbing frames, cracking patios and terraces. Bodies floated in the swimming pools. Slit trenches had been dug across City Park. A primary school burned, set alight by skirmishers trying to dislodge a sniper. Only the golden arches stood from a shelled-out McDonald's; the mortar duel had shifted focus to a Roman Catholic church. Pitched battles were fought for strategically significant and heavily defended gas stations.

But for old ties, Sugardaddy would not have spared Gaby the *pickni* and crew. He was General Sugardaddy now, of the Starehe Center Division, with heavy- and light-mechanized units and infantry under his command. His orders were to spearhead the push all the way to terminum, clearing everything from his path to establish free access to the Chaga. They were halfway there already. In the night, the Starehe Division had exterminated the

Soca Boys, but the Ebonettes had dug in at the end of the Murang'a road and were resisting forcefully. The generals of the right and left divisions, whose task it was to protect the flanks, were sending what troops they could spare to aid the assault, but they were coming under heavy attack from the United Christian Front to the west and the Nyayo Alliance to the east. Terminum brought the enemy fifty feet closer every day.

While his lieutenants ordered a *pickni* and assembled a crew, General Sugardaddy filled out the four and a half years since Unit 12. Rose was up at the front. She did not breed Chaga dogs anymore. She had command of a mechanized scouting unit. M'zee was three years gone into the Chaga. Sugardaddy had always thought that the old man's heart's true home was in that other world. He had heard that M'zee was working with the new immigrants in the Black Simba towns that were growing up ten, fifteen miles beyond terminum. A great nation was building in there. Perhaps M'zee's was the greater work, in the end. Moran was dead. They had hanged him for Bushbaby's murder. On the anniversary of the hanging, Rose went to the grave, squatted and pissed on it. And he, Sugardaddy, the king of cool, was a warrior. There were only a few now who remembered him by that name, fewer who dared to use it. He wished he could go back to the years when he was that name. He was not sure he liked to be a general, and feared.

Gaby wondered if General Sir Patrick Lilley was ever visited by such doubts.

"Since you must tell the world something, tell it the truth about us," Sugardaddy said. "It is not for greed or power or territory that we fight. It is so we can open a way to the Chaga, and hold it open so that all the people who wish to go, or have nowhere else to go, may go safely. It is our future we are fighting for. Our nation."

Then he drove off to war in his personal *pickni.* Gaby never saw him again.

But it is still killing, she had wanted to say to him. There is no end to killing and the excuses men make for it. I have seen a dozen tiny wars like yours, General Sugardaddy, and heard the reasons men have made for them, and they are as convincing and as false as yours. The true reason is that men make war because men love it. The Chaga-builders come eight hundred light-years to learn what it is to be human and the bad news from Planet Earth is that men kill because it gets them wet.

Mojo the driver was taking the *pickni* into the city center now. He did it because he could. No one would stop him. No one would even look twice at him. He could drive up and down Moi Avenue past all the other Tacticals who anywhere else would blow your lungs out of your back, but not here, because even carrion dogs need somewhere to sniff and lick each other's asses. He wanted to show off to the white bitch and her piece of meat that the Black Simbas earned respect from the street. He played lecherous bumper tag with a Lambretta scooter on which two young women were riding. He would crawl up beside them, touch his tongue to his upper lip, pass. They would dart past on the inside and wrinkle their noses at him. He finally put them behind him in the traffic on City Hall Way. Beside him, Gaby watched a young beggar on a trolley push his way along the gutter. His design was resourceful—a fruit box screwed to a skateboard. Without warning, he pushed himself out in front of the *pickni.*

''The beggar!'' Gaby shrieked. Mojo floored the brakes. The kid on the skateboard disappeared under the hood ornament that had once been one of those plastic lions rampant that the middle class with no taste put on their gateposts. ''Oh Christ, you've hit him.''

The kid's face rose over the top of the radiator grille. He was standing on his two feet. He was smiling. In his hands was a pump-action shotgun. He threw himself flat on the hood, blew both barrels through the windscreen. Noise. Glass. Blood. Gaby screamed, thinking she was dead. The blood and meat sprayed over her right side were not hers.

The skateboard kid rolled off the hood to cover. A Lambretta engine squealed. There were two shotgun blasts from the back of the *pickni.* The scooter dashed past. The girl on the back had produced a pistol-grip shotgun from her backpack. She reloaded as her driver turned the scooter for another pass. The Lambretta circled the *pickni,* pumping shot after shot after shot into the gun position. The rear window streamed blood on both sides. Missaluba extricated her Kalashnikov from the footwell and threw open the door. The Lambretta driver kicked it closed as she sped past. Missaluba barely avoided losing fingers and face.

A big blue Plymouth convertible drew up alongside. In it were men with Afro haircuts and big guns. The driver and passenger covered Missaluba while the men in the backseat jumped out and hauled her down on to the concrete. The skateboard kid and the shotgun girl from the Lambretta pulled Mojo's faceless body out of the truck and dragged Gaby over the blood-slick vinyl and shoved her into the rear seat of the Plymouth. A man in the skinniest tank top Gaby had ever seen frisked her. He tutted and shook his head at the caliber of her ammunition, like a Christian Brother teacher finding a vibrator in a schoolbag. Disapproving, but impressed. Missaluba and Faraway were kneeling by the side of the *pickni.* The skateboard kid and the Lambretta girl pressed shotgun muzzles to the backs of their skulls.

"Take her," said the front-seat passenger, a bald-headed man with a drooping mustache, round shades and a long leather coat. The Lambretta girl kicked Missaluba in the kidneys and quickly cuffed her hands with plastic cable grip. She went into the trunk of the big blue Plymouth.

"What about him?" the skateboard kid asked. He wanted to shoot Faraway. He wanted to shoot him very much. He wanted to blow his head up like an exploded melon, spraying red flesh and black seeds of wisdom.

"Leave him," the leather coat said. "He is tribe. We go. Now."

The skateboard kid flipped up his board, caught it with one hand and jumped into the back of the car beside Gaby. The Plymouth smoked away from the shattered *pickni.* There was blood, glass and shotgun cartridges all over City Hall Way, and Faraway standing in the middle of them in his bright orange color-of-the-day jacket. The Lambretta picked up its passenger and wove off through the traffic.

The man with the bald head and the drooping mustache in the leather coat turned in his seat to Gaby.

"Good morning, Ms. McAslan. Sheriff Haran's regards, and he wishes you to come with us to discuss your account."

60

They took her up the front stairs. At some time a bullet had killed one of the neon waterfalls flanking the door. The bouncer did not stand outside anymore, but scrutinized the street from a metal slit.

The balcony bar smelled of sweat, stale cigarettes and the high-end tang that remains when the characteristic chemicals of expensive perfumes neutralize each other. The main ceiling lights were on. You could see the cigarette burns on the carpet. Down in the white-tiled pit, rows of shower heads sprayed steaming hot water over twenty naked men languidly soaping each other. Gaby wondered, as she always had, where the Cascade Club bought its water.

Haran was on his throne in his glass-floored office at the top of the stairs marked PRIVATE in two languages. Leathercoat and the Skateboard Kid sat Gaby in a chair facing him and stood by the door. They did not think that she might try to escape. They just wanted to look scary. Haran had one of them give her a moist wipe to clean the blood and brain off her face. When her condition no longer nauseated him, he spoke.

"I'm disappointed. Really. I have to hear from others that you are back in my country. Gaby, I would have thought you would have called on your old friend and ally before now."

"You killed those Black Simbas. You fucking murdered them. They never stood a chance."

Haran sat back in his ebony throne and contemplated the woman before him.

"We are at war, Gaby. You yourself have realized this, by choosing sides."

Gaby turned in her chair to accuse the Skateboard Kid.

"He wanted to shoot Faraway. He wanted to blow his fucking head apart."

"He is tribe," Leathercoat said. "I would not let him do it."

"But it was exceedingly unmannerly of him," Haran said. "My own tribal brother. Flesh of my flesh. Would you like me to have him killed, by way of apology?"

He would, she knew. It would be a cheap price for Gaby's moral anguish.

"I don't want any more killing. I'm sick of killing and dying, do you understand? I'm sick of it always being the easy option."

"There, Simeon," Haran said. "Now you owe the *m'zungu* your life."

"What do you want, Haran?"

"Always to the point, Gaby. Very well. The posses are finished. The East African teleport is in tatters. The network of agents, operatives and enforcers has collapsed. There is no demand for the commodity I supply anymore. Therefore, according to the laws of economics, I should relocate my industry to a place where materials and markets are plentiful."

"You want out."

"I speak to you without shame or guilt. I want out. I will get out."

"So you're leaving Mombi to face the shit."

"Mombi thinks there is a place for the likes of us in the new Kenya. I have always lacked her patriotic fervor. Perhaps I lack her vision too. But what I know is that there is no place for Haran in this new nation. I will get out. You will get me out."

"You blow people away in the middle of City Hall Way on the long shot that I can somehow take you out as hand luggage? Sick joke, Haran."

He rippled his fingers. Gaby could hear the joints cracking.

"Excuse me if I do not laugh, Gaby. The news agencies have been getting their local people exit visas from the UN. I believe it should still be possible to make a late application directly to East Africa Command."

"If you know so much about it, then you'll know it's impossible without an affidavit from the station chief."

"Gaby, I have refrained from mentioning this so far, but I feel I have to remind you that you were forced to leave this country with your affairs unsettled. You will recall the considerable investment I put into opening the way for you to break the Unit Twelve story; an investment for which I do not think it is unreasonable to expect a return."

"You're calling in your marker."

"You owe me, Gaby. I anticipated there would be a problem with obtaining a new visa, so I will settle for a visa that has already been issued to someone else."

"Now you *are* joking."

"Shall I show you how my sense of humor works? I believe I

shall.'' Haran nodded to Leathercoat. He and the Skateboard Kid left the glass-floored room. They were gone some minutes. Haran sat unmoving, looking at Gaby over the tips of his touching fingers. If Gaby had had a cigarette, she would have stubbed it out in his eye socket. When she heard the enforcers' feet on the stairs, they sounded heavy, burdened.

They came into the office with Missaluba, the Black Simba bodyguard, between them. They had stripped her down to panties and epoxied her to a large sheet of melamine. They leaned her up against the wall of the office. She struggled, but the adhesive bond was permanent. Her lips had been glued shut.

''Remain in your seat, Gaby,'' Haran said. Leathercoat moved behind her chair to ensure her obedience. Haran opened a drawer and removed an object, which he set on top of the ebony desk. It was a heavy-duty staple gun. Gaby had seen her father use such to staple wire fences. It could drive a half-inch staple clean into a solid pine post.

''Hurt her,'' Haran said.

The Skateboard Kid took the staple gun and went to the woman glued to the board. He pressed the muzzle of the gun to her left nipple. He pulled the trigger. The woman grunted and tried to thrash on the melamine board, but the glue held her immobile.

''I will get out, Gaby. You will get me the visa.''

''Oh Jesus. Oh fuck. Haran, I can't give you anyone else's visa, they've got photographs.''

''Hurt her some more.''

The Skateboard Kid pierced the other nipple and put a staple into the palm of each hand. Gaby wailed as if the staples had been driven into her own meat.

''Why will you not help this woman?'' Haran said. ''Is it because she is black? Or is it that she is African, and her life is cheaper than a European's? Or is it because she is a woman that has not had children? You must hate her very much to let her suffer such pain.''

She matters, Gaby thought, head bowed. But so do the people you are asking me to betray. All I have is a choice of evils, and I am too white, too European, too sterile in my womb to be able to decide between them.

She looked at her feet and shook her head. Her hair fell around her face, a covering veil.

"So. Hurt her a lot."

Smiling, the Skateboard Kid put a neat row of staples, two inches apart, into the woman's body from forehead to pubic bone. Gaby surged from her chair, roaring and raving. Leathercoat pushed her back. The Skateboard Kid was meticulous in his work. When the Black Simba girl tore the skin off her lips in a cry of agony, he stopped what he was doing to staple them together. Gaby threw every name and curse at him, but the Skateboard Kid kept stapling, kept smiling. He had a hard-on. When he finished the vertical line, he started on her breasts. He swore when the gun ran out of staples after the first breast and he had to reload. The Black Simba girl had stopped screaming. She hung silently from the melamine board, insane with pain.

"Stop it," Gaby whispered. She could not look at the thing on the white melamine board. "Save her. Help her."

"I am afraid you have left it a little late for that," Haran said. He had watched the slow crucifixion impotent of interest or arousal. "All you can do is determine when it will stop hurting. Her death is yours. I hope you have the courage to give her it quickly."

Gaby looked at the young woman's eyes. Look what you have let happen to me, Missaluba's eyes said. Look at this good body of mine, that I loved to live in, that was so fine and useful; look at how it has been ruined because of your cowardice, so that all it can do is die. All this that has carried me through my twenty years of life is spoiled and wasted, all the things it wanted and hoped for are sold cheap because of you.

"Kill her!" Gaby shouted. "For the love of God, kill her. I'll get you your visa. I'll get you Faraway's visa. Oh Christ forgive me."

"That is good Gaby, but it is not adequate. I must have my faithful deputies to manage my new operation. There must be someone in your organization who has a group visa. Dependents? A family? Relatives?"

Gaby buried her face in her hands.

"Tembo," she whispered. "He's taking his family out. Oh Jesus God, what am I doing?"

"Where can I find him?"

She wrote the address on the slip of paper Leathercoat offered.

"Don't hurt them. You hurt them, you bastard, and I will hunt you down and kill you as slowly as you killed her."

Haran looked at the slip of paper and gave it to the Skateboard Kid.

"Do not be melodramatic," Haran said to Gaby. "You will do nothing." To his deputy, he said, "This is a family man. He will be easily persuaded. You do not need to use force with him or his loved ones. The threat is sufficient."

The Skateboard Kid left on his mission. Gaby threw her head back, imploring any God at all to burn up her soul that had been torn out by the roots. She closed her eyes.

"Haran. Your end of the bargain."

She heard two shots in rapid succession. They were shattering in the confined office. When she dared to open her eyes, she was alone in the glass-floored room.

They left her there with her horror and fear and guilt. The doors were not locked. Her guilt kept her prisoner. She thought of the life she had ended. She had killed that woman when she let the first staple be driven into her body. She had always thought she was one of the brave and the pure, who hated violence so much they would rather die than kill. How simply her illusions had been revealed. You can kill by inaction as much as action. You can kill by silence as easily as words. You can kill by good intentions and the love of friends. You can kill by deluding yourself that the devil keeps sloppy accounts.

She thought about the Skateboard Kid coming to the crowded house two streets from terminum. She saw Mrs. Tembo and Sarah and Etambele and After-the-Rains. She saw the Skateboard Kid standing among them and promising hideous things, and the children shrieking in fear.

She vomited on the glass floor. She willed herself to die, if it would do any good. But it would not. Dying never did any good. Nothing came from violence but more violence. Judgment was given on Gaby McAslan: traitor and murderer.

They found her lying on her back on the glass floor next to the dried vomit, staring at the ceiling. Leathercoat and the Skateboard Kid pulled her to her feet. She went meekly with them down to the main bar and through the back ways to the terrace café around the courtyard garden. There were no customers today. The waiters in white jackets with silver trays were all gone. The slow ceiling fans were still, the fountains in the garden silent. Haran was sitting at a large glass-topped bamboo table on which stood an Ethiopic scripture case; the very fine one that had cost Gaby half a month's wages, with half a month's wages stuffed inside it, five years ago. Mombi sat opposite him, flanked by possegirls in lace and black leather. In the between years Mombi had grown from enormous to monstrous. She was a moon now, a satellite swathed in black silk. She nodded to Gaby as the deputies seated Gaby at the table. Leathercoat stood at her shoulder, the Skateboard Kid took a seat beside Haran.

"You will be pleased to know that the piece of data was extracted and is currently undergoing image processing," Haran said.

"So whose face did you have to stitch up the middle?"

"As I told you, family men possess wisdom. You should have known that I would not hurt a child."

Then what had Missaluba the Black Simba been? You are old when the wasteland warriors start looking young.

"I have what I require." Haran smiled his reptile smile. "Your debt to me is discharged. Our relationship is ended. You are free to go." The Skateboard Kid held the scripture case out to Gaby.

She took a deep breath.

"You know what he's planning to do," she said to Mombi. The big woman looked sideways at Gaby but did not speak.

"Gaby. Be wise. Be thankful. Be free. Please leave," Haran said. Still, the Skateboard Kid held out the scripture case.

"You know what this piece of data is that he wanted from me?"

"Gaby, while you were my client you enjoyed my protection. Now you are not, and that obligation is ended. Jackson, please escort Ms. McAslan from the premises."

Leathercoat swung back the tail of his leather coat to free his gun. Gaby was quicker. She hit him in the balls with the side of her fist and, as he doubled up, pulled out his gun. She found the safety, cocked the hammer, pointed it two-handed at Haran's head. The Skateboard Kid dropped the scripture case and drew his weapon. It was big. He was cool, and smiling. He could hold it on a white woman one-handed, without trembling. But he was that second too slow and that made it a standoff and not a clean blow-away.

"Haran, tell him to put it down. Tell him to put it flat on the table. I can kill you. I will kill you."

"I am pleased to say that you have surprised me, Gaby. I am impressed. But what does this prove? Maybe I will die. You certainly will. More deaths, Gaby. Needless deaths."

Gaby licked her lips. Her tongue was so dry it clung to her lower lip.

"You know he's going to run out on you," she said to Mombi. "That piece of information he wanted from me; it's an exit visa. He made me betray a friend and his family to get it. He's going out of this place tomorrow, Mombi, on the last plane. He's leaving you, to sink or swim. He doesn't give a fuck, Mombi. Everything you've worked together to achieve, all the trust you've built up, it doesn't matter to him. His own hide does. He's getting out and you can go to hell."

"Gaby, you are boring me," Haran said. Leathercoat climbed to his feet, face contorted in testicular agony. Haran waved him away from Gaby, away from the Skateboard Kid's line of fire. "She is lying, of course."

"Why should I lie, Mombi? He let me go, why should I stay and put myself in front of his bullets for a lie? He's running out on you, Mombi. You can't trust him."

The Skateboard Kid held the gun as steady and sure as death and justice. Haran looked at the beautiful Ethiopic scripture case on the glass table.

"Kill her," he said.

"No." Mombi's leather girls were hideously fast. One stood off the Skateboard Kid, the other covered Leathercoat. Gaby's arms ached, but she held the bead on the bridge of Haran's nose. "I will not allow it. Give her back the visa of her friend," Mombi said.

"You believe this white bitch over me?" Haran said.

"Yes," Mombi said. "Get her her paper or I will kill your men and the *m'zungu* will shoot you where you sit."

Haran smiled. It was like the skin peeling back from a skull.

"Fetch the visa," he said to Leathercoat. To Mombi he said, "Now you show yourself for the fool you have always been. There is nothing here for us, can you understand that?"

"The fool is the one who thinks he can run from the Chaga forever," Mombi said. "It will catch you in the end. That is why you will stay with me, Haran. You will come with me into the

Chaga. There is a new network growing in there; its mesh is fullerene carbon, not optical fiber, but it can still feed fishermen with the skill to cast it and trawl its rich catch. You will work with me, Haran. We will reclaim everything that has been taken from us. We will succeed beyond all our dreams of greatness. It is the future in there. To stay out here is to be pushed into the past. You will not make it out here, Haran. There is nothing left out here but more and more of this. You should thank me, that I still offer you this after you try to betray me."

Leathercoat cautiously placed two sheets of paper on the glass tabletop.

"Put them in the box," Gaby said. "Give the box to me."

"Go now," Mombi said. "Get your friend out of the country, since he has decided he must go. Haran will not harm you. You are under my protection now."

Gaby lifted the Ethiopic scripture case one-handed and cautiously backed along the balcony. The gun was fluttering now. The pain in her right arm was incredible.

"Go!" Mombi ordered.

Gaby turned and ran. She ran through the back rooms, and through the Cascade Club, where the bar staff washed glasses and the boys played down in the pit. She ran down the steep street stairs. She met a posseboy coming up. She shouted at him, waved the big gun. He flattened himself against the wall as she exploded out onto the street and saw a phalanx of camouflaged *picknis* and army-surplus APCs advancing down the street.

She stopped dead. The vehicles stopped dead. The wind stirred the lion's-head Black Simba cartel banners on their pennons and aerials. The door of the lead *pickni* opened. A black man wearing a fluorescent orange jacket stepped out.

"It seems that you do not need John Wayne and the Seventh Cavalry to come over the hill to rescue you," Faraway said. "But I think they are going to come over the hill anyway, because they have wrongs to right."

Gaby ran and hit him like a free kick from the edge of the box. Faraway held on to her. He had always been a better goalkeeper than his cool allowed. He whirled her away through the battle lines as the Black Simbas advanced on the Cascade Club.

"I got it," Gaby said, holding up the scripture case. "The visa. I got it." Then the shakes started. Faraway just caught the scripture case in time. He took Gaby to the main street and through the crowds of spectators hoping to see blood to a coffee stall. He bought her sweet milky Kenyan *chai* and sat her on the curb until she could talk through the shivering. He eased the gun out of her hand, looked at it, set it aside.

"I got out, Faraway," Gaby whispered. "I got Tembo's visa back. Mombi made him give it to me. Don't let them hurt Mombi; she saved me. They can do what they like to Haran."

The sound of heavy-automatic-weapon fire came from across the avenue, and was answered by the short flat barks of shotguns and handpieces.

61

Day Zero.

The crowd outside the gates on the airport road had been the worst Gaby had ever seen, but she had managed to push the Landcruiser and its passengers through, past the soldiers who looked as if they knew that they could only hold the wire so long. She had thought that once they were inside the airport, it would be all right. She was wrong. The crowd inside the departures hall was worse.

They stood in the lobby between inner and outer doors. Tembo clutched his exit visa. Mrs. Tembo clutched After-the-Rains. Sarah clutched her best doll; Etambele clutched her favorite toy, which was a matted furry pencil case. They stood with their identity badges pinned to their clothes and looked at the crowd. It was almost religious; so many people so close in such a confined space. Souls wedged in a glass-and-concrete box, awaiting exodus, or judgment.

"Oh my God," Gaby said.

Doubtless important PA announcements went unheard and unheeded over the babel of voices in the concourse. The people were too densely packed to obey them.

"There are people in white uniforms at the check-in desks," Faraway said, seeing over the heads of the crowd. "We have the camera with us, the news-team trick might work again."

"With children and luggage?" Gaby asked. She took a deep breath to prepare herself for the annihilation of the crowd. Faraway plunged into the crowd, swinging one hundred thousand shillings of video camera like a riot baton. Tembo and his family tucked into his slipstream. Gaby took the rear guard, waving a microphone and shouting, "SkyNet news team! Let us through, please!" The way Faraway smiled as he elbowed you away from the check-in desk, you would feel he was doing you a personal favor.

"Five to travel," he announced to the woman in UN white at the desk, who did not care if people jumped the queue as long as her ticket out was safe in the back pocket of her pants. She checked the exit visas and tapped information up on her screen. She took such a long time doing it that Gaby wanted to drag her out of her little booth and press any key, every key, that might do something. The woman studied the words on her screen for a long time, and the visa for a longer time. She took Tembo's passport and examined it for the longest time. She checked the names of wife and children against the passport and the exit visas and the screen. She checked the photo badges against the passport and the visa and the screen. Then she gestured for them to put their bags on the scales. Baggage allowance on the relief flights was one piece each, adult and child. Tembo and Mrs. Tembo had managed to reduce it all to two big cases, which they dragged, and a backpack for Sarah. Etambele had not wanted to be left out, so she had a backpack too, a little cloth one Mrs. Tembo had sewn together. It held her doll's clothes, one dress and her washing things. Gaby did not think she could be so merciless with personal possessions. Take little, leave little, lose little was her professional motto. The UN woman looked at the bags but did not move to weigh or tag them.

Gaby was about to scream.

Faraway was about to hit the woman with the camera.

Tembo was fidgeting from foot to foot.

Mrs. Tembo was transfixed with a dread that had begun with the Skateboard Kid and would not end until she breathed in the clove breezes of Zanzibar.

Sarah and Etambele looked about to burst into tears.

The woman at the desk rattled through a box of rubber stamps, picked one and looked at it. Then, so suddenly that everyone almost missed it, she stamped the visas, tagged the bags and printed out boarding cards.

Tembo beamed as if Jesus had touched his brow. Mrs. Tembo hugged him, her children, Faraway and even Gaby. Faraway shepherded people and bags through the departure gate.

Down on the field the big Antonov mass lifters were wingtip to wingtip, winding black threads of refugees into their cargo bays. Blue-helmets with clipboards waved the people along the edge of the apron. Gaby's hair blew in the hot back blast from the taxiing airlifters. Tembo and Faraway fought with the suitcases. Mrs. Tembo pressed the precious boarding passes closer to her than even After-the-Rains. Sarah and Etambele struggled determinedly onward with their backpacks.

A blue-helmet stopped the line while a plane moved off its stand onto the taxiway. He checked Tembo's exit visa and Gaby and Faraway's press cards and sent them to the next aircraft. It was a little An72F. It had a Cyrillic name stenciled on its side. *Dostoinsuvo.* Gaby knew it would be all right now. She could trust them to Oksana's care, the shaven-headed, shaman-angel of the turbofans. A woman was standing at the foot of the tail ramp collecting boarding passes. And Gaby realized that this was it. They were leaving her. She hugged Tembo.

"You are the best goddam cameraman I ever worked with," she yelled. "I will miss you like death."

"There is no death," Tembo yelled back. "Jesus has beaten it, ten nil. We will meet again, as surely."

"Thank you for saving us once, and then saving us again," Mrs. Tembo said.

That is the way to think of it, Gaby thought. Twice-saved. That way the Black Simba kid's death does not go for nothing.

Faraway hugged Mrs. Tembo, who pretended to be scandalized, and the children, and then Tembo. He held his dear friend a long time, like a man does who knows he will never see this dear friend again.

"It will be good in Zanzibar," he shouted. "It is like paradise down there in the spice island. Maybe not your paradise, but my paradise. Sun, sand, cool palms, cool beer, warm nights, hot hot big-breasted women who smell of cinnamon and cloves. Listen, I can hear them weeping for your great gift, Tembo."

Tembo and his family gave their cards to the woman and they went up the ramp into the belly of the big plane and Gaby could not see them anymore. She and Faraway stood back and waited for the plane to fill and the ramp to close. They shut their ears to the astounding blast of Lotarev engines lighting up at once. *Dostoinsuvo* moved off its stand. Until now Gaby had not been certain Tembo and his family were safe. She waved, knowing it was supremely unlikely she would be seen. The plane turned at the end of the runway, made its run and took off.

"Ah," Faraway said, watching the smoke trails turn over the distant towers of Nairobi. He sounded like a man who has felt part of his body die.

"You'll see him again; you're his deputy station manager, for goodness' sake."

"I will not see him again. I am not going to Zanzibar. I have been decided on this for a long time, Gaby. I told you that night at Tembo's when he and I tried to make an African out of you: when the time came, I would take my chances with the Chaga. I am not leaving. The Chaga is the future. It is Kenya as she should be. I want to be part of that. Tembo has children to fear for; he has made the right choice for him. But me, what kind of future could it be without the incomparable Faraway?"

"You pick your moments, man."

"Some things there is never a good moment to say." He smiled. Gaby could not resist it. "Sure you know that the only reason I stayed so long is because I thought I would get the chance to *fiki-fiki* the woman of my dreams. So I go to the new world happy now, because how many men in this world have made the woman of their dreams howl like a jackal?"

"You." She play-punched him.

"Gaby, I know you do not love me. I do not need you to love me. I am happy, like I said. It does not hurt me that you still love Shepard—I have seen you try to hide the look on your face every time his name is mentioned. I heard you shout his name when the bomb went off on Jogoo Road. At least you had the good manners not to shout it when my bomb went off inside you. Listen, I am such a great guy, I will tell you where you can find him. He is at the Kenyatta Conference Center. They are clearing out every last trace that UNECTA was ever there. Hurry. You may still catch him before he leaves for here."

She found herself running.

She found herself pounding through the incongruously deserted arrivals hall, a running woman with ten cleaners waltzing polishing machines over the mosaic floor.

She found herself struggling into her color-of-the-day vest as she hooted her way through the evacuees outside the main gate. She hoped she had not killed anyone as she rammed the zebra-striped Landcruiser toward the open sunflower of the Kenyatta tower.

Two Polish Sokol utility helicopters flanked the entrance to the center. White UN trucks were scattered around them. A mobile crane was trying to lift the bronze UNECT*Afrique* emblem off its plinth. People bustled like city-building termites in and out of the doors with trolley loads of documents and filing cabinets. The cordon of soldiers stopped Gaby halfway across the square.

"Press," she said, waving her DF108 in the soldier's face and pointing to her orange jacket. He politely barred her way. Incredible, that nations gave people like this license to kill in their name. She emptied a golden stream of Krugerrands out of her purse into her hands. "All right. How much?"

Two did it.

She grabbed a civilian loader by the arm, swung her around, sent her armful of document folders spinning across the colored tiles of the square.

"Dr. Shepard. Where is he?"

The woman frowned. Gaby left her to her scattered files and arrested a tall Sikh with a UNECTA badge pinned to his turban.

"Dr. Shepard. I have to find him."

"Fifteenth floor."

This time, as on that first morning when she had stood awed in this cavernous foyer and felt she was a member of a great invisible communion, no one gave Gaby a second look. She pressed the elevator button, pressed it again, hit it three times as if that would make it come any faster, but all it did was go up and keep going up, so she took the stairs. After five flights she slumped against the window, gasping. The thought of Shepard finishing up up there and pressing the elevator button to go down gave her strength for another five. Panting, heart smashing against her ribs, she leaned her forehead against the glass. She could see the imperceptibly curving horizon of terminum across the northern suburbs. The pillars of the hatching towers, each as tall as the Kenyatta building, receded into the distance like the watch towers of some monstrous rampart. Like Jake before him, Faraway was bound for that. Did it have to take all the men she cared about? Tembo. She had done right by Tembo, in the end. Children made things different, difficult. She saw columns of smoke rise up across the city. Things burning down there. Killings. She thought about the vengeance the Black Simbas had visited on Haran and his posse. She had seen the smoke go up from the Cascade Club when they torched it, but she did not know what had happened to Haran. She hoped he was dead, and Mombi had survived to make it across the line into the colored country beyond.

She closed her eyes, willed her heart to slow its beat.

Shepard.

She kicked open the door to the fifteenth floor and fell through it.

"God," she whispered, "I'm dying." She picked herself up and ran along the curving corridor, opening each door she came to and shouting "Shepard!" into the room. Every room was the same; a pie wedge of carpet, glass wall and abandoned tube-steel office furniture.

"Shepard!"

She could have missed him. She could have been around this corridor a dozen times. Where were all the people? The Sikh had said they were up here, clearing out fifteen. They had moved on. They had moved down. Elevator well. They might still be moving stuff into the elevators. Check there. She did and saw the sliding doors close on an elevator load of civilians laden with cardboard boxes. At the front. Right between the closing doors. Looking right at her.

"Shepard!"

He recognized her. His eyes widened in surprise. He opened his mouth to speak. He started forward. And the doors sealed in front of him. Gaby wailed and hit the call button with the heel of her hand. The illuminated numbers above the door rapidly diminished, stopped abruptly at eight. Gaby rushed out of the elevator lobby back to the stairs. Fifteen. Fourteen. Easier to go down than up, but not much. There's a lot of gravity in that central stairwell. Don't look down between the handrails. Thirteen. Twelve. Turning onto eleven, she saw it out of the window and stopped dead.

The big bat-winged thing came in silent as a secret wish across the smoky skyline of Nairobi. It did not seem natural in the air; it seemed to fight and dodge the air currents, sideslipping and swooping and warping its leather wings. It flew by defiance, and thus Gaby knew with fundamental certainty that it was going to hit the tower. It was going to hit the tower two levels below her, on the ninth floor. She knew she could not make it. She stood on the eleventh-floor landing and watched the thing swell to fill her vision. Bat wings obliterated the view. She cried out and covered her face. The thing hit the Kenyatta tower like an artillery shell. Gaby reeled toward the big drop at the center of the stairwell as the building shuddered. She stared into the abyss and threw herself back. Clangings and distant crashings of falling objects rebounding from the stairwell walls came from beneath. Gaby ventured as close as she dared. She could hear a high-pressure hissing; water lines broken, or the doodlebug releasing its spores?

The thing had demolished outer and partition walls and had wedged itself into an office adjoining the stairwell. From tenth to eighth floors the stairs did not exist. Sulfur-yellow flowers were already breaking out across the concrete walls; the carpet of the shattered office was bubbling into a stew of pseudo-fungi. Slimy ropes of Chaga-stuff hung down the stairwell. Already it would be working on the elevator cables. There was no other way down. She was trapped.

Towering un-ferno.

She thought that was a pretty good joke to think up when you are climbing for your life from voraciously devouring Chaga. Up. It was the only way. The only hope. By twenty-two, her legs were screaming. She stumbled into an office that looked over Parliament Square. The cordon of soldiers was running to their carriers. The convoy of trucks was forming up and moving up. The helicopters had started their engines. She picked up a tube-steel chair and smashed the window. No one looked up. She threw the chair out. No one saw it fall.

"You cannot leave me here!" she yelled. "Shepard, you cannot do this to me!"

He had seen her. He knew she was here. He would be watching to see who came out of the foyer. He would not abandon her. What would he do? He could not come up the tower to rescue her. Helicopter.

She climbed, delirious with exertion and pain. The top. To the top. Top of the world, Ma. GIRL REPORTER IN SKYSCRAPER RESCUE THRILLER. She could not remember how many floors there were in the Kenyatta Conference Center.

The stairs ended on her and she opened the door. Sun. Light. Wind. Heat. Altitude. Vertigo. She was in the center of the central flower at the top of the tower. Steel petals inclined away from her. Don't look at the edge. Don't look up. Don't look down. Then what do you look at?

A helicopter lifted past, close enough for her to feel the

downdraft. It turned to the west, toward the airport. Gaby took off her orange press jacket and waved it over her head.

"See me, you fuckers! It's me. I'm still here. Come and get me. Come on, Shepard, don't let me down now."

Gaby waved her orange jacket and shouted and shouted and shouted.

florida storm warning

62

The crab ran along the tide line, hunting. It scuttled in and out in time to the gentle run and flow of the foam-edged water. Its legs left little pinpoint prints in the white sand. The sand was not native to this place. It had been brought, like the rest of the long, narrow peninsula, by truck from another place. It was part of the contract that the builders environmentally enhance the two-mile strip of landfill trash. Between the white sand and the edge of the grass, you could see the bones of the thing: the cans and the cars and the twenty million black plastic refuse sacks. That was what made it such a good place for the crabs, and the gulls, and the waders in the shallow water between the peninsula and the shore.

Nothing on the tide today. Not even a rotting condom washed up from the resort hotels down the coast. The crab ran up the beach to clamber through the trash line. It did not do this because it thought that trash was better than tidewater. One set of stimuli replaced another; that was all. It was only a crab. It was a big bastard; its shell was the size of your hand, and the color of a hard dick. It wore its fighting claws the way a punch-drunk middleweight gone to fat wore his gloves. The crab gobbled air with its feeding mandibles and tasted it. It darted sideways and tugged at something wedged under the creased black belly of a trash sack. A rat had died here and rotted. The crab tore and tore. It tore a leg right off with its battle claws.

The gull had been watching the big crab from a hover twenty feet up, waiting for its moment to swoop and steal. It saw the crab wave the rat leg in its claws. It dived. It crawked in its throat at the crab, flapped its wings, stabbed with its beak. It was bigger, smarter, meaner; all the crab had was a thick shell and dumb obstinacy. It held on. The gull danced after it, pecking. The crab backed all the way up onto the grass. The crab could go as easily backward as forward or sideways. The gull did not let up. The crab led the gull across the tough salt grass. At the edge of the concrete it made its stand. The gull stabbed and weaved. The big crab held up its fighting claws and circled.

Suddenly all the birds in the tidewater flew up at once in a clatter of wings. The crab fought his corner. The gull paused in its assault and put up its head. It sensed the disturbance that had made the others take to the wing. It gave a fuck-you caw and jumped into the air. The crab was too dumb and too greedy and too short on senses to learn from what had spooked the gull. It chewed its rotting rat leg. It was only when it felt the rumble through its legs that alarm penetrated the dumb. It ran, chewed leg held high. It looked for crevices and crannies. There were none in the tough grass of the artificial peninsula to hide a crab this big. It reversed onto the concrete. It was that dumb.

The wheels missed it, but the fire got it. Three thousand degrees of liquid hydrogen combining with liquid oxygen cindered it: the blast bowled the wisp of chitin ash down the runway.

The circling birds came down, flock by flock, into the shallow water in the lee of the peninsula. In the big trailer park a mile to the south, the people whooped and cheered and applauded as the vapor trail of the HORUS carrier body curved skyward.

"Ten miles out, fifty thousand feet," said a fat man with a beard in an ugly hat and a T-shirt with *Fort Lauderdale in '10: World SF Convention* printed on the front. He was watching the sky with a pair of binoculars.

"Carrier separation in mark twelve minutes," said an equally fat bearded man wearing an equally ugly hat. His T-shirt had a picture of an old-style space shuttle and the words *National Astronautics Society: Per Ardua Astra.* He had a radio jacked into his ear.

The people followed the HORUS upward. There were five thousand of them in the trailer park this day. Thousands more watched from other approved viewing areas, or the beaches, or the offshore pleasure cruisers. But the serious ones, the true BDO freaks, were at the trailer park. It was like a festival. There were license plates from forty-eight states of the Union and beyond on the ass-ends of Winnebagos, RVs, trailers greater and lesser, station wagons, pickups with tents in the back, monster trucks, motorcycles. A nomad village of tents had grown up along the dune side of the park. Family-sized trailer tents, one-man pup tents. Folding gas barbecues, Sterno stoves, campfires of scavenged driftwood carefully ringed with stones. Boots set outside for the night. Terra-cotta beer coolers evaporating in the shade. Awnings, windbreaks, sunshades.

It was a festival of space. Like all the best festivals, it was free. The acts up on the big stage were the daily HORUS launches, but like any festival worth going to, it was down in the tent-and-trailer town among the sex and drugs and booze and free philosophy and easy conversation that the real action was found.

The people were moving away from the viewing stage. The chase planes were coming in to land on the two-mile artificial peninsula jutting out into the ocean. The hyperbola of smoke was blowing away on the breeze from off the sea. Clouds clung to the horizon; a tropical storm was moving out there in the Atlantic. The meteorological satellites were tracking its progress up the Gulf Stream. The odds were slightly over even that it would come ashore. Heavy-weather warnings were in force from Fort Lauderdale to Daytona Beach. If it hit Kennedy, it would shut down the HORUS launch program for days, and the free festival down in the trailer park. The name of the tropical storm was Hilary.

''Launcher separation successful,'' the man with the ear radio said. ''*Isaac Asimov* is climbing into transfer orbit. Unity rendezvous in twenty-seven minutes.''

His fat friend smiled and nodded sagely.

Gaby McAslan walked back to the SkyNet news van. It was a good angle; the incongruous fusion of Right Stuff and Hippy Chic. The guys in the van much preferred it to the hotels where the rest of the world news were bivouacked. But then Gaby reckoned they got action every night, in the back of their SkyNet U.S. van. Right now the men were comparing the tape unfavorably with those of previous launches.

''Night ones are best,'' said the one who called himself Rodrigo. ''Whole fucking place lights up like a fucking Christmas tree.''

''Here's that stuff you asked for,'' said the other, whom Rodrigo called The Man, though he was years younger. ''What you doing with this anyway?''

''My job,'' Gaby said, and took the minidisc recorder and pinhead mike. Pinhead Mike would be a better name for The Man than The Man. They were both jerks. Not for the first time since coming to cover the BDO story, Gaby wished she had her Kenya team with her. That could not be; both her men were prisoners of the Chaga; Faraway literally, Tembo in that he had been refused a visa to enter the United States. ''Potential biohazard threat from exposure to mutagenic substances,'' the consulate in Zanzibar had said. ''You are a black African'' was the truth. The race and fear barriers were going up already. Gaby had been closer than Tembo to Chaga-virons in the last days of Nairobi, but she was the right nationality, the right race, the right color not to get turned back at the yellow line.

In her room in the Starview Lodge across the lagoon, Gaby wired up and pulled on the ugly uniform she had bribed from the chambermaid at the Kennedy Ramada. She checked herself in the mirror. The recorder was invisible. She had reception call her a taxi to the Ramada. The SkyNet car would have been dangerously obvious. The driver dropped her at the staff entrance.

UNECTA had come in force to the Kennedy Space Center to stage-manage humanity's close encounter with the Big Dumb Object. They overwhelmed the capacity of NASA's launch facility. A dozen hotels, motels and travel lodges as far south as Canaveral had been seconded to house the overspill of BDO people and their inevitable entourage of media and society hangers-on. The Kennedy Ramada was the hub of UNECTA*Space*'s operations. No press or celebrity sniffers here. The doormen and bellboys had the scent of a journalist's soul, and the men in suits they summoned had hard hands. Now that Ellen Prochnow—Chief Executive of UNECTA*Space*—had taken residence in the Presidential Suite, the hard hands had been backed up with big guns. Which was the reason Gaby McAslan in her bribed chambermaid's uniform was hurrying through the kitchens and store areas before someone realized they did not recognize her.

The material had been hard picked—a hint, a clandestine meeting, a file copied, a database hacked—and painstakingly assembled, but Gaby now had the evidence to put to Ellen Prochnow. UNECTA*Space* was part-funding Operation Final Frontier with payoffs from biotech corporations and the armaments manufacturers, seduced by the prospect of developing weapons systems from Chaga biological packages. The humane bomb; that destroys the enemy's ability to wage war without harming humans. Winnable wars. All the letters, faxes, interviews, depositions, codes and passwords on the disk in her breast pocket. Care to comment, Ms. Prochnow?

Gaby nodded to Gloria, her inside woman in the corridor to the service elevator.

"She is in, I assure you," Gloria whispered.

Your husband has probably already snorted the two thousand dollars I paid you up his nose, Gaby thought. Was the makeup a little too heavy around the left eye? Cover. You need cover. She ducked into the laundry room and grabbed a hanger trolley of clothes ready to be returned to their owners.

"Next car, please," she told the room valet waiting on the next floor up. All Irish people can do convincing American accents. The illuminated numbers blinked on and off above the door. Gaby amused herself by looking through the clothes on the rail.

She hit the emergency stop button.

Gaby took the hanger down and examined the garment closely. The print on the T-shirt was faded from years of washing, but it was clearly a teenage nun with her habit up, luxuriously masturbating.

Gaby sat in the corner of the elevator for a full minute, staring at the T-shirt while the call-button lights flashed. She put the T-shirt back on the rail, went down to ground, pushed the trolley through the lobby to the reception desk and asked for a pen and paper.

"Give that to Dr. M. Shepard, please," she said. She left the trolley by the desk and went out the front door past all the staring, political-space-BDO-Chaga people. She had caught a glimpse of a television in the public lounge. A glimpse was enough to identify Ellen Prochnow's unmistakable First Lady of Space styling, and the words LIVE RELAY in the bottom right corner.

Thanks a lot, Gloria.

63

Another country, another press conference. So many amphitheaters of seats, so many tables and chairs and carafes of water and nervous scans of the seventh row and the clear of the throat before the "Good morning, ladies and gentlemen." Getting old, Gaby McAslan. Getting cynical. Getting weary. One last big miracle and wonder and that will do me, all right? Getting lonely, in your seventh seat of the seventh row, with all these faces around you you know so well but never become more than faces.

Has he got that note yet?

No. Don't think about that. Think about Rodrigo and The Man going to get her that contact with the Pink Underground. That would be a hell of a story to break. The symbs were breeding subcultures like clap in a brothel; it was politically inevitable that there would be gay communities springing up in the vast chagas of Ecuador and southern Venezuela. Not surprising that there should be a secret underground railroad funneling white *norte* homosexuals across terminum. No homophobia or persecution there. No fear of the Scourge.

Weeks could pass now without thinking about Jake Aarons.

She thought about Shepard again. It is only two hours since you left him that note. He probably hasn't got it yet, let alone meditated on his response. Just what is he doing down here anyway?

Ellen Prochnow was taking this press conference alone. She had never been shy about being seen on the pale blue screen. That was a Chanel suit. Style never goes out of fashion, Coco had said.

God, what if Shepard didn't show?

Ellen Prochnow did the scan of the seventh row. Hi. It's me, the one with the red hair, right? You don't know me yet, but by the time Any Questions is over, we'll be better acquainted. A whole lot better. Ellen Prochnow did not do the nervous throat-clear. She was a professional.

"Good afternoon, ladies and gentlemen." The half smile was very good. "Welcome to the Kennedy Space Center for the briefing on Operation Final Frontier Mission 88. Most of you probably know who I am"—small laughter—"but for those who have been on some other planet than this or the Big Dumb Object, I am Ellen Prochnow, Chief Executive of UNECTA*Space,* and I'll be introducing you later to the crew and expedition team of Mission 88, the HORUS *Arthur C. Clarke.*''

How many biotech salarypersons among them, Ellen? Gaby thought. How many weapons analysts?

''First, the latest on our Big Buddy up there. As of eleven-thirty GMT September eighteenth, the Big Dumb Object is in a trailing position to Earth at a range of seven hundred and twenty thousand miles, slightly under three times the distance between the earth and the moon. The Swarm has dropped into a trailing position fifteen thousand miles behind the BDO and we are assuming it has become dormant. Estimated Time To Earth Orbit is two hundred and fifteen hours thirty-eight minutes. Achieved Earth Orbit will be on Thursday, September twenty-seventh at 10:22 GMT; that's about twenty past five in the morning EST, or Last Jack Daniel's and Then I'll Get Some Sleep, Florida Journalists' Time.''

Don't smile at your own jokes, Ellen.

She rattled through the reports on the state of the Big Dumb Object. What little *Gaia* could photograph through the five slit windows that ran the length of the cylinder indicated that the ring mountain baffles had solidified into partition bulkheads five miles thick, though gravitometric analysis seemed to indicate the presence of large spaces up to three miles in diameter inside the walls. *Gaia* was being retasked for low-level passes over the window slits to attempt to map the interior prior to human exploration. Yes, alien intelligences were a possibility. Even the Chagamakers themselves. So was Harvey the six-foot invisible white rabbit. Any more questions?

Not yet, Gaby thought. Wait until the Great White Major Toms are smiling for the cameras before you pull out your *j'accuse.*

''You can pick up the latest releases from *Gaia* and the Hubble and Chandrasekahr telescopes at reception on the way out,'' Ellen Prochnow said. ''I'd like now to introduce to you the crew and mission team of the space plane *Arthur C. Clarke.* This will be Mission 88 of Operation Final Frontier, HORUS launch thirty-four from the Kennedy Space Center. Ladies and gentlemen, please welcome Commander Phillippa Gregory, orbiter pilot Damon Ruscoe, Flight Engineer McAuley Trudin of the *Arthur C. Clarke,* and her mission team.''

People applauded. Gaby expected them to come on in a high-kicking chorus line but it was just another load of smiling, waving bald-headed astronauts in white coveralls with UNECTA-*Space*'s crescents-and-Earth logo on breast and back. The shaved heads were something to do with preventing hairs drifting around Unity, Gaby had heard. The station was already well over capacity, and Final Frontier people were being shipped up faster than the space engineers could bolt new sections on and fill them with air. Gaby liked the idea of the success or failure of first contact hanging from a stray, free-floating pube. The hairlessness suited the blacks much better than the whites, who all looked grim and refugeelike. So which is the weapons expert? Gaby thought, leaning on her folded arms and watching the mission team shuffle out from the wing and form a semicircle behind Ellen Prochnow. You, big black man with the happy expression? You, little white woman with the look of naked terror on your face? You, Captain Lantern-jaw Marine-face with the much-too-nice-eyes that give it all away?

You?

You.

"You," Gaby breathed at the twelfth coverall from the end. "You cannot do this to me, not here, not now."

64

There was a launch that night. It was only an SSTO freighter—they barely gave the things mission numbers, they were that lacking in glamour—but it made a lot of noise and sent up a mighty impressive pillar of flame across the lagoon. The space junkies and rocket fetishists who had not gone across the causeway to Trailer Park were crowding around the Starview Lodge's telescopes on the upper level to ooh and ahh. Gaby had the terrace bar to herself. The other journalists derided her for her choice of the hippy, dippy, New-Agey Starview Lodge over less eclectic expense-account hotels down the coast and across the lagoon. Gaby stayed here because Gaby liked the vibes and the clientele. It reminded her of Africa. It reminded her of the Watchhouse. Its keel had been laid the same year that Unity's had been welded together in low orbit, and it had grown in symbiosis with the renascent space age. Nowhere else did they hold nightly

BDO-viewing parties, as socially and aesthetically charged as any Japanese cherry-blossom-watching picnic. And there were no newspeople.

"Expecting someone?" Nice Eddie the bar boy she did like asked her.

"Hoping someone," she said, and sucked her piña colada and watched the faintly luminous pillar of cloud from the rocket launch blow away on the wind from the ocean. It was getting up; Tropical Storm Hilary must be dithering between strange attractors out in the Bahamas. Gaby waved her swizzle stick in the air. Come, storm come. If a butterfly's wings in Beijing could summon up a hurricane, surely a swizzle stick with a Saturn Five rocket on the end at the Starview Lodge could command Hilary to storm hard against this coast, rock this wooden ark of a hotel on its moorings, rage over all the HORUSes and launchers and SSTO over the water and press them to the ground, and blow Shepard back to me. Blow me hours, blow me days of him, before he gets into his rocket and flies away from me.

He was taking his time coming. But he was still politely late.

Gaby sought out the BDO in the sky. That bright star in the belly of Pisces, resting on the edge of the world. How would it look when it went into orbit? They were talking about a position halfway between the earth and the moon. She looked at that great light in the sky and tried to calculate apparent diameters. A bright blur. Maybe even a recognizable cylinder. It would go through phases, like the moon. It was a moon. Fourteen-day orbit.

What will it look like to Shephard, in Unity, or on High Steel, that hair-raising surf shack of girders, solar panels and environment tanks they had built out there as the final stepping-stone to the BDO? Too big to be a spaceship; a planet on your doorstep. That was probably the only way to look at it and stay sane.

She ordered another piña colada from Constantin, the bar boy she did not like. He was impolitely late now. And he had managed to shaft her question to Ellen Prochnow. Stand up and play Wicked Witch of the Seventh Row in front of the man you begged to come and see you and tell him how sorry you are, how you've changed, how you've found him in your thoughts every day.

Bamboo wind chimes clocked against each other. Blow

wind, come to me. Listen to me, I cannot lose him to cosmic irony.

Up on the telescope deck they were talking passionately about centrifugal gravity.

"Any messages for me at reception?" she asked Nice Eddie.

"Not last time I looked."

"Could you look again?"

He looked again. There were still no messages.

"He's late," Nice Eddie said.

He is three piña coladas late, Gaby thought. Three piña coladas late is looking-like-he-isn't-going-to-show late. It's he-doesn't-want-to-see-you late. It's this-is-the-end-of-it-Gaby-McAslan late. The fourth piña colada is the longest one, the one over which you work out what you are going to do with the rest of your life now. It would need to be the longest one Emilio at the bar ever shook. She did not have a plan if he did not come. It is a terrible universe, she thought, that such tiny moments, such atoms of decision, are the fulcrums on which whole lives and futures swing. Strange attractors of the soul; like that storm she had tried to charm with her swizzle stick.

He was not-going-to-show late now. He was never-going-to-show late.

"He didn't turn up," Nice Eddie said as she picked small change out of her purse to leave as a tip.

"Doesn't look like it, Eddie."

She stood up to leave. And there he was, asking directions at reception. The girl was pointing right at her. The strength went out of her legs. She sat down, suddenly terrified. She realized that she did not know what to say to him.

She found herself scrabbling in her bag for cigarettes that had not been there for five years.

"Gaby?"

"Oh. Hi." Caught, flustering. "Sit down, oh sit down; Eddie, a Wild Turkey with branch water, isn't that what it is? And I'll have another piña colada, I did remember right, didn't I? It is Wild Turkey?"

"You remember right."

She found she was doing anything but look at him. She forced her eyes toward him. He is not a man who suits having no hair, she thought. It made him look like an impostor of himself. He had bought a new outfit, one of those Indian-inspired two-pieces that were the fashion. It did not flatter him much either, but he looked comfortable in it.

The hideous idea that a woman had bought it for him froze her heart.

"I like what you've done with your hair," Gaby said, trying to restart.

Shepard ran his hand over his scalp.

"Still a bit gray and scaly. I like what you've done with yours."

Gaby smiled self-consciously and touched the soft curls.

"Got fed up with the old 'Joni Mitchell Sings "Big Yellow Taxi' " look."

"Shorter suits you," Shepard said. "I'm sorry I'm so late, I'm sure you thought I wasn't coming. They sprang a surprise meeting on us. Seems Hilary out there has decided she'd like a vacation on the coast and they wanted to warn us in case they had to push the launch date forward."

"Can they do that?" Nice Eddie brought the drinks. Shepard paid for them in space-center scrip.

"Personally, I don't think so. They've rescheduled the *Gene Roddenberry* launch, which is Mission 86, for oh-nine-thirty tomorrow, but the speed this storm's coming, I don't think they'll even make that. Forecast says its due to hit about twenty miles south of Canaveral around oh-seven-hundred."

Oh Shepard, they've got you talking like them, Gaby thought.

"You weren't on the flight roster," she said. "It was a hell of a surprise finding you in the lineup at the press conference."

"Hell of a surprise finding myself in that lineup." Shepard took a long draw from his drink. The wind was stronger now, lifting the paper coasters, rattling the paper lanterns. It is blowing in from Africa, Gaby thought. "Every mission specialist has a backup. Day before yesterday Carl Freyer went down with some mystery virus he caught off a hotel air-conditioning system—that's the risk you run when you exceed the capacity of your quarantine accommodation—and they need someone with specialisms in Chaga nanochemistry and in-field experience. They gave me five days to get my stomach muscles up to high-gee liftoff standard. Four hours a day in the gym, the rest in centrifuge training, practicing suit maneuvers in the water tank, or team building. I can hardly move, I am so stiff and sore."

''You're actually on the expeditionary force.''

''Not the first wave. Not the ones who go up to the door, knock, and then wait and see if anyone answers. I'll be going through with the second wave; Teams Yellow and Green, once the beachhead is established.''

''I can't imagine what it will be like.''

''Neither can I. The boy from the plains states, up on the Final Frontier. Riding the High Steel. Scares the fuck out of me, Gaby.''

Scares the fuck out of me too, Gaby thought, listening to the rattle of the wind chimes and the voices from the deck above. All the things I want to say, I need to say, I have practiced for four years and nine months, are in here and all that comes out is shallow, bland, polite, pleasant drinks conversation. I'm scared to say them, Shepard. I'm scared to have my words rip you open again.

''How did you know I was at the Ramada?'' Shepard asked,

''Journalistic cunning.'' No, she would tell nothing but the truth tonight. ''I was trying to sneak up to Ellen Prochnow's suite—I've evidence I want to present to her that arms corporations are payrolling Final Frontier for seats on the shuttles and first refusal of the expedition findings. I didn't get to see her, but I did find a certain well-remembered T-shirt with a picture on the front of a female member of a religious order engaged in auto-erotic practice.''

Shepard laughed. It had changed with the years. It was a dark, wise laugh now, with old blood in it.

''And by the way, thanks for sending the helicopter back for me,'' Gaby continued. ''It saved my ass.''

''I remember an old riposte to that quite well,'' Shepard said. ''I couldn't leave you stuck up on top of the Kenyatta Center with the Chaga climbing up underneath you.''

''Never got a chance to thank you. By the time I got to the airport, you were gone. So my ass thanks you now.''

Shepard raised his glass to her.

''I accept your ass's thanks. What the hell were you doing up there anyway?''

''Came to see you,'' Gaby said. Came to tell you I was sorry, that I was wrong and bad and cruel and hurt you because I was hurt and that I wanted it all back the way it was when it was right and good and dirty; she did not say.

Shepard hesitated. He is going to change the subject, Gaby thought.

He changed the subject.

"Was it bad, afterward?"

"Yes. At the end, very bad. It was killing, all killing; killing for the sake of killing. They threw everything they had at the Simba Corridor, but the Black Simbas held it open for two months. Half a million people went up it into the Chaga before they pulled it in after them. Faraway—do you remember him? The tall Luo with the dirty mind. He stayed with me until the very end."

"I remember him," Shepard said. The look on his face was that of a man taken by his memories to a place he does not wish to go.

"When they started shelling the airport and the UN stopped the relief flights and it was really scary, he got me out. We managed to put a call through to the coast before the net crashed; then he drove me cross-country at night, through the skirmish lines, to a place where they could put down a plane to pick me up. Do you remember Oksana Telyanina?"

"Was she the one who was some kind of mystic; a shaman, was that it?"

She was the one said she could put an An72 down anywhere, Gaby thought, and she could. After the night of bouncing across the hostile bush, never knowing when they were going to run into another armed scouting party and whether they would run out of Krugerrands before they ran out of people they had to bribe, it had been incomparable glory to see that ugly, beautiful jet coming out of the dawn light, down onto that dirt road, and the red dust pluming out behind it. It took more than natural power to fly like that. It took more than natural friendship to grant a favor like that.

"And Faraway?" Shepard asked.

"He stayed behind." She saw him, with the dawn light full on him, standing on the hood of the 4X4, waving ecstatically as *Dostoinsuvo* made her takeoff run. Smiling. He had been smiling, even at the end. "But he's all right. He's doing good. He's some kind of mover and shaker in the new nation. When the East African teleport came back on-line—the Green Net, they call it—he got in touch with me. The thing's up to handling data transmission. Some folk get love letters. Faraway sends me lust faxes."

"I can't imagine what it's like in there," Shepard said. "That sounds strange coming from someone who's seen as much and been as deep as any other human. It's the tourist thing, nice to visit, but I can't imagine living there."

"They say there are hundreds—thousands—of independent, self-sufficient communities all across what used to be the White Highlands. If you don't find what you want in the place you're at, you take a few like-minded friends, find a spot that suits you and the thing will grow you a customized village. The Ten Thousand Tribes is the current sound bite."

"But we lost Nairobi. Tsavo, Amboseli, the Mara. Kilimanjaro, Kirinyaga, the Rift Valley. All gone. I miss them. I'm not certain that what we've been given in exchange compensates. How long before Mombasa goes?"

"It's got a couple of years." And Kikambala, and the banda there, and the beach where your children played, and the reef where they swam, when it was as good as it could ever get. You are not talking about the Chaga taking things away. You are talking about time, and change. You are talking about death. She knew that if she did not say them now, the things would go unspoken forever, and it would be as dead for them as if he had thrown her note away and never come to the Starview Lodge.

She laid her hands on the table, palms up. They were trembling.

"Shepard, I'm sorry. I hurt you. I was crass, insensitive, selfish, treacherous, crazy; I was a hundred different sins that night, all of them deadly."

"You found the one wound, and you went right for it."

"I always do. It's a talent of mine. It makes me good at football and terrible at relationships. I can't help it, I probably won't ever be able to stop it, pressing them where it hurts most. But I don't do it deliberately. Shit, Shepard, it only works on people I love."

"Like now?"

"Does this hurt?"

"Does it ever not?"

"How long is ever?"

"Four years and nine months and I forget the days."

"Oh shit," Gaby McAslan said. "I think I'm going to have to cry now, and my mascara will smudge and everyone will know. Did you really think of me all that time, Shepard? You can lie to me about this. I won't mind, but try and make it sound convincing."

"Who's lying?" Shepard said.

"Liar," Gaby whispered. "Do you forgive me?"

"Long ago."

"Then why the fuck," Gaby said in a voice so low it could hardly be heard over the rising wind, "did it take you four years nine months and you forget the days to tell me?"

"A thousand stupidities. A thousand mistrusts. A thousand fears. Men are emotional cowards."

"You were scared? Of me?"

He said nothing. Fair comment, she thought.

"That's a pretty lame excuse, Shepard."

"What's yours?"

"I didn't know if you would talk to me, let alone forgive me."

"Me, forgive you? But when I saw you that instant in Nairobi, in the Kenyatta tower . . ."

"When I came looking for you."

"Exactly."

They looked at each other over the table. The wind from out of Africa set the candle flames bickering in their glass jars and bamboo blinds billowing.

"Do you remember in old Tom and Jerry cartoons when Spike the dog used to do something dumb?" Gaby asked.

"And his head would turn into a braying jackass's?"

"Exactly."

"Hee-haw, hee-haw."

"I am going to cry now," Gaby McAslan announced.

While they made fools of themselves and each other, the voices from the telescope deck had grown louder, as had the noise from the main bar, which had gradually filled until all you could see were people's backs pressed against the glass. Suddenly someone discovered there was an outside, and the doors slid open and the people inside poured outside. They rushed to the rail. They seemed to be expecting an event.

"*Robert A. Heinlein*'s coming down early because of the storm." Shepard had to raise his voice. As he spoke miles of runway lights went on across the lagoon. Pentagrams and hexagrams of power, section by section. A hush fell over the spacewatchers. "Is there someplace quieter we could go?" Shepard asked. "Someone's bound to recognize my hairstyle and want to talk to me about space."

"There's my room," Gaby said. "It's down by the pool. No one goes there, it's not on the space side of the hotel. We don't have to go into my room; we can just sit around the pool if you like."

They agreed to sit on the edge of the pool with their feet in the water. Gaby listened to the stratospheric rumble of the chase planes up on the edge of the storm, hunting the incoming shuttle with battle radar.

"How can you contemplate this?" she asked. She watched the circles of ripples spread out from her gently moving ankles and interfere with each other.

"They say it's just like a bus with wings."

"That pulls four gees, with five hundred tons of high explosive up its ass."

"If you got the chance, you'd do it too."

Without a second thought, she said to herself.

"Aaron's coming down for the launch," Shepard said.

"How old is he now?" Gaby asked.

"Almost sixteen. Terrifying amount of growing in four and a bit years. He likes me to think he's coping well, he's cool, he can tough it out, but he's overcompensating. He was at the age when children use their bodies instinctively when it was taken from him, and he tries to make up for the loss with wheelchair sports: archery, basketball. He wants to train for a marathon. He pushes himself too hard—he's just a kid still." Shepard emptied his glass and set it to float in the pool. The ripples carried it out into the deep water. "There's an operation they want to try. It's something they've developed in Ecuador from symb technology. They can splice symb neural fibers onto human nerve endings. If it works, he would walk again, run again. Be like he was. He won't admit it, but he's scared of it. I think he likes to be extraordinary. I think he's afraid to go back to being an ordinary archer, an ordinary basketball player, an ordinary long-distance runner. Is that a terrible thing to say about your son?"

"Shepard, I don't know what to say about Aaron, and Fraser. It just seems . . . wrong. That most of all. Wrong; an offense against nature. It's not meant to happen like this. Parents aren't supposed to outlive their children. Parents aren't supposed to bury them and grieve for them and try and live the rest of their lives while thinking every day about what they should have been doing, where they should have been, what they should have achieved and experienced."

"It was the clothes that killed me," Shepard said. "Going through the closets, gathering all the things he used to wear; the shirts and the pants and the T-shirts and the shoes and the underwear. I couldn't see them without seeing him in them; all these clothes he had chosen because he liked the shape or the color or the pattern or the fashion, that he loved to wear. Laying them out and thinking, he won't change into this T-shirt anymore, or put on these short pants, or decide he feels like wearing this hat today. Things for which he has no more use. I gave them all away. I couldn't even bear the thought of Aaron in them as hand-me-downs.

"It's like a fire underground, Gaby, that's been burning down there in the dark for years, that dies down in one place and you think maybe it's gone out, but it's just moved somewhere else. There are coal-mine fires in Pennsylvania that have burned down under the earth for whole lifetimes."

"I envy you that fire," Gaby said. "Really. Truly. My ovaries kick me every time you mention their names, Shepard. I goggle at babies in buggies. I linger in children's clothing stores; the sad woman by the zero-to-six months who's too scared to pick up and feel that cute little red dress. My biological clock is saying 'Hurry up now, it's time.' Looming thirtysomethinghood. I always envied you your kids, did you know that, Shepard? I used to think I envied their claim over you; now I know it was that they were kids that I envied. I'm tired of having nothing outside of me to care about."

The wind was blowing hard now, flapping their clothes, ruffling the surface of the pool into wavelets that swamped the whiskey glass and sent it to the bottom of the deep end.

"Gaby," Shepard said, "come and swim with me." His voice was thick with want. He stood up, took off his Indian-style suit that did not really flatter him. His body was as hairless as his head. "It's how we train for free fall. Swim with me, Gaby. I love to see women in water. Women swimming."

Dizzy with anticipation, Gaby stripped down to her panties and followed Shepard into the pool. He was waiting for her in the deep water where the whiskey glass had sunk. She swam toward him, pleasuring herself in the slide of water past her body. So, wet women do it, Shepard? She trod water beside him.

"Shepard, in all those years, was there ever anyone else? Is there anyone else now?"

"No one it would break me to lose. You?"

It would be too complicated to explain about Faraway, and she had still not clarified her feelings about the thing with him. It had seemed like a breaking of something or a curing. A healing. A whole-ing.

"The same," she lied.

The HORUS orbiter *Robert A. Heinlein* passed over the Starview Lodge and the man and the woman treading water in the deep end of the pool with a mighty rushing sound. It thumped down on the main runway across the lagoon. Gaby heard the space-watchers at the back of the hotel cheer and clap. She wriggled herself close to Shepard, tucked her fingers into the waistband of his shorts.

"All body hair?" she asked innocently.

"Let's find out," he said.

Gaby yelled with laughter. The wind gusted and boomed around the Starview Lodge's many eaves, and the water of the pool became a dance of droplets as the rain came striking down.

65

Aaron came down from Minneapolis on the second day of the storm. He made it in an hour before they closed the airport. Gaby hardly recognized the lean, fit, almost-sixteener in a wheelchair. He remembered Gaby. He seemed glad to see her. His memories of her were all good; he happily shared them with Gaby as she drove the hire car through sheets of gusting rain to the Ramada where Shepard had reserved a room. She wondered how he would take the news that she was moving into the Ramada at the same time.

Tropical Storm Hilary's visit to the coast would not be soon forgotten. She blew in to the south, moved north, thought about heading back out to sea for a day or two, then decided she liked the south and went down there again. She left behind her a litter of gutted trailer parks, snapped palm trees, felled billboards, roofless Pentecostal churches, de-awninged gas stations, shorted power lines, breached sea defenses, scuttled pleasure cruisers, Pearl-Harbored marinas and thirty-foot yachts in supermarket parking lots. In the five days of her progress, she dumped three months' rain on the dry coast.

Gaby McAslan never looked at a swizzle stick again without a prick of awe at the power eight inches of fluorescent plastic could wield.

As she had prayed Hilary wrecked the HORUS launch program. When the wind dropped beneath forty, the occasional SSTO struggled toward the gray clouds, cheered on by space junkies in waterproofs and plastic rain sheets. The UNECTA hotels filled up with newspersons drinking out the storm and shaven-headed Final Frontiersmen moping nervously around the corridors in their UNECTA*Space* white sweats, like a convention of Bad-Ass Buddhists. Gaby spent as much of the storm as she could in bed with Shepard. When she could not be there, she took Aaron to look at rockets in the rain, or view the launches with Rodrigo and The Man, or watch the figures in bulky white spacesuits way down in the deep-water training tank, or moving in the Virtual Reality simulators like old men practicing Tai Chi.

"Quick, Gab, infect me with something nasty but non-lethal," Shepard said as the television weather girl declared that Tropical Storm Hilary had bottomed out and was filling from the south, wind speeds were dropping and the whole system was predicted to spin itself to nothing over Bermuda.

"You're right about Aaron," Gaby said, rolling herself up in Shepard's sheet. "He tries too hard."

"You've noticed it," Shepard said from the bathroom. He was plastered from head to toe in UNECTA*Space* depilatory cream. Yellow storm light shone through the cracks in the racing gray rain clouds.

"When I've been out with him, yes. Everything is too much. Nothing is relaxed, natural. Shepard, I don't think it's himself he's doing it for. I think it's you."

"What do you mean?" he shouted over the sound of showering.

"Remember, back in the Mara, when you said that Fraser would be the one would make hearts and break hearts and everything would come to his fingertips, but Aaron would have to work hard for everything he wanted to achieve, but because of it, the world would know his name?"

"You've got a long memory."

"I think living up to that expectation is the most important thing in his life. Everything he does is to prove to you that it is worthwhile for him to be alive while Fraser is not—that he can be not just Aaron, but Fraser too."

Shepard stepped out of the bathroom. He looked more alien than ever, naked, smooth, wet.

"Oh no, Gaby."

"It's the damage that we do and never know, Shepard."

He shook his head, and started to pull chin-ups on the shower rail.

On the television news the anchorman reported that the Swarm's new position fifteen thousand miles behind the BDO and inactive status were now confirmed. ETTEO was now one hundred and twenty-two hours twenty-seven minutes.

They ate that night at the Starview Lodge, because the food was great and undersubscribed and there was no better place to watch the *Ursula K. Le Guin* come down out of orbit. The space junkies were soft people and gave Aaron a place right at the rail. As they watched the landing lights come on block by block, Shepard said, "I'm sorry about the Unit Twelve thing, Gaby. I did my best."

"I know. T.P. told me that you'd leaked it to Dr. Dan. You didn't have to resign for me, though. It scared me, Shepard; that's why I was so insane that night. For the first time I was utterly helpless. I couldn't do anything to stop them. I was disappeared. I was annihilated. I was an unperson. Nothing. It was like being dead, Shepard."

The spectators all began to cheer as they caught sight of the black delta of the orbiter in the clear yellow evening sky that had come behind the storm.

She knew that would be the last evening. They called him at midnight for the preflight medicals, tests, briefings. Gaby and Aaron said all the good-byes they needed to say in the hotel lobby. The mission coordinator was getting ratty because they were taking so long to say them.

"Mind Aaron."

"Aaron can mind himself."

"I never asked; where do you go after AEO?"

"Back to Tanzania. T. P. Costello has talked UNECTA into

taking me on one of your deep patrols. I'm going in to see these Ten Thousand Tribes, meet the people of the future, get their faces on television."

"I'll be in touch when I get back."

"And how long will that be?"

Shepard shrugged. "Ask the Evolvers. But when I do, I'd really like to see Ireland with you; the places you talk about; the Watchhouse, the Point, and your people too."

"Go with God, speed skater."

"I'll write."

"Ha-ha."

"Watch me."

The minibus door slammed.

Gaby and Aaron ate and drank and talked in the hotel bar until they could see dawn streak the sky outside the glass lobby. There was no Heineken, but Gaby reckoned Aaron would be all right on Miller. It was the right kind of drink for a kid whose father was about to rendezvous with an alien artifact. They found, sometime just before dawn, that they got on fine for a son and a lover.

In the morning they talked with Shepard in the White Room on a videophone. Both agreed that he looked petrified. They did not repeat the farewells of the night before. Farewells did not carry over videophone, and anyway, to them he had already left the planet.

Shepard had got them complimentary passes to the executive viewing area inside the space center. Gaby fought with a NASA official about access for Aaron's wheelchair and intimidated him into giving them seats next to the presidential box, which today was occupied by Ellen Prochnow. Gaby noted this, and also the neat NASA binoculars everyone was given. She wondered how many pairs they expected to get back.

It was a good day for a launch, hot and clear. High pressure had come in on the tail of Hilary. Some pools of rainwater still stood on the grass beside the taxiway but the main strip had been dried during the night by special vehicles. Heat haze boiled off the concrete. The HORUS was a dark predatory shadow, as improbably elongated as a hunting insect, moving within the shiver of the haze. It glided from the big hangar, along the taxiways to the end of the main runway and turned.

At T minus sixty seconds on the big countdown display, the tractor unit disengaged and dashed like a photophobic beetle for its blastproof bunker. The digits clicked down on the big counter. Everyone resisted the temptation to count along with the final five. This was not New Year. The clock reached zero.

A mile and a half down the runway, nothing happened in response to this.

Then Gaby screamed because it seemed to her as if the spaceship had exploded in a ball of smoke and flame. Then she saw a black shape hurtling out of the fire toward her. The tricks of the heat haze were dispelled. It was big. It was fast. It was riding on a tail of fire, coming right at her. Gaby's heart leaped as the carrier body passed in front of the stand and quite unexpectedly, quite improbably, quite magically, lifted into the air.

The noise was louder than anything she had ever heard in her life. She could scream her head off and no would know. Shc did. She watched, roaring in exuberance, the launcher go up, and keep going up, in a beautiful asymptotic curve, the HORUS orbiter clinging to its back like a thrilled child. The smoke blew away on the wind from the south, but the spaceship kept climbing, over the artificial peninsula of the launch runway, over the tidewater waders and the gulls and the big crabs, over the space freaks and the rocket fetishists down in Trailer Park, over the day-trippers in the jolly boats, over the green water of the Gulf Stream, still climbing. Nothing could bring it down now.

"Ten miles out, fifty thousand feet," said the fat bearded man with the ugly hat in the T-shirt with *Fort Lauderdale in '10* on it.

"Carrier body separation in mark twelve minutes," said the other fat bearded man, with the equally ugly hat and the T-shirt with the old-style shuttle on the front.

In the executive viewing stand the people who had seen all this before were leaving for their corporate hospitality suites, but Gaby McAslan's face was still turned to the sky. She watched the brilliant speck of the rocket exhaust until it disappeared into the high blue.

"Fucking hell!" she shouted to Aaron. "Bloody fucking hell! Wasn't that the greatest thing you ever saw?"

"Are you crying?" Aaron asked.

"Of course I am," Gaby said. Then she saw Ellen Prochnow

gather her entourage around her and head to the door of the presidential box. Fumbling in her handbag, Gaby ran along the row of seats, tried to get over the low partition wall.

"Hey! Excuse me! Ms. Prochnow! Could you spare me a wee minute of your time?"

the tree where man was born

66

Hi Gab.

I said I'd write.

I'm sorry my face is so puffy—you're going to be seeing a lot of it; there isn't much to look at in this little confession booth they call the Personal Communications Space—that's free fall for you. Everyone ends up looking like a Bond villain. Three hundred Ernst Stavro Blofelds, hurtling round in their mad space station eight hundred miles above the earth.

This is Space, Day One. If I shift the camera a little, there, can you see it? Mother Earth, up there above us. That's the orientation I seem to have chosen. Most others orient themselves the other way up; feet down toward the Earth. I'm probably heading for vertigo and even more nausea than I'm feeling right now: everything you eat sits right on the bottom of your esophagus and won't shift. Also, everyone else is metric and this down-home hayseed is still yards and miles. I'm trying to adjust, but I just can't *feel* a mile.

See that? There goes Baja California. It's always Baja California, isn't it? I could watch the planet turn above me all day, which is why they limit you to ten minutes in here. It's a major recreation, Earth-watching. They've got a fully equipped Gaiaist contemplarium out in number two hydroponics tube. Hover in lotus, listen to whale song and watch the great green mother of us all spin before you. A Jodo Tendai chanting group time-shares it with a free-fall yoga class. I promised myself before I left that I would not turn into one of these astronaut-mystics who find being beyond the envelope of atmosphere and gravity a religious revelation, but it would be very easy to succumb to a Zen state of disconnectedness with worldly things. Never could manage lotus, though. Something wrong with my left shin.

What you once told me about airline booking computers is doubly true for space shuttles. They put me next to a cetologist—God knows why they think they need a whale expert at the BDO, I suppose they want to cover every possibility—who was even more shit-scared than me but was damned if he was going to show it. He talked all the way through the prelaunch checks about how mutations were appearing in the whale populations that had responded to the Foa Mulaku call and that this was clear evidence that the cetaceans were at least as intelligent and worthy of species vastening as humanity. When they actually lit the engines, he put his hands over his head and yelled all the way up to carrier body separation. His exact words to me were, ''Well, that was more fun than Magic Mountain.'' I don't think he meant the Thomas Mann novel.

The real story, according to Shepard. It was like being strapped into a windowless tube that suddenly accelerates and doesn't stop and all those things they teach you about puffing your breath and not fully collapsing your lungs and pulling your belly muscles and tightening your sphincters all go straight out of your head because you cannot see where you are going, you have no idea where you are, you don't have a clue what the hell is happening and you want it to be over like you've never wanted anything else to be over but at the same time you don't because what happens next may well be worse. It seems like forever until carrier body separation, and that is like the bottom falling out of an express elevator leaving you clinging to the walls. The gees drop off a little, so it's only a linebacker sitting on your chest and not a sumo wrestler, but that's worse, because you feel underpowered, that you don't have the speed to make it, that at any minute this blacked-out bus on wings is going to fall out of the sky.

And that's exactly what it does. The words *throttle back* do not appear in the HORUS pilot manuals. They give it full thrust until they've burned every drop of fuel in the tanks, and then they switch to glide. You go from multigees through HESO to free fall. Emphasis here is on the word *fall.* Everyone screamed. We all thought the engines had failed and we were plummeting to earth. Burn and crash. Quite a lot of barfing. Some had already shat themselves in fear when *Clarkie* launched. You're sitting strapped into your seat trying to dodge globes of floating puke with the place smelling like a sewage pit and the pilot tells you that *Arthur C. Clarke* has achieved Earth orbit and is moving into a transfer trajectory that will bring it to Space Station Unity in forty-nine minutes.

They say it's worse going back down.

You'd think that at however many billion these things are apiece, it wouldn't burn the budget to put in a few windows.

Got to go now. Next soul due for video confession. I love you, Gaby. I miss you and Aaron like hell and it's only nineteen hours. It's a real temptation to touch the screen and ask you to touch it back and pathetic saccharine stuff like that. More tomorrow. See ya.

Space, Day Two.

Ernst Stavro Blofeld here.

The beautiful spiral of cloud above my left shoulder is Tropical Storm Hilary, spinning off across the Atlantic in the general direction of Ireland. It's rapidly filling, so our weather watchers say; the far southwest should get a couple of inches of rain and a few tiles off the roof. You're from the northeast, isn't that right?

Space, I am discovering, is like camp. You don't sleep enough, you don't eat right, you don't wash, you feel tired and puffy and constantly wondering where the hell you are. The cocoon bag they give you to sleep in is comfortable enough—weird, weird dreams, Gaby, I didn't know I had them in me—and would be positively cozy for two, but two minutes after you tumble out, someone else tumbles in. We're so overcrowded we're running a hot-bagging system. Three shifts of eight hours in the sack. I hope the woman before me doesn't have any nasty little habits for me to discover. Likewise, I hope I don't leave any for the guy who comes after me.

It's bad enough that everything looks stupid in free fall—eating, sleeping, talking, excreting, exercising with those dumb rubber bands, but in Unity it's stupidity at close range. Intimacy is a necessity, privacy an inconvenient aberration. Going to the bathroom; not only can you hear every grunt and groan and ah! but everyone has his or her own personal colored nozzle for the cocksucker, as we guys call it, and God help you if you use someone else's. This is much worse than using another person's toothbrush. There have been serious fights, I hear. Everything and everyone is in your face all the time. I'm surprised there are any faces left uneaten.

There's a guy, he's been here about a month longer than me, a Team Red boy; he has a Grateful Dead disc he just has to play at full volume at every possible occasion. Winning converts to the One True Music, he says. One True Music up his ass, if I get the chance. I'll have to wait in line, there are fifty others want to throw him out the air lock, no questions asked, or if they can't get him, his disc will do. In space no one can hear the Dead.

The Japanese team members cope with this best. I suppose all their lives are lived so close to others they want to bite faces off, but etiquette forbids.

Unity is strange, in that it's a place with an inside but no outside. You don't see anything as you go through the pressure link from the HORUS; it's just a big tube after a tiny tube after a middling-size tube. We could as easily be at the bottom of the sea, or the center of the earth, as eight hundred miles up in space. It's a hard place to envision whole—you get a much better idea from the television, where it looks mightily impressive, this mile-and-a-half tangle of construction beams, solar panels, tanks, environment modules. From the inside it's the odd boom, or a bit of a solar array, or a manufacturing core glimpsed from a tiny window. It's very easy to get lost in; the passages seem to move around and reconnect while you're not looking. There is a grain of truth in this; every shift you wake up to find the engineers have bolted on a new section or opened a lock into a pressure body you never knew existed. Ironic, that it takes the advent of the BDO to push space exploration into a renaissance. This place, the HORUS shuttles, High Steel, the intra-orbit tugs; these would have been intolerable budget leeches fifteen years ago. We could go to Mars right now, if we didn't have more interesting places to go. The BDO giveth us our reason to go into space, and it taketh away.

Someone's coughing politely outside. One last impression, which was actually a first impression. On arriving at Unity, what's the first thing that hits you? It smells of fart. Three hundred people in a space designed for one hundred and seventy-five at a pinch, an overstrained air-conditioning system and all that high-protein, high-carbohydrate food? Someone's dropping one every second of the day—you are not going to believe this, but over in Hydroponics One they hold see-who-can-fart-themselves-the-furthest contests. Fart, feet and piss. They never tell you this on the television.

More tomorrow. Love you.

It's me again, Gaby. It's Unity. Day Three.

I'm just back from a BDO-watching party down in the Remote Sensing. Direct feed from Hubble and our own, smaller, observatory. The orbital telescopes can achieve such fine detail you can see *Gaia*'s shadow passing over the bright end, like a flea on Mt. Rushmore. It brings home what a big mother that thing out there really is. We can see the mountains on the outer skin, watch the shadows lengthen and shrink as the object spins away from the sun. What's most amazing is the sense of color. This thing makes Jupiter look dowdy. Bright as a beer can thrown into space.

I'm not afraid of it. It won't send hosts of destroying angels across the earth, or open its vial of plagues, or smash the planet apart into crumbs. It's come here for us. For humans. And while this gift from the powers in the sky draws ever closer, we cling to the walls of our little cocoon, hairless apes squabbling about the Grateful Dead and who's doing it with whom, and when, and where, and in what position, and who's using whose pissing tube. I find this tremendously reassuring. The Evolvers have come eight hundred light-years to learn the concept of irony. It only took us Americans two and a half centuries.

There's a cunning caste system in operation up here. It's based on the length of your stubble. The smoother your pate, the lower down the order you peck. Top of the tree are the Suedes, with about three or four weeks of growth all over. It's pernicious; I found myself acting like an old sea dog, handing out unhelpful tips and scornful looks to the virgins up off the *Jules Verne* and the ESA HOTOL that docked yesterday, keeping to myself anything that might be useful or important. It'll end in hazing rituals. I hope not to be around for that. Herd instinct and team bonding are survival tactics in as extreme an environment as this. Space stations, and jails. Even within groups, it's shape up or ship out. I get waves of hostility from the rest of Team Green because I refuse to adopt the same spatial orientation as them in group exercises. My "up there" is their "down here" and vice versa. Unity Thought Police. This beef will get back to them, and I'll be in real grief. The grapevine up here violates special and general relativity.

There's another kind of caste division, more deeply rooted, and that's between Spacers and Passengers. Spacers are the crew of Unity, its construction workers, system engineers, tug and shuttle pilots, anyone who works with space as their raw material. The rest of us are Passengers. Grunts. Breathing their hard-worked-for air, pissing out their expensively recycled water, leaving our skin flakes floating in their pods and passages. They swing through the tubes like you're not there, push in front of you when you're in the line for the food dispenser or the john, talk over you when you are *trying to record a private letter,* pull you up on any one of a hundred imaginary violations of space routine that of course threaten the lives of every soul aboard and are *complete militarist Nazis who are jealous because all they do is drive the taxi, we're the ones who get to see the show.*

There's a place I've discovered—I won't call it private, because nothing is in this shell of fools—but it's undercrowded, and it has a window on the docking area. There is a lot of free time when you're a Passenger. With mine, I like to watch spaceships. Didn't your friend Oksana once tell you that time spent watching airplanes is time exceedingly well spent? That goes double for spacecraft. There is seldom an hour that you don't find something moored to the docking unit. Mostly they're those brutal little SSTO robot freighters—our lifeline to the mother world, without which we really would be eating each other's faces. I watch for the HORUSes and HOTOLs as they come out of the atmosphere blur at the edge of the world. They're beautiful things. They seem to fly on space, surf on it, like the old Silver Surfer; that it happens in absolute silence and the slowness of Zen drama makes it all the more beautiful. To me, the tugs are the most interesting. Nothing to look at, except, I suppose, a certain fitness-for-purpose aesthetic in the ungainly agglomerations of engines, tanks, construction beams and heavy grappling arms. What fascinates me is that they're deep-space creatures. The space planes, the freighters, they're Earth things; their job is purely to get through that layer of air. The tugs could never exist in gravity and atmosphere; they are absolutely designed for space. They interest me primarily because in a very short time I'm going to know one—or rather, the environment pods they pick up—a whole lot more intimately. They're moving us out. Teams Yellow and Green are being rotated up to High Steel. We leave tomorrow at 20:30, in two pods. I'm in the second ship. I may not have time to talk to you tomorrow—there's quite a lot of prepping needs to be done before the flight, you spend the fifteen hours muffled up in an air bag and they reckon it's best to knock you out for it. So it's likely the next time I'm talking to you will be from High Steel.

By the way, I've been using your name as a blunt instrument

to ward off undesired advances—I've had several, with a lot of spare time and free fall to experiment with, what do you expect?—and it seems opinion is divided whether you're Christ or Antichrist over the Ellen Prochnow thing. Paranoia breeds like thrush bacteria up here, no one believes her denials, but at the same time no one wants to be checking their neighbor's scalps for 666s or McDonnell Douglas Aviation. So we are a pretty congeries of mistrusts. Don't worry, I'm not going to accept any of the offers I've been given.

Shit. Well over time. Love. Bye.

Hi, Gaby. It's Day Five and this is High Steel.

Another white plastic interior, with a rectangle of stars over the left shoulder. Space travel is very disappointing. You go from one white plastic tube to another, where you get gently pushed and shoved around a little, and then a timeless time later you are taken out of this tube and put into one exactly identical. Absolutely no sense of going anyplace. Thank God they knock you out. Kmart economy spacesuits, air bags. They'll keep you alive in case the pod depressurizes or the tug lets go of it, and if the end gets torn off and you spill into space, they'll broadcast distress calls, so theoretically someone can come and pick you up. Though what they pick up after days in an inflatable mummy floating through space is one for the psychiatrists. If you die in space, where do you go? Nasty, nasty little thoughts like this creep into your head and will not creep out again.

It's a bad sign that after Unity, the first thing you notice about High Steel is the stink. Twelve accommodation modules, a mile of solar paneling arrays, an engineering plant and an APR on a boom, halfway to the moon. The earth is frighteningly small and distant. It looks like a planet now, and that is not comfortable. The moon is frighteningly big and close. It looks like a planet too. Biggest, closest and most frightening of all is the BDO. It looks like the fucking end of the world.

BDO before me, Chaga below me. I can see Africa from here. Clouds cover much of the equatorial regions; I can see the path of the monsoon, curling up from Madagascar, across the Indian Ocean, beyond the horizon. Through breaks in the cloud, I can see the outlines of the Chagas scattered across the continent; circles and clusters of circles, merging together. I can see you,

Gaby. How are you, down there in Tanzania? Up here in my bubble of air and stink and plastic, I feel old, fragile and scared.

The mainframe is shaking again. The tug engines must be firing. High Steel is being moved into a station-keeping orbit, ten miles above the bright end of the Big Dumb Object. From that distance it will look bigger than the earth does from Unity. I am going to have to get my spatial orientation sorted out by AEO: hovering above, or floating in front of a three-hundred-mile-long cylinder should be psychologically survivable. What is not is to imagine that it is poised over you like the hammer of God.

There is another link between you and me, Gaby, apart from visions of Africa. There are Changed up here: the free-fall adaptations with four hands. They are incredible; I feel like a brick in an aquarium next to them. This is how the future is going to look? That's scary too. There are four of them up here, three are South Americans, but one is the boy you found in Unit 12—Juma. I knew about him, Gaby. I knew about all of them; Peter Werther, the Moon woman. I lied to you. I'm sorry, I had no other choice. And you were right—funny how you can remember every word and nuance of the worst days of your life—I did give you that diary to get you into bed, and I regretted it the moment I had done it, because I knew you would pry into the mystery of the disappeared pages. It wasn't until long, long after—years after you left Kenya—that I realized that I had done the right thing for the wrong reasons. The diary had led you to bust Unit 12 wide open, and reveal all its paranoid little secrets that I wanted to but could never disclose. Rather late for self-justification, you would say.

I'm sorry I sound a little melancholy on this installment; everyone is a bit down, nervous, tense, expectant. The BDO is sixteen hours from AEO and here we are, sitting in our tin can far above the earth, realizing how pitifully unprepared we are. And I feel far from home. I miss gravity. I miss water. I miss air, and wind. I miss you. I miss Aaron. I'm not sure the BDO compensates for all this missing, but the next time I talk to you, it'll be here.

Day Six, Gaby. It's here.

AEO was two hours fifty minutes ago. You've seen the pictures. Everyone on the planet has seen the pictures. This is how it felt to be there.

When you sized me up and seduced me with your question-and-answer that time in the Mara, you told me I was a thing of earth and plains and big skies and empty lands with not a lot of room left for God. Pretty astute, Gaby. Religion has never played a great part in my life. But the BDO was the closest I have ever come to a genuine religious experience. I told you I wouldn't get mystical on you. I'm not. It was genuine awe of a God with real muscle and a hell of an FX budget.

That tense, depressed feeling I told you about last time deepened as ETTEO decreased. High Steel hit its orbit first; we had seven hours of looking out at that thing coming down our throats. Half an hour before AEO we just quit whatever job we were meant to be doing and found someone to be with. You need someone to hold you when the sky falls. What little apes we are, clinging to each other in our tin can. I was with a woman called Clarissa from Team Yellow. We found a window, wedged ourselves into it and just held each other and watched the thing keep coming. That's what the pictures can't convey, Gaby. It kept coming, and coming, and fucking coming and you think, that's got to be all of it, but it still kept coming. Floating there in twelve accommodation modules, a couple of solar sails, an air plant and three tugs, you felt like it was going to swat High Steel like a mosquito. What I said about the launch from Kennedy, that was nothing, Gaby. That was fear of something; that you are going to die. This was existential terror, the fear of you don't know what could happen. People were praying, Gab. Some were crying, in fear, awe, love. Tears float in zero gee. I gripped Clarissa so hard I left bruises.

And then I felt High Steel move. You've heard the theorists, that it got caught in a gravitational eddy from the mass-momentum drive as the BDO stabilized its orbit. What it felt like, Gaby, was every part of everything around you, and every part of yourself, down to the atoms, held by something and gently but firmly pulled. Like falling, with nothing to hold on to, except the human body next to you.

I'm not asking your forgiveness for this, Gaby. You would do the same with the first human body that floated by.

I thought we were coming apart; all that was happening was High Steel was being dragged into an orbit in line with the BDO's axis and spun up to match its rotation. We're turning in time with BDO.

So: the arrival of the BDO. What did it feel like? It felt like God had come. In every sense of the word, polite and impolite. The fearful depression that gripped us during the orbital approach has been burned away by a sense of quasi-spiritual euphoria and activity. We're here, we're alive, we've got holy work to do. It's almost as if the BDO *approves* of us. We're learning to live with the thing ten miles off the starboard bow. The way to look at it is that it's a new moon for Earth. Isn't that a gorgeous thought? Two moons rising. From High Steel you can't see that it's a cylinder, and by a trick of spatial perspective you can push it away from you so that it becomes a world far below you, and the mottlings and patterns on the facing end are continents and oceans.

What they really are is Chaga. Vacuum-adapted Chaga, carpeting the hills and valleys of the forward end and cylinder sides. This close, you can make out individual details; some of the formations are thousands of feet high. They diminish in size toward the edge. In a way, I find this riot of alien life almost homely: I've spent much of my professional life looking out from high windows across vast discs of Chaga. It's actually smaller than many of the longer-established terrestrial symbs—certainly much smaller than the Nyandarua–Kilimanjaro–Mt. Elgon Chaga. That puts it into perspective.

Our three tugs are out mapping the exterior. Two are working the cylinder body—one has a specific mission to move along the windows and photograph as much information about the interior as possible, but its view is largely obscured by clouds—and the third is hovering over the forward end, running full-spectrum scans of the surface, probing for possible means of ingress. God, I am starting to sound like them. Good joke, though: it comes all this way and forgets to build a front door. I don't think so somehow. First-wave Team Red are out there in the tug pod, ready to go in if they find an entrance. Team Yellow is down in the air lock, preparing to enpod for tug pickup. We're on orange alert, the call could come at any time. Horribly seductive, this style of talking.

Hold on. What? Shit. Jesus Christ. All right. Sorry, Gab. Got to go. Team Red just lucked out.

No, Gaby. Your eyes deceive you not. Take a good look, Gaby, because nobody on the planet ever got a videogram like this. I could look at it all day, and a day here lasts a week. Why didn't they pack poets or writers or musicians on Operation Final Frontier, folk who could do justice to this place and not just measure it and analyze it and record it. I'll put the camera up here so you can see the cylindrical land behind me. I really haven't an awful lot of time; now we're on the ground, there's always something needs doing or reporting or observing. From Zen indolence to karoshi. But the Passengers are paying their fares now.

The story so far. I got abruptly called away from my last note to you because Team Red out there over the forward end suddenly found a mile-wide section of spin axis opening up in front of them. It was the classic sci-fi cliché: "The door dilated." Like the aperture of a camera. After half an hour obtaining permission from Earth, they moved the tug into the opening. What they found inside, as you've doubtless seen on the television, was an air lock about three miles long—that's what the cavities in the partitions are—and at the other end of it is this. A cylindrical buckyball jungle, sixty miles deep, four hundred and fifty round.

It's a good thing, I suppose, that a lot of these Right Stuff astronauts have had imagination bypasses. If it had been me, coming through with the tug into free-fall atmosphere, I'd still be there, turning with the world, blissfully out of my head. What they did do was dump Team Red's pod down in the microgravity on the lip of the inner air-lock door, and cycled out back to High Steel.

We came through this morning. Just in time; High Steel was getting mighty stinky with Unity moving its troops up to the front as fast as it can get tugs turned around. I could have killed the stupid accountant who decided it was not economically viable to put windows in tug pods. You cannot see it on the television monitors. Did I say that to you once, back in the Mara? You used to video things all the time. I bet you never watched any of them.

There's an unexplored land down there bigger and wilder than all the game reserves of Kenya.

When you step outside and touch it with your eyes, that's when you see it. You can do this, here. It violates every sensibility of space exploration: zero gravity, but atmosphere. Too thin to be breathable, but sufficiently warmed by the light through the five slit windows to allow an almost shirtsleeves environment. Three layers, a breather mask, and a tether so that you don't get taken away on the funny winds that get spun up by the Coriolis force.

The pseudo-gravity well steepens quickly; seventy miles straight down gives you time to do a lot of screaming.

What did I feel when I stepped out of the pod air lock? Unreality. Sheer human disbelief. A valley one hundred and fifty miles wide you can visualize—complete with rivers and a couple of landlocked small seas—but the mind will not permit a *cave* the same size. It will not accept that the forests and rivers are hanging over your head, and it categorically will not allow *seas* up there. The waters above the earth, wasn't there something about that in Genesis? So you tell yourself that it's all a stage set, a complex glass shot for a Hollywood sci-fi movie; after all, here you are in sweatshirt and jeans, this can't be an alien world. But then the details start to work on you. The lakes glisten. The clouds move in odd spirals around the curving land. You can see the shadow of rain falling on the buckyball jungle. If there were anything down there that made a noise, you could hear over seventy-five miles, you could hear it. You want to tear off your breather mask and give a great shout and wait for the faint echo to come back to you from the partition wall sixty miles away. It is real. You are here. And that makes you feel very small, yet at the same time very big. Do you remember we talked about that feeling, the night at Tsavo when they'd just discovered the fullerene clouds out at Rho Ophiuchi? You asked me if I'd ever stood under the stars and lost and found myself in their distance and vastness. That's what I feel here: this cylindrical land so completely dwarfs me that I am virtually annihilated, but I'm here, I witness this, I interpret it, I express it, I am the reason it has been conceived and constructed from the ruins of Hyperion. I matter. The BDO is the product of a technology that looks like magic next to ours, but we made it. We're here. We matter. Small, big. It's like the angels, who, for all their divinity, are ultimately no nearer an infinitely high and holy God than humans are. This artifact may be an entire world, but measured against the stars, the spiral arms, the galaxies, the expanding universe which we share, it's as small as I am. We're both tiny bright beacons of sentience. We both need someone to hold us against the dark. And so we cling to each other. Symbiosis.

So, here we are. Now, what do we do?

They've brought new accommodation modules up from Unity—much bigger than the standard tug pods—and they've got *windows.* We're building camp one up here on the lip of the air lock. About a hundred feet inward, the land drops away on a cup-shaped curve to the main cylinder. Seventy-five miles, downhill. Team Red are about ten miles downslope. Easy going in the light gravity; when it gets stronger, the slope decreases. We shouldn't be surprised, this place was built for us. But it's not too easy: no stairway to heaven, no elevator to hell. If we want to learn what the Evolvers have to show and tell us, we have to work for it. Team Red wants to make breathable air before they set up camp two, just under the snow line. Tomorrow, they'll go down through the clouds into the forest beneath.

Tomorrow, I will follow them. Team Green is going down to the curving land. Love to you, Gaby. Wish me well, wish me a thousand things. Funny, I'm not scared anymore. I've got land under my feet, I can draw strength from that. I've got to go now; as I said, there's always something to do here, and there's a tug going back to High Steel in ten minutes that can take this disc—there, can you see it? The tug holding station up there in the spin axis. Hope this letter finds you, wherever you are. Love to you, Gaby McAslan.

I've just heard. Message from Team Red. They say there are *figures,* moving down there in the mist.

Gaby McAslan ejected the disc from the PDU and rested her chin on her arms on the Landcruiser's steering wheel. The letter had come through to Tinga Tinga at five-thirty that morning after ten days lost in the limbo of Operation Final Frontier Control. She had requested the communications people to alert her at any time if anything came through. Good people. They used to bang people out of bed in the old game-lodge days for an arthritic elephant scratching its ass against a tree, she thought. How much more so, then, for news from another world?

The track had been rough but easily followed, even in the dark. Glittering pairs of eyes had fled from her headlights. Gaby could not say why she had to go alone up to the ridge to watch the disc. Sense of ritual. Sense of propriety. Sense of the romantic. Sense of the spiritual, of connectedness with the land, and the huge sky that hung close over it, and Shepard, above it all.

An edge of light lay across the eastern half of the world. New day. Always a miracle. The moon was already down. The brighter stars and planets still shone in the softening indigo. None challenged the BDO, a brilliant oval of light just past the zenith.

A pair of binoculars would resolve it into a half-shadowed cylinder. Two moons is gorgeous, Shepard.

The sky brightened. Gaby fiddled with the car radio, found Voice of America. Early-morning music. She poured coffee from the flask the woman on Tinga Tinga's outdock had given her because it got cold out there on the high savannah. She sipped the gift and watched the land open up in front of her. Down these bluffs and across the valley was the Chaga, never sleeping, never ceasing, drawing closer to her at fifty feet every day. Today she would embark on her expedition into the unknown country; down the valley, across terminum, into the land of the Ten Thousand Tribes and the beautiful, startling, wonderful, bizarre nation they were growing in there. There were faces she wanted to see, in there.

All the room to be all the things we can be. All the things we have the potential to be. The door to the nursery was open. Two million years of childhood was over. Now would come the storms and changes of puberty, the struggles for identity and selfhood and mastery of adolescence. How long they might endure, what the maturity that would come when they had passed might be like, Gaby could not conceive. She did not imagine it would be as long as childhood—certainly, it would be harder—but the teenage millennia would be dazzling.

The coffee was mighty good.

The PDU queeped. A call, from Tembo back at Tinga Tinga. He looked and sounded poked out of bed and wondering what the hell she was up to out there in the wild. Word from the Miyama orbital telescope, via T. P. Costello in Zanzibar. Phoebe, the eighteenth moon of Saturn, had just disappeared.

Gaby laughed long and hard at that good joke by the powers in the sky. Perhaps they had come to Earth to learn irony. Nice one, all you bright stars. And here's a better one. The good news from Earth. She sat back in the Landcruiser's seat and rested her fingertips on her belly. It was three days since she had tested positive. It had been much quicker than she had planned. Already she imagined she could feel the life budding in there, turning over and over in the free-fall waters of conception. What a world you're going to live in, kid! What a future you're going to have.

She was glad the conception had been so stunningly sudden. She could go down to the Chaga with Tembo and the UNECTA team without fearing that its spores might change it.

She was not sure whether that would be a good or bad thing in this new world.

The darkness was almost gone now. Light filled up the land, spilled down the sides of the bluffs into the valley, touched the tops of the tallest hand trees and pseudo-corals of the Chaga. It was changing in there too, losing its shape and structure as it grew closer to humanity's needs and societies. Symbiosis, growing together. Hugging in the big big dark.

The upper limb of the sun touched the horizon. Only the BDO could rival it now, and it would soon fade. The sky was a high, deep blue, clear and clean. Gaby emptied the rest of her coffee out the window of the car and made to start it. She stopped herself.

A lion had come out of the thorn scrub down the bluffs and was working its way up the hill to the crest. It was an old female, sag-jawed, sag-bellied, strong and scarred. It sniffed at the Landcruiser's tires. Gaby sat, not moving a muscle, hardly breathing. The old lioness moved to a slab of smooth rock beneath a big baobab overlooking the valley. She sniffed the rock and sat down. Gaby watched her, lying under the tree, looking out across the brightening land.

After a time a second lion came and lay down beside her.

postface

"In science fiction, everything should be mentioned at least twice . . . with the possible exception of science fiction."

—Samuel R. Delany, *Triton*